ALSO BY
KATEE ROBERT

Dark Olympus

Neon Gods

ELECTRIC IDOL

KATEE ROBERT

sourcebooks
casablanca

To Jenny. It's a pleasure

to share an Id with you!

Published by Sourcebooks Casablanca, an imprint of Sourcebooks
P.O. Box 4410, Naperville, Illinois 60567-4410
(630) 961-3900
sourcebooks.com

Cataloging-in-Publication Data is on file with the Library of Congress.

Printed and bound in the United States of America.
LSC 24

THE RULING FAMILIES OF
Olympus

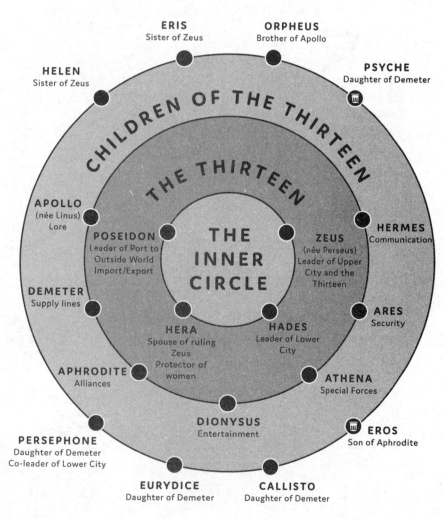

ERIS
Sister of Zeus

ORPHEUS
Brother of Apollo

PSYCHE
Daughter of Demeter

HELEN
Sister of Zeus

CHILDREN OF THE THIRTEEN

THE THIRTEEN

APOLLO
(née Linus)
Lore

HERMES
Communication

POSEIDON
Leader of Port to
Outside World
Import/Export

THE
INNER
CIRCLE

ZEUS
(née Perseus)
Leader of Upper
City and the
Thirteen

DEMETER
Supply lines

ARES
Security

HERA
Spouse of ruling
Zeus
Protector of
women

HADES
Leader of Lower
City

APHRODITE
Alliances

ATHENA
Special Forces

DIONYSUS
Entertainment

EROS
Son of Aphrodite

PERSEPHONE
Daughter of Demeter
Co-leader of Lower City

EURYDICE
Daughter of Demeter

CALLISTO
Daughter of Demeter

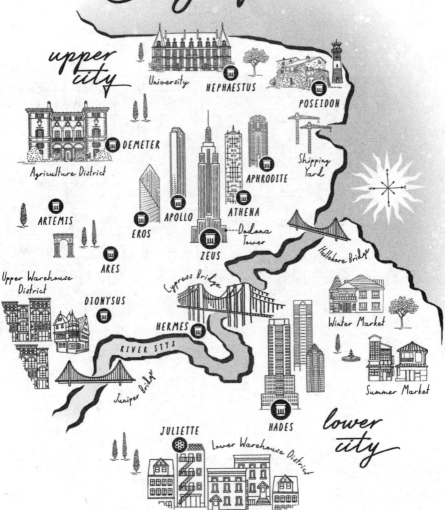

PSYCHE

ANOTHER NIGHT, ANOTHER PARTY I DESPERATELY DON'T want to attend.

I try not to clutch my sickeningly sweet drink as I drift around the room's perimeter. As long as I keep on the move, my mother won't zero in on me. One would think the events of the last few months would be enough to give her ambitions pause, but Demeter is nothing if not driven. She's successfully married off one daughter—yes, she's taking credit for Persephone marrying Hades—and now she's turned her sights on me.

I would rather gnaw off my own leg than marry anyone here. Every single one of them is closely connected to a member of the Thirteen who rule Olympus: Zeus, Poseidon, Demeter, Athena, Ares, Hephaestus, Dionysus, Hermes, Artemis, Apollo, and Aphrodite. The only two missing are Hades and Hera—Hades because he possesses a legacy title and not even Zeus can command his presence at these events, and Hera because our current Zeus is unmarried, which leaves Hera's title empty.

It won't stay empty for long.

For sure a large room, it's remarkably claustrophobic. Not even the giant windows overlooking Olympus can combat the heat from so many bodies. I'm tempted to step outside and freeze for a bit just to get some fresh air, but then I'll be trapped if someone decides to make small talk. At least in the main party, I can keep on the move.

Tonight isn't *officially* a marriage mart, but you can't tell that from the way Aphrodite parades person after person in front of our new Zeus where he lounges in the throne that used to be his father's. It's large and gold and gaudy. It might have suited the father, but it doesn't suit the son in the least. I'm not one to judge, but he lacks the commanding charisma that the last Zeus possessed. If he's not careful, the piranhas of Olympus will eat him alive.

"Zeus," Aphrodite trills. She's been moving back and forth to the throne enough times for me to get a good look at the bright-red dress that hugs her trim figure and contrasts with her pale skin and blond hair. This time, she's towing a young white guy with dark hair behind her. I don't recognize him on sight, which means he's a friend or a distant cousin or has the dubious favor of being one of Aphrodite's pet projects. She beams at Zeus as she cuts through the crowd. "You simply *must* meet Ganymede."

"Psyche."

I nearly jump when my mother appears behind me. It takes all my control to paste a passive smile on my face. "Hello, Mother."

"You're avoiding me."

"Of course not." I most definitely am. "I went to get a drink." I hold up my glass to prove it.

Mother narrows her eyes. Unlike Aphrodite, who seems determined to cling to every last drop of youth she can manage, my mother has allowed herself to age gracefully. She looks like exactly what she is—a white woman in her fifties with dark hair and impeccable style. She clothes herself in power the way some people clothe themselves in jewels. When people look at Demeter, they are instantly at ease because she exudes an aura that promises she'll take care of everything.

It's how she won the title in the first place.

When it came time to craft my own public persona, I looked to her for inspiration even if I took my image in a different direction. Personal experience taught me early that it's better to blend in than to stand up in front of a crowd and make a target of yourself.

"Psyche." Mother takes my arm, angling us toward Zeus's throne. "I am going to introduce you to Zeus."

"I've met him before." Several times in fact. We were introduced ten years ago when Mother took over as Demeter, and we've been attending the same parties ever since. Up until a few months ago, he was still Perseus, heir to the title *Zeus*. Best I can tell, he's nowhere near the predator his late father was, but that doesn't mean he's not a predator at all. He's grown up in the glittering viper's nest that is the upper city. You don't survive this long without being at least a little bit monster.

Mother's hand tightens on my arm and she lowers her voice. "Well, you're going to meet him again. Properly. Tonight."

We watch Zeus barely glance at Ganymede. "It doesn't look like he's interested in meeting anyone."

"That's because he hasn't met *you* yet."

I snort. I can't help it. I know my strengths. I am pretty, but I am no traffic-stopping beauty the way my sisters are. My true strength lies in my brain, and I highly doubt Zeus would appreciate *that*.

Not to mention I have no desire to be Hera.

But then, it doesn't matter what *I* want, does it? Mother has plans upon plans, and I'm the best candidate of her remaining single daughters. For all my internal dramatics, I suppose there are worse fates than being one of the Thirteen. As Hera, the only danger I'd truly face is from Zeus. At least *this* Zeus doesn't have a reputation for harming his partners.

I manage a smile as my mother guides me through the crowd toward the gaudy throne and the man occupying it. We're only a few feet behind Aphrodite and Ganymede when Zeus catches sight of us. He doesn't smile, but interest lights his blue eyes and he flicks his fingers at Aphrodite. "That's enough."

A mistake.

Aphrodite turns toward us. Her gaze flicks over me, instantly dismissing me, before turning to my mother. Her rival, though the term is far too mundane for the amount of loathing these two women hold for each other.

"Demeter, darling, I *know* you're not thinking of *this* daughter as a potential marriage candidate." Aphrodite makes a show of looking at my body. "No offense, Psyche, but you're hardly the proper type to become Hera. You just...don't fit in. I'm sure you understand." Her smile goes sugary sweet and does nothing to dampen the poison of her words. "If you'd like, I'm more than happy to send over the health plan I recommend to all marriage hopefuls while I work on their matches."

Wow, she's not even trying to be subtle. Lovely.

I don't have a chance to respond because my mother's grip tightens on my arm and she's turning a brilliant smile at the other woman. "Aphrodite, *darling*, you've been around long enough to learn to take a hint. Zeus dismissed you." She leans forward and lowers her voice. "I know rejection stings, but it's important to keep your chin up. Maybe you can work on another marriage for Ares instead. Lower-hanging fruit and all that."

Considering Ares has to be over eighty and is practically knocking on the doors to the underworld, it's no wonder Aphrodite practically shoots fire out of her eyes at my mother. "Actually—"

"What are we talking about?"

The question comes from a tall, dark-haired white woman as she steps between Aphrodite and Demeter with a confidence only a member of the Kasios family can pull off. Eris Kasios, daughter of the last Zeus, sister of the current one. She weaves a little on her feet as if she's had too much to drink, but the sharp intelligence in her dark eyes is undimmed by alcohol. An act, then.

Both Aphrodite and my mother straighten, and I can see the exact moment they decide it's in their best interest to be polite. Aphrodite smiles. "Eris, you look stunning tonight as always."

She's telling the truth. Eris wears her customary black—a long dress with a deep V in the front that dips nearly to her belly button and a slit up one side that flashes leg with every step she takes. Her dark hair falls around her in waves that seem effortless, which is just an indication of how much time she put into them.

Eris grins at her, a slice of crimson lips curving in a way that has the small hairs rising on the back of my neck. "Aphrodite.

A pleasure as always." She turns toward me, and her glass tips, sending green liquid that smells like black licorice to splatter both Aphrodite's red gown and my mother's green one. Both women let loose little shrieks and jump back.

"Oops." Eris presses a hand to her chest, her expression perfectly sincere. "My gods, I'm so sorry. I must have drank too much." She weaves a little on her feet, and my mother jumps forward to grab her elbow, nearly running into Aphrodite attempting to do the same.

No one wants Zeus's sister to collapse in the middle of a party and make a scene, potentially embarrassing him and putting an end to the night's festivities.

They're so busy ensuring she stays on her feet that neither of them notice her look at me and...wink. When I stare, Eris jerks her chin in a clear command to make an escape while I can.

What is *that* all about?

I don't stick around to ask. Not with Aphrodite already aiming those barbed arrows she calls words in my mother's direction and Demeter stepping right to the line in the sand between them. When they get going like this, they can keep it up for hours, just snipe, snipe, sniping at each other.

I glance at Zeus, but he's turned away, speaking to Athena in a low voice. Ah well. If Mother is so determined to introduce me properly to Zeus, it looks like tonight won't be the night.

Or maybe I'm simply looking for a good reason to escape.

I don't stop to worry about my mother. She can handle Aphrodite. She's been doing it for years. "Excuse me," I murmur. "I have to use the ladies' room." No one pays me any attention, which is frankly just perfect.

I'm already moving, slipping through the crowd of tuxes and luxurious gowns in a rainbow of colors. Diamonds and priceless jewels glitter beneath the lights scattered throughout the room, and I swear I can feel the eyes of the portraits lining the walls follow me as I move. Up until a month ago, there were only eleven—and one frame kept empty for the next Hera—each depicting one of the Thirteen. As if anyone needed the reminder of who rules this city.

Tonight, all thirteen are finally here.

Hades has been added to the mix, his dark painting a direct counterpoint to the lighter tones of the other twelve. He glowers down at the room the same way he glowers at the people here when he actually chooses to be present. I wish he were here tonight, if only because that means Persephone would be here, too. These parties were so much easier to suffer through when she was at my side. Now that she's gone, ruling the lower city at Hades's side, being in Dodona Tower is tedious in the extreme.

It will be so much worse if I'm Hera.

I let the thought go. There's no point in worrying about it until I know the shape of my mother's plans and how receptive Zeus is to them. In the corner, I catch sight of Hermes, Dionysus, and Helen Kasios gathered around a high table. They look like they're playing some kind of drinking game. At least *they're* enjoying the party. They don't have anything to lose in this space, moving through the power games and carefully veiled threats as naturally as sharks through water.

I can fake it—I'm rather good at faking it—but it will never be instinct the same way it is with people like that.

Without breaking stride, I push open the door and head out

into the quieter hallway. It's after business hours and we're at the top of the tower, so it's deserted. Good. I hurry past the evenly spaced doors with their floor-to-ceiling curtains bracketing each one. They creep me out, especially at night. I never can seem to escape the feeling there's someone hiding there, just waiting for me to pass. I have to keep my gaze straight ahead, even as a low rustle behind me has my instincts screaming to run. I know better; it's my own footsteps echoing back, giving me the impression of being chased.

I can't outrun myself.

I can't outrun *any* of the danger waiting for me back in the main ballroom.

I take my time in the bathroom, bracing my hands on the sink and breathing deeply. Cold water would feel good on my face, but I won't be able to properly fix my makeup and going back with even a hair out of place will have the predators circling. If I become Hera, those voices will get louder, will be inescapable. I'm already not enough for them, or, rather, I'm *too much*. Too quiet, too fat, too plain.

"Stop it." Saying the words out loud grounds me, just a little.

Those insults aren't my beliefs. I've worked hard for them not to be. It's only when I'm here, having my face shoved in what Olympus considers perfection, that the toxic voice from my teenage years rears its ugly head.

Five breaths. Slow inhales. Even slower exhales.

By the time I get to five, I feel a little more like myself. I lift my head but avoid looking at my reflection. The mirrors here don't tell the truth, even if those lies are only in my head. Best to avoid them entirely. One last breath, and I make myself leave the relative safety of the bathroom and move back into the hall.

Hopefully my mother and Aphrodite will have either finished their spat or taken it to some corner of the ballroom so I can return to the party without getting drawn back into the drama. Hiding in the hallway until it's time to leave isn't an option. I refuse to give Aphrodite any indication that her words affected me in the slightest.

It takes two steps to realize I'm not alone.

A man staggers down the hallway toward me, coming from the direction of the elevators. For a brief moment, I consider ignoring him and heading back to the party, but that means he'll be shadowing my steps. Not to mention there are only two of us out here and there's no way to pretend I'm doing anything but ignoring him. He doesn't look too good, either, even in the low light. Maybe he's drunk, a little pregame party that went too far.

With an internal sigh, I slip my public persona back into place and give him a tiny smile and a wave. "Late arrival?"

"Something like that."

Oh shit. I know that voice. I take great pains to avoid the man it belongs to.

Eros. Aphrodite's son. Aphrodite's *fixer*.

I watch him approach warily, stepping out of shadow as he comes near. He's as gorgeous as his mother is. Tall and blond, though his hair has a distinctive curl that would be cute framing any other face. His features are too masculine to ever be something as harmless as *cute*. He's tall and has a strong body, to a point where even his expensive suit can't hide how broad his shoulders are, how muscled his arms. The man is built for violence with a face that would make a sculpture weep. Apt, that.

I catch sight of a stain on his white shirt and narrow my eyes. "Is that blood?"

Eros looks down and curses softly. "I thought I got it all."

No point in examining *that* statement. I need to get out of here, and fast. Except... "You're limping." Staggering, really, but not because he's drunk. He's speaking too clearly for that.

"I'm not," he answers easily. Lies easily. He's most assuredly limping, and that's most certainly blood. I know what that means; he must have come straight here from committing some violence on Aphrodite's behalf. The very last thing I want is to get involved with *those* two.

Still, I hesitate. "Is it your blood?"

Eros stops next to me, his blue eyes holding no emotion at all. "It's the blood of the last pretty girl who asked too many questions."

PSYCHE

EROS AMBROSIA THINKS I'M PRETTY.

I shut down *that* useless, foolhardy thought immediately. "I'm going to pretend that's a joke." Even though I know better. There's nothing more dangerous in Olympus than being a pretty girl who manages to enrage Aphrodite enough that she sends her son calling.

Especially a pretty girl who might stand in the way of her plans to secure her *choice for the next Hera.*

"It's really not."

I can't tell if Eros is being serious or not, but better to err on the side of caution. He obviously doesn't want to talk, and spending any more time in his presence than strictly necessary is a terrible idea. I open my mouth to make some excuse to go back into the bathroom to hide until he's gone, but that's not what comes out. "If you go in there injured, someone might decide to finish the job. You and your mother have more than your fair share of enemies in that room." Surely I don't have to tell him that any perceived weakness will have those enemies descending like wolves to a slaughter?

Eros raises his brows. "Why do you care?"

"I don't." I really don't. I'm just a fool who doesn't know when to quit. No matter what else is true of Eros, he didn't choose to be a child of one of the Thirteen any more than I did. "I'm also not someone who wishes you harm. Let me help you."

"I don't need your help." He turns and heads back the way he came, in the direction of the elevator.

"I'm offering it all the same." My body makes the decision to follow him before my brain can catch up, my legs moving on their own and carrying me further from the relative safety of the party. Stepping into the elevator feels like stepping past the point of no return. I wish I could say I'm overreacting, but Eros's reputation precedes him and it's...very, very violent and very, very dangerous. I clasp my hands in front of me and fight the urge to babble.

We only descend a few floors, and then he leads me through glass and stainless-steel offices to a door that opens easily beneath his hand. It's only when we're closed in together that I see it's a fancy bathroom. Like the rest of Dodona Tower, it's minimalist with black tile floors, a few stalls, a tiled-in shower, and a trio of stainless-steel sinks. There's even a small area near the door with a pair of comfortable-looking chairs and a small round table between them.

"You seem to know your way around here rather well."

"My mother often has business with Zeus."

I swallow hard. "There were bathrooms upstairs." Closer to the relative safety of the party.

"This one has first-aid stuff." He starts to lean down to open one of the cabinets beneath the sink and winces.

That prompts me into motion. This is why I'm here: to help, not to watch him struggle. "Sit down before you fall down."

I'm surprised when he doesn't argue, just limps to the chairs and sinks onto one of them. Thinking about this whole situation too hard is a mistake, so I focus on the task of figuring out how badly he's hurt, patching him up, and getting back to the ballroom before my mother sends out a search party.

Considering last time one of her daughters went missing at a Dodona Tower event, said daughter ended up crossing the River Styx and throwing herself into Hades's arms...

Yes, better not to be gone too long.

As promised, there's a first-aid kit in the cabinet below the sink. I grab it, turn around, and freeze. "What are you doing?" My voice comes out squeaky, but I can't help it.

Eros stops in the middle of taking off his shirt. "What's wrong?"

Everything's wrong. I've been moving in similar circles to this man for a decade, but I've never seen him anything less than perfectly pressed and polished and downright gleaming at these parties. His beauty is breathtaking and almost too perfect to be real.

He doesn't look too perfect right now.

No, he's all too real. Impossible to keep the mental fence I have around Eros as *dangerous playboy* when he's peeling off his shirt and revealing a body carved by the gods. The exhaustion on his face only makes him more attractive, which I might find horribly unfair later, but right now I can't find enough oxygen in this room to breathe.

Panic. That's what I'm feeling. Pure panic. It's not attraction. It can't be. Not to *him*. "You're stripping."

Beneath the white fabric, I can see that someone—likely Eros himself—has slapped a scattering of bandages across his chest. He gives me a charming smile that's only slightly strained around the edges. "I was under the impression you wanted me out of my clothes."

"Pass." I blurt the word out, my hard-won public persona nowhere in evidence.

"Everyone else does."

Weirdly enough, his arrogance calms me. I take a breath, and then another, and give him the look that comment deserves. Banter. I can do banter. I've been trading artful insults with people like Eros for my entire adult life. "Am I supposed to feel sorry for you? Or are you bragging? Please be clear so I can adjust my reaction accordingly."

He bursts out laughing. "Clever."

"I try." I frown. "I thought your leg is injured."

"It's just a bruise." If anything, his charming smile ramps up a few notches. "Trying to get me out of my pants, too?"

If him being shirtless is enough to cause this uncomfortable reaction, I most certainly don't want him to lose any more items of clothing. I might combust, and if the embarrassment doesn't kill me on the spot, it will hand Eros a weapon to use against me. "Absolutely not."

He finishes shrugging out of his shirt and gives a rough exhale. "That's a shame."

"I'm sure you'll live." I set the kit on the table and eye his chest. Some of the bandages have already come loose, and there are red smears where the blood made contact with his shirt. What *happened* to him? Did he get into a fight with a rosebush? "These need to be redone."

"Go for it." He leans back and closes his eyes.

I'm about to make a sharp comment about him having me do all the work, but the words die in my throat when I peel back the bandage to find... "Eros, this is a lot of blood." I can't tell how serious the wounds are with the mess between the blood and bandages, but some of them are still bleeding.

"You should see the other guy," he says without opening his eyes. Confirming what I already suspected.

Is the other guy still alive? No need to ask that question. The fact that he's here at all means he was successful in whatever his task had been. I finish removing the bandages and sit back, examining his chest. There are at least a dozen cuts. "I'm going to need to clean this or the new bandages won't hold."

He waves a hand. Permission.

I don't allow myself to think as I rise and dig around beneath the sink until I find a basket of clean washcloths. I wet two of them and bring the dry ones over to try to mop up the worst of the mess. It takes several long minutes to clean it away.

Which is right around the time I realize I'm essentially giving Eros Ambrosia a sponge bath.

I sit back abruptly. "Eros, some of these might need stitches." They don't look nearly as bad as they did before I cleaned him up, but I'm not a doctor. Surely he has one on staff like every other household of the Thirteen. I don't understand why he didn't call that person instead of trying to show up for this blasted party.

"It's fine. It'll hold until the end of the night."

I frown down at him. "You can't be serious. You're prioritizing attending a *party*, rather than finding a doctor and getting the medical attention you might require."

"You know better than anyone why I need to." At that, he finally opens his eyes. They seem even bluer than before, and a strange look passes through them. It must be pain, because there's no way that Eros Ambrosia, son of Aphrodite, is looking at *me* with desire.

Despite myself, my gaze flicks to his mouth. He's got a very nice mouth, lips ·curved and sensual. It's really a shame he's a dangerous murderer.

To distract myself from such foolhardy thoughts, I stand and move to the sink. It feels remarkably like running away, but I'm just washing the man's blood from my hands. I glance at the mirror and stop short. He's staring at me with the strangest expression on his face. It's not the desire I've already convinced myself I imagined. No, Eros is looking at me like he's never seen me before, like maybe I've acted against his expectations.

That can't be right, though. It doesn't matter if I've occupied the same parties and ballrooms and events as this man for the last ten years; there is absolutely no reason for Eros to think of me at all. I certainly don't spend much time thinking about *him*. He might be gorgeous, even for Olympus, flawless enough to have his likeness plastered across every billboard if he wanted the work, but Eros is *dangerous*.

I dry my hands and move back to the seat across from him. Somehow, without all the blood in play, this feels even more intimate. I push the thought away and get to work bandaging him. Though I half expect him to push my hands away and do it himself, he stays perfectly still, barely seeming to breathe as I carefully apply bandage after bandage. There are about a dozen cuts, all said and done, and despite my assertion that he needs to see a doctor, most of them are small enough that they've nearly stopped bleeding.

"You're rather good at that." His low voice is filled with edges. I can't tell if he's accusing me or merely making a comment.

I choose to take it at face value. "I grew up on a farm." Sort of. It was technically a farm, but it wasn't what people picture when they think of so-called farm life. There was no quaint little house with a faded red barn. My mother might have expanded her fortune with her three marriages, but she was hardly starting from scratch. We were an industrial farm and the setup reflected that.

His lips curl, something light flickering in his eyes. "Are there a lot of stab wounds on farms?"

"You admit it, then—that you were stabbed."

Now he's actually smiling, though there's still pain evident on his face. "I admit nothing."

"Of course not." I realize I'm still too close to him and back up quickly, moving to the sink to wash my hands again. "But to answer your question, when there are a variety of large machines, not to mention various animals that take exception to foolish humans, injuries happen." Especially when one possesses adventurous sisters like I did. Not that I'm going to tell Eros *that*. This interaction has already been too intimate, too strange. "I need to get back."

"Psyche." He waits until I turn to face him. For a moment, he looks nothing like the confident predator I've worked so hard to avoid. He's simply a man, tired and in pain. Eros touches one of the bandages on his chest. "Why help Aphrodite's pet monster?"

"Even monsters need help sometimes, Eros." I should leave it at that, but his question felt so unexpectedly vulnerable that I can't help the impulse to soothe him. Just a little. "Besides, you're not really a monster. I don't see a single scale or fang to speak of."

"Monsters come in all shapes and sizes, Psyche. You should know that by now, living in Olympus." He starts to button up his shirt, but his hands are shaking so badly, he fumbles it.

I move before I have a chance to remember why this is such a terrible idea. "Let me." I lean over and button him up carefully. My fingers brush his bare chest a few times, and I'm certain I imagine the way he hisses out an exhale in response. Pain. That's all it is. Eros is certainly not responding to *my* touch. I hold my breath as I finish the last button and move back. "There you go."

He climbs to his feet. I watch closely, but he seems a little steadier than he was earlier. Eros pulls his jacket on and buttons it up, hiding the worst of the bloodstains. "Thanks."

"Don't thank me. Anyone would do it."

"No." He shakes his head slowly. "They really wouldn't." He doesn't give me a chance to respond to that. Just motions to the door. "Let's go. Head up without me; I need to find a replacement shirt." He hesitates. "It wouldn't be good for us to be seen returning to the party together."

It really wouldn't. It would get Olympus's gossipmongers chatting, and Aphrodite and Demeter might stroke out in pure rage in response. The very last thing I want is to be linked to Eros in any way, shape, or form. "Of course."

As we step into the hall, Eros presses his hand to the small of my back. The contact jolts through me with the violence of lightning in a bottle. I miss a step and he moves quickly, catching my elbow and keeping me from ending up on the floor. "You good?"

"Yes," I manage. I don't look at him. *Can't* look at him. It was difficult enough to ignore this unfortunate spark between us while I patched him up. I don't like my chances with him standing so close, one hand on my lower back and the other cupping my elbow. I should most definitely not...

I lift my face and Eros looks down and, gods, we're so close. This is a mistake. At any moment, I'll pull away and put a respectable amount of distance between us and it will be like this strange little interlude never happened. At...any...moment...

A bright flash sears my eyes. I jerk away from Eros and blink rapidly. Oh no. *Oh no, no, no, no.* This can't be happening.

Except it is happening. My vision clears slowly, and any hope I have of pretending some light bulb shattered at random goes up in smoke. A short white man with bright ginger hair and a camera in his hands stands a few feet away. He grins at us. "I *knew* I saw you get in the elevator together. Psyche, care to comment about what you're doing sneaking away from Zeus's party to get alone time with Eros Ambrosia?"

Eros takes a menacing step toward the photographer, but I grab his arm and fight for a smile. "Just a friendly little chat."

The man doesn't miss a beat. "Is that why Eros's shirt is buttoned up incorrectly? And you looked like you were about to kiss in this picture?" He's gone before I can come up with a lie that might make sense.

"We're fucked," I breathe.

Eros curses far more creatively than I have. "That about sums it up."

I know how this goes. Before the end of the night, pictures of me and Eros will be plastered across the gossip sites, and people will start theorizing about our *forbidden romance*. I can see the headlines now.

Star-crossed lovers! What will Demeter and Aphrodite think of their children's secret relationship?

Forget stroking out in rage. My mother is going to *kill me*.

EROS

TWO WEEKS LATER

"BRING ME HER HEART."

"My chest is healed up just fine. Thanks for asking." I don't look up from my phone as my mother paces from one side of the room to the other, her skirt swishing about her legs. Knowing her, she chose her clothing today to maximize her dramatic flouncing.

She's nothing if not a showwoman.

The phone isn't the distraction I'd like it to be. In the two weeks since the party, the speculation and gossip about me and Psyche Dimitriou hasn't died down. If anything, our refusal to make a public comment about it has only fanned the flames. There's nothing Olympus loves more than a good story, and the children of two public enemies hooking up is nothing if not a good story. The truth doesn't matter when there's a compelling lie to be told.

Not to mention the photographer got a stellar shot.

In the picture, we're standing so close, nearly in an embrace, and she's looking up at me in question. And me? The look on my face can only be described as *hungry*. I wouldn't have done something as foolish as to kiss Psyche in that hallway, but no one looking at our image will believe it.

"Stop playing with your phone and look at me." My mother spins on her tall heel and glares down at me. She's fifty, and though she'd skin me alive for saying as much, no wrinkles or gray hair betray her. She spends a fortune to keep her skin smooth and her hair a perfect icy blond. Not to mention the countless hours with her personal trainer to accomplish a body twenty-year-olds would kill for. All in the name of her title, Aphrodite. When one has the role of the matchmaker of Olympus—the peddler of love—one must meet certain expectations.

"Eros, put down that godsdamned phone and listen to me."

"I'm listening." My bored tone betrays my waning patience, but I'm already tired of this conversation. We've had some variation of it about a dozen times in the last two weeks. "I already told you what really happened."

"No one cares what really happened." She's almost screeching now, her carefully curated smoky tones going high and sharp. "They are dragging your name through the mud by attaching it to that upstart's daughter."

I don't point out that the title Aphrodite has no more legacy than Demeter's. The only titles in Olympus that pass from parent to child are Zeus, Hades, and Poseidon. The rest of the Thirteen come to them as adults, in ways both aboveboard and clandestine. My mother can't stand the fact that she was appointed by the last Aphrodite, while Demeter was chosen through a citywide election.

The people chose Demeter, and she's never let my mother forget it.

"It won't be long before the next scandal hits. Just be patient."

"*You* don't tell me what to do, Son. *I* give the orders, and you obey." She stops in front of me and glares. "This is your mess. If you'd done the last job properly, you wouldn't have been photographed with *that girl*."

"Mother." I don't know why I'm arguing. Once my mother goes on a rampage, it's all but impossible to divert her. It's one of the reasons people step so carefully around her. Even *I* have to step carefully around her. She might present our relationship to the public as adoring mother and loyal son, but the truth is far less appealing. I am Aphrodite's knife. She tells me where to go, what revenge to exact, and I follow along like a fucked-up toy soldier. My input is never asked for and sure as fuck never heeded. I *told* her that we needed to wait to deal with Polyphonte instead of rushing into things the night of that party, but Aphrodite pushed the subject.

She always pushes the fucking subject.

"Her heart, Eros. Do *not* make me ask again."

I swallow back my irritation, but only barely. "You're going to have to be more specific, Mother. Do you *literally* want her heart? Do you have a silver box all picked out for it? Maybe you can stick it on your mantel next to my graduation photo."

She makes a sound suspiciously like a hiss. "You are such a little shit." This is the Aphrodite she doesn't show anyone else in Olympus. Only I get the dubious privilege of witnessing what a monster my mother truly is.

But then, I'm not one to throw stones on that subject.

I don't see a single scale or fang.

I nearly flinch at the memory of Psyche's soft voice. I really thought she was smarter than that; she'd have to be a fool to move in nearly the same circles I have for ten years and *not* call me a monster.

I make a show of turning off my phone screen and giving my mother my full attention. "You've decided on this course of action, so don't be shy now."

Another person would flinch in the face of my mild tone with the threat of violence threaded beneath it. Aphrodite just laughs. "Eros, darling, you really are too much. After that stunt Demeter pulled last fall with her other daughter and Hades, she really thinks she can bypass me completely and set up *Psyche* as the next Hera. Over my dead body. Or, rather, over *hers.*"

My chest goes strangely tight, but I ignore it. "If you're so furious at Demeter, then do something about her, rather than the daughter."

"You know better." She flicks that away with her fingertips. "Both mother and daughter need to be taught a lesson. Demeter has been throwing her weight around, thinking she's anything other than a glorified farmer. This will bring her down a notch."

Only my mother would consider the death of a child to be bringing someone down a notch.

But then, she'll do anything to maintain her power. Aphrodite is responsible for a number of things, but her most popular task is arranging marriage between the rich and elite within Olympus. The Thirteen and their families, yes, but also those in the wider circle of influence that never quite make it into the parties at Dodona Tower.

With Demeter inching in on her territory, it's no wonder my mother's head is about to explode. She arranged all three marriages for the last Zeus—the fucker kept killing off his wives, which suited my mother quite nicely as she loves a wedding and hates everything that follows. Securing a new Hera for the new Zeus is her top priority, and it seems like Demeter is determined to launch Psyche into the position of Hera without consulting Aphrodite.

I try to picture it, but my mind rebels at the thought. All I can see is the line of concentration between Psyche's brows as she bandaged me up. Surely someone foolish enough to show kindness to the son of their enemy is the same kind of someone who will be eaten alive in the position of Hera.

I clear my throat. "How's Zeus doing these days? Does he not like any of your eligible options?" Up until a few months ago, he was Perseus, but names are the first thing sacrificed at the altar of the Thirteen. Once upon a time, we were friends, but Olympian life has a way of forcing people apart. The older we got, the more Perseus became embroiled in training to become the next Zeus. And me? Well, my life took an equally dark path. We're still friends, I guess, but there's a distance there that neither of us can quite recover. I don't even know where to begin to try.

I let the thought drift away. Perseus has been Zeus's heir for his entire life. He knew he'd take the title when his father died. If it happened a bit earlier than anyone expected...well, he's more than capable of handling it. It's not my problem. It *can't* be my problem. After all, *I* didn't kill the man.

"Don't change the subject," she snaps. "Ever since Persephone ran off and shacked up with Hades, Olympus is unbalanced. Now

Demeter thinks she's going to pair up another daughter with another legacy position? What's next? Marrying off that feral older daughter of hers to Poseidon?" She huffs. "I think not. Someone needs to check Demeter, and if no one else will step up, then we'll have to."

"You mean *I'll* have to. You might be demanding a heart, but we both know that I'm the one doing all the work." I have no desire for someone to start calling for my head, so I try to keep the murders to a minimum. It's so much easier to remove an opponent with a well-placed rumor or simply observe them until their own actions provide the ammunition for their downfall. Olympus is filled to the brim with sin, if one believes in that sort of thing, and no one in the Thirteen's shining circle is without their fair share of vices.

Except, apparently, Demeter's daughters.

They've tried hard to stay out of the spotlight, and it even worked...at least up until a few months ago. Ever since the old Zeus decided he wanted Persephone for his own—for all the good that did him—Olympus has gone rabid for the Dimitriou sisters. After all, Persephone's story seems like an epic one for the ages, the kind of shit the gossip sites eat right up. Zeus drove her right into Hades's arms, which in turn brought Hades out of the shadows of the lower city. No one saw *that* coming.

Zeus and the rest of the upper city like to pretend Olympus stops at the River Styx. Hades was something of a dirty little secret only the Thirteen and a few choice others had knowledge of. Now he's out in the open and the entire power balance of Olympus is in flux. It will be months yet before things settle, possibly longer.

Hades's romance with Persephone has only amped up Olympus's fascination with the Dimitriou sisters. They're all attractive, but none of them quite *fit*. Persephone always had her eyes on the horizon, her determination to find a way out of the city clear to anyone with a drop of perception to their name. Callisto, the oldest, is just as feral as my mother claims. She's constantly getting into fights or saying things she shouldn't, a blatant refusal to play Olympus's power games that people both resent and are drawn to. Eurydice, the youngest, is pretty and sweet and far too naive for someone in this city.

And then there's Psyche. It's not just that she's different physically from her sisters—she's just flat-out *different*. She plays the game and plays it well, all without seeming to. She's got this unassuming thing going on, but I've been watching her long enough to notice that she never makes a move by accident. I can't prove it, of course, but I think she's got just as savvy a brain in her head as her mother does.

None of *that* explains what happened the night of Zeus's party. If Psyche were really as conniving as her mother, she never would have let herself get caught alone with me. She wouldn't have patched me up. She wouldn't have done *any* of the things that happened from the moment I saw her in that hallway.

I don't have much of a moral center, but even I think it's shitty to reward her kindness by ending her life.

"Eros." Mother snaps her fingers in front of my face. "Stop daydreaming and do this task for me." She smiles slowly, her blue eyes going icy. "Bring me Psyche's heart."

"Have you really thought this through?" I raise my brows,

working to keep my expression disinterested. "She's rather beloved by hundreds of thousands of Olympians—at least according to her social-media follower counts."

I realize my mistake the second Aphrodite sneers. "She's a fat girl with little style and no substance. The only reason MuseWatch and the other sites follow her around is because she's a novelty. She's not even close to my league."

I don't argue with her because there's no point, but the truth is that Psyche is gorgeous and has a style that sets trends in a way Aphrodite can only dream of. Which is exactly the problem. My mother's decided to take down two birds with one stone. "I wasn't aware you were in competition."

"Because we're not." She waves that away as if I'm foolish enough to believe her. "This isn't about me. This is about you." She props her hands on her hips. "I want this taken care of, Eros. You have to do this for me."

Something in my chest twinges, but I ignore it. If I believed in souls, my actions would have guaranteed I'd sacrificed mine long ago. There is a price for power in this city, and with a mother in the Thirteen, I never had a chance at innocence. If you're not at the top of the Olympus power structure, you're being crushed beneath someone else's heel as they use you to get ahead. I have no choice. I was born into this game, and the only option is being the best, the scariest, the one people would do anything to avoid fucking with. It keeps both me and my mother safe. If it means that sometimes I'm required to do these little *tasks* for her? It's a small enough price to pay. "I'll see it done."

"Before the end of the week."

That doesn't give me much time at all. I stomp down on the flicker of resentment and nod. "I said I'll see it done and I will."

"Good." She twirls away, her skirt once again flaring dramatically around her, and strides out of the room.

That's my mother, all right. Here for the proclamations of revenge and heavy with the demands, but when it comes time to actually do the work, she's suddenly got somewhere to be.

It's just as well. I'm good at what I do because I know when to be flashy and when to fly below the radar. Aphrodite wouldn't know how to be subtle if her life depended on it. I wait a full thirty seconds before I push to my feet and walk to my front door. If she changes her mind and comes back to spout off some more bullshit, she'll be pissed to find my door locked, but I don't like being interrupted once I get to planning.

And frankly, it's good for my mother to be foiled from time to time. She controls so much of my life, it's important to have at least one space that is Aphrodite-free—even occasionally. As much as I chafe at being under her control, my options are limited. My mother is one of the Thirteen. No matter where I reside in Olympus, the fact remains that she holds all the cards—all the power—and I am merely a tool to be picked up at her leisure.

I'm no saint. I've long since made my peace with my path in life. But fuck if it doesn't smother me sometimes, especially when Aphrodite gives an order that feels especially cruel. Psyche *helped* me, and now my mother's commanded *my* hand to be the one that strikes her down.

I head through the penthouse to what passes for my safe room. I use it to store things I don't want nosy guests—or Hermes—to get their hands on. She's tried at least a dozen times to break into it, and so far my security has held, but I'm all too aware that eventually she might prevail. Still, it's the best option available to me.

Once I lock *that* door, I sit behind my computer and consider my options. This would be so much simpler if Aphrodite just wanted to make a nonlethal example of Psyche. She might be crafting a reputation as an influencer in that quiet way of hers, but reputations are easy to burn to ash. I've done it dozens of times over the years, and no doubt I'll do it many more. All it takes is some patience and the ability to play the long game.

But no, my mother wants her literal heart. How very Evil Queen of her. I shake my head and bring up my files on the Dimitriou sisters. I have files on all the Thirteen and their immediate families, as well as close friends. In Olympus, information is 90 percent of the battle, so I work hard to keep myself informed. Since the party two weeks ago, I've taken a particular interest in Psyche, and I can't even blame my mother for it.

Psyche didn't have to help me.

She would have been so much smarter to turn away and pretend she never saw me. Anyone else would have done as much. Even some of the people I consider friends would have made that choice. I don't blame them for it. In Olympus, it's every person for themselves.

I click through the most recent articles on MuseWatch. Persephone visited her family last weekend briefly and caused quite the stir because she brought her new husband with her. The Hades-Demeter alliance is one nobody saw coming, and it's feeding into my mother's paranoia. She had the last Zeus on a leash, but his son hasn't taken the bait she keeps dangling in front of him. It's got her worried.

I stop on a picture of Psyche and her sisters shopping. The Dimitriou sisters seem to genuinely love and support each other. They might dip their toes into playing the power games, but they mostly hold themselves separate. I don't know if it's because they think they're better than the rest of us or if the rest of us are just so naturally insular that we didn't exactly welcome them with open arms when they first showed up. My mother likes to label the whole family as social climbers, and more than a few within the Thirteen's inner circles have taken to doing the same.

But if that were true, Persephone Dimitriou wouldn't have braved crossing the River Styx to try to get away from a marriage with Zeus.

And Psyche wouldn't have helped her.

Even I'm not sure exactly what happened that night, but I know Psyche was involved—and it wasn't to play the part of the rational party convincing her sister that this marriage would help their family's position. If they were any other family, Psyche would have taken advantage of her sister's absence and placed herself in front of Zeus as a candidate for the new Hera.

Instead, she helped her sister. Just like she helped me.

I study the image of Psyche. She's got long, dark hair and full lips that always seem curved in a secretive smile. Looking at her, I can't blame the gossip sites for being so obsessed: she seems comfortable in her body, and that kind of thing is sexy as fuck.

She's extremely photogenic, but the pictures still don't do her justice. There's something about her presence in person that makes people sit up and pay attention, even when she's dimming her light as best she can the way she always seems to at the parties we've both attended over the years.

She wasn't dimming herself in the hallway or down in the bathroom where she patched me up. I don't think it was on purpose, but I caught a glimpse of a bright and inquisitive mind behind that pretty face. She might play as if her looks are all she has going for her, but she's smart. Too smart to get caught alone with me, and yet she took that risk and got burned. Why? Because I so obviously needed help. *Because even monsters need help sometimes.*

All this leads me to one very unfortunate conclusion.

Psyche Dimitriou might actually be what passes for a unicorn in Olympus—a good person.

I curse and close the window. It doesn't matter if she's hot or that I respect the way she's so effectively dodged the power games since her family arrived on the scene or that she's *nice*. My mother has a task, and I know the consequences of failing.

Exile.

Being left with nothing. *Being* nothing.

Aphrodite likes to remind me that the only thing I'm good at is hurting people. Even recognizing the blatant manipulation for what it is...she's not wrong. I don't know how to run a corporation like Perseus. I don't know how to charm people and put them at ease like Helen. Fuck, I'm not even that good at breaking and entering like Hermes.

Not to mention more than a few victims of Aphrodite—of *me*—have suffered exile. If I end up sharing their fate, I don't like my odds of lasting a year without one of them tracking me down and taking their just revenge.

Best not to think about that too closely. I'll take care of the task, and then I'll find a few partners and lose myself in a week of fucking and drinking and anything it takes to numb me out completely. Just like I always have.

With another curse, I pick up my phone.

A chirpy female voice answers. "Eros, my favorite little sex god. It's my lucky day."

Normally, it's difficult to keep a smile off my face when I'm dealing with Hermes. She's incorrigible and the only one of the Thirteen whose presence I actually enjoy. I don't feel much like smiling today. "Hermes."

She gives a sigh. "So it's business, then?"

"It's business," I confirm. It's not always business with Hermes and me. She and I have hooked up a few times over the years but ultimately settled into something resembling friendship. I don't necessarily trust her—her title is practically spymaster, after all—but I like her.

"All business and no play makes Eros a dull boy."

"We can't all spend our time playing jester in Hades's court."

She laughs. "Don't be mad just because Hades banned you from his sex dungeon. You would have done the same thing in his position."

She's right, but that doesn't mean I'm about to admit it. The only reason Hades let me come and go across the River Styx without an issue was that we had something of a mutually beneficial relationship. He controlled the information I reported back to my mother. I enjoyed his hospitality. That all changed when Persephone entered the scene. She expanded his allegiance from himself to his now wife—and her mother, Demeter.

Seeing as how Demeter and *my* mother hate each other, that means I'm persona non grata in the lower city these days. When Hades cut me off, he cut off my main outlet to blow off steam. Not that that matters now, but Hermes always did know how to find a person's buttons…and then do jumping jacks on them. "I have a message I'd like you to deliver, but it's delicate in nature."

A pause. "Okay, you have my attention. Stop toying with my emotions and tell me what you're up to."

I force a small smile as I sketch out what I need from her. Hermes's role in the Thirteen is a little bit messenger, a little bit spy, a little bit agent of chaos for her own amusement. Her only real allegiance is to Dionysus, and even then, I'm not sure that friendship would hold if things got really intense. He's not my aim, however, so I have no doubt she'll do exactly as I request.

When I finish, she gives a merry laugh. "Eros, you sly rake, you. I'll have the message delivered by morning." She hangs up before I can respond.

I sit back with a sigh and rub my chest. No matter my personal thoughts on this, things are in motion. It's too late to go back and change the past; I can only do what I've always done—come out on top.

Psyche Dimitriou will be dead before the end of the week.

PSYCHE

"I SWEAR TO THE GODS, IF MOTHER GETS ONE MORE PARTY invitation, I'm going to pull a Zeus and throw myself out a window."

I pause in the middle of sorting through the dresses in the rack in front of me. None of them are right. They're all pretty in a pale sort of way, but this designer has a nasty habit of merely adding inches to their plus sizes instead of actually taking into account how different my curves are from a size two. I had heard they'd gotten better with the new spring line, but obviously I was misinformed.

That irritation matters less than what my sister is spouting off behind me, within easy eavesdropping range of everyone in this shop. The *last* thing we need is more of a scandal, especially right now. The rumors about me and Eros have held on longer than I expected—it's been a slow news month in Olympus and that *was* a truly excellent photograph to get the gossip mill churning—but they will pass. Or they will pass as long as we keep our heads down and our mouths shut. Eros has all but disappeared from the public eye; smart of him. I don't have that option, so the only other route is to go on about my life as if I'm not the subject of everyone's conjecture.

Today, that means shopping.

Just my luck that my eldest sister is feeling overprotective and decided to tag along. I turn around and level a look at Callisto. As always, she's dressed in a pseudo grunge look that makes her appear like a model on her day off. We share the same dark brown hair and hazel eyes, but Callisto's beauty is sharp enough to cut while mine is a softer variation. She's never had to deal with Mother trying to *gently* guide her to try some new diet, but any resentment I felt about our differences is ancient history now.

What *isn't* ancient history is how godsdamned reckless she is.

I march over to where she's sprawled on the waiting area couch and lean over her. "Keep your voice down."

Callisto narrows her eyes. "What do you care if these lemmings hear? I'm only speaking the truth."

It's been a little over two months since Zeus's "accidental" death and Olympus is still reeling. Making a joke about it will be in poor taste twenty years from now, but right now it's a great way to attract the kind of headline we do *not* need at the moment.

Dimitriou daughters mock the former Zeus's death!

On the heels of the Eros photograph, Mother might actually follow through on one of her many threats to toss her frustrating daughters out the nearest window. I'm sure Perseus—er,

Zeus—would be delighted by that. We're under strict instructions to avoid making him angry, and Callisto seems to have taken that as a challenge to see how far she can push things. Normally, it would be a minor irritation, but we're under a much heavier spotlight right now. I still can't believe I was so foolish as to get caught alone with Aphrodite's son. I've received no less than three of Mother's lectures about my irresponsibility and how this will affect my prospects with Zeus.

Having my name struck from the list of Zeus's potential partners is hardly a great loss in my opinion, but I'm smart enough not to say that out loud.

Unlike my sister.

I lean down farther and lower my voice. "You know everyone is watching us right now. Stop trying to stir the pot."

Callisto lifts her brows, completely unrepentant. "If you'd stop babysitting me, I'd do something to get the focus off you. It won't take much, and I'll even enjoy it."

"Callisto, no." Her idea of *help* is usually the exact opposite. Even though I know better, I can't help but ask, "What would you even do?"

"Oh, I haven't thought about it too hard. Probably shove Aphrodite into traffic. Maybe I'll get lucky and her asshole son will be with her. A two-for-one bargain."

Of course. I don't know why I even asked. "If you piss off Zeus and Mother, *I'm* going to be the one who has to clean up the mess. Please don't—for my sake."

She opens her mouth like she's going to snarl, hesitates, and finally curses. "Okay, fine. I'll play nice, but I'm serious about not wanting to attend the next party. Now that Persephone's off living her happily wedded bliss, Mother doesn't let me make excuses anymore."

I don't point out that there have been several parties since Persephone moved to the lower city, and Callisto never let Mother bully her before. She's doing it for me, so I won't have to face the vipers alone. Really, she's the only one capable of it. After having her heart broken by Orpheus, Eurydice is too fragile to deal with the backstabbing of the glittering crowd that surrounds the Thirteen—and she wasn't all that good at it before. She's too likely to take everyone at their word and assume innocence while surrounded by people who lie as easily as they breathe.

Callisto doesn't have that problem. Then again, Callisto is much more likely to stab someone with a salad fork—or shove them into traffic, apparently. The former is something she actually did at the party before last; it was the reason Mother relented and let her stay home recently. That reminds me... "How *is* Ares? I haven't seen anything on MuseWatch about him." Now that I think about it, I hadn't seen him at the last party, either.

"I'm sure he's fine. It was only a surface wound." She flicks her hair off her shoulder. "If he hadn't called Persephone a fickle w—" She curses. "I refuse to repeat it. If he hadn't called our sister *that*, it wouldn't be an issue."

"It's only words, and Persephone could care less what anyone on this side of the river thinks of her—family excluded, of course."

"She doesn't care, but *I* care." Callisto examines her fingernails. "They might fight with words, but eventually they'll figure out that I don't stop there."

"Insults and assault are two very different things." Though, honestly, I don't think Mother smoothed this one over the way she has with Callisto's…missteps…in the past. If she had, we would have heard about it, but after the initial lecture, it never came up again.

"Are they?" She shrugs. "Could have fooled me."

There's no getting through to Callisto. She might consent to attending the endless parties Mother is dragging us to, but she'll never play the game. I still haven't quite figured out how she's pulled *that* off, but it's something I can't replicate. "If I go try on a few dresses, will you behave yourself?"

She shrugs a single shoulder. "There's no one in here that pisses me off, so odds are good."

They'd only stay good for as long as that remained true. I straighten. "There's this little thing called self-control. You should try it sometime. You might even like the results."

My sister laughs. She might be just shy of vicious to everyone outside our little family unit, but she laughs like an angel—or a siren, more accurately. I catch the saleslady peering with interest in our direction and barely manage to resist rolling my eyes. "I'll be quick."

"Good idea."

I grab the most promising options off the rack and head back into the changing rooms. They're large enough for several people to fit in each one, which makes sense because so many of the upper crust of Olympia seem to dress themselves by committee. Maybe I would, too, if any of my sisters showed any interest in fashion. Callisto ignores it and Eurydice dresses in whatever is available. Persephone is the only one who used to enjoy it, just a little, but those shopping trips with her are in the past. She's too busy running half the city with her husband now.

I don't begrudge Persephone her happiness. I truly don't. But I miss her. Her infrequent trips to this side of the River Styx are never enough, and Mother already has an issue with Eurydice visiting the lower city so often. If I started doing it as well, her head might actually explode. Especially now.

No, for better or worse, my options are limited.

I strip out of my dress and try on the first dress. As I suspected, it's a terrible fit. It clings in places it's not meant to cling and is baggy through places it shouldn't be baggy. I sigh and peel the disappointing garment off.

"That's godsawful. I expected better of Thalia."

I freeze in the middle of hanging the dress up. I know that voice, but even as I tell myself it's not possible, I look in the mirror and meet the gaze of Hermes. She's a petite Black woman with natural hair who favors quirky wide-frame glasses and has the gift of mimicry. Today her glasses are bright red and she's wearing purple glittering pants, an orange hoodie with the picture of a cat on the front of it, its eyes bugging out, and red Chucks. I suppose when you're one of the Thirteen, you can do whatever you want and people just accept it. The benefit of power. Hermes, in particular, doesn't seem to care what anyone thinks of her. She appears to enjoy shocking people and challenging their expectations, which would be enough to make her interesting to me, but she's one of the Thirteen, so I try to steer clear.

There's no steering clear now.

I don't try to cover myself, don't blush, don't react in any way that would tell her I'm nonplussed by this development. "Hello, Hermes."

"Hi, Psyche." She leans down and stares at my breasts. "Is that a Juliette bra? It's exquisite. And I'm not just saying that because your tits are a ten."

I strive for patience. I haven't spent much time interacting with Hermes, but the few conversations we've had felt like walking through a minefield blindfolded. Persephone likes her, but Persephone has enough power now that she *can* associate with members of the Thirteen without worrying about being steamrolled. I'm not that lucky. There's no good reason for Hermes to be here, but I hope against hope that it's merely her curiosity that brought her around, rather than her official duties. "What can I help you with?"

"Maybe I just showed up to chat."

I don't let out a sigh of relief. Not when she's got *that* mischievous look in her dark eyes. "Did you?"

"Nope." She grins at the look on my face. "Okay, yes, fine, you caught me. It's official business. I have a message for you."

Damn it, that's what I'm afraid of. "A message that couldn't wait until I'm dressed."

She shrugs. "Sorry, love. It's marked urgent. You know how these things are."

I do, but mostly in theory. I've very intentionally dodged the worst pitfalls the upper crust of Olympia has to offer. In theory, I possess a fraction of power since my mother is Demeter, but the truth is far more complicated. Even within the Thirteen, there are hierarchies. The legacy titles—Zeus, Hades, and Poseidon—stand apart. The status of the rest fluctuates depending on the year, the season, sometimes even the week. Seniority counts for something, as do the responsibilities of certain titles—Ares with Olympus's personal army, for example. Add in alliances and feuds and petty grievances, and one wrong move can have half of Olympus turning on you.

We all watched it happen with Hercules. As a member of Zeus's family, he should have been nearly untouchable, but he pushed too hard to reveal the seedy underbelly of the shining upper city's politics. Every single one of them turned on him as a result. The official story is that he left Olympus of his own power, but since everyone's afraid to even mention his name now, the message is crystal clear.

Cross the Thirteen and they will wipe you from existence.

I bite back a sigh. "Okay, let's hear the message."

Hermes straightens and clears her throat. When she speaks, a man's voice emerges from her lips. "This mess isn't going to blow over anytime soon. There's only one way to keep our mothers from feuding. Meet me tonight at Erebus. Come alone."

I know that voice. "Eros." What is he *thinking?* The last thing we can do is risk being seen together. The paparazzi that fuel MuseWatch are too savvy to miss an opportunity like this, even if we meet somewhere neither of us normally frequent. Being caught in one chance encounter is one thing, but two? It will incite an inferno of gossip.

"Why wouldn't he just call me if he wants to talk?"

Hermes raises her brows. "And risk you deciding to record the conversation and use it against him?"

She has a point, but still... "There's nothing stopping me from doing that anyway."

"Maybe he'll *pat you down*—in a very sexy manner." Hermes bounces on her toes. "You know, I have to ask. Were you banging in the bathroom at the party two weeks ago?"

"No." My mind offers up the image of Eros with blood on his shirt, his low voice saying, *It's the blood of the last pretty girl who asked too many questions.* He's Aphrodite's fixer. Has Aphrodite decided *I'm* a problem in need of fixing?

No, that doesn't make sense. There are a thousand ways to bury someone in Olympus without ever having to physically harm their body or put yourself in direct contact with them. Even as Demeter's daughter, I'm hardly untouchable, but if Eros wanted to *fix* me, he could do it. He certainly could do it without potentially implicating himself by meeting me in person.

I go through the motions of trying on the next dress. It's just as bad as the first. Gods, I hate it when designers are lazy. Focusing on that small irritation clears my head enough that by the time I turn to face Hermes again, I'm no longer in danger of losing control. "I assume he needs no reply."

"Nope. Your reply is showing up tonight—or not, as the case may be."

I have to show up. I don't have a choice. He's right about us needing to talk about the picture and a plan going forward. If Aphrodite is as furious about it as my mother is, it makes sense to ensure the gossip sites have something else to focus on so that they forget all about us and our so-called forbidden romance.

Still... We can't afford a second picture of us. The location Eros gave is in the upper warehouse district, a neighborhood most of the Thirteen avoid, which means most of the paparazzi avoid it as well. We *should* be okay, but that doesn't mean I'm about to take that for granted.

I consider Hermes. Using her services is a risk. She's loyal to no one but herself—and maybe Dionysus—and that means I can't take the secrecy of any message for granted. There's nothing stopping her from standing on some karaoke stage and singing out the dirty laundry of all the people in the room, which is something I heard she did about a year after she took over as Hermes. No one took her seriously up to that point, but *that* event ensured everyone saw her for the threat she is.

Actually, that gives me an idea...

"Hermes, would you be willing to engage in a little friendly deception? In your professional capacity, of course."

Her smile is crafty. "You know, you Dimitriou women keep surprising me. I'm willing to do this *friendly deception* for free since you're entertaining me."

I don't know if that's better or worse, but I'm not one to look the gift horse in the mouth. "Go out tonight."

"I was already planning on it. Dionysus has some *excellent* new products that I'm dying to try."

I ignore the interruption. "Go out tonight and post something about it. Tag your location. Make people believe I'm with you. Then give them a merry chase." There's no better alibi than one of the Thirteen. Who's going to call Hermes a liar? No one. At least not to her face. If the paparazzi are busy chasing Hermes, thinking

I'm with her, they won't be sniffing around the upper warehouse district. Eros and I will be able to talk in peace.

"Consider it done." She shakes her head. "Olympus is never dull with you and your sisters around."

"I could do with a little less excitement." I don't mean to say it, but once the words are out, there's no taking them back.

Hermes heads for the changing room door. "Chin up, Psyche. You're a savvy girl. I'm sure you'll come out on top." She opens the door and twists to look at me. "Maybe you'll even end up coming *on top* of Eros. For real this time." She's gone before I can form a reply, her laugh trailing behind her.

It's just as well. What am I supposed to say to that? Eros might be as gorgeous as a god, but that man is a monster right down to his core. He's my *enemy*.

I'm tempted to call Persephone and get her opinion on this whole situation, but if I loop her in, she'll be barging through my door and threatening Eros before I finish the call. Better to call her in the morning and update her once I hear what he has to say. Maybe we'll even come up with a solution that will make everyone happy.

The fluttering feeling in my stomach is nerves, of course.

I'm certainly *not* looking forward to seeing Eros again.

EROS

I ARRIVE AT THE MEETING SPOT OVER AN HOUR EARLY TO scope out the place. Erebus is a little hole-in-the-wall pub on the edge of the upper city warehouse district. We might still be on the north side of the River Styx, but this area is a different world from the carefully curated central city where most of the Thirteen live. Proximity to Zeus's place of business, Dodona Tower, is seen as a point of status, and every street in the surrounding blocks is a cold and clean combination of concrete, steel, and glass. Uniform and attractive enough if you're into that sort of thing.

The area around the upper city warehouse district is where people go for a little illicit fun when they don't have the strength or the balls to cross the river to the lower city. Here is where Dionysus rules, and there's plenty of vice to go around. People also tend to look the other way and mind their own business when they're in the area, which suits my purposes.

I have to play this carefully. This bar is small, but it's been built into the space between two buildings so it has lots of nooks and crannies filled with shadowy tables. I have one staked out near the back, and I've tipped the bartender well to look the other way during what comes next.

No matter what this task entails or what my mother wants, I have no desire to make Psyche actually suffer. I'm sure Aphrodite would like me to drag her into an alley and get to work with a dull knife, but all Psyche will feel is a sleepiness and then nothing at all.

It's the bare minimum she deserves.

I sit back and rub my hand over my chest. Now is not the time for doubts or guilt or any of that bullshit. I've done worse to nicer people, all because they got in my mother's way or she decided they were threatening her position. The public might think murder is the greater evil, but they haven't seen a young up-and-coming person have everything stripped away. Their beauty, their status, the respect of their peers. It's so fucking *easy* to dismantle someone's life if you have the right information, the right resources.

All that being said, not even I can convince myself that killing Psyche is a mercy.

It never used to be like this. I only went after people who deserved it, people who actively threatened my mother. I was a hunter of monsters, of people who intended to harm the only family I have in this world. Until one day I looked up and realized I'm the biggest monster of all. I'd sacrificed too much, had erased too many lines for morality to be anything more than a theory.

There was no going back.

There *is* no going back.

I sense the moment Psyche walks into the bar. The few patrons go silent and watchful. No matter that she's dressed down in a pair of jeans and a black coat that covers her to the knees, she's beautiful enough to stop traffic. She moves through the bar slowly, surveying each table before those hazel eyes finally land on me.

It's a good thing she's still a fair distance away because I suck in a breath at being the sole focus of this woman. I was too distracted the night of the party to properly appreciate her sheer presence. Even in pain and pissed the fuck off, I'd still enjoyed the way her gray dress hugged her generous figure and gave a tantalizing glimpse of her large breasts and ass. Especially when she leaned over me to change my bandages.

Focus.

She crosses to my booth and slips into the seat across from me without hesitation. Despite myself, I like that she's not cowering or flinching. She walked in here with confidence, and I get the feeling that she approaches every situation the same way. It's too damn bad she can't brazen her way through tonight. "Psyche."

"Eros." She considers me for a long moment. Is she comparing and contrasting how I look now versus the last time we spoke? The only time, really, aside from a handful of greetings over the years at various parties. Even as children of the Thirteen, we hardly move in the same circles. The Dimitriou women hold themselves apart. Another thing about them that drives Aphrodite up the wall.

Psyche leans back slowly. "Most people send an email when they want to meet me. You're efficient enough to have figured out my phone number. Why bother with Hermes?"

Because an email can be hacked and a phone can be traced. No matter what everyone believes about Hermes, she takes her title and her role seriously. If a message is meant to be secret, it stays that way. Not even the legacy titles can compel her to share a message.

If Psyche is murdered, I want nothing tracing it back to me.

If? What the fuck am I talking about *if*? Her fate was sealed the moment my mother demanded her heart. No, before that, when she showed me kindness despite the fact that anyone else in that party would have turned away. Even my friends would have pretended not to notice the blood or the limp. We all operate under the carefully balanced lie that I am nothing more than Aphrodite's playboy son. A little too free with his charms, a little too hard to pin down in anything resembling commitment.

No one talks about what else I do for my family.

Or who pays the price.

There is no room for doubt about the price to be paid tonight. The only way forward is through. It's not like I haven't done worse. My hands are covered in the blood of my mother's enemies, both real and imagined. I've long since made my peace with the fact that I'll never get them clean. I'm no longer particularly inclined to fight that uphill battle for sainthood. It's Tartarus for me.

I lean forward and prop my elbows on the table. "I'm sure Hermes already told you this, but I'd prefer to have this conversation in person."

"She mentioned it." Psyche shrugs out of her coat, revealing a thin black sweater that hugs her tits to perfection. "How's your chest?"

I blink. "What?"

"Your chest. The one that was covered in cuts two weeks ago." She nods at me. "Did you manage to find a doctor?"

My hand goes to my chest before I can stop the impulse. "Yeah. It wasn't as bad as it looked."

"Lucky you."

"Sure. Lucky." It was a sloppy mistake on my part. If I hadn't been rushing the job to make it to the party on time, I never would have lowered my guard enough to let Polyphonte's father get that many strikes in. "But then, I walked away from that fight. Not everyone did."

Psyche takes a slow breath. "Like a pretty girl who asked too many questions?"

Right. I did say that to her, didn't I? I don't bother to smile. "My mother takes exception to a lot of pretty girls in Olympus." Pretty people, really. Gender matters less than beauty and attention, and Aphrodite wants the lion's share of both for herself.

"Who was it?"

"Knowing won't make a difference."

Psyche gives me a sad little smile. "Indulge me."

I meant it when I said knowing wouldn't make a difference. It won't save her. It won't change what happens here tonight. "Polyphonte."

She frowns. "I don't know that name."

"No reason for you to." Polyphonte hadn't climbed the social ladder high enough to attend Dodona Tower parties. Fuck, she hadn't climbed high enough to do more than endanger herself. The little fool thought she could take on Aphrodite without consequences. Even if she hadn't crossed my mother, she would have sent someone else important into a murderous rage within a month. She had too big a mouth and too little caution.

"Eros..." She shakes her head, her expression turning inward. "Never mind. I suppose it doesn't matter."

I suddenly desperately want to know what she almost said. Was she going to mention the way she caught me staring at her mouth? She'd bitten her lip in response to that look. I don't think she even realized she did it. Just like I don't think she realized she glanced at my mouth for several long seconds before she shook off the moment. If we were anyone else, in any other situation, I might have kissed her then.

I might have pulled her down onto my lap and coaxed all the wariness right out of her. First with a kiss, and then a slow seduction that we both would have enjoyed entirely too much.

I shake my head. What the fuck am I thinking? Even if I had crossed that line, it would just make this situation that much worse for both of us. "You're right. It really doesn't matter."

"Like I said." She clears her throat and straightens. "Okay, let's get down to business. You wanted to meet to talk about how to guide the media attention away from us. Well, away from you specifically. I'm sure Aphrodite isn't happy about the whole situation, and you're not exactly as practiced at dealing with this stuff as I am. I have a few ideas."

I blink. "Excuse me?"

"That *is* why we're meeting, isn't it?"

I might fucking kill Hermes for putting *that* thought into her head. I told the woman to get Psyche here, no matter what she had to say, but I didn't expect her to use Psyche's own good nature against her. My stomach drops. "You showed up here because you think I need your help to manipulate the media into chasing after someone else." As if I haven't done that very thing on my own before.

The little fool rushed here, threw herself right into my trap without a second thought, because she believed I needed her help.

I think I'm going to be sick.

Psyche goes still. "Isn't that why we're meeting?"

"No," I say almost gently. Gods, I hate myself right now. "That's not why we're meeting."

She clears her throat. "You're here in your official capacity, then."

"Yeah." The word comes out like an apology.

A beat of silence. Another. She draws herself up. "Surely she can't be that furious about a single photograph?"

"Actually—"

Psyche continues as if I haven't spoken. "Then again, I suppose it's not that simple. She and my mother have been feuding for a decade, and she won't like that Demeter is stepping on her toes. The why doesn't matter. The bottom line is she's got nothing to ruin me with. I have no skeletons in my closet. Which means she'll make some up." She folds her arms on the table beneath her breasts. "So what's on the agenda? Will you fabricate some seedy sex scandal? Maybe even attempt to exile me, though good luck with that. My mother won't stand for it."

She's obviously not taking this seriously, and I suddenly need her to be. I don't know why. My job would be significantly easier if she thought this wasn't literally life or death. And yet I find myself telling her the truth. "Aphrodite doesn't want you ruined. She wants you dead."

Psyche goes pale.

I expect tears. Begging. Maybe even for her to try to run. She does none of those things. After taking a moment to collect herself, she merely squares her shoulders and holds my gaze. "Eros, you strike me as a not-unintelligent man."

"Thanks," I say drily. Experience had given me a map of how this conversation would go, and Psyche hasn't performed to expectations at all. Against my better judgment, a sliver of curiosity wedges itself through my determination to see this through. I knew she was different from anyone I've dealt with previously. I suspected she was formidable, but she's even more than I could have guessed.

"You must realize who I have in my corner. If you do something to me, Persephone will rip you into a million pieces, and Hades will stand by to ensure no one stops her from doing it." She leans forward, and I can't help glancing at where her impressive cleavage presses against the V of her sweater. "That's not even getting into what *my* mother will do. Unlike Aphrodite, Demeter has no problem getting her hands dirty when the situation calls for it."

"Are you saying your mother murdered the last Zeus?"

"Of course not." She snorts. "That's an unsubstantiated rumor and you know it. Let's not pretend your mother wouldn't have pounced on the story and run with it if she had even a shred of evidence."

She's not wrong. Still, I find it interesting that she didn't flat out say Demeter is innocent. The official story might be that Zeus somehow *accidentally* broke the window in his office and *accidentally* fell to his death, but everyone knows it's fiction.

None of that matters, though.

This is quickly spiraling out of control. "Psyche—"

"I'm not finished." She eyes the drink I ordered for her, the one containing the sedative that will knock her out and ensure she feels no pain. "There's one additional element that you need to consider before we go any further. My mother is arranging a marriage between me and Zeus. I can't imagine he'll thank you for killing the future Hera."

Understanding dawns, bringing with it frustration hot enough to burn me to ash. "If that were settled, this would already be squashed." Not even Aphrodite would dare go after the future Hera.

"Maybe, but it's still a very large risk to take. As I said before, you strike me as a smart man, so you must have considered this already."

That's quite the backhanded compliment. Against my better judgment, admiration snakes its way through me. She came in here expecting one thing, but she's pivoted with barely any hesitation at all and is well on her way to outmaneuvering me. "If I hadn't, I wouldn't be all that smart, would I?"

"Exactly." Psyche tilts her head to the side. "With all that said, I have a question for you."

I sit back with a curse and wave my hand. "By all means, don't let me stop your brilliant monologue."

"Thank you." She gives me a small smile that almost combats the fear lurking in her hazel eyes. I had a lot of assumptions about this woman when her family first appeared on the scene ten years ago, and those assumptions only seemed to be confirmed in the intervening years. Between her helping me at the party and this conversation, I'm forced to admit that I might have been dead wrong.

She's not a vapid social influencer whose only hobbies include spending her mother's money and taking pretty pictures for her followers. There's a cunning brain in that pretty head, and she's using every bit of her intelligence in an attempt to get out of this situation alive.

Psyche tucks a strand of her dark hair behind her ear. "If stability is so important that Demeter, Hades, and even Zeus are all invested in seeing it happen, do you really think that they'll stand back and let your mother's petty feud go unchecked? They might be willing to look the other way when her targets are outside their immediate circle, but I am not some poor socialite who no one has ever heard of. I'm Demeter's daughter. If you harm me, they will take action. They'll crush her, and you with her."

She's not wrong. When the majority of the Thirteen get on board and agree with one another, they're nearly an unstoppable force. It's too damn bad it won't make a difference for the woman sitting across from me. "Cute story. Even if it's true, it won't matter."

At that, her smile dies. "What are you talking about? I just named a good number of the major players in this city, and I imagine Poseidon will throw his support behind them as well since he seems to hate all the jockeying for position. That's all three of the legacy titles. Surely your mother is smart enough to know when she's been outmaneuvered. Surely *you* are. No logical person would continue down this path against these odds."

I bite back a sigh. That's the crux of it, isn't it? "Bold of you to assume my mother and logic have ever been on speaking terms. Do you know her at all?"

She opens her mouth, seems to reconsider whatever she was about to say, and finally frowns harder. "I thought the petty, vengeful thing was an act."

My life would be so much simpler if it were, if my mother didn't live to see the downfall of anyone who crosses her, even in passing. "She's more than capable of dealing with the fallout." One way or another. I don't know how she'll manage it, but I already know what she'd say if I brought this to her.

Your job isn't to think, Son; it's to punish who I tell you to punish.

Kill the girl and carve out Demeter's heart in the process.

Psyche goes even paler. "You really mean that."

"I do."

"I just came here and told you that I can marshal a good number of the Thirteen against you, and it doesn't matter how many moves I make because the person giving you orders cares more about her personal vengeance than she does about her son's life." She stares up at me, searching my face for something that she'll never find. "She's the reason you were hurrying to the party, isn't she? That you didn't go to a doctor first? I bet she was furious you were late."

Psyche's hitting a little too close to the truth. "It doesn't matter."

"Of course it matters. You were *hurt.* Even my mother, with all her machinations and ruthlessness, would care if one of us were injured."

I give her the look that statement deserves. "I would say that supports my point, not yours. But it doesn't matter, because no one will pin this on me. *You* made sure of that." I pull my phone out, find the app I want, and open it. Then I set it on the table between us. Psyche leans over and scrolls through a few posts, going paler and paler. I already know what she'll see. Hermes and Dionysus and a curvy brunette apparently having the time of their lives on the town. The brunette's face is never quite in the picture, but she's close enough to Psyche's body type and hair style that everyone will believe it's her. "These photos are all tagged and time stamped. No one even knows you're here."

"Hermes does."

"Hermes is playing her own game. She's not on your side. She's not on anyone's side but her own." I reclaim my phone. "And she won't come forward with the truth for the very reasons you just listed. She's as invested in stability as Zeus and the rest. She won't give up any information that will start a war." Hermes is chaotic enough that normally I wouldn't pretend I could guess which way she'd jump, but I *know* this is the truth.

Ultimately, she serves Olympus just like the rest of the Thirteen.

Psyche's bottom lip quivers a little, but she makes a blatant attempt to firm it. "You deserve better than to simply be your mother's weapon, Eros."

"Don't bother trying to appeal to my humanity. I have none."

She leans forward and lowers her voice, hazel eyes pleading. "I helped you two weeks ago. I didn't have to and we both know it. Maybe you don't have humanity, but surely you believe in the scales being balanced. Are you really willing to repay my help with violence simply because it made your mother mad?"

"Psyche." Damn it, I shouldn't have said her name. It feels too good to do it, makes me want things not meant for me. "Stop. Nothing you say will make a difference."

For the first time since she sat down, true fear comes to life in her eyes. She came here ready to help the son of her mother's enemy and pivoted into a truly spectacular argument that would have worked if I were anyone else, if she hadn't already been the instrument of her downfall because she trusted me enough to create an alibi for her location. It's been so long since I've been challenged, so long since someone has even tried to fight back, to outmaneuver me.

So long since someone showed me even a shred of kindness.

I find myself reaching out and covering one of her hands with my own. Her skin is startlingly warm. "For what it's worth, it was a good try. You gave it your best shot."

"Strange how that doesn't make me feel better." She stares down at where I touch her. "I'm going to need you to take your hand back now. I hardly want comfort from my murderer."

Something pricks me and I remove my hand from hers and use it to rub my chest, the feeling from before when she patched me up getting stronger. What the fuck is this? Surely I'm not having an attack of conscience *now*. I can't save this woman. I might be my mother's preferred weapon, but I'm hardly the only one. If I refuse to do this, she'll send someone else, and they won't care if Psyche is terrified and in agony at the end. They'll simply cut her down.

"Is this what you did with Polyphonte? Met her for drinks and then took her out back and killed her? I guess kudos to her for putting up a fight, but obviously she wasn't successful. How many times have you done this, Eros? Is that really the life you want?"

"Stop." The word comes out harsher than I intend it, but I

know what she's doing and it won't work. I didn't intentionally put myself on the path to become my mother's pet monster, but I'm here now and there's no going back. "I meant what I said before. You can't talk your way out of this."

She runs her fingers through the ends of her hair, twisting it in a way that looks almost painful, but her expression is eerily calm. "I wanted kids. That seems so foolish now. Why would I want to bring kids into this world? But I did. I thought I had more time. I'm only twenty-three."

Fuck. "Stop," I repeat.

"Why?" Something sharp and angry breaks through the calm. "Does it make me seem more human to you? Harder to pull the trigger?"

Yes. And it was already a herculean effort before. "It doesn't matter what I want." I don't mean to say that, but I haven't meant to say a lot of things when it comes to this woman. She's so fucking brave, and it just kills me that I've been ordered to snuff out this light. But there's no other option.

Unless there actually is a way to repay her earlier kindness...

No. It's a terrible idea, and hardly foolproof. My mother is like a terrier with a bone when it comes to her vendettas. She won't let anything get in the way of punishing both Psyche and Demeter by removing Psyche. If I try to stand in her way, she'll just go around me and kill Psyche anyway.

"Promise me that you won't hurt my sisters."

I drag myself out of my traitorous thoughts and stare at her. "You know I can't do that." When she narrows her eyes, I relent. "Look, Persephone is as safe as possible because she's married to

Hades, and no one wants the boogeyman of Olympus showing up on their doorstep. Callisto is likely safe for a similar reason—no one wants to fuck with her kind of viciousness. She doesn't play by the established rules, and that's enough to make most enemies think twice. And Eurydice..." I shrug. "All she has to do is have a prolonged stay in the lower city and few people can even get to her. It's not like Hades or Persephone are going to invite my mother's people over the river to harm her."

"Is all this supposed to make me feel better? You could just promise not to hurt them."

I give her the look that statement deserves. "You wouldn't believe me."

"You could give me your word."

I know she's still trying to make herself more human to me, to prick my nonexistent conscience, but when's the last time someone actually gave a damn about my word? My mother's tasks have dragged my name through the mud, deserved though that may be. No one trusts me, because all it takes is pissing Aphrodite off and her will overrides mine. She points, I take care of things. My word doesn't mean a fucking thing.

Maybe that's why I find myself asking, "If I gave you my word, would you believe me?"

"Yes."

The word feels like she reached across the table and punched me in the chest. There isn't a shred of doubt in those three letters. If I gave my word, she would believe me; it's as simple as that. I stare at this woman who defies all my expectations. I had half convinced myself that her taking care of me that night was a fluke or at least something I could push aside. It's not a fluke, though. Her showing up here tonight is proof of that.

Psyche really is a good person who's somehow managed to survive Olympus politics.

And my mother wants me to extinguish her flame.

I swallow hard. "Seriously?"

"Yes," Psyche repeats. She stops twisting her hair and gives me her full attention. "*Are* you giving your word?"

I shake my head slowly. "I can't promise you anything."

"Oh." The disappointment on her pretty face cuts through me like a knife. I am not a good person. I never had a chance to be one, and it's not like I fought my fate all that hard once the path unfurled beneath my feet. But killing Psyche? The idea of it made me uncomfortable before, but after this conversation, it makes me physically ill.

I...can't do this.

Maybe I do have a soul, dusty and unused though it is, because the thought of ending Psyche's life feels so fucking repellent to me, I'm about to do something unforgivable. I take a drink of my vodka tonic, the burning of the alcohol doing nothing to clear away the sudden determination taking root inside me.

A wild plan takes root, one reckless in the extreme. Defying my mother is a risk, but it's one I'm willing to take. Psyche has already risked herself for me twice. Surely I can meet her halfway? I'm not good like she is, though. It's not kindness that has me speaking. It's pure selfish *want*. "There might be another way."

PSYCHE

IT SEEMS A PARTICULARLY CRUEL TWIST OF FATE THAT GAVE
Eros Ambrosia the face of a golden god and no heart to speak of.
He sits there, somehow finding the single beam of light in this
dark hole of a place, and looks at me with nothing in his pale-
blue eyes. No guilt. No sympathy. Not even anticipation for what
comes next. There's no bloodlust there, either—just a certain sort
of weariness as if he's already tired of this song and dance and just
wants to get the whole thing over with so he can go home and go
to bed.

He's wearing nearly the same expression he was when he
thanked me for helping him.

I refuse to hope he's actually offering me a way out, but I'm
approaching a desperation that makes me foolish. I thought I was
so incredibly clever, creating that false timeline with Hermes so that
Eros and I could plot together. What was I *thinking*? The first thing
I should have done was go to Persephone. Just because Eros wasn't
a total monster to me two weeks ago doesn't mean he's safe.

If I had known I was in danger, I would have fled to the lower city and taken what protection Hades and Persephone have to offer. It would only be a temporary solution, but at least my life would be extended past tonight. That extra time would have given me the opportunity to think my way out of this mess, preferably without getting my mother involved.

If she finds out that Aphrodite essentially took a hit out on me, she'll go after the woman with everything in her arsenal. And my mother has *many* things in her arsenal. She might not have killed the old Zeus herself, but she certainly set up the sequence of events that ended in his death. She's also the sole reason that his death was ruled an accident instead of murder. She helped pave the way for Hades himself to reenter society. She has some kind of dirt on Poseidon that ensures he backs her at least half of the time. But even with all that power at her disposal, she will throw caution to the wind and might do something truly foolish like trying to run Aphrodite over with her car. Something with no *plausible deniability.*

If I had known…

But then, it doesn't matter. Playing what-if is a recipe for disaster. I made a mistake. Just because I didn't know the cost doesn't mean I'm exempt from paying it.

Eros is watching me so closely, I almost forget myself and take a sip of the drink that was waiting for me when I got to the table. Knowing what I do now, it's definitely poisoned, though whether it's a lethal dose or just something meant to incapacitate is up for debate.

"There might be another way," he says again, as if reassuring both of us.

After everything he's said, suddenly he's offering me an alternate option. *Why?* Is this another way to torment me? I want to scream in his face, to throw this poisoned drink at him and watch it drip down his perfect features. Maybe I'll get lucky and it will burn his skin, distracting him long enough for me to run.

I glance around the bar. It's even dimmer than when I arrived, and people have begun to filter in. This place is as far from the shining streets around Dodona Tower as a person can get and stay in the upper city. It's also in an area I'm not overly familiar with. It's entirely possible that all of these people are on Eros's payroll— *Aphrodite's* payroll—and the moment I try to flee, they'll catch me and haul me back to him.

No, I am out of options and we both know it. I try to swallow down the panic making it difficult to think. "What other way?"

"You're not going to like it."

He says it so flatly that I have to laugh. "Right. Because I like the idea of being murdered so much more."

Finally, he seems to steel himself and says, "Marry me."

I blink. The two soft words don't morph into a sentence that makes sense. If anything, the longer they stand between us, the less comprehensible they are. "I'm sorry, I misheard you. I could have sworn you just said 'marry me.'"

"Because I did." There's still no emotion in his eyes, no reaction to indicate what he's thinking. I'm used to being able to at least pick up *something* from the people around me. Even the best liars have tells, and I've spent enough time drifting through Olympian parties to pick up on most of the major players' over the years. It's a matter of survival and I'm very good at it. I know that

Ares scratches at his beard when he wants to throttle someone. I know that Perseus—Zeus—gets colder when he's buying time to respond. Even the last Zeus, while not transparent, got louder and more boisterously happy when he was furious.

Eros gives me nothing.

I catch myself reaching for the drink out of instinct and push the glass to the far side of the table. "That's not funny."

"Who's laughing?" He sighs as if already tired of this conversation. "There are consequences for failing my mother, and I'm not willing to bear them. I can't walk away without either killing you or marrying you."

A hysterical giggle escapes, and I grab *his* drink and down it. Vodka tonic. Of course it is. I shudder. "That's ridiculous. Why are those the only two options? If you don't want to kill me, surely there's something else you can do."

"There's not." When I just stare at him, he rolls his shoulders a little. "Look, if I marry you, that ties me to Demeter as much as it ties you to Aphrodite. She won't be able to exile me without causing a stir, and if you suddenly turn up dead, there's no plausible deniability there. If we make it believable, everyone will assume that it's a love match between two rivals' children. As the last two weeks have more than proven, the media loves that Romeo and Juliet shit."

"You're not exactly convincing me with that comparison. Romeo and Juliet both died."

"Semantics. You know I'm right."

I rub my throat where I can still feel the burn of the alcohol and try to think my way through this. Marriages of convenience are hardly unknown in Olympus, especially among the families of the Thirteen. Everyone is constantly jockeying for power, often in the form of alliances, and using a marriage to seal an alliance is an ancient practice. It's just... Even with my mother's obvious machinations, I honestly thought I would avoid being married to someone who actively wants to harm me. It's the lowest bar possible, but here we are.

"You're serious?" I finally ask.

"Yes."

There's no reason for this to be an elaborate trap. He already has me in the upper warehouse district, and from the look of the streets around here, there are plenty of alleys for him to drop my dead body in with no one the wiser. *I* paved the way for that to happen without consequences, and I have no one to blame for my naivety but myself.

No, the only thing that makes sense is that Eros is actually offering to marry me. He's right, in a way; if we played things correctly, we'd be untouchable. There's little Olympus loves more than gossip. A secret marriage between Eros and me would send them into a frenzy, practically crawling over one another to ensure they're the first to get an exclusive scoop. The buzz *still* going on about that single photo is more than proof of that. From there, it's child's play to get people on our side, rooting for us to go the distance. If someone harmed either of us at that point, Olympus would have a riot on its hands and not even the Thirteen could quell it. They'd be forced to answer some uncomfortable questions about what happens out of the sight of the public, and no one wants that.

Even Aphrodite.

So, yes, the plan might work. There's just one glaring issue. I press my lips together and consider Eros. He's attractive, yes, but there's an aura of danger that even his flawless looks can't dispel. "No one would believe that you've lost your head and married *anyone* in a whirlwind affair. You're too cold. You don't play the game with the media, and they resent you for it."

"I don't play the game because it bores me, not because I'm incapable."

He's confident enough that I almost believe him, but this could backfire half a dozen ways, and that's just off the top of my head. I know *I* can fake it; it's what I've been doing since my mother became Demeter and dragged our family out of its idyllic country life and into the snake pit that is Olympus. "Prove it."

The change is almost instantaneous. Eros smiles at me, and it's as if the sun just came out from behind a cloud. It warms his eyes and lights up his face. He leans across the table and takes my hands. "I love you, Psyche. Let's get married."

I break out in goose bumps and my heartbeat picks up until I can hear it in my ears. Even knowing this is fake, I can't help reacting. "That'll do, I guess," I say faintly.

Just like that, he flips a switch and the coldness creeps back over his face and eyes. "Like I said, I can fake it."

I don't want to do this, but my options are between bad and worse. Which means I don't actually have a choice. Still, I can't help pressing him. "Why would you do this? Why not just do what your mother wants?"

"Unlike my mother, I am capable of putting my emotions aside and thinking logically." I almost snort at that; I can't imagine Eros having emotions in the first place. He continues, watching me closely. "Your mother will go off the deep end if something happens to you, and she'll turn the city upside down until she finds the culprit. There's the smallest chance she might actually figure out the trail leads back to me. That's not my idea of a good time."

When he puts it like that, it does makes sense. He might not be able to stop his mother, but he's aware enough to realize that *he'll* be the one paying the consequences if he goes through with this. "That's the only reason?"

He looks away, the first sign that he might be in anything other than perfect control. "I don't have a conscience, so don't get any funny ideas."

"Of course not," I murmur.

"It feels shitty to do this after you helped me." He speaks so softly, the words are almost lost in the general murmur of the bar around us.

I can't decide if him acknowledging that makes this situation better or worse. It's obviously not something I can try to use as leverage, not when he's been very clear about his intentions. It doesn't matter if he thinks it's shitty; he'll still do it. I sigh. "I'll agree on one condition."

"You seem to be under the mistaken impression that you have anything to negotiate with."

Fear tries to clamp around my throat, but I muscle past the instinctive response trying to stifle my words. I can't afford to let fear rule me right now. I only have one chance to pull this off, and

I have to get whatever promises from him that I can. "We both know I do."

After a long moment, he looks at me and inclines his head. "What's your condition?"

"You won't harm my family. Not my sisters. Not my mother. I'm not dodging this bullet only for one of them to take the hit."

He hesitates but finally nods again. "You have my word."

I don't know if that's enough, but it's not like I can have a contract drawn up and... Speaking of contracts. *Fuck.* "I also need a prenup."

"No."

I have two years before I turn twenty-five and gain access to the trust fund my grandmother set up for me. It's not an insignificant amount of money; people have been killed for less. Then again, I suppose Eros has something similar in his name. No matter what else is true about Aphrodite, it's common knowledge that her fortune rivals even Poseidon's. One of the perks of that particular title is the money is attached to *Aphrodite*, not to the person who holds it. But the last three people to be Aphrodite ensured that their children were well taken care of, so there's no reason to believe this one has done any differently. "Why not?"

"Because this is a whirlwind romance and people deeply enough in love to sprint to the altar aren't smart enough to write up prenups beforehand."

Damn it. He's right. "Fine."

"If that's settled, let's go." Eros rises from the table and holds out a hand. "My car is around back."

I cautiously slip my hand into his and allow him to tug me out of the booth and to my feet. I half expect him to release me, but he simply laces our fingers together and heads for the dark rectangle of shadows in the back of the room. As we get closer, it resolves into an exit. It's not until we're walking down the dim, narrow hallway and through the grimy back door that I realize this could all be a trap.

I dig in my heels, but Eros easily hauls me along behind him without missing a step. He's stronger than he looks. Panic rears its ugly head and I try to regulate my breathing. "Eros—"

"I gave my word, Psyche." He pulls me out into the freezing night air. The ground is slick beneath my boots, but he doesn't seem to have any trouble with it. "I know that doesn't mean shit to most people, but it does to me."

I obviously haven't learned my lesson, because I honestly believe him. Even knowing he can lie so effectively, the strange look on his face when I said I'd take his word as truth is enough to convince me he means it.

I've made my choice. It wasn't much of a choice, but I'll stand by it. It's not until I'm climbing into the passenger seat of his fancy sports car that the implications of what I've agreed to really sink in.

Eros starts the engine, and I look at him. "We can't tell anyone the truth."

"Who would I tell?" He says it so casually, as if it's obvious that he has no one close enough to want to trust with what's really going on. I know he doesn't have siblings, but surely he has friends? I've seen him with the Kasios siblings regularly, but friendships in the upper crust of Olympus are often more political alliances than anything else.

Eros pulls out from behind the bar and onto the street. "That means no telling your sisters."

"It's a little more complicated than that. My sisters aren't going to believe I had a secret whirlwind romance. We tell each other everything."

"Everything?" He pulls up to an intersection and looks at me. The red from the stoplight plays over his cheekbones and jaw, highlighting his sensually curved lips.

Gods, the man is beautiful. I keep expecting to get used to it, but every time I look at him, it's a shock to my system. That will wear off. It has to. I can't imagine being in close contact with him for a prolonged period of time and still being affected on this level. There are plenty of beautiful people in this city who I don't lose my head around. He'll number among them within a week. I hope.

Did he say something?

I give myself a shake. "Yes, everything. They won't believe a secret relationship."

"Make them believe, Psyche. If word gets out that this is anything but genuine, we'll both pay the price."

The sheer weight of what we're doing has me slumping back in the uncomfortable seat. I shift, but it doesn't get better. "How long?"

"How long what?"

"How long are we doing this?"

"As long as it takes."

I stare at him. "That is nowhere near specific enough."

"Fine." He shrugs. "Until my mother is no longer Aphrodite."

That seems more reasonable, but it could still potentially be a long time. There are only three ways for one of the Thirteen to stop holding their title—death, exile, or retirement. I can count on one hand how many have chosen the latter option in the entire history of Olympus. A scattering more have had that option forced on them because health or mental deterioration made it impossible to do their duties. The odds still aren't in our favor. Aphrodite won't step down voluntarily, and she's in her fifties. If left unchecked, she might be around for decades.

I can't be in a fake marriage for decades. I *can't*. I've barely let myself dream of love and a family and everything that entails. If I spend twenty years married to Eros, that will nuke those dreams. The knowledge leaves a weight in my chest that is difficult to speak past. "You won't kill Aphrodite."

"She's a monster, but she's my mother." He takes another turn, guiding the car north. "I won't allow you to do something to put her in danger, either."

That limits our options considerably. I turn and stare out the window. The farther from the warehouse district we get, the more the buildings lining the street change. The bars disappear from the windows. The streets become more pristine and look less grimy. As we enter the blocks around Dodona Tower—Zeus's seat of power—the storefronts take on a uniform look that's as soulless as it is flawless.

Several blocks northwest of the tower, Eros turns into an underground parking garage. I manage to stay silent until he parks and turns off the car. We sit there for a moment, the air seeming to gain weight between us. I can't look at him. This is too dangerous, too volatile. Words bubble up, escaping before I can think better of them. "You know, it strikes me that I've already broken the rule about going to a secondary location with someone who means me harm."

He gives me a strange look. "Do you always make bad jokes when you're nervous?"

"No. Never. But then, I've never been threatened with actual death before, so there's a first time for everything."

"We'll talk inside."

I follow him out of the car and look at the space around me. My mother's building is quite a bit farther from the city center, and although it's nice, it's very clear that our neighborhood isn't as interested in keeping up with the Thirteen's idea of what beauty entails. Mother likes to stay close to the agriculture district so when there are inevitable issues, she's a short drive away. Our neighborhood and home are expensive but understated.

There is nothing understated about this place. Even the parking garage reeks of wealth, from the line of hideously expensive cars, to the bright lights displaying everything, to the glassed-in elevator area. There is even a security guard in a glassed-in booth, a white man in a nondescript black uniform. I glance at Eros. "Is this security really necessary?"

"Depends on who you ask." Eros opens the glass door to the interior room that houses the elevator and steps back, allowing me to precede him into the space. He slides an arm around my waist, and I nearly levitate right out of my skin. It takes everything I have not to shove him away, to relax against him as if touching Eros is something that I do all the time.

We step onto the elevator and I barely wait for the doors to close before I try to move away. Eros only tightens his hold on me. "There are cameras."

Right. I should have thought of that. Of course there are cameras covering every inch of the public space in this building. I speak through gritted teeth that I hope look like a grin. "We haven't started this yet."

"We started it the second you said yes. Relax and stop grinding your teeth." He smiles down at me—his liar's smile with warm eyes and sweetly curved lips. "We're in love, after all."

EROS

TOUCHING PSYCHE WAS A MISTAKE. SHE'S SO FUCKING SOFT that I have the nearly unstoppable urge to run my hands all over her body and... Fuck, I need to get a hold of myself. Being attracted to her is useful for the lie we're about to pull off, but losing control is unacceptable.

My mother is going to be furious.

I shouldn't relish that knowledge. She holds most of the cards and I have so few that there's a very real chance she'll throw caution to the wind and exile me for this. No matter how reckless she is, she'll know this marriage isn't the real thing. Not that she'd care one way or another. To Aphrodite, it doesn't matter if I'm hopelessly in love with Demeter's daughter or playing some deeper manipulation. She only cares about her endgame.

No, the one we need to convince is Demeter herself. I need her in my corner, and I need it yesterday. If she's on my side—our side—then she can step in and protect us in a way even I can't manage. I am only a son of Aphrodite. Demeter is one of the Thirteen and has more alliances and power than anyone.

There's a reason Aphrodite hates her so much, after all.

My mother would hang me out to dry if she thought it would serve her long game. Demeter threatened to starve half the city to get Persephone back from Hades—and then followed through on that threat. If not for Hades's foresight, people might have died. So, yeah, we need to convince Demeter that we're hopelessly in love so that her legendary overprotective motherly instincts kick in. An impossible ask, but if anyone can pull it off, it's me and Psyche.

The elevator stops at my floor and the door slides soundlessly open. The entire floor is my penthouse suite, so there's just a small room here with a single door. I release Psyche and unlock the door. "Welcome home."

I expect her to keep showing her nerves and her claws in equal measure, but she turns a happy smile on me. "Thank you, baby. I'm so happy."

It's a lie. I *know* it's a lie. That doesn't detract from the power of my response in the least. I rock back on my heels and have to clench my fists to keep from reaching for her. She hates me and I don't know how I feel about her in general, but there's just enough chemistry between us to make things complicated. I haven't missed the way her gaze keeps flicking to my mouth as if she can't stop looking at my lips.

I wasn't imagining her attraction the night of the party.

I'm not surprised; I have access to a mirror, after all. My looks are as much of a weapon as anything else in my arsenal. People see a pretty face and they're conditioned to expect certain things, which means they often don't look for the danger beneath the surface. If Psyche is among those who find me attractive, all the better. We're going to be up close and personal for quite some time.

Maybe I shouldn't look forward to that. I sure as fuck shouldn't already be considering how quickly I can get my hands on her again. I have to be better than this. For our scheme to work, neither of us can afford to be distracted.

Psyche steps into my home and whistles. "You really went full-on millionaire playboy when you decorated this, didn't you? How crass."

The cloud of lust around my head dissipates a little. I try to see my penthouse from her point of view. It's filled with expensive things, yes, but so is her mother's home, I'd wager. "What's wrong with it?"

Her lips quirk and she sweeps a hand to encompass the entire room. "How narcissistic do you have to be to have a hexagon-shaped foyer with mirrors on *every single wall*?"

"They're not on every wall. Just four of them." The other two house the door to the elevator and the door leading deeper into the penthouse. My skin heats, and it's not desire to blame this time. "My mother feels strongly about making a first impression."

"More like your mother enjoys being the center of attention, even if she's the only one in the room." She says it with a straight face. Before I can come up with a response, Psyche moves to the nearest mirror. They're massive things that stretch from floor to ceiling and nearly the width of each part of the wall, all framed by stylistic metal. "Eros, these are ridiculous." She brushes her fingers along the frame that is designed to look like clustered feathers. "Gorgeous work, but utterly ridiculous."

"You're being judgmental right now." I sound defensive, but I can't help it. Just like I can't help watching Psyche and her many reflections move about the room, pausing before each mirror so she can see the different frames. Feathers, daggers, jagged hearts, and a cluster of arrows.

Psyche touches her finger to the arrow point. "Sharp."

"Like I said, my mother likes to make an impression."

Psyche shakes her head. "Okay, give me the tour. I need to know what other monstrosities this place holds before we move forward."

I know she's using humor to deal with the unexpected turns this night has brought her, but it still irritates me. "I don't *have* to marry you, you know?"

"Except I kind of think you do. You don't seem the type to do anything without a good reason—and it's not because I was nice to you for fifteen minutes at a party once. You don't have to tell me, but let's stop pretending that this is one-sided, yes?"

That's the problem; I'm not sure I *do* have a deeper reason for embarking on this with her. Maybe she doesn't realize what a big deal that moment was because she's used to moving through life, dealing out small kindnesses on a regular basis. That's not *my* world. If I admit as much, she'll laugh in my face, and I can't blame her for it. What kind of monster am I that I hesitate to crush a single rose? I don't like the idea of the world without her bright presence in it. If I want to keep her alive, to keep her uncrushed, this is the only option available to us.

If I were a good man, I would offer to find her a way out of Olympus. Exile is harsh, but she's a smart woman who will shortly have access to a giant trust fund. She would miss her family, but she would land on her feet. My mother doesn't give a fuck about anything outside the city limits—not when it's so damned difficult to get in and out of Olympus—so it's as foolproof a plan as possible.

Except that puts Psyche right out of my reach, too.

I want her. Want her with an intensity that doesn't make sense but that I can't deny. I mean to have her.

I drift after her as she snoops around my place, making cute little disparaging comments about the bold black tile that floors the entire place and the thick dark-red curtains that bracket the floor-to-ceiling windows and the mirrors that populate every room. She even pokes around inside my fridge before giving me a long look. "You have a chef. Interesting. I would have thought you were too paranoid to let many people into this place."

I prop my hip against the kitchen counter and cross my arms over my chest. "What makes you say that?"

"Your fridge is fully stocked. If you ate out all the time, you'd have takeout containers, or it would be empty. Your vegetables are all fresh, which suggests they actually get utilized."

All great deductions, but it doesn't explain how she leaped straight to chef. "And?"

Psyche somehow manages to look down her nose at me despite being a good six inches shorter. "Please, Eros. Someone as high maintenance as you are doesn't cook for yourself."

"Someone's making assumptions again."

She frowns at me, and even her frown is cute. "Don't tell me you cook."

"I cook. I'm good at it, too." When she keeps frowning at me, I find myself elaborating. "You were right about my not liking people in my space, and cooking is one of the ways I wind down."

Her frown fades, replaced by a look of intense curiosity. "And the other ways?"

"I work out." I watch her face closely. "I fuck."

Her complexion goes a bright tomato red, which is fascinating in the extreme. The only other time she's looked ruffled is at the thought of her death. That I've affected her supports my growing suspicion that she's just as attracted to me as I am to her.

"That won't work."

I blink. "It's worked just fine for me up to this point."

"I'm sure it has." She recovers quickly and waves that away. "Sex is a great stress reliever."

I push off the counter and stalk in her direction. Slowly. Giving her plenty of time to see me coming and decide what she's going to do about it. "Do you fuck, Psyche?"

"That's really none of your business." Her voice goes a little breathy as I stop in front of her and lean forward, planting my hands on the counter on either side of her generous hips. "What are you doing?"

"Practice." I'm a godsdamned liar, but it's as good a reason as any. "You can't jump every time I get within touching distance. No one will believe that we're fucking like rabbits if you do." Every time I say the word *fucking*, she flinches a little bit. That won't do. That won't do at all.

She reaches up cautiously, almost as if she expects me to bite her, and gingerly places her hands on my chest. "There? Can we continue the conversation now?"

What conversation? I can't string two thoughts together with her hands on me, and she's not doing anything but planting them on my pecs as if preparing to shove me off her. I fight a valiant battle with my body to keep from reacting like I'm a horny teenager being touched for the first time. I was never this ridiculous, even when I was sixteen. It doesn't speak well to my sanity that she affects me on this level. We're in trouble.

Kiss her.

Seduce her.

That will get it out of your system.

I ignore the whispered temptation and try to focus. "What conversation?"

"You can't have sex with anyone." Her fingers shift a little against my shirt. "I'm not polyamorous and everyone in my family knows it. They also realize that I'd gut my partner before I stayed with them after they cheated on me. You can't be with anyone else while we're married."

I honestly hadn't planned on it. Sex is exactly what I labeled it: a tool to help me let off some steam and wind down. I have a good time. My partners have a good time. Everyone has clear expectations. It might sound like I'm a user, but the truth is that I'm no prize and everyone in Olympus knows it. Anyone I try to date has to deal with the mother-in-law from Tartarus, and that's not even touching on my reputation as her fixer. I'm the guy they fuck, the guy who gives them a ride on the wild side before they move on to safer choices to settle down with. That's the way it is, and it's always been enough for me.

That doesn't mean I'm about to confess that truth to Psyche without prompting. Not when this is just another negotiation. "Psyche." I like the way her name tastes on my tongue. I suspect I'll like the way *she* tastes even more. "I have needs."

"I suggest you get familiar with your hand, then." She has a stubborn set to her brows that I enjoy far too much. "Or, if you want to get fancy, I'm more than capable of purchasing you one of those toys that mimic your hole of choice."

That surprises a laugh out of me. "Will you be content with your hand or a little buzzy toy?"

"I have had dry spells before. More often than not in recent months, those dry spells have been the rule rather than the exception." She shrugs as if it's a fact of life and not a godsdamned tragedy.

I slide my hands closer to her, pressing my forearms to her hips. She jolts a little, and I raise my brows. "The surest way to have you settle into the idea of me touching you is through exposure therapy. Sex will speed up that process."

She blinks those big hazel eyes at me. "I'm sorry, I must have misheard you. I thought you just suggested sex with you as exposure therapy."

"I did."

"You really have a high opinion of yourself, don't you?"

I can't tell if she's being sarcastic or not, so I ignore the question. "I'm attracted to you. You don't find me overly repulsive."

"Wow, you really *do* think highly of yourself."

"I'm stating facts. Sex is the easiest way to fast-track to the results we want." The easiest way to get exactly what *I* want.

Maybe it'll be just another sexual encounter. Desire, sex, wake up the next morning with that need purged. We never have to do it again; we're more than capable of sharing the same space without making things uncomfortable. She's too good at playing the game to do otherwise, and control is never something I've had an issue with.

Until now.

"No. Absolutely not. I don't know what you see when you look at me that makes you assume I'd happily have sex with a man who was set to murder me an hour ago, but I have higher standards than that." She puts the slightest amount of pressure against my chest. "Back off, Eros. Now."

I do as she asks, allowing her to push me several steps back. I want her in my bed, but I want her there willingly. "We can't leave this apartment until you manage not to startle when I touch you."

"I'll be fine by morning." She makes a show of looking around. "Now, do you have a spare bedroom?"

"Psyche." I wait for her to look at me. I do have a spare bedroom and it's more than adequate for her needs. But I want Psyche in my bed, and I'll play dirty to get her there, even if it's just to sleep. "I meant it about exposure therapy. If not sex, then sleeping next to each other will do in a pinch."

"No."

"It's nonnegotiable."

"There are plenty of couples who don't share bedrooms. My mother and her second husband never slept together."

I raise my brows. "The existence of you and Persephone suggests otherwise."

She's so damn cute when she blushes. "I'm going to pretend you didn't say that. Stop trying to distract me."

"Love match." I speak the words slowly. "If we've lost our minds enough to rush through with a marriage, then it would be strange if you flinch every time I get close enough to touch you."

"I'll work on it. We don't have to sleep in the same bed to accomplish our goals."

I'm already tired of this argument. "You don't want to play?" I motion behind me. "There's the door. I won't hurt you, but my mother *will* send someone else. If you want to try your chances surviving the week, you're more than welcome to." It's a bluff. I can't let her leave. Not when the consequences for both of us are so damn high.

She looks at me like she hates me, but I can live with that, because she turns toward the hallway leading deeper into the house. "Let's finish the tour of this monstrosity of a penthouse."

PSYCHE

AFTER SEEING THE REST OF EROS'S PENTHOUSE—EACH room more expensive and sleeker than the last—I finally manage to pry him off me and hide in the master bathroom. It's just as ridiculous as the rest of the place with a tiled walk-in shower large enough to fit six people with a dozen showerheads in various strategic locations. The tile is rather pretty, though I'll never say as much out loud. It almost looks like rose quartz, which shines attractively against the slate-gray tile on the floor. The sinks are both a shiny black and deep with faucets that are motion activated. Of course they are.

And the mirrors.

Gods, there are so many *mirrors* in this place.

I might own more than my fair share of mirrors back in my mother's home, but this is truly above and beyond. They're all massive and have ornate framing. Maybe they wouldn't be so overwhelming if there was literally any other decoration in this place. But no. Just mirrors and minimalist furniture that has me feeling like I wandered into some strange art gallery. It's attractive and expensive but ultimately soulless.

I'm sure it says something about Eros, but I'm too tired to connect the dots right now.

I brush my teeth with the spare toothbrush he found for me, mostly to give myself something to do, and stare at my reflection in the main mirror in this room. It's a large horizontal one that stretches across the full length of the counter, the frame a simple black metal that shines against the tile. I sigh. This entire night has turned my plans on their head, but there's nothing to be done. I know when to roll with the punches, even if this one is a knockout. There's a way out of this eventually, but the only path forward right now is to marry Eros.

Marry Eros.

I might laugh if I had the breath for it. I knew he was attractive. I have eyes in my head. *Of course*, I knew he was attractive. Knowing still didn't prepare me for the force of his personality when he turns all his attention in my direction. He's not warm—I don't think he's capable of true warmth—but the sheer sexuality he exudes is enough to melt all my logic away to base need.

The reason I jump every time he touches me isn't because I find the contact repulsive. It's the exact opposite. Every time his fingers brush me or he wraps his arm around me, I feel like I've been struck by lightning.

He wants to have sex.

He wants to *sleep together*.

Being self-aware means I know all my weaknesses with the same thoroughness that I know my strengths. I am smart and savvy and excellent at crafting a public image for myself. I am also lonely and exhausted and not very good at separating sex from emotion. I learned that with my first boyfriend and took the lesson to heart. Hooking up casually might be for other people, but I'll never achieve it. I get too entangled. As a result, I have to carefully vet anyone I'm interested in, which is why my romantic life has been relatively barren the last year or so. If I can't trust a person to really be into *me*—instead of either trying to curry favor with my mother or attempting to use me in some other way—then I can't afford to sleep with them and have my logical brain sidelined.

I'll need every bit of logic and foresight and craftiness I am capable of to survive this marriage with Eros. I can't afford to misstep in a way that will bring my guard down.

No matter how attracted I am to him.

I close my eyes and straighten. Okay, I've made that decision. Now I just need to stick to it. I can do this. I've been dealing with strong personalities since I was born; that label fits everyone in my family and all the people I've met living in Olympus. I'll just handle Eros the same way I'd handle everyone else. All it requires is finding the right angle to leverage in order to get Eros to do what I want.

To shift the power of this partnership in my direction, at least a little.

With that in mind, I head to the door and open it... Only to find Eros stretched out on the bed, wearing nothing but a pair of lounge pants. I stop short. He was handsome in a tux and perfection in an expensive gray suit. He shouldn't be able to get better than perfection. It's not logical in the least, but somehow Eros in lounge pants is so much worse. He's *barefoot*.

I stare at his feet. They're nice feet, I think? I'm not exactly a person who has strong opinions about feet, but this casual vulnerability symbolizes a kind of intimacy that has every alarm in my head blaring a warning. "What are you doing?"

"It's late. I'm tired." He pats the bed next to him, the muscles in his arm flexing, which draws my attention to how nice his chest is, which leads me down…

I jerk my gaze away from his hips. "We still have to talk."

"We'll talk in the morning. There's nothing left to say tonight." I can't really see his blue eyes from here, but there's a set to his mouth that tells me this isn't a battle I'm going to win. Eros pats the bed again, this time in a blatant command. "Come here, Psyche."

I'm going to spend a significant amount of time sleeping next to him. I suppose it's logical to start tonight. "Normally I sleep naked." Gods, why did I just say that out loud?

"Normally, so do I. However, you've taken sex off the table for the time being, so I think it's prudent to keep some clothing in place."

Prudent. I swallow down a borderline hysterical laugh and pad to the side of the bed. I know it's all in my head, but the closer I get to him, the thicker the air seems around me. Whether it's pulling me in or pushing me away is up for debate. I reluctantly undo my jeans. I might be too exhausted to fight him on sleeping arrangements, but there's one thing I can't let slide. "Correction: I've taken sex off the table permanently."

"It's open for discussion."

"It's really not." It can't be. I slide out of my jeans, achingly aware of how intensely Eros watches me. Getting anything close to naked with a new person is awkward and makes me feel so fucking vulnerable in a way I hate. And that's with someone I trust enough to get physical with. I brace myself as I look at his face, not sure what to expect. I've seen the people Eros surrounds himself with. They are all the peak of what Olympus considers physical perfection. Thin bodies. Flawless skin. Beautiful in a very specific way.

I am hardly that. It's something that I'm reminded of constantly, especially with the public life I've chosen. There's no escaping the way societal expectations scrape against my reality.

I love my body. I've fought so incredibly hard to love my body, even if some days that feels like an ambition instead of truth. I'm still painfully aware that not everyone feels the same.

After a short debate with myself, I take off my sweater, leaving me in a tank top and panties. As I refuse to sleep in a bra, I wrestle my way out of it without removing my shirt.

There's nothing else to stall with, so I finally look at Eros.

He's staring at me as if he wants to consume me bite by bite, savoring each morsel. Every muscle in his body is locked, and there's no mistaking the hard length pressing against the front of his lounge pants. Lust. It's pure lust, and it's so strong it feels like it's filling up the room between us.

I cannot, under any circumstances, let him touch me again.

I clear my throat. "Scoot over."

"It's a king-sized mattress. There's plenty of room." He has that mild tone again, and the only verbal sign that he's affected is a slight deepening of the timbre. "Stop arguing and get in my bed, Psyche."

The only thing worse than sliding beneath those blankets is standing here and letting him devour me with his gaze, so I obey. For a moment, I foolishly assume that Eros will sleep on top of the covers and give us the illusion of separation, but he stands long enough to peel back the comforter and sheets and climb into bed next to me.

This is a bad idea. Correction: this is such a terrible idea that *bad* doesn't begin to encapsulate it.

Tomorrow...

I shoot up to a sitting position. "I have to make some calls." Anything to prolong the need to turn off the lights.

He moves faster than I anticipate, looping an arm around my waist and pulling me back against his chest. "Stop."

I freeze. Holy shit, I can feel his cock pressing against my ass, and that's not even getting into all the bare skin shifting against *my* bare skin and, gods, it's been so long since I touched someone like this. Surely that's why my body is strumming happily in this new position even as my mind screams *danger ahead.* "What are you doing, Eros?"

His breath ghosts against the sensitive spot behind my ear. "Instead of making those calls, we're going public with our relationship."

"We don't have a relationship." I don't know why I'm arguing. This is the plan, after all.

"We do now."

I close my eyes, but that only makes the spell his proximity weaves stronger. He's still got his arm around me, which means his forearm is pressing against my breasts and, gods, my nipples are pebbling beneath my shirt. "We talked about this. There's no way my sisters will believe our relationship, especially if we go public before I tell them I'm, ah, in love with you."

"What they believe matters less than the perception we present." Did his lips just touch my skin? I can't be sure. All I know is that I'm fighting back shivers.

"It will never work. It's hardly even a plan."

"You're arguing simply to argue and you know it. You're more than capable of handling Persephone and the rest of your sisters in whatever way you see fit." He shifts, his arm rubbing against my breasts ever so slightly. "Besides, your sisters wouldn't do anything to put you in danger, so they'll play along until they have a chance to talk to you face-to-face."

He's not wrong. I hate that he's not wrong. I consider this for a long moment, running through scenarios. "You're proposing going public on my social media." It makes sense. With a single picture, we can announce our relationship and get ahead of any repercussions from Aphrodite. This only works if all of Olympus buys our love story, and for that to happen, all of Olympus needs to know it's happening.

"Yes. Mine is sadly neglected."

It might be neglected, but he has nearly as large a platform as I do. It's good to be Aphrodite's son with the face of a god and a mysterious personality to match. But he's right. If one of us were to announce our relationship to the world, it would be me.

I open my eyes. I'm going through with this. I've already committed. Now it's simply a matter of doing it right. "Okay. Give me a few."

Eros watches with something akin to amusement as I climb out of bed and move around his room, turning on some lights and turning off others. I use my phone to shoot a few test shots of him, and then curse him inwardly for being so photogenic that every photo looks like it should be in some magazine about millionaire playboys on their off-time.

It takes moving the lamp on the nightstand onto the bed to get the light I'm looking for. It's not perfect, but it's close enough. And really, no one expects perfect for the kind of shot we're creating.

I drag forth what little courage I have left and crawl back into bed with Eros. He smooths my hair off to one side and tugs the strap of my tank top down a little so my shoulder is bare. I almost yank it back up, but we're going for intimate and a little sexy, so it works.

I angle my phone and snap a few photos, trying not to jump when he kisses the spot where my shoulder meets my neck. "Stop that."

"Got to make it good for the camera."

I flip through the pictures. "You're taking advantage and you know it. That's a terrible angle to see your face."

Eros tugs me even closer to him, and then his hand cups my jaw, turning my face to his. "Get the camera ready," he murmurs, his gaze on my lips.

I shouldn't. It's a terrible idea. The absolute worst. But I check the angle of my phone and then turn back to him. I only intend for it to be a quick kiss and snap a few pictures as soon as his lips touch mine.

Eros isn't content with that. He nips my bottom lip, sharp

enough to draw a gasp from me, and he promptly takes advantage of the opening to slip his tongue into my mouth. He tastes like the peppermint toothpaste I used in the bathroom, and he kisses me like this is just the opening battle in what he expects to be a long war.

I melt. There's no other word for it. I drop my phone and dig my hands into his curly hair, allowing him to deepen the kiss even as a small voice in the back of my mind calls me seven different kinds of a fool.

If he pushed things or went too fast, then maybe reason would have intruded and put a stop to this foolishness, but Eros seems content to simply kiss me until we are both breathing hard and I'm shaking. His cock is a long length against my hip, so hard that I have to fight myself to avoid reaching for him.

When he finally lifts his head and stares down at me with eyes gone dark from desire, he looks almost as shocked as I feel. The expression shifts away almost instantly, replaced by fierce determination. He eases back slowly enough that I have to bite my bottom lip to remind myself that this is fake, that I most certainly cannot reach for him and drag him on top of me to finish what that kiss started. It's only when he's a precarious six inches away that he speaks. "Your words say one thing, but that kiss says something else entirely, Psyche. Sex is still up for negotiation and you know it."

EROS

BY THE END OF A SLEEPLESS NIGHT SPENT LYING NEXT TO Psyche, I'm cursing myself for not letting things spin out of control the way we both wanted. She was right there with me, arching to press as much of her lush body against me as she could. It would have taken the slightest movement to tip us over the edge.

I don't know why I held back. I refuse to examine my reasoning.

I flip through her social media, mostly to distract myself from the temptation to tug the sheet down past her chest and just *look* at her. She's too fucking sexy. Being this close and not touching her feels like my blood is simmering with no signs of cooling down anytime soon. Backing off last night was more difficult than I'll ever admit, especially when her hands started shaking where she gripped my hair and her hips made little seeking movements.

Best not to think about that right now. I'm liable to be walking around with a permanent case of blue balls as it stands; no need to make it worse.

Despite posting the photo so late, it already has thousands of comments and even more likes. The comments snag my attention. I frown, go back to the top, and start scrolling slowly, reading every single one.

What is this shit?

Next to me, Psyche stirs. I note her going tense, but she relaxes pretty quickly once she realizes I've maintained the careful space between us. She yawns, her hand covering her mouth. "What's got that look on your face?"

I grip my phone tightly, enough that there's a very real danger I'm going to crush the damn thing. "What the fuck is wrong with people?"

"You're going to have to be more specific."

I almost turn the phone screen to face her but think better of it at the last moment. It doesn't matter if she's more than capable of seeing this shit on her own; I'm not going to show it to her. "People are saying some fucked-up shit about that photo."

"Oh." Her expression falls a little, but she shrugs it off quickly. "The first and most vital rule of the internet is to never read the comments. That is exponentially more important for anyone who doesn't fit the traditional views on beauty or is marginalized in any way, but the truth is that even the thinnest, most gorgeous models get people being terrible in their comments. Trolls will be trolls."

How can she say it so casually? More, how long did it take her to build up that impressive wall between her and the assholes in the comments section? I glare at my phone. "It's not right."

"No, it's not. But you can't do anything about it, and getting upset over some stranger whose opinion I don't care about is counterproductive."

I glare harder at my phone. "Maybe you can't do anything about it, but—"

Her hand covers my mouth, the light touch scattering my violent fantasies. Psyche gives me a wary look. "I'm sure you weren't about to tell me that you can find out who these people are and threaten them in some way."

Since that's exactly what I was about to say, I keep my mouth shut.

She doesn't lower her hand. "We have bigger battles to fight right now." She picks up her phone with her free hand and shows it to me. There are so many texts and calls that the notifications disappear off the screen. "Now, we need to talk—and *not* about strangers on the internet."

The only reason I haven't heard from my mother yet is because she checked herself into the spa yesterday afternoon and will be there all weekend. It's something she does monthly, and by some *strange* coincidence, these occasions often line up with a particularly unsavory task she's given me. Aphrodite would never be caught without an alibi, and in this case it will work in our favor. Though she has her assistant post a few photos through the spa trips, she intentionally makes herself damn near impossible to get ahold of.

I sigh against Psyche's palm and wrap my fingers around her wrist, easing her hand from my face. "We need to get married as quickly as possible." Before my mother checks out of the spa and realizes what we've done. "A girlfriend is still disposable. A wife isn't."

She makes a face. "Yes, I understand. We're in agreement

there." Psyche glances at her phone. "We'll do the cute dating stuff for the public after the ceremony to really sell the romance."

I don't ask for clarification about what *cute dating stuff* is. It's not my forte and I'll be the first to admit it. Right now, the wedding ceremony takes precedence. The less time we give my mother to react, the better. Still... "I meant what I said last night. We're not leaving my apartment until I can touch you without you startling."

"You're touching me right now."

I give her a look. "You know what I mean."

She sighs. "Fine. But I need to return these calls, or my sisters and mother will be knocking at your door." Psyche glances at my bedroom door. "I'm honestly a little surprised Callisto isn't already here. She's learning some restraint now that she's almost thirty."

More like I have the best security money can buy, and while Callisto Dimitriou is formidable, she's no Hermes. I fully expect to see *her*, though. Sooner rather than later. "There will be interview requests."

"I already have six." She scrolls through her phone as she sits up. Her tank top is dangerously low, her large breasts stretching the fabric to the point where it'd simply be kinder to take it off. Psyche sighs without looking at me. "Stop staring at my chest. It's distracting."

I can't stay in this bed with her. If I do, I'm going to seduce her and we're not going to leave this room for days. I'm starting to come to terms with the knowledge that one night with Psyche won't be enough. I could have spent all night kissing her. The realization isn't a comfortable one. "I'm going to take a shower."

Maybe jacking myself will give some relief. I can't be expected to think straight when I've been nursing a hard-on for something like six hours straight.

Except when I step under the water and wrap my fist around my cock, all I can think of is Psyche. How sweet she tastes. Her big tits and full ass. How good her lips would look wrapped around my cock. I come with a curse.

Fuck.

I'm not normally so impulsive as to change a plan at the last moment, but I can't deny how right it feels to get dressed and walk out to find Psyche in my bed, typing away on her phone. Her hair is a little messy and she's pulled on her jeans, but she looks almost at home here. Dangerous thoughts. So incredibly dangerous. I finish buttoning up my shirt. "Let's eat."

"I'm not hungry." She doesn't look at me. "I have some things to take care of before the call with my sisters in thirty minutes. I also need to figure out how to get my stuff from my mother's home without running into her because that's not a conversation I'm ready to have yet. Or running into *your* mother. Though I can't say I've ever accidentally ended up at the same place as Aphrodite, Zeus's parties excepted." She holds up a hand when I open my mouth. "I realize that we need to get the physical-touch thing figured out, but I also have exactly zero changes of clothes."

I shrug. "I'll buy you more."

That gets her attention. She lifts her head to frown at me. "That's ridiculous."

"You said you don't want to go home and deal with your mother yet, and I doubt you want to be wearing yesterday's clothes when you do. Not to mention it's not exactly safe to be wandering around Olympus before we're actually married. Simple solution: new clothes."

"Eros." She speaks slowly as if talking to a child. "You might be able to walk into any place that carries menswear and find your size, but I don't have that luxury. The shops are better than they were a few years ago because I get so much press for the designers who do decent plus-sized clothing, but there are only two or three that I'd trust to have what I need in stock, and even then, it'd only be a handful of items. Buying me a whole new wardrobe isn't possible on short notice, not without going through twice as much work as it would be to get my actual clothing."

I hear what she's saying, but I don't like it. "That's ridiculous. Why wouldn't they have a wide range of sizes to fit all their customers? You're hardly the only woman's who's..." I wave my hand at her.

"Fat."

I bristle. "I didn't say that."

"It's not an insult. It's just a word." She shrugs again. "It's also the truth. And while I appreciate your enthusiastic defense for plus-sized sizing everywhere, there's little you can do about it at the moment. I need *my* clothes."

I want to keep arguing because Psyche not having everything she needs at the tip of her fingers aggravates me. She's right, though. We don't have time for this shit. "Talk to your sisters. Win them over and convince them to distract your mother so we can get in and get out while she's not in the house."

"*We?*"

"Yes, we. I'm not letting you out of my sight."

Psyche sets down her phone with exaggerated care. "You don't have to follow me around like a shadow. I have nowhere to run and I've given my word that I'll do this."

I give in to the gravity of her presence and cross to stand in front of her. I like the little line that appears between her brows when she frowns at me. I even like that her mind is already whirling ahead of this conversation to what she needs to accomplish next. That's not going to stop me from slamming her back into the here and now. "I can't keep you safe if I'm not with you, Psyche."

"Do you really think your mother will regroup that fast?"

More like I *know* she's capable of it. Even without me helping her, Aphrodite hasn't held power for so long without good reason. She's a formidable enemy. "I think it would be a large waste of time and effort if we went through all this negotiation and then she had someone rig an explosive to your car while you're out running errands."

She frowns at me. "That seems extreme."

"We've gone over this. There's a reason a very public romance and marriage is the only option." I lean down, bracing my hands on either side of her hips. She manages to keep her jolt to the barest flinch, but the reaction is still readily apparent to anyone who watched us closely. I drop my gaze to her mouth and she licks her lips. It's not quite an invitation to kiss her again, which is just as well. She's right. We need to focus, especially through the first few days of this. The next forty-eight hours will make or break Olympus's belief in this whirlwind romance. "We'll have the ceremony tonight."

Her hazel eyes go wide. "Tonight?"

"The sooner, the better. If you can convince your family, they are more than welcome to attend. I'll have two witnesses as backup."

"Who are your witnesses?"

Instead of answering, I press a quick kiss to that little line between her brows and rise. "You have twenty minutes until breakfast is done."

"I said I'm not hungry."

"It's going to be a long day, Psyche, and you need the calories to keep your energy up." I pause in the doorway. "It'd be a damned shame if you swooned when I put my ring on your finger and I had to carry you to our marriage bed."

She makes a face. "That's not funny."

"No, it's not. Twenty minutes." I close the bedroom door behind me and walk down the long hallway and into the kitchen. I'm not even surprised to find Hermes standing at the stove, her dark hair done up in two puff buns on the top of her head. She's wearing skintight overall shorts and a cropped top with a picture of...Krampus? Also knee socks with little trees on them. I cross my arms over my chest and lean against the counter. "Breaking and entering is a crime."

"For most people. With me, it's practically my love language." She uses the skillet to flip what appears to be a passable omelet. "Speaking of love languages, imagine my surprise to see that devastatingly romantic picture of you and Psyche on her social media." She shoots me a brilliant grin. "Congrats to the happy couple. I'll officiate the wedding, of course."

That takes one task off my list, but I know Hermes too well to accept this gift without looking for barbs attached. "Why?"

"The Dimitriou ladies are so *interesting*, don't you think? When they first arrived on the scene, I thought they were like the other boring social climbers, but I've changed my mind. I think they're going to turn Olympus itself on its head."

I don't know if that's a terrifying thought or a welcome one. I glance back down the hall, but my bedroom door is still shut. "I changed my mind about killing her. This is the only option."

"Careful, darling, or I might think you've developed a nasty condition called a conscience." She pulls a plate out of my cupboard and slides the omelet onto it.

"Wouldn't dream of it." It has nothing to do with a conscience and everything to do with taking what I want. I want Psyche, have wanted her since she took care of me in that bathroom in Dodona Tower. I can't have her if she's dead. That's all.

Hermes sits on my counter and starts eating the omelet. "You'll need two witnesses. Her sisters won't do it."

"You seem rather sure of it." I am, too, but I'm curious enough to keep Hermes talking.

She takes a bite and makes a face. "Too much prosciutto. Ugh." She chews slowly enough to try my patience. "They'll be too busy looking for an opportunity to get her away from you. You'll have to find your witnesses yourself. I don't suppose your mother is in a generous mood?"

I give her the look that statement deserves. "I'm going to ask Helen and Eris."

Hermes freezes and then bursts out laughing. "The balls on

you, Eros. Gods, it's a shame you make a better friend than a romantic partner—and that's not saying much because you're a shitty friend. But life with you would never be boring."

I don't bother to argue about my being a shitty friend. I am, and we both know it. "It's a good play."

"Oh, undoubtedly. Not even Zeus can argue against the marriage if his sisters stand as witness." She grins. "I'll bet you a grand they say no."

"I'll take that bet." I motion at the door. "Now get out. I have calls to make, and you need to find a suit or something to wear tonight because this getup isn't fit for the occasion. For fuck's sake, Hermes. Christmas was nearly two months ago."

"Christmas is a state of mind." But she hops off the counter and pushes her plate into my hands. "I got it. Fancy duds. I'll invite Dionysus."

The woman cannot help but stir the pot every chance she gets. I roll my eyes. "You know better, Hermes."

She keeps walking, talking over her shoulder at me. "He probably won't show up, on account of the fact that he hates you. But I'll invite him because *I* am a good friend, and it would hurt his feelings if I didn't."

"Dionysus isn't my friend just because he's your friend."

"Can't hear you. Bye!" She finger waves in my direction and then she's gone. A few moments later, I hear the front door close. I stalk to it and flip the locks. I've made my peace with Hermes showing up whenever she damn well pleases. The woman is 90 percent cat; she comes and goes when she feels like it and helps herself to my food and booze regardless of whether I'm in the house to offer it or not. It's annoying and weirdly endearing in a way no one but Hermes could pull off.

She's agreed to officiate, so that's one less call I have to make. I head back in the kitchen, clean off Hermes's plate, and get to work on making breakfast for me and Psyche. It's going to be a long fucking day.

PSYCHE

"YOU WHAT?"

I bite back a sigh and focus on my phone. It's divided into three squares, each depicting one of my sisters, all with varying expressions of fury and disbelief on their faces. Eros, damn him, was right. This isn't going to be an easy sell. "Eros and I are getting married. Tonight."

Callisto's camera moves as she paces back and forth in her room. "I'm going to kill him."

"You can't threaten to kill everyone who pisses you off," Persephone says. "But in this case, I'm inclined to agree. Or break his legs, shove him in a box, and have him shipped out on the next boat leaving Olympus. I'm sure Poseidon wouldn't notice."

"Please stop threatening violence against my fiancé," I say mildly.

Eurydice watches me, her eyes shadowed with sorrow. "It won't work, Psyche. Aphrodite hates us because of Mother, and Eros is the weapon she uses to punish the things she hates."

I know that better than all three of them at this point. I fight back a shiver. "My mind's made up. Please support me in this." I start to say that it's true love, but the lie sticks to my tongue. "Aphrodite's and Mother's opinions on the marriage don't matter."

"That's a bit shortsighted."

I give Persephone a look. "Says the woman who ran away from Zeus and hooked up with the boogeyman of Olympus. Let's not cast stones."

My sister seems entirely unconvinced. "Hades didn't earn his reputation. Eros has."

I can't argue that, so I go with the only thing I can. An honest plea. "I'm asking you to support me in this. I'm choosing to marry Eros, and I won't change my mind."

Eurydice looks like she's going to cry. Callisto is the exact opposite; she has the same dangerous expression on her face as when she stabbed Ares's offending hand or when she started that bar fight not too long ago. And Persephone? She's watching me as if she's never seen me before. Finally, she says, "If you were in trouble, you'd tell us, wouldn't you?"

Not in a hundred years. Not when I'm up to my eyeballs and sinking fast. There's nothing they can do to help, and if they try, all it will do is provide more opportunity for Aphrodite to remove me permanently. Worse, she might turn her vengeful gaze on my sisters, too. Dragging them down with me would be the height of selfishness, and I refuse to do it. So I hold my sister's gaze and lie. "Of course."

She sighs. "Mother is going to have a heart attack when she hears this."

"No, she won't, and you know it. She's been looking for a way to stick it to Aphrodite for years, and once she calms down, she'll realize this marriage is the perfect way to do so." Even if it means I won't marry Zeus the way she obviously wanted. I can't afford to think about *that* too hard right now.

"'When she calms down' is one rather large caveat." A puppy appears in Persephone's screen, a cute little black mutt that licks her chin and makes an eager yipping sound. She pets his head distractedly. "Not now, Cerberus. I'm talking."

Callisto curses. "This is bullshit. I'm not supporting this." She hangs up before I can get a word in edgewise.

Eurydice shakes her head. "I'm sorry, Psyche. But you're going to regret doing this. I can't support it, either." She hangs up, too.

I bite back a sigh. It's no less than I expected, but hope springs eternal. Persephone is still petting Cerberus in a contemplative way. She finally says, "I trust your judgment. I don't think this is the right course, but I suspect you're not telling me everything. Last night, you were tagged in half a dozen posts around town with Hermes, and this morning, surprise, you're marrying the son of our mother's enemy."

It's everything I can do to keep my guilt off my face. "To be fair, half the Thirteen are Mother's enemies."

She doesn't smile. "You went along with me when I asked for your support while I stayed with Hades after fleeing Zeus. You gave me the time and trust I needed to figure things out. It'd be hypocritical in the extreme not to support you right now, too."

I snort. "I'm so glad you've come to that conclusion."

"Hey, I love you and I'm worried about you. I am really

tempted to come pull a Callisto, break down his door, and haul you over the river to the lower city."

If I thought for a second that would work... But it won't. Persephone already told me that she's seen Eros in the lower city, and even revoking his invitation might not be enough to keep him out. It's difficult to cross the River Styx without an invitation, but it's not impossible. The barrier in place is a slightly weaker version of the one that surrounds Olympus as a whole. Like Poseidon with the external barrier, Hades has some control over who comes and goes from the upper city to the lower city. It's not a perfect system, though.

Not to mention the fact that Eurydice and Callisto are here, both ideal backup targets for Aphrodite's wrath. Next time she orders one of Demeter's daughter dispatched, Eros might not take the time to have a conversation. He might simply strike.

I can't let that happen.

"I want this," I repeat for what feels like the twelfth time.

"If you change your mind, we'll get you out." No telling if she's talking about her and her husband or her and our sisters, but neither option is a good idea. "We'll be at the wedding, though. Hades and I." Persephone hesitates. "Do you want me to try to convince Callisto and Eurydice to come as well?"

"No, it's okay." I can't blame them for not wanting to attend our sham of a marriage ceremony, even if it stings. "But if you could invite Mother out to brunch, I'd really appreciate it. I need to get my things from the penthouse, and I can't do that if I run the risk of seeing her there." Time might have tempered my mother's impulse control, but Callisto comes by her rage honestly.

I wouldn't put it past the two of them to lock me in my room until I see reason, which would just make this situation even messier.

"Consider it done. I'll text you when it's confirmed."

"Thank you."

She gives me a small smile. "Be careful, Psyche. Eros is dangerous in the extreme."

I understand that far better than she ever will. I try for a smile in return. "I know. He's a monster. But after tonight, he's *my* monster."

We hang up pretty quickly after that, and I take a few minutes to try to put my appearance to rights. Eros, thankfully, has a whole cabinet full of hair and skin products, but most of it is unfamiliar to me. I comb my hair and twist it up into a messy-chic crown around my head. I keep a small selection of makeup in my purse for touch-ups, which is a lifesaver right now. By the time I exit the bedroom, I look like a woman who just had an unexpected sleepover with her partner but still put together. It will have to do.

A divine smell draws me into the kitchen to find Eros finishing up a hash with potatoes, peppers, and fried eggs. It's heavier than what I'd normally eat for breakfast, but I accept the plate he passes over and take a seat on one of the stylish iron stools that flank the kitchen bar. They're not exactly comfortable, but they are pretty. I take a few bites, enough that Eros stops watching me and digs into his own meal.

We eat in a strangely comfortable silence, interspersed by our respective phones buzzing with notifications every few seconds. Eros gives his a dirty look. "How do you put up with this shit?"

"It's necessary." I learned early on that power is the only thing the upper crust of Olympus respects and that I'd never attain it by trying to imitate them. I had to go my own way while still playing the game—a careful balance that exhausts me more often than not. But it was working, at least until Aphrodite turned her vengeful gaze in my direction. I scroll through the notifications. Several are from my mother, growing increasingly irate. Another few are interview requests. "How long do you want to make them wait for interviews?"

He hesitates and finally says grudgingly, "I bow to your expertise in this."

Surprising that he'll willingly give up even this much control. I ignore the strange flare of warmth in my chest at the trust he's placing in me. "I say we give it a week. A few pictures of the wedding, a few outings where they see us being the loving couple in public, and they'll be so frothing at the mouth to get an exclusive scoop that they won't bother to ask hard questions." I have just the interviewer in mind for it, too, but I haven't heard from her yet.

"Okay." He stretches and then his hand lands lightly on the spot between my shoulder blades. I don't flinch this time; I'm too busy trying not to melt as he trails his fingers over the nape of my neck. "I like your hair up."

"I assure you that your preferences have absolutely nothing to do with how I'll dress or act in the future."

Eros chuckles, the sound low and strangely happy. "You are a constant surprise, Psyche. I like that, too."

I don't shrug off his hand. Even as I tell myself it's practice for being in public, I know I'm a liar. I like the weight of his palm against my skin. I like how tenderly he traces his fingers down my spine. Believing that he's actually affected and not simply adjusting to me the same way I'm adjusting to him...

He's not. I'm no psychologist, but if Eros is a sociopath, I wouldn't be surprised. He doesn't seem to have the moral brakes most people do. Or maybe that's just a side effect of being raised from birth by Aphrodite. Nature or nurture, the bottom line is that if he has emotions beyond amusement and irritation, he keeps them hidden deep down. And lust. We can't forget about lust. Eros has that in spades.

Even so, this is all a lie, a game, even.

I don't look up from my phone. "Why are you doing this?"

"I don't want you dead." He says it so simply, I flinch.

"What's so special about me that *I* get spared?" He has bodies in his past. He's admitted as much. "Is it because I'm Demeter's daughter?"

He snorts. "No, that's hardly a mark in your favor."

"Then *why?*"

Eros stares hard at his plate. "I've done a lot of stuff I'm not proud of, hurt people who I thought were enemies at the time, only to find out later that the only thing they'd ever done wrong was to piss off my mother." He shrugs. "After a while, it didn't matter *what* they'd done, only that she commanded them to be punished."

I still don't understand. "But she commanded *me* to be punished."

"Yeah, she did." Eros stabs a piece of potato. "But like I said, I don't want you dead. This is the only other way."

I have no reason to trust him. None. He's given his word, yes, but Olympus is filled with liars and cheats. Even my mother has been known to commit to a shady deal when the situation calls for it. Everyone in the city thinks that she and Hades have an alliance; they don't. Instead, she traded her help for Hades's attendance at six events each year. He shows up at her side, and people make the assumptions my mother wants them to make. It's not the truth, though. The upper city might have forgotten how far she was willing to go to return Persephone to her engagement with the old Zeus, but Hades hasn't.

My mother is arguably one of the gentler hands when it comes to Olympian power games. Aphrodite has neither a soft touch nor a subtle bone in her body. Eros wouldn't have survived this long in this city without being a little bit of both liar and cheat. I certainly haven't. There's plenty he's not telling me about his motivations. For all that, I trust that he's as intent on this marriage as I have to be. All the other details will fall where they may.

It's our job to ensure they fall where we want them to.

My phone buzzes as a text comes through. A welcome distraction from how good it feels to have Eros touching me.

> **Persephone:** We're meeting in an hour at Poppy's. She's furious about that photo. Between the one last night and the other, she thinks you've been secretly dating behind her back. Good luck.

Our plan is working. This is what I wanted. So why do I feel so sick about it?

I type a quick thank-you and push my chair back. "My mother will be leaving the penthouse in about thirty minutes." She'll want to get to Poppy's early to ensure she has her preferred table. My mother isn't predictable when it comes to many moves she makes, but there are certain things I can reasonably assume she'll do. One of those is maneuvering to get the best table in any restaurant, maximized for seeing and being seen.

Eros grabs both our plates and heads for the sink. "Let's go."

"We really don't—" I cut myself off at the look on his face. It's clear he's not about to let me out of his sight, and I honestly don't know what I'd do if I got a little distance from him. I've committed myself to this, yes, but if there was a chance to find another way... I am who I am, which means I am my mother's daughter. I will always be looking for the best path forward, even if that means pivoting unexpectedly.

Not to mention if he's serious about the threat his mother offers, I actually need him to look out for me. I haven't survived the last twenty-four hours only to fall *now*, when survival is on the horizon. "Fine. Let's go."

It takes us five minutes to get our shoes on and into the elevator. There's a different security person waiting at the floor of the parking garage with Eros's car, a white woman with bright-red hair and even brighter lipstick. She smiles at him, and the expression only dims the slightest bit when she sees me. "Morning, Eros."

"Morning." He barely glances at her as he holds the door open for me and whisks us down to the aisle he parked in last night. Except instead of going to the tiny sports car, he walks past it to a dark sedan. It's still the height of luxury, but it's surprisingly understated. When I raise my eyebrows, Eros looks away. "The Porsche isn't practical if we don't want to draw attention." His shoulders hunch the tiniest bit. "And you weren't comfortable in it."

There is absolutely no reason for that sliver of thoughtfulness to have heat flushing my body. None at all. I'm not so starved for attention that my head will turn over such a small thing. And yet... "Thanks," I say softly.

If I didn't know better, I'd think he's blushing as he unlocks the doors and we climb into the car. We don't speak as we pull out of the parking garage, and I'm grateful for the silence because it allows me time to get my head on straight. I don't need to be overanalyzing Eros's motivations for switching vehicles. I need to think and strategize about what I'm going to pack and what I absolutely can't live without. Doing it in one trip is going to be a challenge, but I'll figure it out.

I don't question the fact that Eros knows where I live. I can pinpoint the buildings of all of the Thirteen and most of their inner circles and families. It pays to be aware of these things, and so everyone is.

"Where should I park?"

"The street."

He makes a face. "That's more exposed than I'd like to be."

"I know, but it's a risk we have to take." The security people who work for the building monitor our comings and goings and report them to my mother, and the last thing I need is for her to decide we need to be detained so she and I can have a sit-down. There's no avoiding it indefinitely, but I want Eros and me to be beyond the point of no return before Mother gets involved. Like Aphrodite, even she will have to recalibrate once his ring is on my finger.

Speaking of... "We need rings."

Eros expertly parallel parks in a spot small enough that I would have said it was impossible. He turns off the engine. "The jeweler will be at my place at two this afternoon with a selection. I just need your size."

Of course he's thought of that. I tell him my ring size and watch as he shoots off a text. My phone is still blowing up with notifications, but I've silenced it so I can work through them when I have time. "I don't know if Callisto is there, but I don't want a confrontation."

"You don't have to worry about it."

I give him the look that deserves. "I think we've already established that violence is definitely something you're capable of."

He transforms before my eyes. The coldness disappears from his face and he gives me a charming smile. "I would never harm anyone the love of my life cares about."

I dig my nails into my palm, using the bite of pain to remind myself that this is fake. No matter how intensely my heart flutters when he looks at me like that, it's all an act. I may need to get my damn heart looked at soon, though. Surely skipping beats this regularly isn't healthy. "Let's get this over with."

"After you, beloved."

EROS

I'VE SEEN THE OUTSIDE OF DEMETER'S BUILDING PLENTY OF times, and I have the blueprints of the penthouse she shares with her daughters—just like I have blueprints for all the buildings of people who could eventually be my mother's marks. It's still a different experience to walk into the lobby. I count half a dozen carefully concealed security people, which means there's likely another half dozen on the premises, if not more. Demeter's taking no chances, though she's not the type to want to rub the presence of security in her guests' faces.

Or maybe it's her daughters she's worried about.

In any other situation, the security people would be an annoyance, but right now they're actually an asset. My mother won't strike here, won't send her people here. It's too risky, with too little reward. Psyche is safe as long as we're in this building, and I can relax a little.

She heads past the main elevators and down a short hallway to a different one. She presses her palm to the pad next to it, and a moment later, it flashes green. Interesting. The doors slide open and she steps inside. "I'm going to put together a suitcase, but I need you to haul out some of the other things."

Curiosity grabs me by the throat. Her social media always looks so effortless. I don't fuck with that shit for the most part, but even I know the more natural it appears, the more effort it actually takes. I'm about to get a peek behind the curtain.

It shouldn't matter. Her savviness at presenting a compelling story to the world is an asset I intend to utilize. That's it. Watching her stage that "spontaneous" photo with us in my bed was a revelation. She went about it with a single-minded focus that I find entirely too sexy, and that was done with a few lamps and her phone. I want to see how she works when she has all her tools at her disposal.

I would wager that Psyche was being entirely genuine the night we were first photographed together, but she's a different kind of genuine when she's creating compelling fiction for Olympus to consume. And consume they do. I check my phone. The likes on that picture of us are well over a million at this point, and it's not even noon. Truly, she's brilliant at what she does.

The elevator doors open into a surprisingly welcoming foyer. The walls are a deep green that should be overwhelming, but combined with the light-gray tiled floor, they actually create an appealing balance. There are a few pieces of furniture—two tall-backed chairs in an understated floral print and a long, dark wooden table with a variety of drawers—that seem to invite guests to sit down and have a chat. In the fucking foyer.

Next is the living room. It's more of the same. Bold walls, light floors, and furniture that looks remarkably comfortable. There are books scattered on the coffee table centered between a long couch and another pair of chairs: genre fiction books with their spines creased from reading. It's all too possible to picture Psyche draped over the couch, a book in her hands, relaxing with her family.

This place feels like a home.

How novel.

My mother uses her living room as a place to entertain guests, which means she always strongly discouraged me from spending leisure time there growing up. That's what bedrooms are for; personal space that can be hidden away behind a closed door. She keeps her game face on at all times, even in the relative privacy of the shared spaces of my childhood home. I was expected to do the same.

I want to find an excuse to poke around, but Psyche's leading me up the floating stairs, and the prospect of seeing *her* room overrides all else. If Demeter's daughters treat this entire penthouse as personal space, what will Psyche's actual personal space reveal?

I stop short in the upstairs hallway. It takes Psyche several steps to realize I'm not behind her and stop as well. She turns with an impatient sigh. "I know the temptation to snoop is nearly overwhelming, but please keep up. We don't have much time."

She's right, but it's like my brain has skipped. I stare at pictures lining the walls. They're artfully arranged, of course, but they're *personal*. Staged photos in large frames with Psyche and her three sisters in coordinating clothing, starting from when they were very small and continuing to what looks like a recent one. They're interesting, but what really catches my eye are the unstaged photos in smaller frames peppered throughout.

Psyche and Persephone, their arms thrown around each other's shoulders, their hair in pigtails, and Psyche missing her front teeth.

A preteen Callisto holding up a fish nearly as large as she is, a happy grin on her face that is entirely unfeigned.

All four girls dressed up in costumes. Eurydice a fairy. Callisto a knight. Persephone an angel. Psyche a princess.

My chest hurts. Why the fuck does my chest hurt? They're just pictures. Obviously Psyche's always been good at pictures; she's the most photogenic of all her rather photogenic family. There is no reason for some undefined barbed emotion to lash through me at the photographic evidence of her happy childhood. It certainly shouldn't be made worse by the fact that Demeter has said photos prominently displayed, if in a part of the penthouse where only family would spend time.

"Eros?"

I give myself a shake. "I'm good."

"Are you?" Psyche's brows draw together, worry lingering in her hazel eyes. "What's wrong?"

"Nothing's wrong." It should be the truth. I dredge up my charming smile, but Psyche only frowns harder in response. Right. She knows I'm lying, and she won't be fooled by a fake smile. I curse. "Nothing should be wrong. It's not relevant."

"Are you sure?"

"Yes."

She looks at me for a moment longer but finally nods. "Okay, let's hurry." She turns and continues down the hallway, leaving me to follow.

I give the photos one last long look and then leave them

behind. Maybe it shouldn't be so novel that Psyche and her sisters had a good childhood, but this is Olympus. I was raised on power games, and I learned to lie around the time I learned to walk. It's the same with Helen and Perseus and their siblings. Those of us both fortunate and unfortunate to be born into Olympus politics were in a sink-or-swim situation from a very young age.

My mother, in particular, tolerated no missteps.

No wonder kindness comes so naturally to Psyche; she had an abundance of it growing up.

She stops in front of the third door, drawing me from my thoughts. Anticipation curls through me. This short visit has already been a treasure trove of information about this woman. Her bedroom will be the ultimate look behind the curtain. Psyche opens the door and steps into the room, leaving me to follow.

It's...a mess.

I stand in the doorway and take in the stacks of clothing draped over every available surface. There's an antique vanity with countless jars and tubes of makeup and skin-care and hair-care stuff. "You sleep in a closet."

"This is a bedroom."

"Is it? I can't see a bed anywhere. All I see are clothes."

"Shut up." She follows a small path of cleared floor deeper into the room. "I have a system."

"I highly suggest you find a new system, because I can't live like this." The thought of all this clutter, system or no, is nearly enough to make me break out in hives. I expected this room to be more of the attractive, welcoming vibe that permeates the entire penthouse. This is pure mayhem. I edge my way a little into the room and poke the pile of clothes balanced precariously on what I assume is a chair. "I'm marrying a chaos monster."

"Then I guess we're both monsters."

"Cute." I resist the urge to continue prodding the mound of clothing and focus on her. "But we both know that's not true."

"Yes, yes, you're the biggest, baddest monster in the room. Stay on task." She disappears through another doorway and returns with a giant suitcase. Another trip through the doorway and she's got a variety of bags that look like lighting equipment. These she thrusts into my hands. "Hold these, please."

"I've seen photos of your bedroom. It doesn't look like this." For all my teasing, the bed is clear—but it's not the one I've seen pictured.

"Oh. Yeah." She drops the suitcase on the bed and starts picking through the piles of clothing and tossing stuff into it. "I use Persephone's bedroom. She's kind of a neat freak and she's got a nice aesthetic going on in there. Plus, she never posted photos of inside our house even before she moved to the lower city."

I watch three more dresses land on top of the suitcase, colorful fabric spilling out, before I lose it. "For fuck's sake." I'm not a clean freak, as she put it. I like my shit in order because it simplifies my life, but I'm hardly going around with a label maker or having a meltdown when something gets moved. That said, her complete disregard for anything resembling order is making my right eye twitch. I set the lighting equipment by the door and carefully wade to her bed and start folding.

"What are you doing?"

"Ignore me and keep packing." It's kind of strange to be

handling women's clothing. It's a completely different sensory experience from my stuff, and most resist normal folding, so I have to resort to strategic rolling to get them into some semblance of order. I try very hard not to think about Psyche wearing any of the items, especially not the silk dress that slides over my palms as I wrestle it into submission. It would look great on my floor after I tugged it off her shoulders and...

Focus.

The suitcase is half-packed when she gives me a long look. "I just have a few more things. Grab the equipment and I'll meet you downstairs."

"Nice try. No."

"Eros, I'm about to start digging through my underwear drawers. Give me a little space."

I start to argue, but stop when something else occurs to me. "A wedding dress."

"What?"

"You need a wedding dress."

Psyche frowns, but then curses. "I need a wedding dress. *Shit.* This will never work. There's not enough time." She keeps going, words tripping over themselves as she spirals. "Oh gods, no one is going to believe we're really doing this if such an important piece isn't involved."

I grab her shoulders. "Psyche, look at me."

"Guess I should start picking out my gravestone because—"

I don't think about the implications of my actions. I just kiss her. She tenses, but before I can pull away, she's melting against me, her hands instantly going to my hair and her body pressing to mine. Now's the time to stop, to recalibrate this conversation for a solution. I've headed her panicking off at the pass, so I've accomplished what I set out to do. We just need to break the kiss…

I'm not ready to give up the taste of Psyche yet. She's so fucking sweet on my tongue. Another reminder that she's unlike anyone I've ever met. Cunning and oh so careful about her public image, but beneath that, she's soft and funny and so fucking sweet.

A good man would do anything to preserve this woman's soft center. He would battle her demons and enemies alike to create a world where she could let down her barriers and live happily without the armor. He would get her the fuck out of Olympus, would promise her safety without any selfish gains for himself, would put her up on a pedestal and worship at the altar of her daily.

I'm not a good man, though.

I'm a fucking monster.

I want Psyche for my own. A desire that was kindled that first night but has grown beyond control in the last twenty-four hours. I don't care if she deserves someone just as sweet as she is. I want her chained to me, and I'll rip out the throat of anyone who thinks they can take her away.

I cup her jaw and angle her head back a little, taking the kiss deeper. Claiming her in this tiny way. Marking her as mine, even if we're the only two people who will know it. She makes a little whimpering sound that goes straight to my cock. It would be nothing at all to nudge her back onto the bed and keep kissing her until we forget all the reasons this is a terrible idea.

Except we aren't in my penthouse, with a locked door between us and the rest of the world. I can't seduce Psyche into letting me do everything I want to her because it's only a matter of time before we're interrupted, and *that* will ensure I never get to touch her again.

Unacceptable. Nothing will keep me from this woman...not even my own selfish urges.

Reluctantly, I lift my head. She blinks those big hazel eyes at me, her lips plumped even more from our kiss. It's almost enough to have me tasting her again, but reason chooses that moment to take control. I drag in a ragged breath. "Tell me your measurements."

She blinks again. "What?"

The pure satisfaction coursing through me at the realization that I've affected her just as much as she affects me is worrisome. Just another piece of evidence showcasing just how out of control I am right now. I push it away and try to focus on the here and now. "Your measurements. I need them."

She licks her lips, her gaze still distracted. "Um, we talked about this. It's not—"

"Your measurements, Psyche." I coast my hands down her sides to grip her hips. "Unless you want me to take them myself. You'll have to strip down, of course."

She takes a large step back, breaking our contact. "That won't be necessary." She rattles off a series of numbers that I promptly memorize. Psyche's face has gone red, and she won't quite meet my eyes. "Is that everything?"

"Yeah." I grab the lighting equipment. "I'll wait for you at the car."

"Thank you."

It takes more effort than I would have dreamed to turn and

walk away from her. I retrace my steps to the living room and take the elevator down. Though I half expect Callisto to appear, I don't run into anyone as I stride to my car and tuck the equipment into the trunk. There's room for her suitcase and not much else, but we'll make it work. After a brief debate with myself, I decide making the call from the car is better than standing on the street and waiting for Psyche. There's not as much foot traffic here as there is around my place, but I'm still drawing stares. It's only a matter of time before someone takes a photo, posts it, and then the paparazzi show up. The last thing I need is anyone overhearing this conversation.

Not to mention the tinted windows hide me from anyone who might be walking by and give me a good view of the entrance of Demeter's building.

I scroll through my contacts until I find Helen Kasios— daughter of the last Zeus, sister to the current one. I had to call her anyway, so this will kill two birds with one stone. She doesn't make me wait long before she answers. "Since when do you date someone seriously enough to be internet official?"

Of course she's seen the photo. At this point, nearly everyone in Olympus has seen the photo; that's the entire point of it. I take a silent breath and gear up for the first of many performances. "Psyche's special."

"Uh-huh. Don't get me wrong; all the Dimitriou women are characters, and if anyone could turn your head, it's a strong personality, but that doesn't change the fact that if we were *friends*, then you'd have told me you were dating someone."

She's not exactly wrong. I know my mother hoped that I'd end up marrying either her or her sister, but we've never been more than friends. And we *are* friends, or as close to it as is possible for people like us. "I didn't think you'd approve."

"Liar." She doesn't sound pissed, just amused. "This reeks of a scheme. It's fine. You don't have to tell me the details. I assume you're calling because you need something."

"You wound me, Helen."

She laughs. "That would require you to have a heart that could be wounded."

She's got me there. I glance at the entrance to Psyche's building. I don't have a heart, but my future bride does. It's my job now to ensure it stays safely within her chest. Helen will help with that, even if she doesn't know the full story. I drop the charming persona, strangely grateful to do away with the bullshit. I can maintain the act indefinitely, but there's a certain relief in being able to be my true self. I'm allowed the freedom with so few people. "I need two favors."

"Granted, but I want one in return."

I snort. "You haven't even heard what they are yet."

"I don't need to. I'm bored. After Eris decided to stir the pot by spilling absinthe on *both* Demeter and Aphrodite at the last party, Perseus has got us all under lockdown so we don't bring any more shame onto the family name—as if that were even possible after our shitshow of a father." She makes a derisive noise. "I need a distraction, and whatever you have going on will do nicely."

"And for your favor?"

"I'll figure it out later. Just tell me what you need."

Giving open-ended favors isn't exactly my style, but I highly doubt Helen will decide to use it against me. Beyond that, if she were in trouble, I might bullshit a little but we both know I'd help.

"I need the contact information for that clothing designer in the lower city you like to use. The one who pisses my mother off."

"Juliette. Sure. I'll text you her number." My phone beeps a second later with the text in question. "That was boring. What's the second thing?"

Best not to beat around the bush. "I need you and Eris to stand as witnesses at my wedding. Tonight."

She's silent for so long, I have to resist the urge to check to see if the call dropped. It hasn't. Helen just needs time to process. When she finally draws in a long breath, I brace myself. She doesn't disappoint. "Eros, I say this with all the love in my withered heart, but *are you out of your fucking mind?* Dating her is one thing. *Marrying* her? Your mother is going to stroke out. Gods, my brother is going to stroke out, too. And likely Demeter. You're going to take out three of the Thirteen in a single act. It's brilliantly ruthless but reckless in the extreme, and you're not reckless."

Not usually, but then there's nothing usual about this situation. "Will you do it or not?"

"I'll do it." She doesn't even hesitate. "I don't know what you're planning, but I'll do it. Eris will, too."

I don't bother to ask her to confirm. If there's one thing Eris can be guaranteed to do, it's show up when there's chaos in the wind. A wedding between me and Psyche is the very definition of sowing chaos. "We're doing it at my place tonight at seven."

"We'll be there."

"Helen... Thanks. For showing up. For not asking too many uncomfortable questions. For all of it."

She huffs. "It's really sad that you're even a little surprised that I would, but I can't exactly blame you. This is Olympus, after all."

"Yeah." The rules are different here, at least for the circles we move in. Having a person you trust enough to ask for a favor is the most valuable thing in the world—and about as rare as the Golden Fleece of legend.

We hang up quickly after that, and I glance at the clock and then the front door to Psyche's building. She's taking her sweet time, but I have one more call to make before I go hunt her down. This one goes even quicker. Apparently Helen sent Juliette a text right after she sent me one, so the designer is expecting my call.

I explain what I need and give her Psyche's measurements. She mutters to herself for a few minutes, and I can hear her flipping through hangers on the other side of the line. "I have several items that might suit. You'll have to come to me, though. I don't give a fuck who your mother is—that's a mark against you, to be perfectly honest—or if the bride is one of my clients from time to time. I'm not crossing over into the upper city."

I silently curse, but I should have expected this. My mother helped drive Juliette out of the upper city. I can't remember why, only that it was one of the rare cases where she handled things herself instead of having me do it for her. Not that it matters. Aphrodite's feuds can be as petty as they are long-reaching. At best guess, the designer either refused to work with her or clothed a rival better than Aphrodite for some event.

Then again, this might be something of a blessing in disguise. Psyche is infinitely safer in the lower city than she is in the upper city right now. From there, we'll go right back to my place, get married, and remove the target from her back once and for all.

I inject as much charm into my voice as possible. "How soon can we show up?"

"Give me an hour to make some adjustments, and then I'll need another hour to ensure whichever one she picks is fitted properly." She gives me the address of her place. "Be prepared to pay for disrupting my plans for the day."

"Of course."

She hangs up just as I catch sight of Psyche hauling two suitcases out the door. I climb out of the car and hurry to her side. "Packing light, I see."

"You're the one determined to move me in with you. This is barely half of what I need to survive." She follows me to the car and watches me wedge one suitcase into the trunk and the other into the back seat. "We need to leave. Persephone texted letting me know that her brunch with our mother is finished."

I hold the door open for her, ignoring the strange look she gives me, and then walk around to the driver's seat. "Call her back."

"Persephone? Why?"

"We need an invitation to the lower city, and we need it now."

PSYCHE

I DON'T KNOW HOW EROS GOT JULIETTE'S INFORMATION, but an hour later, we're driving onto one of the three bridges in Olympus to meet her. Each of them have a particular feel, and Cypress Bridge calls back to our Greek roots. There are tall pillars lining it, and in the light of the late morning, they give the impression of crossing into another world.

My ears pop as we cross the River Styx, but that's as uncomfortable as things get, thanks to Persephone's invitation. Without it, moving from the upper city to the lower city isn't impossible, but it's significantly more uncomfortable. Or that's what everyone says. I've never tried it myself. The few times I've visited my sister in her new home, I've been welcomed.

We're not headed to that house today. Eros guides us south along the river to the lower city warehouse district. It looks nearly identical to the one in the upper city—each block populated with massive warehouses, the streets with very little foot traffic. It's strange how determined the upper city is to pretend the lower city is actually lower, when really it's not that much different. At least on the surface.

In reality, the differences run bone deep.

I know my sister loves it down here, but I don't understand this side of the river. Surely the people here aren't actually as transparent as Persephone makes it sound? How do they go through life without the defense of a public image in place? It boggles the mind. Then again, I suppose they take their cues from Hades. He's a very different kind of ruler than any Zeus has ever been.

Eros circles the massive block and parks in front of a warehouse that looks indistinguishable from the rest of the others in the area. I recognize the subtle sign above the door, though. *Juliette's.*

He turns to look at me. "Get whatever you need. Spare no expense."

"Eros—" Maybe he doesn't realize how expensive Juliette's custom pieces run, but I'm not mercenary enough to take him up on this offer.

"I mean it." He shuts off the engine. "Image matters, remember?"

Right. Our image. *My* image. That's what he's worried about. He's not some besotted man with a black credit card wanting to treat his partner. This is all about the plan. "Of course it matters." I step out of the car before we can continue the conversation. He's right; I need to keep my eye on the prize.

The prize being my life.

Juliette's warehouse might seem like all the others on the outside, but it's a completely different world inside. Right off the door, there is a stylish sitting room with a variety of chairs and reading material. The rest of the space is divided into two. The front half for racks upon racks of clothing, arranged by style, size, and color. The back is her work space, and only a fool tries to check it out without an invitation.

She must have been watching for us because she appears immediately, striding down the space between two racks as if it were a runway. If she were anyone else, I would think she's putting on a show, but this is just Juliette. She started her career as a model, and while she may have moved to the fashion side of things, she's still naturally aware of her surroundings and subconsciously putting forth her best angles.

Not that the woman has a bad angle. She's a tall Black woman with cheekbones sharp enough to cut and a focused air about her that speaks to how she made it to the top of her field. She meets my gaze and smiles. "Congratulations on your engagement."

I manage to smile back, and it almost feels natural on my face. "Thank you. And thank you for working with us on such short notice."

"Of course." Juliette motions toward the changing rooms tucked against the far wall. "I have a few options picked out that I think would suit."

If she says they'll suit, I believe her. The woman is truly a master with fit, fabric, and style. There's a reason I have a few of her pieces in my suitcase currently, though she's expensive enough that I try to ration my purchases for special occasions. A wedding is nothing if not special, I suppose. "Thank you," I say again.

"You." She turns dark eyes on Eros. "Go sit down or wait outside. I don't want you wandering about the place and distracting me." There's no give in Juliette's voice. Or on her face, where she's barely concealing her dislike for Eros. When he obediently walks away, his footsteps echoing in the large space, she turns to me. "It's not my job to ask questions, but I hope you know what you're doing."

I hope I know what I'm doing, too. Confiding in anyone, especially a near stranger, is out of the question, though. Instead, I offer her a bright smile. "I do."

Juliette gives me a long look and finally nods. "Let's get to it."

She sends me into the changing area with six dresses. It takes me ten minutes to eliminate four of them as possibilities. They all fit perfectly, but they just don't feel right for the image I plan on projecting. Plenty of people spend years dreaming of their wedding, and when I was a little girl, I was no different.

Once we moved into the city, I set those dreams aside. Oh, I always hoped I'd end up married one day, but with every year that passed, the reality of our situation sank in further. The only people I can trust in Olympus are my sisters. Even my mother has her own agenda, and more often than not, she asks for forgiveness instead of permission when she ropes us into her schemes.

A part of me always dreamed of walking down the aisle to my partner, of putting together a small but tasteful wedding of our closest friends and family, one that had nothing to do with the press or social media or the judgment of others. A marriage that *I* chose, rather than one set up for political gain like my mother wants.

That dream has turned to ash now.

I study the remaining two dresses. One is what I would have chosen for that dream wedding. It's a fitted white dress in a mermaid style with exquisite lace and beading over the bodice and hips and thighs before flaring out in layers of tulle that create a short train.

The other is a deep merlot color that's breathtakingly striking. It's got a structured sweetheart bodice that does impressive things for my breasts. The fabric gathers on my right hip in a burst of silver roses, the flowers appearing to be swept along, with silver petals trailing down the full skirt. Tiny sleeves create an off-the-shoulder look that seems more designed to show off my shoulders and chest than cover anything up. Silver stitching creates a V along the top of the bodice, finishing the look.

It's bold and untraditional, and even though it's not the right color of red, it still makes me feel like it's been dipped in blood.

In short, it's perfect.

"Juliette."

She steps into the changing area and raises her brows. "It wasn't my first choice when I put these options together, but it's a showstopper."

I stare at myself in the mirror. My coloring allows me to pull off a wide variety of palettes, but I usually keep to a subtler neutral with pops of brightness. A look that doesn't scream for attention but also isn't hiding. No one can look at me in this dress and see anything other than a statement.

Choke on that, Aphrodite.

"I'll take it."

Juliette nods. "Give me a few moments." She circles me, tugging the dress in a few places and pinning the hem a little higher. "I can have this done in an hour or so. Do you want to wait?"

It's not a good idea to linger in the lower city. Persephone might be willing to let us be here, but Hades doesn't like Eros, and there's always the risk he'll override my sister and revoke his invitation. "I'll ask my sister to bring it when she comes tonight."

"Works for me." Juliette pins one last piece and nods. "Okay, I'm finished. I don't need you anymore."

I smile. "Thanks for the rush order on this."

"Don't thank me. As I told Eros, I plan on charging for my disrupted plans. Triple my going rate sounds fair."

The amount is more than a little staggering. I can't believe Eros agreed to that. I don't even really require a wedding gown for this marriage, except for the fact that we need it to look real. But he didn't have to pay out for one of the best designers in Olympus to make it happen. "Definitely fair."

"Also, before I forget." She pulls something out of her pocket. It's a swatch of fabric the same color as the gown. "In case you need to find a matching palette."

"Thank you." Such a small detail, but one I hadn't really thought of in the midst of this whirlwind. "I really appreciate it."

I dress quickly and then head through the aisle of clothing to the waiting area situated near the entrance. Eros lounges in one of the chairs, glaring at his phone. He glances up as I approach, his blue eyes hard. "You should really limit who's allowed to comment on your shit. These people are toxic as fuck and have too much time on their hands."

I almost miss a step. I'm not foolish enough to assume that he's expressing actual concern. More likely, guessing by the comments I normally see on my posts, he's pissed by proxy. We're a unit, at least for now, so an insult against me is an insult against him. I fight for a smile. "I told you not to read the comments."

He rises and falls into step at my side, moving just ahead to open the door for me. I send a quick text to Persephone, confirming that she's good with ferrying the dress to me, which she is. That done, we head back across the river. I don't mean to breathe a sigh of relief as we cross the River Styx, but Eros shoots me a strange look when I do.

Embarrassment flares. "I know it's just part of living in Olympus, but the River Styx has always creeped me out."

"You're not alone. It's a kind of barrier, a reminder of how isolated we are from the rest of the world. That would unsettle anyone who brushes against it." He reaches across the middle console and sets his hand on my thigh. I stare at it, waiting for some kind of explanation, but Eros just keeps driving, his gaze on the road.

Oh. Right. The whole getting-comfortable-touching-each-other thing. I can't deny that I'm failing terribly at this goal. It's not even that I'm afraid he's going to hurt me. I know he's capable of it, of course, but that's not the problem.

The real issue is that every time he touches me, it feels like he's hooked me up to a live wire. I can be a great actress when the situation calls for it, but I haven't managed to act natural a single time we've made contact. It's something the gossip sites will glom onto without hesitation—some out of spite, some out of curiosity. Neither is good for us.

Or maybe I'm looking for an excuse to take something I most certainly shouldn't want.

I slowly, hesitantly, place my hand on Eros's. It feels like his palm scorches me through my jeans, like his fingers are making imprints against my skin even though he's not gripping me at all. I'm achingly aware that he's a few short inches from the apex of my thighs, and it's everything I can do not to clench my legs together. I've never been affected by someone like this. I don't know if it's the danger heightening my desire or the simple fact that I shouldn't want this man, almost husband or no.

"You're so tense, you're practically vibrating out of your seat."

The comment stings. "I'm doing my best."

His tone is mild. His words aren't. "Your best isn't good enough. We have mere hours to make this work. As enjoyable as it is to kiss you every time you start spiraling, you have to be able to handle me touching you."

A hot feeling flares across my face, but I can't tell if it's shame or desire. "I'm aware of that."

Eros takes the turn to his block and then again into the parking garage. "The offer still stands."

No need to ask for clarification. There's only one offer on the table right now, and it's one I most definitely shouldn't accept. I stare down at the way his hand looks on my thigh. Broad palm, blunt fingers, perfectly maintained nails. It's as handsome as the rest of him, but there are calluses on his palm. A small external indicator that he's not entirely as he seems.

The heat suffusing my face flares hotter, lower. It feels like Eros has sucked out all the air in the car, and he hasn't even done anything. The only time I've felt this discombobulated was when I held hands with Jenny Lee in seventh grade. Hot and clammy and desperately not wanting to do anything to make the contact cease. It hadn't ended well for me then; I'd dredged up all my bravery and leaned in to kiss her, only to discover she was holding my hand as a friend.

Eros doesn't want to be friends with me, but the sensation of walking a tightrope over a pit of crocodiles is identical. One wrong move, and humiliation will be the least of my worries.

He parks and we climb out of the car. Eros allows me to grab one suitcase, but he takes the other and the lighting equipment. He's got a strange look on his face, but I don't know him well enough to recognize if it's just a default distant expression or if something's actually bothering him. He locks the door to his penthouse behind us and leads me down the hallway to one of the doors we passed the night before.

It opens into a perfectly nice spare bedroom decorated in cool gray tones. A king-sized bed takes up one wall and there are two doors on the opposite side of the room, leading to a decent-sized walk-in closet and a bathroom that is only slightly smaller than the master bath. And, of course, there's a giant mirror in between the doors, reflecting our images back at us.

Eros sets my stuff on the bed, and I follow suit. He turns to me. "You can have the spare bedroom."

Relief has me weaving on my feet. It was one thing to sleep next to him last night, but I can barely comprehend doing it every night. "Thank the gods."

Eros's lips curve, but it's not a nice smile. "Don't misunderstand. You can put your shit in the spare bedroom. Make it as cluttered as you want it, but keep it confined to here. That's the *only* thing staying in the spare bedroom."

My relief fizzles out like a deflated balloon. I want to yell at him, which is precisely why I can't. It's just proving that I'm not prepared to do this all the way. Damn it. I *have* to do this 100 percent. I thought I could cut corners, but today's proven that's an impossible ask. There's only one solution.

I glance at my phone. It's nearly one. "What time is the jeweler getting here?"

"Two."

"Plenty of time, then." I walk out of the spare room and down the hall to the master. I'm achingly aware of Eros shadowing my steps, and when I glance over my shoulder, I find his gaze on my ass. Strangely, that gives me the confidence I need to pull my shirt over my head. "Let's do this."

He stops short. "I'm going to need you to elaborate."

I start unbuttoning my jeans. This would be a lot less awkward if he was stripping, too, rather than staring at me as if I'd sprouted a second head. "You were right, I was wrong. We need to rip the bandage off, and we need to do it now. So let's trade orgasms and be done with this so we can convince people we're a real couple."

EROS

I DON'T KNOW WHAT CHANGED ON THE RIDE BACK TO MY place, but now I understand what Psyche was silently chewing on. She peels off her jeans, leaving only a pair of lace panties and a nude bra. The sight of her steals my breath. She doesn't have the Photoshop finish that so many people in Olympus chase; she's got curves and a scattering of stretch marks and an ass I want to take a bite out of. Holy fuck, this is actually happening.

Still...

I clear my throat, concentrating on holding my position and not lunging at her like a fucking animal. "Just this morning, you said it wasn't necessary."

"I know." She shrugs and twists a lock of her dark hair around her finger. "Look, the truth is that I don't separate sex and emotions all that well. The very last thing I want is an emotional entanglement with you. It would make an already messy situation messier, and neither of us needs that."

No reason for that to sting. No reason at all. This is merely a business arrangement, if one she didn't enter into voluntarily. It's only reasonable that she doesn't want to become emotionally entangled with me.

That, and the fact that I'm a fucking monster.

I take one step into the bedroom and close the door softly behind me. "What are you proposing?"

"A one-time thing." She reaches behind her for her bra hook and hesitates. "Trial by fire and all that."

"I can assure you that it will feel better than a trial by fire." I move toward her slowly. I already know once won't be enough for me—not by a long shot. She won't thank me for saying as much, though. Psyche feels the chemistry, too. If she didn't, she wouldn't melt for me every time I kiss her. On that note... "Kissing remains on the table for the future."

She opens her mouth like she wants to argue but finally shrugs. "You're right. You've been photographed multiple times with your tongue down someone's throat, so they'll expect you to do the same with me."

That slows me down a little. "How closely did you follow gossip about me before this?"

"As closely as I follow gossip about every person in Olympus who might become a threat someday."

It's not quite an answer, but we have plenty of time for me to dig into that later. No reason to think she spent the last two weeks doing a deep dive on me and my history and scouring the gossip sites for tidbits about me the same way I did about her. Right now, I have a nearly naked Psyche standing in front of my bed. Only a fool would pass up this opportunity. I close the distance between us in two great strides, stopping just short of touching her. She doesn't flinch away this time. She simply unfastens her bra and lets it drop to the floor.

I allow myself to look first. Psyche is a fine wine, and like any fine wine, I plan to enjoy her in stages. She's fucking gorgeous— gorgeous enough to make Aphrodite jealous, which isn't an every-day occurrence. I push that thought away before it can ruin my mood. Instead, I focus on the woman standing before me. She holds perfectly still and lets me look my fill, as if that's something I can accomplish in the hour we have available to us.

Another time, I promise myself. Another time, when we have more hours at hand, I'll convince her to stand before me like this and let me look as long as I want.

I sift my fingers through her mass of dark hair, brushing it back and out of the way. Her breath catches as I coast my thumb over the slope of her shoulder, and she shivers a little. "We don't have much time."

"We have as much time as we need," I murmur, continuing my path down her arm, all the way to her wrist. Her skin is so fucking soft, I want to follow the path with my mouth. Instead, I bring her hand up and place it on my shoulder. Then I repeat the process with her other arm and hand.

"Eros." Her voice has gone ragged. "Stop teasing me and *touch me*."

Another day…

But this isn't another day. I might have countless ways I'd like to play out a seduction of Psyche Dimitriou, but the truth is that we are on limited time and I have to proceed accordingly.

I cup her big breasts, nearly groaning at the way they overfill my palms. Her nipples are a pretty dark pink and I can't deny myself any longer. I bend down and capture one with my mouth.

She whimpers and then her hands are in my hair. I doubt Psyche will ever admit it, but I think she likes my curls. She sure as fuck likes to use them has a handhold at the first opportunity she gets.

I switch to her other nipple, playing with her until she's shaking in my arms and arching to meet my mouth. Psyche tastes like a godsdamned dream. She also smells like a fucking cookie. I press my nose to her skin and inhale. "You smell so good, I want to eat you up."

"How very cannibal of you." She's too breathy to make the comment as dry as she obviously intends. "It's my lotion. It's—"

I look up at her. "Psyche."

She nibbles her bottom lip. "Yes?"

"I don't fucking care what kind of lotion you use." I urge her the last step to the bed and guide her down onto her back. Slowly. I have to move slowly, because if I snap my leash, I'm going to be inside her in two seconds and that's not what I want for this. I never have control issues. Never. Every seduction I've ever enacted is a carefully choreographed dance between me and my partner—or partners. I never fall on them like a beast intent on ravishing.

A beast I can feel howling inside me.

I'm actually in danger of faltering now, when it matters the most.

That's why I go to my knees next to the bed instead of joining her there. This is better. Safer. No matter what she said earlier, I don't intend for this to be a one-off. Psyche makes a surprised sound but I ignore it, focusing on easing her panties down her legs. Her thighs shake, as if she's not sure whether she wants to close them or open wide. It doesn't matter. I can see her perfectly just like this, her pussy glistening in an invitation I have no intention of rejecting. "I'm going to kiss you now."

"I'd rather we just got to it."

I almost laugh. Might laugh if I wasn't dying for a taste of her. "I've changed my mind."

Psyche tugs on my hair. "Get up here."

"We're not having sex right now." I can't trust myself to go there with her, not like this, not right now. Not when my hands are shaking, and it's everything I can do to hold myself back. She deserves flowers and romance and more orgasms than she can count. She doesn't deserve to be shoved down onto the mattress and ravished by a fucking beast.

I don't know if I'm capable of giving her what she deserves.

No, that's a lie. I already know I'm destined to fail if that's my goal. All evidence points to Psyche and I existing in entirely different realms. Even in this. *Especially* in this. She said she has trouble separating sex and emotions. I can't think of a single time sex has made me feel anything but physical pleasure.

I am going to fuck this up.

"Eros, please."

"Psyche." I press my forehead to her soft stomach and exhale shakily. "Just let me make you feel good for a little bit. Please."

"If you want to, I guess—" Her words morph into a throaty

moan as I lean down and drag the flat of my tongue over her pussy.

Fuck me. She tastes even better here than she does everywhere else. I slide my hands up her legs and grip her thighs, pushing them wider. More. I need so much more...

I drag myself back from the edge in time to grab my phone. Psyche props herself up on her elbows and looks down her body at me. Does she like the view from up there as much as I like it from down here? Hard to say. She frowns. "What are you doing?"

"Setting a timer."

She blinks. "Why?"

"Because I'm about to get distracted eating you out and I don't want to make the jeweler wait."

Another of those slow, shocked blinks. "Eros, the jeweler won't be here for forty minutes."

"I know." I curse softly. "It's not nearly enough time."

Then there's no more time for talking. I want to feel her coming all over my face and I want it now. Psyche is stubborn, so I want to make this so good, she'll forget why she tried to put a limit on this. Or that's the plan.

Any *plan* goes right out the window at my second taste of her. She tenses, but then seems to give herself over to sensation. Between one breath and the next, her legs fall open and she has her hands in my hair again. Giving herself to me. Trusting me to make her feel good. It's a heady feeling to have all of Psyche at my disposal.

I watch her closely as I work her with my tongue, exploring her slowly while I figure out what she likes. She's not quiet about what she enjoys, which is a delight to discover. She has no problem tugging on my hair to guide me to her clit or moaning and whimpering when I land on a slow vertical stroke with the flat of my tongue. I keep doing it, building her up to an orgasm that has her shaking and damn near ripping my hair out of my head. I relish the sting, the clear loss of control.

I keep my gaze on her flushed body as I move down to pepper light kisses and love bites on her inner thighs. She's completely relaxed right now, but I still have time left and no interest in stopping until the alarm sounds. I work my way back up her thighs, intensifying my touch, and then lift my head so I can part her pussy with my fingers.

She's so wet, I have to tighten the chain on my control. I want in, want it so bad I'm shaking more than she did when she came all over my face. My cock is painfully hard, and I'm not even remotely ashamed to have a small wet spot on the front of my pants from the pre-come. Of course I do. This woman hits all of my buttons. It'd be so easy to reach down and undo my pants, to wrap my fist around my cock and jack myself.

Too bad I don't trust myself enough to do it, no matter the relief it would bring. I have to keep my pants on. No exceptions.

I lick my lips, tasting her there, and push two fingers into her pussy. She gasps and arches her back, and I nearly orgasm on the spot from the way she clamps around me. And then it doesn't matter because she's coming again, milking my fingers in a way I'd kill to have her milk my cock.

Soon.

The alarm goes off long before I'm ready to stop, but I manage to lift my head. I crawl up her body and catch her mouth. She clings to me as I kiss her, and for a moment, I actually consider ignoring the alarm to keep this going.

No. Damn it, no. We have a plan; we have to stick to it. Too much is riding on us pulling this off for us to let lust get the best of us before we're able to actually speak our vows. Reluctantly, I break the kiss.

Psyche makes a sound of protest and tries to pull me back down to her. "More."

"The jeweler."

She goes still. It's amazing to see her pull herself together, putting away her desire and focusing on the endgame. Her body tenses and then relaxes. Her grip on my hair loosens. She can't quite banish the heavy-lidded look from her eyes, but she manages to smooth out her expression a bit. Slowly, oh so slowly, she removes her fingers from my hair. "Right. The jeweler. We need rings for the ceremony." Her voice is only a little ragged now. She recovered so quickly, far faster than I'm able to.

"Yes."

She licks her lips. "Then you should probably get off me."

It's only then that I realize I'm still pressing her into the mattress. She cradles me between her thighs, her heels locked at the small of my back. "If you want me to get off of you, you should probably release me."

I like the way she blushes. I like it a lot.

It still takes far too much control to move off her, and then it only gets worse because I can see her again. If a normal Psyche is a temptation I'll never be able to resist, a pleasure-sated Psyche is like mainlining the most addictive drug on the planet. I want her again, as soon as possible, as many times as we can manage before our bodies give out.

I take a step back, and then another. "I'm going to change."

"Good idea," she says faintly, her gaze on the front of my pants. "I should get dressed."

"Yes."

We stare at each other for a long moment, the tension building into an almost visible thing. It feels like she's hooked a magnet up to my gut—or, more accurately, my cock—and it's pulling me in her direction even now. We break at the same time, me heading for the closet and Psyche darting out the door in the direction of the spare bedroom.

It's only once I change into clean clothing and have my shit put back together that I can admit the truth. She might not want to get entangled, but it's pretty damn clear that I already am. I've never been that close to losing control before, not with any of my other partners. But then, she's proven again and again in the short time we've spent together that Psyche Dimitriou isn't like anyone else in Olympus. No wonder my mother wanted to extinguish her bright light. She's smart and savvy and far too good for a man like me.

I don't give a fuck.

After tonight, she's mine in truth.

PSYCHE

AFTER TWO WORLD-SHATTERING ORGASMS IN QUICK succession, the rest of the day goes by far too quickly, the hours slipping away as Eros and I get everything in order, until it's time to get ready for the ceremony.

For my wedding ceremony.

Persephone arrives with both my dress and her glowering husband. Hades is rather attractive—a tall white man with dark hair, dark eyes, and a really nice beard—but the only person he seems to smile at is my sister, and his do-not-fuck-with-me vibe is enough to keep everyone at a distance. He loves Persephone to distraction, and that's enough for me. He doesn't have to be a cuddly teddy bear as long as she's happy. And she really, really is.

It's too bad I don't have the same fate ahead of me with my very own monster of a man.

Eros has disappeared, saying something about getting some last-minute details in place. He's promised me that Aphrodite is still ensconced in her spa weekend—he even called to check in with her assistant earlier—but I can't help worrying that she'll show up in time to put a stop to this whole charade. But I trust Eros, at least in this.

When Aphrodite checks social media after her weekend away, there will be consequences, and they will come down on Eros's shoulders. I can't help feeling…bad for him.

My mother won't be any happier when she finds out about this hasty marriage. I might not know the details of her plans for me, but they don't include a marriage to Eros. That's for damn sure. Even she can't fight it once we're legally bound together. But once she works through her anger? She'll already be examining the angles for how she can spin the situation to benefit her.

On the surface, our mothers aren't that different. Both are powerful and ambitious and ruthless to a fault.

The difference?

My mother might try to move me around like a pawn on the chessboard that is Olympus, but she actually loves me. She won't let love get in the way of power, but she also wouldn't expect me to show up for a party after being cut up and then be furious because I was late.

And there was the shell-shocked look on Eros's face when he studied the photos of me and my sisters in the penthouse. It's possible that I'm completely off the mark and projecting, but he looked almost flabbergasted at how happy we were in those photos. My childhood wasn't perfect—Demeter is a difficult mother to have, even under the most ideal circumstances—but I had my sisters and we *were* happy a lot of the time. It wasn't feigned in those photos.

What must it have been like to grow up with a mother who only saw him as a tool to be exploited and nothing else?

I give myself a shake. I'm projecting. I have to be. No matter how much I hate Aphrodite, surely I'm not seeing the whole picture. She must love her son, even if she demands such horrific things from him.

Right?

"Psyche? We don't have much time."

I push my wayward worries away and focus on my sister. "You're right. Let's get this started."

We leave Hades in the living room, studying the place like he's a general looking over a battlefield, and retreat to the spare bedroom to get me ready. Persephone keeps the conversation light as she pins my hair up in an artful style and I put my makeup on, but when it's time to reach for the dress, she hesitates. "I know I've asked you this already, but are you sure?"

No. Not even a little bit. I wasn't sure before this afternoon, but now that I've had Eros's mouth all over me, I feel rattled right down to my bones. "Yes."

My sister snorts. "I knew better than to ask."

"Hey, let's not throw stones. It was only a couple months ago that you shacked up with a man everyone thought was a legend and refused to let me help you."

She lifts her chin. "That was different."

"Maybe, but I trusted you to know what you were doing. You promised to give me the same benefit of the doubt."

For a second, I think she might keep arguing, but she finally sighs. "I really don't like the shoe being on the other foot."

"It's hard to stand by and let people you care about take risks."

She gives me a bittersweet smile. "When did you get so smart?"

"I have two pretty great older sisters as role models." My throat goes tight, and I have to turn away or I'm going to cry and ruin my makeup. This might not be the wedding of my dreams, but I'll ensure it's a believable one. I drop my robe and step into the gown, turning so my sister can fasten the back.

"This is really gorgeous. Not what I expected you'd choose, but it's perfect." She does me up quickly, her voice thick. "You look like a goddess."

"Maybe a nymph."

She laughs. "You always do that. If today's your wedding, then you will damn well believe that you look like a goddess."

There's no point in arguing. The truth is that I *do* look good, and I *did* choose this dress with the intention of making a statement. It's far too late to change my mind about this, just like it's far too late to change my mind about the wedding itself. "You're right. I look like a goddess."

"There you go." She looks away. "There's one more thing."

Alarms blare in my head. Persephone might not be as confrontational as Callisto, but she's more than able to hold her own. For her to be exuding guilt right now... This won't be good. "What did you do?"

"Don't be mad."

"Persephone," I say slowly, grabbing patience with both hands. "I can't promise you that I won't be mad until you tell me what you've done."

"I, ah, might have mentioned this event at brunch."

At brunch.

With *our mother*.

"Tell me you didn't."

She's got that look on her face again, the stubborn one that says I'll never win this argument. "If anyone can understand political maneuvering, it's our mother. Give her the benefit of the doubt."

I stare at her. I stare at her long enough that Persephone has the grace to blush and look guilty. "Give her the benefit of the doubt?" I repeat. "That's quite the statement coming from you. You know what she did in an attempt to remove you from Hades's grasp. Do you really think she'll be any less ruthless when it comes to me?"

"That was a different situation."

"You keep saying that. I keep not believing you." I start to reach to twist my hair but stop before I make contact. "She was trying to introduce me to Zeus."

"*What?*"

"Even if Mother can appreciate political maneuvering, she had plans for me." Plans I wasn't entirely opposed to, even if I wasn't thrilled about them. "In her eyes, Eros is going to be a downgrade." The words feel a little like a betrayal, but that doesn't make sense. If I wasn't forced into a choice between death and marriage to the man, I never would have consented to his ring on my finger.

Right?

"Psyche, I—"

A knock on the door interrupts us, and it's just as well. I give her one last glare and turn in that direction. "Yes?"

"We need to talk."

Eros.

Gods, I hate how my heartbeat picks up just hearing his voice. I move toward the door even as I tell myself to plant my feet. "It's bad luck to see the bride before the wedding."

"Neither of us is the superstitious type." He lowers his voice. "Open the door, Psyche."

I ignore my sister's huff of displeasure and do exactly that. For a moment, all I can do is stand there and stare like a fool. He's wearing a tux that highlights his golden skin and blond hair.

I want to tear it off with my teeth.

Holy crap, where did that thought come from?

I'm so shocked at myself that I don't tense as he steps into the room and slides his arms around my waist. "You look divine."

"You too." I sound distant and strange, but I'm fighting so hard to keep my grip on him light and not wrinkle the fabric of his shirt. "What's going on?"

He smiles at Persephone. Even knowing it's an act, I can't help being drawn into his aww-shucks expression. "If I could have a moment alone with my wife?"

"She's not your wife yet."

Eros stares at my sister for a moment. "You're protective of her. I understand, but—"

"*Do* you understand?" Persephone draws herself up. She's never looked more like a queen than she does in this moment. More like our mother. "You don't have siblings, Eros. I'm not even sure you have friends. Do you really understand what it's like to care about someone so much, you'll burn the city down if they're hurt?"

"That's enough." They both look at me, and it's everything I can do to keep my voice even. My sister isn't wrong to be protective of me, but if this was a real relationship, I would *never* let her talk to my partner like that. "That's enough," I repeat.

"I just want you happy."

"Then support me in this."

She hesitates for so long, I think she might continue arguing, but finally Persephone squeezes my shoulder and moves past us out of the room.

Eros releases me once the door is shut, and even then it seems reluctant. At least he drops the happy groom act. "Your sister doesn't like me."

"Are you really surprised?"

"No." He gives himself a little shake and refocuses. "I co-opted a room downstairs. It's normally used for... Well, I honestly don't know what it's used for, but it's ours for the wedding ceremony."

"Okay." He didn't need to kick my sister out in order to tell me that. "What else?"

"My mother called." He says it so neutrally, I half think I misheard.

I jerk back a step. "What? I thought you said she was still at the spa."

"Apparently some well-meaning soul managed to get in contact with her. She's too far away to stop it, but she knows." His mouth twists. "She left a colorful voicemail."

"Let me hear it."

He shakes his head. "That's not necessary."

"I don't care if it's necessary or not, Eros. Either we're full partners in this charade or we're not and there's no point in getting married." I make myself hold his gaze. "Let me hear the voicemail."

For a long moment, I think he'll keep arguing, but he finally sighs and pulls out his phone. "It's not pretty."

I take his phone and pull up the voicemail. My hands are shaking as I push the Play button. Immediately Aphrodite's voice permeates the room. For once, she doesn't sound sweetly poisonous. She's too furious.

"What part of 'Bring me her heart' did you not understand, Eros? Why am I hearing that you're going to *marry* the woman?" She draws in a harsh breath. "I thought you could follow simple orders, but apparently even that's beyond you. It must be that, because I *know* you're not trying to play white knight to her damsel in distress. You're not capable of it."

I flick a look to Eros, but he's got his face arranged in an unreadable mask.

On the phone, Aphrodite's voice is vibrating with rage. "I was willing to do this the nice way, out of respect for you obviously having a soft spot for the girl, but you've spit in my face. She'll pay the price. Your bluff about marrying her isn't cute, and now she's going to suffer for it. Before the end, she'll be scared and alone and in pain, and it will be *your* fault."

My chest is too tight. There isn't enough air in the room. I march to the window, intent on wrestling it open, only to find that it doesn't open at all. "What the fuck?"

"Psyche." Eros takes the phone back and then catches my hands, bringing them to his chest. "I won't let my mother harm you."

I give a harsh laugh. It hurts my throat—or maybe that's just the tightness there that isn't dissipating. "I think we've more than established that you can't control your mother."

"She won't harm you," he repeats. "I promise. After tonight, it will be a moot point. You'll be beyond her grasp."

I shouldn't believe him. All these years surviving in this cutthroat city, and I've never had an issue with keeping my emotions in check. The only time I let down my walls is around my sisters, and even then not always entirely. They're dealing with their own stuff, after all. We've taken turns propping one another up when the situation gets tough.

Trusting someone outside that tiny circle is unthinkable.

Eros isn't promising to prevent his mother from killing me out of the goodness of his heart. It wouldn't further our mutual goals if she managed to do something to stop the wedding. He's invested in marrying me, and if I don't fully understand his reasoning, I can at least trust that it's what he wants. That knowledge should comfort me, but it rings hollow.

"I believe you." I clear my throat. "I suppose now's a good time to tell you that Persephone told my mother about the wedding and she *will* be attending."

Eros stares at me a long moment, and then he throws his head back and a laugh booms forth. The sound surprises me so much, I jump, but he's too busy laughing his ass off to notice. He actually has to wrap an arm around his waist to maintain his upright position.

I cross my arms and wait him out. "By all means, get it out of your system now."

To his credit, he doesn't make me wait long. He straightens and shakes his head. "We're going to have to up our game to stay one step ahead of our mothers. This should be interesting."

"Interesting. That's one way to put it."

Eros moves to the door, but he stops before opening it. "Trust me."

"In this, I do." It's almost the truth. I can't afford to lean on Eros, can't afford to assume our endgames match up. But I can trust that he is as invested in getting this marriage off the ground as I am, fake relationship or no.

He gives me a slow smile, heat slipping into his eyes. "And, Psyche? I meant it when I said you look divine. I want to eat you right up. Again." He slips out the door before I can formulate a response.

What is there to say?

I've already established that Eros is a consummate liar and that's he's cold down to his very soul. It doesn't matter how warm his eyes get when they look at me, how intoxicating his smile. I can't trust it.

It didn't feel fake when he had his mouth on me earlier, though. When his hands shook as he gripped my thighs and his voice went rough and low. In that moment, it felt like he wanted me just as much as I want him. More, even, because he didn't seem to be fighting his reaction.

A lie. It has to be a lie. We needed to rip the bandage off, so that's what we did. If I still desire him, there's a logical conclusion as to why. Adrenaline and pheromones. A physical response is normal under these less-than-normal conditions. That's all.

I've almost managed to convince myself that it's the truth by the time I step into the elevator to take me down to the room Eros has claimed for the event. Persephone is at my side, and she's doing the beaming-sunshine thing she does whenever we have to deal with the Thirteen. I try to draw myself in, to push everything that matters to me down deep and lock it away so that nothing that happens tonight can hurt me.

I try...and I fail.

How can I lock everything away when I'm one giant exposed nerve right now? I know I have to do this, but expectations about the wedding I always wanted are crashing against the reality of this moment, and it hurts so much more than I expected. It feels a whole lot like grief.

The elevator doors slide soundlessly open, revealing a long hallway that reeks of money for all that it's gone the same minimalist route that Eros's penthouse leans toward. Brushed concrete floors gleam in the bright light, and the walls are painted gunmetal gray. It might feel like walking through an expensive prison if not for the mirrors.

They line the hallway on either side, stretching nearly from the floor to the nine-foot ceiling. Wrought iron and shining silver create the frames, and I have the near-hysterical thought that if I pressed my hand against one, it would give way and I'd end up in another world entirely.

What is it with this building and mirrors?

Halfway down the hall, a door opens and my mother steps out. She's dressed in an elegant gown that covers her slim body from neck to wrists to ankles, and the silver and structure in the bodice and hips give the impression of armor. She's twisted her dark hair, so similar to mine, back from her face and her makeup is, as always, flawless.

It takes every ounce of courage I have to keep walking next to my sister until we stand before Demeter. She surveys me from head to toe and back up again. "If you wanted to make a statement, you've succeeded with that dress."

Persephone gives my hand a squeeze. "I'll see you inside." She slips through the door, leaving me to face Demeter alone. *Coward.* But then, I was always going to face my mother alone in this. I chose this path, was *forced* to choose this path because I wasn't good enough to outmaneuver Aphrodite.

This time.

"Mother—"

She lifts a hand and shakes her head. "We are due for a discussion, but not here. You're set on marrying Eros?"

Something like relief courses through me. No matter what else is true of Demeter, she's not one to waste a valuable asset. My marrying Eros gives her a direct line to Aphrodite, or, rather, a direct way to constantly needle and undermine the other woman. She might have learned her lesson about selling her daughters into marriage without their knowledge—and that's a rather large *might*—but if one of us is foolish enough to stumble into a marriage with a powerful person, she's hardly going to stop it. "Yes, I'm set on it."

"Then let's go." She pivots to face the door and holds out her elbow. "I'll be damned before any of my daughters walk down the aisle alone."

We don't really talk about my father—about any of our fathers. Three marriages resulting in four daughters, and every one of our fathers disappeared off the face of the earth within weeks of the divorce. Or, rather, they disappeared out of Olympus. If not for the rather active social media accounts of her ex-husbands, my mother might have a reputation as a black widow. As it is, my sisters and I are pretty damn certain she paid off our fathers and ensured they found a way out of Olympus.

I suppose I could blame her for my not having a father figure, but the truth is that my mother never goes with a stick when a carrot will work just fine. My father chose to take her money, take passage out of Olympus, and never look back. Why would I mourn the loss of such a selfish man in my life?

So, yes, it's entirely apt that my mother be the one to walk me down the aisle and give me away to my new husband.

I slide my hand into the crook of her arm. "Thank you, Mother."

"You are my daughter, Psyche. More than the others, you are the apple that doesn't fall far from my tree. I trust that you have a reason for doing this." She shoots me a severe look. "You should have told me. We could have negotiated for more favorable terms."

Despite everything, I huff out a laugh. "Maybe on my next marriage."

"That's my girl."

EROS

I NEVER EXPECTED TO GET MARRIED. IT'S NOT THAT I HAVE an issue with monogamy, though I've only flirted with it in the past. Something as relatively permanent as marriage is more than just a relationship. It's more than sex, more than moving someone into your space and figuring out how to share it. It's a partnership. An alliance.

But as I stand before the altar, Hermes bouncing on her toes in her silver three-piece suit, it just feels fucking right.

I refuse to examine that sensation too closely.

Instead, I focus on the door opening and Psyche walking through. On the expression on her face as she takes in what I've spent the last few hours putting together.

The room isn't large, which is an asset for this event. There are two pews on either side of the aisle, each capped with a bouquet of crimson roses tied with a shining silver ribbon, a perfect match for her dress thanks to the swatch Juliette provided. The aisle itself is a deep red runner in the same shade. As I watch, Helen walks up to Psyche and hands over another, larger bouquet of the same arrangement.

The shock on Psyche's face deepens as she looks around the room. I see her register that everyone is wearing some variation of red, black, and silver. Even Hades, though his black-on-black suits seem to be the only clothing he owns. A photographer who I hired edges around the room, the snap of his camera the only sound for one long moment.

Then the music rises, a variation of the wedding march that sounds almost like a dirge. From her small smile, she finds it as fitting as I do. Almost like an inside joke between just the two of us.

Psyche takes the first step toward the altar—toward me—and meets my gaze. Her smile widens, and even as I tell myself it's all for show, I can't help the warmth that blooms in my chest. I know this isn't what she wants. If she's like Helen and Eris, she's had plans for her wedding from when she was a little girl, and I hardly expect that those plans included marrying the son of her mother's enemy in front of an audience of five.

I can't change that, but the least I can do is give her this gift. Something photograph-worthy. This wedding might not be a good memory, but at least the publicity in its aftermath won't embarrass her.

She and Demeter make their way to the altar and stop a few steps away. Hermes clears her throat, looking delighted by this whole experience. "Who gives this woman's hand in marriage?"

"I do." Demeter moves forward and places Psyche's hand in mine. She smiles sweetly as if delighted to be here, but her low words drip poison. "If you do anything to bring my daughter harm in any way, I will gut you and leave you for my pigs."

I've heard rumors about Demeter and her pigs, but I've never been able to substantiate any of them. "I'll take that into consideration."

"See that you do." She presses a kiss to Psyche's cheek and then moves to sit next to Persephone in the front row.

We stand before the altar, and all I can do is stare at Psyche. This woman, this brilliant and fierce creature, will be mine in truth the moment I slip my ring on her finger, the moment we both say "I do." This was only meant to be a way to keep Psyche among the living, but sometime in the last twelve hours, it's turned into something else altogether. I will keep this woman safe.

Fuck, I'm just going to flat out keep her.

I barely listen to Hermes, barely manage to repeat the proper words to get this thing done. My hands actually shake as I slip the giant diamond onto Psyche's ring finger. I'm undone.

For her part, my new wife doesn't seem to have the same problem. Her voice is perfectly even as she repeats the same vows. Her fingers are cool against my skin as she slips the ring on. She smiles sweetly at me, and I surprise myself with how badly I want it to be real.

"You may kiss the bride."

I don't hesitate. I step forward, closing the distance between us, and cup her face. If I were a better man, I'd never touch this woman with hands that have committed such violence, but I'm selfish right down to my core. I kiss her, filling that one moment with so much promise, she's melting against me.

Someone—I think Eris—clears her throat, and I manage to lift my head, though I don't drop my hands. I smile down at Psyche. "Hey."

"Hey," she whispers.

"We did it."

She wraps her hands around my wrists and gives me a little squeeze. "We're not done yet."

With that in mind, I lace my fingers through hers and we turn to face the room. Helen and Eris have careful expressions in place, as if they still can't quite believe this happened. I expect I'm going to hear it from both of them later when they have more time. Demeter has an excellent poker face, but I've seen her use that same serene smile before systematically cutting her opponents off at the knees. Hades glowers, but he always seems to glower. Persephone beams, but I don't miss the promise of violence in her hazel eyes.

This marriage is going to set off all sorts of chaos.

Strangely enough, I can't wait.

Hermes makes a happy sound. "I now present to you, Mr. Eros Ambrosia and Ms. Psyche Dimitriou."

Demeter stands and crosses to us. "Congratulations." She takes my hands, her nails digging into my skin even as her expression remains happy. "Welcome to the family."

This was the plan, but I can't help a shiver of unease. There's no going back now. We can only live with the consequences. "Thanks."

"Family dinners are Sundays. No exceptions. See you next week." She presses a quick kiss to Psyche's cheek. "We'll talk later."

"Of course." My wife doesn't look shaken in the least.

Wife.

Mine.

I wrap that possessiveness surging through me in chains of silver and shove it deep. There's no space for feeling this right here, right now. Behind us, Hermes gives a giggle that raises the small hairs on the back of my neck. "Now you've really done it. Aphrodite is going to be so *pissed*." She nudges my shoulder as she walks around me and grins at Psyche. "Good luck with that. Hope you survive to your first anniversary. I left a gift for you up in the kitchen. Enjoy!" She skips down the aisle, moving with the bouncing joy of a child despite the fact that she's at least as old as I am, if not older.

Persephone and Hades are next, though he stands a few feet back and glares at me while she gives her sister a hug. "Call if you need anything." Persephone looks at me. "If you fuck with my sister, my mother's pigs will be the least of your worries."

We watch them leave the room and I chuckle. "Charming family you have."

"You're lucky Callisto didn't show up. She probably would have beaten you over the head with the closest blunt instrument."

I glance at her. "Everyone in Olympus thinks you're such nice girls."

"Everyone in Olympus sees what they want to see." She narrows her gaze as Helen and Eris approach. "Case in point."

Both women have the Kasios family features. High cheekbones, Roman noses, full lips. Helen is built a little more petite than Eris, and her hair is a lighter brown with red undertones, but no one would look at these two and assume they're anything but related. Eris is gorgeous, but Helen is... There are no words for what Helen is. She's got the kind of flawless beauty that brings cities to their knees and sends entire armies to war. She doesn't play it up—if anything, she downplays it—but she still commands the attention of any room she walks into.

Eris raises a dark brow. "Congrats, I guess. Though, since Aphrodite was conspicuously absent, I don't like your odds at experiencing a blissful honeymoon period. She'll be meddling the first chance she gets, and she plays dirty." She gives a wicked grin. "How long do you give them, Helen?"

Helen smacks her sister on the shoulder, her smile strained. "Can you save the doomsday talk for the day after the wedding, at least?"

"Where would be the fun in that? Things are finally getting *interesting.*"

I open my mouth, but Psyche beats me to the punch. She leans against me and smiles at the two Kasios sisters. "You're underestimating Eros if you think Aphrodite can get the best of him."

Eris opens her mouth, but Helen elbows her and glares. "That's enough." She turns a brighter smile on Psyche. "We haven't gotten to know each other, and I'd like to. I'm having a party next Friday. Both of you should be there."

"A party." I feel the way Psyche tenses, but she doesn't show it outwardly. Still, I can't help giving her a little squeeze as I say, "I was under the impression *you're* under house arrest."

"And yet I'm standing right here, my house nowhere in sight." Helen's smile takes on a mean edge, her amber eyes lighting up. "My brother is getting a little too high and mighty since he became

Zeus. We might be related, but he doesn't own me. If I want to have a reasonable sized group of friends over for some light revelry, I'm going to do it."

Eris laughs, the sound promising all sorts of trouble. "If it pisses him off, all the better."

"Don't act like you're above doing exactly that!" Helen nudges her sister. "He told you to behave, too, and *you* spent all yesterday day drinking with Dionysus."

"I like Dionysus." Eris shrugs. "He knows how to have a good time, he keeps his hands to himself, and he has the sexiest friends. It's a win-win."

As much as I normally enjoy their bickering, I am ready for this part of the event to be over. "We'll see you next Friday."

"Good." Helen loops her arm through Eris's and tows her sister down the aisle and out the door.

Now all that's left is the photographer.

Psyche smiles at him, some of the tension bleeding out of her body. Here, she's in her element. "Thank you so much for attending. I'd like a few staged shots in addition to what you already have."

He smiles. "Sure."

I zone out a little as they discuss options. It takes ten minutes before they settle on four shots and then another thirty to get pictures both Psyche and the photographer are satisfied with. He looks up from his camera. "These are great. I can have them cleaned up and to you by tomorrow."

"Thanks." I'm already eyeing the exit. How fast can I get my new wife out of here?

Psyche puts her hand on his arm. "It wouldn't be amiss if

you used this moment to your advantage, Claude." She leans in, smiling sweetly. "If you're going to sell off one of these photos, use the one at the altar, please."

He goes a little green around the edges. "I wouldn't... I didn't..."

"We know how Olympus works." She pats his shoulder. It's a light touch, but he weaves unsteadily on his feet as if it were a right hook. "Just ensure it's *that* picture or I'll be rather upset with you."

"Yes, ma'am," he whispers.

"You may go now."

We watch him practically sprint from the room. I barely wait for the door to close to start laughing. "You're terrifying."

"Oh, hush."

"Truly. You fit right in with your vicious mother and your violent sisters."

Psyche smacks my shoulder. "I am not terrifying. And let's not throw stones when your mother took a freaking *hit* out on me."

I drape an arm around her shoulders. Not because anyone is watching; simply because I want to. This easy banter between us feels good after the tension of getting all the pieces in place for the wedding. "Can you honestly tell me that your mother has never had anyone killed?"

"I—"

"*Honestly*, Psyche."

She glares. "Unconfirmed."

"Exactly. You have to be at least a little bit of a monster to survive and thrive in Olympus. That goes triply for members of the Thirteen themselves."

"You're not wrong, but it's irritating all the same." She gives the door a long look. "The upper crust of the city likes to pretend we're more cultured or refined than anywhere else in the world, but the opposite is true. I mean, look at us. We just got married so your mother will stop trying to have me killed."

There's not much to say to that. She's right. "I know."

"So, yes, maybe we all have to be a little bit monster to survive this city." Her eyes dim, a frown pulling at her lips. "Even more than a little bit if I'm going to be perfectly honest."

"There's no shame in it." I stroke my thumb over her bare shoulder. Gods, why is she so soft? Ten years in Olympus, and she still has most of her heart intact. She's able to mourn the small parts of herself she's sacrificed to thrive, but the city hasn't worn her down until she barely recognizes herself. I envy her in that. Maybe I do have some soul left, because I can't stop myself from trying to chase away the sorrow written across her features. "You're not one, you know."

"Not what?"

"A monster." I smile a little. "I would know, being a monster myself. You might move among us, but you aren't like us at all."

She narrows her eyes. "I can't tell if that's a compliment or an insult."

"It's a compliment. It takes someone special to live among monsters and not become one." We're veering into conversational depths I don't know how to navigate. I need to get us back on safer ground. "Hungry?"

She hesitates but finally says, "Yes. I was too nervous to eat before."

Truth be told, I was, too. It seems silly to get nerves before a real wedding for a fake relationship, but nothing about this situation is as expected. I'm not supposed to want my new wife so much that I'm practically shaking with the restraint required to keep from kissing her again.

Or, if nothing else, it should only be lust coursing through me when I think of her. I sure as fuck shouldn't be wanting to put myself between her and anything that would put that sad look in her pretty hazel eyes.

I clear my throat. "Let's go back up to the penthouse. I'm reasonably sure that no one will fuck with us tonight, so we might as well enjoy ourselves."

Psyche allows me to guide her to the door and down the hallway to the elevator. "They're not supposed to fuck with us at all, not now that we're married."

I didn't want to talk about this until later, especially after I just got done trying to reassure her, but Psyche is too savvy not to notice an awkward change of subject. I already know this woman well enough to know that she won't let me distract her. She'd rather have the full truth out in the open so we can deal with it accordingly.

It still takes far too much effort to answer honestly. "This marriage means my mother won't be able to follow through on the threats on your life. It won't stop her from attempting character assassination."

Psyche gives me a slow smile. "Let her do her worst. I can more than handle her in that field."

I hope she's right.

PSYCHE

TODAY HAS BEEN FILLED WITH EMOTIONAL EXTREMES. I feel like I'm flying apart into a million pieces, and not necessarily in a good way. From those forty minutes in Eros's bed to walking into the room that he thoughtfully pulled together into something resembling a real wedding. He'd themed the colors to my dress, for gods' sake. That kind of attention to detail might only be so that we can sell this fully to everyone in the city, but I can't help thinking that he did it in part for me.

I'm a fool.

To go from that to him casually mentioning that it's likely his mother will continue with her vendetta, at least when it comes to my reputation...

Whiplash doesn't begin to cover it.

Of course I expected this. We've talked about it, at least in passing. But a small part of me had held out hope that Aphrodite would turn away from this path once we were married. I really know better than to believe such a fantasy, but hope springs eternal. It seems rather naive to assume that, thwarted, Aphrodite would move on with her life and focus on some other potential victim.

Naive and selfish.

At least if she's focused on me, Eros isn't having to hurt other people. Now that the worst of the threat is removed, I can handle Aphrodite. I hope. In the arena of public opinion, I'm nearly as capable as she is. I have to believe that. I'm just so godsdamned *tired*.

I don't manage to speak until we're tucked safely back into Eros's penthouse. "I suppose it was naive of me to think that this would be enough to dissuade her."

He keeps his arm around me as we head into the kitchen. There's a bottle sitting on the counter, and I pick it up, mostly to give my hands something to do. A pretty silver ribbon is tied around its neck, the tag simply saying *From Hermes*.

I examine the label. "She's got expensive taste."

Eros reaches around me and flips the tag over. The back reads: *Totally stole this from Hades's wine cellar. So, really, it's from me, Hades, and Persephone.*

That draws a tired little laugh from my lips. "Hermes is a menace."

"She's chaotic neutral personified. She's pretty okay, though." Eros takes the bottle from my hands and sets it back on the counter. "I won't let anyone hurt you, Psyche."

"That's rich coming from you, someone who intended to hurt me twenty-four hours ago." Maybe that's fair, maybe it's not, but I don't care either way. The events of the last two days are rapidly catching up with me. Too much has happened in too short a time. "If this was the plan all along, it's not a half bad one. One cut for marrying Demeter's daughter. A finishing move by killing her."

"Stop it." He takes my hands, his grip light but unavoidable. "Look at me."

I don't want to. I know how well Eros lies when he's motivated. I can't trust a single word, look, or gesture. But when I gaze up at him, he looks terrifyingly serious.

"Psyche, my mother might still be furious, but our reasons for getting married remain the same. She can spit her poison and try her manipulations, but she can't harm you. I will not let *anyone* harm you. You're mine now, and I protect what's mine."

"That's very patriarchal of you." I have no business believing him. None at all. Just because we're married doesn't mean he's anything other than an enemy. He was going to *kill* me. I try to maintain my grasp on that truth, but it keeps bumping up against other truths.

How angry he was about the negative comments on my social media.

His insistence that I have a wedding dress that I'd be proud of.

The fact that he took the swatch and organized the entire wedding, guests and all, around my chosen color palette.

So many tiny, thoughtful things. Things an enemy wouldn't do, even if they were trying to butter up their victim. Now he's telling me he will stand between me and any threat to my safety and I…believe him.

He shakes his head. "I don't really give a fuck if it's patriarchal or not. It's the truth. You're safe with me. I promise."

I don't mean to touch him. Touching Eros is the very definition of a poor choice, but my hands find their way inside his tux jacket all the same. The fabric of his deep-gray shirt is softer than I expect, but that's not what has my legs already shaking. It's the curves and divots of his muscles beneath. He was shirtless in bed with me last night, but the circumstances made it impossible to enjoy the view without restriction.

I can enjoy it now. It's my wedding night, after all.

"Eros."

He holds perfectly still, watching me closely. "Yes?"

"I said only once." My fingers find the buttons in the center of his chest. "What if that once doesn't end until sunrise?"

His eyes flare hot, but he doesn't reach for me the way I suddenly crave. "I want no misunderstandings between us, Psyche. You need something? Use your words and be explicit."

I should have known he wouldn't make this easy on me. Nothing up to this point has been easy; why would this be? I lick my lips and strive for an even tone. "I would very much like to have sex with you tonight."

His slow smile has something more violent than butterflies erupting in my stomach. "One condition."

"I'm not interested in bargaining."

"And yet here we are—bargaining." His grin widens, and I'm startled to realize it's a little crooked. The tiniest of imperfections that somehow makes him even more attractive, something I thought impossible. He leans into my touch the slightest bit. "We'll have sex tonight, and in return, for as long as we're married, you'll give me the opportunity to seduce you properly."

"No." The word slams through my lips before I can call it back. "I already told you why that was impossible."

"Psyche." He practically purrs my name, and I have to fight down a shiver. How can this man do so much with one word? "I'm never going to pressure you to do something you don't want."

Danger. That way lie dragons.

The idea of being seduced by Eros is almost intoxicating enough to have me throwing caution to the wind. Almost. I draw in a ragged breath. "I'd be a fool to agree to that, and you're ridiculous for demanding it. Everyone knows that you don't stay with one partner for more than long enough to quench your curiosity. The only reason you want me so much is because I told you no." If we go further down this path, eventually he'll get bored with me. I know myself well enough to recognize how much that will hurt when he finally fucks his fill and decides he isn't interested in continuing the seduction.

"Is it?" He takes a slow step closer, and I do nothing to stop him. Eros strokes the tips of his fingers over the backs of my hands. "Everyone seems to know a lot about us, all of it projection and carefully concealed lies. *Everyone* knows I'm allergic to monogamy. Just like everyone knows that you're a sweet influencer who doesn't make waves—or have a mean bone in her body."

The point lands just as he intends it to. Olympian gossip might be an elite event, but most people involved play the game and massage their image as needed. I do. Of course Eros does the same; he's already admitted as much. So why is it so shocking that *this* isn't true? "I've never seen you with the same date at two events."

"My reasons are my own, and my past partners have nothing to do with us. You know that, but you're being stubborn."

I search his face, understanding dawning. "Aphrodite is a jealous creature. She wouldn't like sharing your allegiance with anyone, especially a romantic partner."

"Clever girl." His lips curve in a bitter smile. "I don't have to worry about that with you, since my mother already hates you and you're more than capable of handling her going forward."

He says it so confidently, as if it's truth and not just wishing on a star. I am good at what I do. I know that. I've had ten years of practice and it comes naturally to me. But so much of my strength lies in people underestimating me. Even my sisters do it; sometimes they forget I'm playing the same games they are. If I told them I was going toe-to-toe with Aphrodite, they would be terrified on my behalf.

Eros simply believes I can hold my own. There's no hesitation, no doubt. His confidence is headier than any alcohol. It makes me feel bold and reckless and more than a little wild.

Which is exactly why I need to restrict sex between us. "Eros, please," I whisper. If he's able to make me feel so off-center in a single day, a few weeks of sleeping next to each other—of sleeping *with* each other—and I'll be in serious trouble.

"You're the one who opened up negotiations." He keeps up that featherlight touch, tracing over my wrists. "To be honest, though, you have me over a barrel. I want you too badly not to take you up on this."

It's a terrible idea to give him the green light to attempt to seduce me, especially when he's already backed down. If I were smart, I'd capitalize on this, take my pleasure for tonight, and go back to keeping a careful distance between us tomorrow.

I don't know what I want.

Liar.

I ignore the sensible voice inside me. Tomorrow is Future Me's problem. Right now, I am buzzing in my skin, torn in a thousand different directions by too many emotions. I just want to feel, to forget, to cease to exist for a little while. All my problems, all the planning and plotting, will still be there tomorrow. I meet his eyes. "You have yourself a deal. For as long as we're married, you can attempt to seduce me."

He exhales slowly as if giving me a chance to change my mind. When I simply stand there and look up at him, he growls, "Thank fuck." He grabs my hand and tows me down the hall to the master bedroom. "I love this dress. But if you don't tell me how to get it off you in the next thirty seconds, I'm going to cut it to pieces."

Shock and pleasure have me laughing. "Laces in the back. Please don't cut up my wedding dress."

He makes another of those delicious growling sounds and spins me around to face the dresser across from the bed. To face the giant gilded mirror that hangs over it. I stare at it, hardly recognizing the woman reflected there. She looks like a stranger, dressed in her crimson wedding gown with her cheeks flushed from desire. I watch Eros as he moves to stand behind me, his expression a mask of concentration and impatience as he gently tugs the laces loose until the dress sags away from my body. I should help, but I can't stop staring at the picture we make.

"For fuck's sake, it's like one of those Russian nesting dolls."

Eros runs his hands over the corset, guiding my dress past my hips to the floor. Again, he goes to the laces, though this one requires a little more finesse because Persephone is a sadist and laced it up tight.

"You could just leave it on," I gasp. The little jerking motions as he frees the laces are a strange sort of foreplay that I didn't expect, but then I've never had a partner get me out of a corset before.

"No way. I want access to all of you." The last row of laces gives, and he yanks the corset off me. I hear it hit the ground behind us.

I freeze, gripping the dresser hard enough to hurt. He saw me naked just a few hours ago, but I can't help the stab of insecurity I feel. Corsets might look like a dream, but they leave press marks across the skin of my stomach. It's hardly the sexy image I'd choose for tonight.

Eros meets my gaze in the mirror. The naked hunger on his face puts what few doubts I have aside. This man has no reason to lie to me, not about this. Which means he wants me just as desperately as I want him.

He wants to seduce me properly.

"Look at you," he murmurs, closing the distance between us to press his body to my back. "You're so fucking beautiful."

I expect him to go nearly feral the same way he did early today. But apparently my new husband isn't in the mood to rush despite his determination to get my wedding dress off. He sinks his hands into my hair, removing the bobby pins that Persephone put into place one by one. It feels like there's a thousand of them, and he goes after each methodically, dropping them on the dresser next to us. He's barely touching me, his fingers carefully moving through my hair, occasionally pressing to the tight knots at the base of my skull, but it feels like he's doused me in gasoline and lit a match.

I can't stop shaking. I want to reach for him, but I also don't want this slow seduction to stop. And it *is* a seduction, even if I doubt he'd label it as such. I open my eyes, not quite sure when I closed them, to find a look of utter concentration on his face. Every bit of Eros's formidable attention is focused on me. The realization is one of the headiest moments of my life.

This man is mine.

Maybe not in truth, maybe not forever, but for right now.

Once my hair is free to fall down my back in loose waves, Eros moves it out of the way and presses a kiss to my neck. He drags his mouth over the slope of my shoulders, watching me in the mirror. Somehow, this feels more intimate than when he had his mouth all over me earlier today. I can *see* everything. My body. My need. His blatant desire burning hot enough to incinerate both of us.

His teeth graze sensitive skin, but he's oh so careful not to mark me. I can tell even while completely overwhelmed with this experience. And that care, that thoughtfulness, only makes this moment more intoxicating. "Take off your pants," I gasp.

"Not yet."

Frustration adds spice to my desire. "Please, Eros. I need you."

"Not yet," he repeats. He cups my breasts with a rough touch, and if I didn't know better, I'd say his hands are shaking. Surely not. Surely Eros Ambrosia isn't so affected by *me* that he's off his game. It doesn't matter that the look on his face is downright reverent. But then he goes and blows my assumptions out of the water with his next words. "If I take off my pants, I'm going to be inside you, and if I'm inside you, this will be over too quickly. Don't rush me."

My body flushes hot and needy. I arch my back, pressing my breasts more firmly into his touch. I can't doubt his words. Not when he's told me harsh truths and soft ones. He has no reason to lie to me now. He's getting exactly what he wants, after all—what we both want.

I tentatively run my hands up his arms, lingering over the harsh lines of his muscles. We paint quite the picture. Me, naked and soft. Him, clothed and all barely controlled strength. "Touch me."

"I am touching you." His voice is lower than I've heard it yet, rough and tight. "Or do you mean touch you like this?" He moves, bracketing my throat with one hand and sliding his other down to palm my pussy. I've never felt so owned in my life. I've never *looked* so owned.

No, not owned. *Possessed.*

I lean forward a little just to feel the strength in his palm against my neck, just to have him flex his fingers against my sensitive skin.

Eros holds my gaze as he parts my folds and pushes two blunt fingers into me, a slow and thorough penetration. I start to shut my eyes, unable to bear being exposed like this, but he makes a sharp sound. "No. Don't hide from me. Not tonight. Not like this."

I can't handle the sheer heat in his eyes so I focus on his hand between my thighs. It looks as good as it feels. He idly fucks me with his fingers, strumming my need higher and higher. "Look at you," he murmurs. "You're so fucking perfect."

If any other partner said those words—and they have—I would chalk it up to being caught in the heat of the moment. I know I'm attractive, but my beauty doesn't inspire the reverence these kinds of compliments inherently carry.

Except...

Eros sounds like he means it. He *looks* like he means it. He keeps working my pussy in slow strokes as his free hand moves over my body, like he can't touch me enough. Cupping first one breast and then the other, stroking down my stomach, over to squeeze my hip as he makes a growling sound. "Fucking *perfect*." He eases his fingers out of me and moves up to circle my clit. "So clever and ambitious and you hide it behind this pretty face. Do you ever let down your walls, beautiful girl?"

"Eros, please." I don't know what I'm asking for. For him to stop, to never stop, to just make me orgasm without saying words that feel like he's lashing me right down to my soul.

"That's answer enough." Eros nips my shoulder, making me jolt, and slides two fingers back into me. "Let go, Psyche. I want to feel your pussy clamp around my fingers as you come." He presses the heel of his hand to my clit, each stroke rubbing me where I need it most.

I don't last another sixty seconds.

I come hard, the cry barely passing my lips before his mouth is on mine, devouring the sound as he strums my pleasure higher and higher. Wave after wave. Gods, it's too much and not enough, and if I could think properly, I'd be terrified that I'll never get enough.

My knees give out; he doesn't miss a beat. Eros guides me back onto the bed and far enough up the mattress until he can kneel between my spread thighs.

The way this man looks at me.

If I were smarter, I'd find a way to run from him. The heat in Eros's eyes is something like obsession, and being this man's sole focus is dangerous in a way I'm not prepared to deal with. I am strong; I've had to be in order to survive this long mostly unscathed.

I'm nowhere near strong enough to win a battle of wills with Eros if he ever decides he wants to break me to pieces.

EROS

MY HANDS ARE SHAKING. MY WHOLE FUCKING BODY IS shaking. Watching Psyche come apart for me, *feeling* her clench around my fingers as she orgasmed, knowing that she's trusting me enough to let me guide this... It makes me want to fall on her like a ravening beast. To plunge into her until nothing exists but our hard and rough fucking.

She deserves better than that.

I don't put much stock in marriage and all it entails, but Psyche is the type who does. Even if I hadn't forced her hand with this situation, she might not have had a love match. It's nearly unheard of in Olympus, especially among the Thirteen and their families. It's significantly more common to marry for money, power, and prestige. Love doesn't enter into the equation.

Even so, the fact remains that I'm the reason she lost what little chance she had for love. The very least I can do is ensure that she has a memorable wedding night.

I run my hands up her legs and over her rounded stomach.

Having her naked and spread out before me is just as heady now as it was this afternoon. It's how fucking sexy she is, yes, but I keep coming back to the trust she's placing in me. I don't deserve it…but strangely enough, I *want* to deserve it.

"Eros." She half sits up and reaches for me. "Come here."

"Not yet." I haven't taken my pants off yet. I can't risk it. Judging from the desire pounding through my body, centering in my cock and balls, I'm not going to last once I get inside her. I want her to come again, want to feel her shatter at my hands, my tongue, a few more times before we get there.

I want to bind her to me as closely as possible, to have her crave what I can give her as much as I want to give it to her. The only way to accomplish that is by dealing her so much pleasure tonight that she turns to me when she's feeling needy again.

If I have my way, she'll be in a permanent state of need.

I allow her to tug me up to kiss her again. Kissing Psyche is no hardship. She doesn't passively take what I give her. She meets me every step of the way, sparring with her tongue the same way she does with her words. A game of give-and-take and pure pleasure. I enjoy kissing. I always have. But kissing this woman could almost be the main event.

Or it could if I didn't have her naked and writhing beneath me.

I slide down her body, pressing her large breasts together so I can tease one nipple and then the other, moving back and forth between them until she's whimpering and arching, offering herself up for more than a taste. Only then do I shift lower, licking and nipping down the curves of her breasts to her stomach. She tenses the slightest bit, but I'm having none of it. I give this part of her the same thorough treatment I gave her breasts. Each curve, dimple, roll. I meant everything I said; she's perfect and I'll not be kept from any inch of her.

When I finally reach her pussy, her thighs fall open. She's no longer trying to guide me or rush any moment of this. She's letting me do what I want, and I fucking love it. Her trust is just as heady as her taste. Psyche is wet and practically dripping, and I waste no time in dragging my tongue up her pussy to her clit.

Gods, this woman.

Her hands find my hair on the second lick, and she tugs me up to focus on her clit. I'm only too happy to take the silent guidance, especially as her hips rise to meet my tongue. She's moaning and grinding herself all over my mouth, and I have to force my hips still to avoid fucking against the mattress until I come in my pants.

That's the second time today.

I might laugh if I could breathe past the need pounding in my blood. Psyche has stripped away all my art, all my finesse. The only thing that matters is delivering pleasure until she can't take any more. Not even *my* pleasure ranks above that.

When she comes, it's with the sweetest sound I've ever fucking heard. Her back bows and her lips part and... "*Eros.*"

Holy shit.

The monster inside me throws itself against its cage, rattling my entire being. She cried out *my name* as she orgasmed. It shouldn't feel so profound, but there's no denying the surge of possessiveness that stills every thought in my head except the need to get inside her and do it now. I have to press my forehead to her stomach and focus on breathing for a few moments.

It's time.

I force myself to release her and move off the bed. She watches me with eyes gone hazy from pleasure, her desire sharpening as I shuck off my pants and grab a condom from the nightstand drawer. I crawl back onto the bed and resume my position between her thighs. It's a struggle to think past the primal urge to stamp my presence on every inch of her, but I manage. Barely. "Let me have you, Psyche." The words are wrong; they mean too much, reveal too much.

Thankfully, she doesn't seem to notice. She's already nodding. "I don't want to wait any longer."

"Good." I rip open the condom and roll it down my length. Slowly, oh so slowly, I brace myself over her and guide my cock to her entrance. She lifts her hips, welcoming me even as I try to remember why I need to ease my way into this.

Fuck it.

I work my way into her in short, unrelenting strokes. My breath is just as choppy as hers. I think I'm moaning, but I can't fucking tell over the rushing in my ears as I finally, *finally*, sink into her to the hilt. She feels even better than I could have dreamed. Like she's made just for me. I'm too far gone to care about the danger of thinking like that. I can't help thrusting a little, watching her face as I do.

She bites her bottom lip. A clear invitation if I've ever seen one. I'm only too happy to take her up on it, dipping down and claiming her mouth the same way I'm claiming her body. She might not see it that way, but I can't help the way I feel. It's my problem. I'll deal with it later.

I have every intention of going slow, but she digs her nails into my ass, urging me on, and what little control I had left snaps. I slide my arms under her to grip her shoulders to give me better leverage and fuck her in long, intense strokes. I've gone too far already. I can't stop, can't slow down. Even if I wanted to, she's urging me on with a ferocity that puts my own fierceness front and center.

"You feel so fucking good, Psyche." I thrust hard, loving the way she moans in response. "All tight and wet and made just for me."

"Eros." She's gasping and panting and still trying to urge me on. "More. Harder."

I give up doing anything but exactly what she demands of me. I fuck her hard enough that the slap of flesh against flesh fills the room, punctuated by words I can't keep inside. "Once more, beautiful girl. I want to feel you coming around my cock. It feels good, doesn't it?"

"So good." She whimpers and then her nails are on my back, biting in hard enough that I'll be wearing her marks tomorrow. Fierce satisfaction lashes me. There's no taking this back, just like there's no taking back my ring on her finger and hers on mine. No matter what else happens, tomorrow there will be no pretending this was all a dream. We're grounded too firmly in reality.

I adjust my angle, working to give her clit the friction she needs to get there before I do. She's only too happy to help me, pressing her heels to the mattress to grind herself against my pelvic bone. Psyche becomes frantic. "Eros, please. Please, please, please."

"I've got you." I drag my mouth over her shoulder. "I won't stop."

I don't stop. I keep up that careful angle, that intense motion, until she comes apart around me. I want to last. I do. But it feels too fucking good. She clamps around my cock, and it's too late. I drive into her as I come, filling the condom.

I stare down at this woman, at my *wife*. She's always gorgeous, but she looks like a goddess right now, her hair spread around her, her eyes half-shut with pleasure, her lips plumped from my kisses. I'm no photographer, not like Psyche is, but I would give my right arm to take a picture of her in this moment to keep with me always.

"Eros."

If I tell her what I was just thinking, it will freak her out. She's already skittish as fuck around me, and with good reason. The woman showed me kindness once, and then I essentially followed her home like a feral cat and forced her to marry me. "Don't move," I finally manage.

"I don't think I can."

That draws a rough laugh from me. My legs are more than a little shaky as I move off her and stagger to the bathroom to dispose of the condom. When I return, it's to find her exactly as I left her. Again, I'm slammed with the intense desire to keep her like this forever. I want more than a picture to remember tonight by. I want *more*.

I want this to be longer than a single night.

With that in mind, I grab a handful of condoms and toss them onto the bed next to her. Psyche looks at them and then at me, her brows raised. "Someone's ambitious."

"The sun's not up yet."

The smile she gives me contains multitudes. "No, the sun's not up yet." She stretches. "But I'd like a chance to shower off the worst of the wedding before we do anything else."

I offer my hand, a feral part of me crowing in victory when she sets her hand in mine. Such a small thing, allowing me to tug her to her feet, but it feels more significant than that. It feels like we really have started something meaningful. It's foolish in the extreme to let myself believe that. Psyche might like the way I fuck, but she doesn't like me.

She doesn't hate me, though. She's too good a person to let me touch her like this if she truly hated me. That's a tiny ledge to stand on and wish for more, but I've been in more impossible situations and come out on top.

I maintain my grip on her hand and lead her into the bathroom. She doesn't argue as I get the water going or when I follow her into the spray. For a moment, something wary lingers in her eyes. "If you could see the way you look at me. I don't understand it."

"What's there to understand?" I can't shut down my expression now. It's a skill I've managed for as long as I can remember, closing out others and offering nothing I don't intend to. But right here, right now, I'm an open book if she's inclined to read me.

Psyche stares up into my face for a long moment, blushes, and ducks beneath the spray. I'm both disappointed and grateful for the reprieve. Some things are better left unsaid, especially when I'm still not sure how I'm feeling, when I'm riding the edge of control.

But she's here in my shower and I am only human.

I grab the shampoo from her hand. "Let me."

"Eros, that's not necessary."

"It has nothing to do with necessity and everything to do with the fact that I want to." We just had sex. I should be sated, if temporarily. Instead, my need for her only seems to grow stronger. I pour the shampoo into my hands and get to work massaging it into the heavy length of her hair. She stays tense for a moment, but once she seems to realize that I have no intention of rushing, Psyche sighs and relaxes against me.

She might not realize the significance of this, but it's impossible for me not to. She's stopped fighting me somewhere along the way. This woman will never submit, will always be looking at a situation from a thousand different angles, but right now, she's content to let me take care of her.

She...trusts me.

She shouldn't. She has absolutely no evidence to support this. And yet here we are. It feels like a gift, one I certainly don't deserve but will accept nonetheless.

We finish showering relatively quickly, and Psyche makes me wait while she dries her hair, but eventually we end up back in the bedroom together. She stares at the bed. "We don't have to..."

"Psyche." I wait for her to look at me to continue. "I want you. The sun isn't up yet. Do *you* want more?"

It's hard to tell in the shadows of the room, but I think she blushes. "I shouldn't."

"I didn't ask what you thought you *should* do. I asked what you want to do."

She exhales slowly. "Yes, Eros. I want more of you."

Thank fuck. I pull her into my arms and brush her hair back from her face. "See, that wasn't so hard. Let's keep going." I kiss her before she has a chance to fire off some smart-ass response.

Tonight. We have tonight. We can worry about tomorrow in the morning.

PSYCHE

I WAKE UP IN WAVES OF SENSATION. THE EARTHY SCENT OF Eros against my skin. The warmth of him at my back, his arm a comforting weight over my waist, the bed's luxurious sheets and comforter wrapped up around us to ward off the chill. The sweet ache of my body from everything we did last night.

I don't want to open my eyes. If I open my eyes, this is over, and I'm not ready to step back onto the battleground. Later, I'll be more worried about my hesitation, will probably curse myself seven times over for the moment of weakness after the ceremony. Another thing to add to Future Me's tab. A terrible habit I'm settling into.

Eros's arm tightens around me, his hand spreading to press to the spot just beneath my breasts. "Morning."

Now there's no pretending any longer. We're both awake. It's time to get up and talk through our next steps.

Except I don't.

Instead, I arch back a little, pressing my ass to his hard cock. "Morning."

His harsh exhale tickles the small hairs at the back of my neck. "The sun's up."

Damn him for insisting on pulling back the curtain and shining light on this situation. Would it be so hard to ignore the sliver of dawn showing through the window? I sigh. "Then I guess we should be up, too."

"There you go again, using that word. *Should*." His hand skates down my stomach and over to my hip. It's not quite an invitation, but it's not *not* an invitation, either. "You seem tired, Psyche."

I frown at the gray wall across from the bed. "Thanks. That's what every bride wants to hear the day after her wedding."

His low chuckle has me fighting not to arch back against him again. Eros presses a light kiss to my shoulder. "It seems a damn shame to get out of bed before we have to."

I'm already on a slippery slope when it comes to this man. First, I compromised with some of the best oral sex I've ever received before the ceremony. Then, we had entirely too much sex *after* the ceremony. If we push the boundary again, I'm not certain I'll be able to hold out the next time he decides he's in the mood to seduce me.

If the slow heat building in my blood is any indication, he won't need to do much to have me on the verge of begging. He's barely doing anything *now*. I clear my throat. "That's a bad idea."

"Is it?" Eros doesn't move his hand, doesn't shift against me at all. His tone is so dry, he might as well be asking about the weather. "Psyche, I'm *famished*. Let me have a little taste. Nothing more."

Did I think this man was dangerous when he held my death in his cold blue eyes? The joke's on me. He's a thousand times deadlier when he's whispering filth in my ear. I worry my bottom lip. "You say nothing more, but we both know that's not the truth."

He shifts back and I barely get a chance to mourn the loss of his touch before Eros pushes on my shoulder, all but shoving me onto my back. I blink up at him. He looks...concerned? His gaze flicks over my face. "What are you talking about? I thought we were on the same page yesterday. You explicitly told me what you wanted." He hesitates. "Are you saying you didn't want it?"

Despite my best efforts to remain calm, I can't help responding to his apparent distress. "Of course that's not what I'm saying. How many times did I come yesterday? I'm sure your scalp is sore from how hard I was pulling your hair as I rode your mouth. I wanted it, Eros. That's not what I'm trying to say."

Eros blinks at me as if I just popped him on the nose with a newspaper. "Then what's the issue?"

My frustration bursts like a soap bubble. There and then gone in an instant. "The *problem* is that last night was supposed to be a one-off."

He recovers quickly, though there's still some surprise lingering on his face. "We just talked about this. 'Supposed to' is—"

"Do not play word games with me, Eros." I might not actually be angry with him, but frustration sinks its claws into me and digs deep. Of course he doesn't see an issue with twisting our words to stay in bed as long as possible. For him, this is simply pleasure with someone he desires. I wish I was wired like that. "Last night was a one-off," I finally manage. "We were both under an extreme amount of stress, and it's only natural to want to let off some steam."

"Psyche." He says my name slowly, his eyes narrowing. "You

can rationalize your way into damn near anything with that big brain of yours, but do *not* try to include me in those mental gymnastics. I fucked you last night for the same reason I ate your pussy for damn near an hour yesterday afternoon—because I wanted you. Stress, pheromones, or whatever other excuse you're about to spit at me has nothing to do with it."

Now it's my turn to blink. "Of course it has something to do with it, along with proximity. That's biology. Otherwise, we would have been attracted to each other before now."

Eros lowers his head until our noses are nearly touching. "Can you honestly say you've never been attracted to me before yesterday?" He doesn't wait for me to sputter out an answer. "Not once in ten years of attending the same parties? Not even when we were leaving the bathroom and I had my arms around you the night we were photographed?"

It's really difficult to argue with him when he's so close. And so right. "Um."

"Because *I* was attracted to *you*."

So I hadn't imagined that brief flare of heat in his eyes. I don't know if that's comforting or terrifying. My careful wall of logic is crumbling around me. "I meant what I said before; I can't separate emotion from sex. Maybe once, but if we keep doing this, then you're going to hurt me, even if you don't mean to."

"What if I didn't?"

Gods, why is he still arguing? He's already proven that while he's hardly a paragon of virtue, he *does* have some kind of conscience. Eros isn't cruel. He might not care for me, but he can't plan to protect me from his mother and then turn around and wield an emotional knife against me. "This marriage is one of convenience. *You* set that up."

Eros finally sighs. "You're right."

I know I'm right. So why do I feel the faintest sinking in my chest at his agreement. "I know I am. I just..." He's agreed with me. Why am I still arguing?

Eros doesn't move, doesn't try to press his advantage. Surely he knows that it would take a single kiss to make me putty in his hands? He's a smart man; he must know. But he simply watches me, waiting for me the same way he waited last night.

Last night, I could tell myself all the same things I just told him. It was a stress-based decision. We needed to let off some steam. No matter what promise I made, I had no intention of continuing to sleep with Eros.

That's what it boils down to. *Intention.* If I let us blur the lines this morning, what's to stop us from continuing to do so? We're both such excellent liars; throw in sex, and I might start to believe the fiction we spin for the rest of Olympus.

Restricting sex to our wedding night is the only smart way to keep my heart intact.

"It's a bad idea," I whisper.

"Is it? I'm not so sure." He brushes a strand of my hair away from my face. "I know what I said last night about wanting a chance to seduce you properly, but the truth is I'm not going to pressure you. I want you, Psyche. If you were on board with the idea, I'd be okay spending the next three days in this bed."

I drag in an unsteady breath. "That's a lot of sex."

"It'd barely take the edge off." His smile is a little bittersweet.

"I'm well aware that I'm no catch. There's no reason a woman like you would want to be linked to me any more than you already are, and I'll respect that."

The horrible melting feeling in my chest from last night comes back, this time with interest. I'm so busy trying to protect my heart that I never once thought myself capable of hurting Eros. Even a little. I search his face, but for once, he doesn't have a mask in place.

He gives me that crooked smile, still trying to put me at ease. "I can't promise my virtuous streak will hold, especially if you keep looking so fucking sexy, but you're safe from any attempted seduction this morning." He starts to sit up.

I grab his arm, my hand moving almost of its own volition. I stare at where my fingers wrap around his bicep. "Wait."

"You're killing me, beautiful girl." He exhales a shaky breath. "I'm trying to do right by you."

"I know." Still, I can't quite make myself release him. My need for self-preservation battles with desire and something like empathy. I want him. He wants me. I might not be able to hold the careful line between us if we keep doing this, but my reasons for saying no slip away like the tide going out. "Eros."

He doesn't seem to breathe. "Yeah?"

"Would you accuse me of being incredibly fickle if I changed my mind?"

His slow grin is a different kind of foreplay. "I'd say I like you when you're fickle."

I don't get this man. Before this marriage, he could have nearly anyone he wanted in Olympus. Why does he look at *me* like I just delivered his favorite present on Christmas morning? It's so tempting to believe that he wants me that desperately, but allowing myself to believe that is a mistake. Lust and love aren't the same thing, but my brain might get the two confused, especially when it comes to this man.

There's no time to think about that, though, not with him easing down my body, taking the covers with him. I start to close my eyes, desperate to reclaim some of the rapidly closing distance between us, but he nips my thigh as he presses my legs wide. "Don't shut me out, Psyche."

"You ask too much."

"I know." He doesn't sound the least bit sorry, either. Eros's eyes have gone hot as he looks up my body. The way he drinks me in visually is something I don't think I'll ever get used to. He's so contained the rest of the time, but the second I get naked, it's like a beast is looking out at me through those blue eyes.

He dips his head and then his mouth is on my pussy. It's different from yesterday afternoon, when he was a man on a mission, perfectly focused on my pleasure but wasting no time on making me come so hard, I saw stars.

There's none of that furor now.

He's almost lazy as he licks me. This is like the oral sex version of brunch, like he plans to linger and enjoy himself, and I don't know how to feel about that. I've had a variety of partners who had a variety of feelings about oral sex, ranging from a box to check off to get to the good stuff to some kind of strange competition to prove how many times they can make me come. I don't know that I've ever been with someone who seems to love it for its own sake, for the pleasure it brings *them*.

I never guessed how much hotter that would make the whole experience.

Eros lingers over every inch of my pussy, seeming to savor the exploration. It's a slow tease, an idle strumming of pleasure that increases with every lick and then grows again each time he makes that sexy little growling noise against me, his hands tightening on my thighs as if he's beside himself with need. He finally, *finally*, works his way up to my clit and rubs the flat of his tongue over me in little strokes.

I cry out, my back bowing. "More. Please, Eros. More."

His rough laugh nearly makes me come on the spot. I might be able to go toe-to-toe with this man in every other arena, but in the bedroom, I'm hopelessly outmatched. Because it doesn't feel like a match as his tongue plays over my clit. It just feels like pleasure, like two people pursuing the same goal with the same intensity. How am I supposed to remember that he's the enemy when it's everything I can do not to grab hold and ride his face until I come all over him?

He's not the enemy.

The thought should comfort me. Instead, it makes Eros even more dangerous. I can't bring myself to regret saying yes, though. Maybe I will later, but right now this feels too good to stop.

"Stop holding back."

I open my eyes, not sure when I closed them, and lift my head to look down my body at him. "What?"

Eros nods at where my hands are fisting the sheets, and a strange little smile pulls at his lips. "You know you want them in my hair."

I do. I really, really do. Which is precisely why I shouldn't, why I should try to keep some part of me withdrawn.

This isn't a battle I'm going to win, though. It's not even one I *want* to win. I give myself over to him with a cry, dropping back to the mattress and digging my hands into his curls. This man's hair should be illegal. It's so incredibly soft and just long enough to get a wicked grip. My legs fall wider without my having any intention of doing it, and the low sound Eros makes is nearly as much a reward as his tongue sliding into me.

Is this really happening?

Am I, in the soft light of the morning, naked in bed with Eros Ambrosia and rubbing my pussy against his mouth as he tongues me?

There's no room for doubt, for recrimination. Later, I'll worry about how I've changed things between us, smudged lines that desperately needed to remain clear. Right now, I'm dancing on the edge, my body strummed tight with the orgasm bearing down on me. So close...

Eros shifts and then he's pressing his fingers into me. The shock of the penetration, combined with the way he's working my clit, hurtles me over the edge. I cry out, my grip spasming in his hair, but the pleasure doesn't stop. It keeps going, his mouth and hands building up another wave even before the first dissipates.

Oh gods.

"Eros." I tug on his hair, but I might as well try to tug the moon from the sky. "Eros, wait."

He barely lifts his mouth enough to say "One more."

"I can't." *I shouldn't.*

He slows but doesn't remove his fingers. The entire bottom half of his face is wet from my desire, and as I watch, he licks his lips. "That was barely a taste. I'm not done." He pumps slowly into me, penetrating me, possessing me. "Let me have my fill, Psyche. You can go back to hating me later."

I don't hate you. Even if I should. "Okay," I whisper. I don't sound like myself. I don't *feel* like myself. Surely someone else has taken possession of my body—a wanton, reckless creature who cares only for pleasure and the consequences be damned.

Even if I'm the one who will ultimately pay the price.

I lose track of time. Of my fears. Of everything but the two of us in this bed, Eros going down on me like he never needs to breathe, drawing orgasm after orgasm from me.

Eventually he slows. Or I do. I'm not sure. Only that I'm shaking so hard, it's as if I've just enduring one of Callisto's boot-camp workouts. Eros isn't all that composed, either. He kisses his way up my body and then his mouth is on mine, ramping me up despite the intense wave of exhaustion the last orgasm brought.

Maybe I'm not that tired, after all.

I push on his shoulders, and for a moment I think he'll ignore my unspoken demand. He finally leverages himself up and looks down at me. "What?"

What?

He's just shattered me to pieces half a dozen times and *that's* the first thing he says to me?

I almost laugh. I might if I could draw in the breath. "My turn." I shove on his shoulders again.

"No." He frowns. If his breathing wasn't just as ragged as

mine, I'd think he was unaffected. But then, there's no ignoring the hard cock pressed against me, even if he shows no signs of trying to do anything with it. Eros shakes his head as if trying to clear his thoughts. "You don't have to."

My heart gives an almost painful lurch. Eros is always the fixer, the one taking charge and handling things. It's a role he's obviously embraced in every part of his life. But now he's looking at me with this strangely vulnerable expression in his blue eyes, almost confused at the idea that I might want to take care of him, too.

I lick my lips. "I want to. Stop being stubborn and let me suck your cock." I shove on his shoulder again, and this time, he lets me push him onto his back.

"With an offer that sweet, how am I supposed to resist?" The words are right. The tone is close. But the way he watches me move to kneel between his thighs...

There's no distance between us now. It's ceased to exist.

If I'm not careful, what I fear most will come to pass. I'll start to believe the pretty lie about this thing between us, rather than the stark truth.

Worry about it later.

I pull my hair back and wrap a fist around his cock. He's long and has a delicious curve that I enjoyed an *extreme* amount last night. He's also so hard, he's practically throbbing. "Poor baby," I murmur. "This looks like it hurts."

"You could say that." He doesn't move, but the tendons stand out in his neck.

"Don't worry. I'll take care of you." My first taste of him

makes me giddy. No, it makes me drunk. Is this what he feels when he goes down on me? No wonder he was *famished* this morning.

I lick my way down Eros's cock, savoring every inch of him. Savoring his reaction even more. Every muscle in his body looks carved from stone, as if he's straining to hold perfectly still, to submit to my mouth and not take control of this interaction. It's breathtakingly sexy to feel this powerful.

But I don't want his restraint. Later, maybe—when reality sets in and brings regret and a determination to protect my soft emotional center—but not right now. How far will he allow me to push him before his control shatters?

There's only one way to find out.

EROS

THIS WOMAN IS GOING TO KILL ME. I'M TRYING SO FUCKING hard to respect the boundaries she put in place, to play this slow until I can seduce her the way she deserves, can prove to her that she has nothing to fear from me, and Psyche is over here, playing her tongue along my cock, her hazel eyes flaring in a challenge it takes everything I have not to meet.

For a woman who claims we only feel desire for each other as a side effect of stress, she certainly watches me like she wants me to drag her up my body and fuck her until neither of us can walk right.

Again.

I don't wrap her hair around my fist the way I want to. I can't trust myself right now. "You're playing a dangerous game."

"We've already established that on multiple levels." She gives me a slow smile and drags the head of my cock over her full lips. The softest touch that has me fighting not to come on the spot.

"Psyche." I can't keep the warning from my tone. Can't keep the growl out, either.

Her only response is to part her lips and swallow me down. Gods, I might be destined for Tartarus, but the pure pleasure in this moment makes it almost worth it. Who cares what the afterlife brings when I'm being treated to this slice of perfection right now?

Psyche doesn't let me sink into the moment. She releases me and flicks her tongue against the sensitive spot at the head of my cock. She's watching me so closely, I can't shake the feeling that she's *trying* to provoke me.

I want her to. Fuck, I'm enjoying my time with her more than I could have dreamed. She challenges me at every turn, and I didn't anticipate how much I'd come to crave that.

But I promised. "Either suck my cock properly or I'm going to do something we both regret."

"That would be a shame." She holds my gaze as she drags her tongue down my length like she's licking a melting ice cream cone. "Such a shame if you lost control."

She doesn't know what she's asking for.

I don't know if I can resist giving it to her despite that.

I move slowly, giving her plenty of time to react, and wrap my fist around the long length of her hair. "Last chance."

She flicks her tongue against my balls and I lose it. I drag her up my body. Too rough. Too fucking rough. Not that Psyche seems to care. She practically throws herself at my mouth, kissing me with none of the teasing she exhibited during that blow job.

I roll, toppling her back to the bed, and thrust against her. Some dark part of me wants to take her up on the invitation of her lifted hips, her thighs spreading to welcome me. It would be the most natural thing in the world to slip inside her now, to fuck her without anything between us.

Stop.

I manage to muscle down the desire, but only barely. "Do not move."

"Better hurry then." She slides a hand between our bodies and wraps her fist around my cock. "I'm needy."

Shock stills me. I hold perfectly still as she rubs her pussy against my length. The woman is playing chicken with my control. "Psyche."

She shivers. "I really, really like it when you say my name like that."

"You wouldn't if you recognized what it meant." I lower myself onto her, letting my weight pin her in place and keep either of us from doing something unforgivably reckless. Gods, she feels good. Arching and straining and writhing against me. I have to close my eyes to focus. "If you knew what I wanted—"

"Tell me." The sheer need in her voice shreds my control. I can feel it snapping, thread by thread. Her next words only make it worse. "Tell me you're spinning out just as much as I am. Tell me I'm not in the depths alone."

I can't deny the thread of fear in her voice, can't stop myself from wanting to assuage it even if it means I scare her in different ways. I curse. "I want to fuck you bare." Damn it, what am I saying? It's too much, too intense. Not that it matters. I can't fucking stop. "I want to tie you to my bed and help myself to every bit of you on *my* whim. To tease you and fuck you and make you come until you know exactly who you belong to."

She inhales harshly. "I belong to myself."

I know that. It's part of what makes her so unforgivably attractive to me. Just one of the many puzzle pieces that come together to form this woman who I can't get enough of. "You didn't ask me for the truth. You asked what I want."

She turns her face to my neck and kisses my throat. "Get a condom, Eros."

A condom. Right. Because I cannot, under any circumstances, fuck her bare. Not like this, not without a very clear conversation beforehand. One that I've never had before, never needed.

What the fuck is happening to me?

I'm spinning out just as badly as she is. I'm in the depths beside her.

It takes more effort than it should to move away enough to grab the condoms from the top drawer of the nightstand. To stop touching her long enough to tear open the wrapper and roll the condom on.

Psyche doesn't wait for me. She grips my cock and guides it to her entrance. I fight to hold still, to let her guide this, and the effort has me shaking. Psyche, the little asshole, knows it. She keeps hold of me, dipping the head of my cock into her pussy again and again, but never letting me sink more than an inch into her.

"Tease," I growl.

She's breathing just as hard as I am, shaking just as hard as I am. Her hazel eyes hold a challenge I feel right down to my very soul. "Do something about it."

My leash snaps.

I move back onto my knees and grab her wrists, shifting them to one of my hands and shoving them up over her head. She presses against my hold as if she can't help herself, and her lips part in a moan. "Yes, like that."

I'm fighting a losing battle. I want this woman too desperately to do this properly. I haven't actually managed to maintain enough control to seduce her the way she deserves. I just want to fuck and fuck and fuck until my presence is tattooed on every inch of her body. I settle between her legs. "You want me to get rough with you, Psyche? Fuck you like a godsdamned monster?"

She shivers harder. "*Yes.*"

I notch my cock at her entrance. She's soaked and ready for me, but I still have to slow down enough to work my full length into her. It's only when I'm seated deep inside her that I manage to keep talking. "I think you're a little liar."

"What?" She tries to free her hands, but I'm having none of it. If she grabs my ass like she did last night, sinking her nails in, this will all be over far too soon.

I nip her earlobe. "You might belong to yourself, but I think the same dirty little part of you that wants me to fuck you hard also wants me to claim you." I slide slowly out of her and then back in, teasing. "I think you want me to remind this pussy who it belongs to."

"It's temporary." She might be trying to sound assertive, but it almost comes out as a question.

"Temporary or not, you're mine, Psyche." I use my hold on her wrists to leverage myself up a little, pressing them hard to the mattress. "Do you want to see how I fuck someone who's mine?"

"Yes," she moans.

I don't ask again. I loop one arm under her thigh and open her wider for me. And then I hold her down and fuck her. There's no finesse. No seduction. It's pure animal instinct, the desire to claim, the need to make her mine in a way I've never made anyone mine. Not once.

I release one of her wrists. "Touch your clit. Make yourself come."

"I'm already halfway there." But she does exactly as I command, sliding her hand down her soft stomach to circle her clit.

I slow down just enough that I can watch myself slide in and out of her, witness this claiming in the most archaic of ways. Maybe I'll regret this later and I'll want to take it all back. But right now, the only thing I desire is to feel Psyche's pussy clenching around my cock as she comes.

She doesn't make me wait long.

Her back bows and she nearly dislodges my grip on her wrist as she orgasms. I don't break stride. I drop down onto her, rutting away even as unforgivable words spill out of me. Needing to reassure her with my body in a way she'll never allow me to reassure her with my words alone. "Do you feel that, Psyche? I'm the one who makes you feel that way. I'll do it again, whenever you need me. Again and again and again." *Forever.*

At least I keep the last bit internal. Barely.

I come hard, grinding into her as I milk every last bit of pleasure. Too good. It's too damn good with this woman. It's never been like this with anyone else—man, woman, nonbinary. I've had partners aplenty and it's always been fun and mutually satisfactory. I've never had a problem keeping my leash in place.

Sex is great. It's always *been* great. But with Psyche, it feels like the axis of my world has shifted. I don't like it. If I were smarter, I'd call this whole thing off and ship this woman out of Olympus. Triton is someone who knows how to pull that off. He owes me a few favors, and I'd have to call in every single one of them in order to book passage. It's not an easy ask, but it's the best way to ensure Psyche's safety and get her as far away from me as possible.

If she stays here, stays with me, I can't shake the feeling that I'll smother her kind heart in a way she'll never recover from.

But as she stretches next to me and makes a little contented noise, I already know I'm not going to send her away. I'm too fucking selfish.

Psyche is mine.

She just doesn't know it yet.

I manage to drag myself off her long enough to dispose of the condom. I make it quick because I'm not about to leave this bed before we absolutely have to. Thankfully, I fucked Psyche damn near comatose. She rolls slowly to face me as I climb back into bed. "I have a question."

Okay, she's not comatose. I barely manage to resist the urge to kiss her and derail whatever her question is. The truth is that I kind of want to know. "Yes?"

Her gaze trails down my chest before she drags it back to my face. "Is it always like this with you?"

I relax down next to her. "Is what always like this?" I know exactly what she's asking, but I want to hear her say it, to put voice to something I'm barely ready to admit to myself.

We're spinning out and in the depths together.

"Don't play coy, Eros. It doesn't suit you." Her lips quirk, which only serves to remind me what they were doing not too long ago. "This. Sex. Is it always like this with you?"

"I'm going to need you to be more specific."

"No, you aren't. You're just fishing for compliments." She reaches out as if she can't quite help·herself and tugs on one of my curls. Finally, she says, "Is it always so intense? So...overwhelming?"

No. It's never like this. "You're saying sex hasn't been like this before for you?"

She looks away and I allow it. I'm feeling pretty fucking vulnerable all of a sudden, too. Psyche shakes her head. "No, it's not like this with other people. It hasn't been bad or anything, just different."

A part of me wants to shy away from admitting it's the same for me, but the larger part wants to use this knowledge to bind us together even tighter. I press one finger to her chin, guiding her face back to me. "It hasn't been like this for me, either."

"Don't lie to me."

"I won't. I promise. We lie to other people, but not to each other. Not going forward." I hesitate, but the vulnerability in her eyes draws forth the truth. "I seduce, Psyche. I'm actually quite good at it when I'm so inclined. I never lose control enough to be *overwhelming*. Not with anyone but you."

"Oh."

I give her a mock frown. "Oh? That's all you have to say?"

She trails her fingers up my arm and back down again. "Eros?"

"Yeah?"

"We haven't left the bed yet."

I grin and press her back against the mattress. "We sure as fuck haven't."

PSYCHE

I'VE NEVER BEEN A RECKLESS WOMAN. I'VE BENT OVER backward to ensure that I could anticipate any outcome, could be several steps ahead of any opponents. As a daughter of Demeter, carelessness has consequences and so I've avoided it.

Until now.

Spending the day in bed with Eros is a mistake. I *know* it's a mistake, but every time I consider getting up and facing the rest of the world, he kisses me or touches me or, gods, just *looks* at me. And then we're off again, working each other into a frenzy of lust and need. If it were just that, maybe I could convince myself that I haven't veered off the path to the point of no return, haven't driven this plan right off a cliff. Except we spend several hours catnapping, curled around each other as if we're newlyweds in truth, rather than pretending to be simply to serve a purpose.

By the time I can no longer ignore the growling sounds my stomach makes, it's early evening. I shove him back and practically throw myself off the bed. "I need to eat. I need to *shower*."

"I'll join you."

"No!" I scramble back a step, panic rising because of how badly I actually do want him to join me. I need distance, and I need it now. "Give me a few, okay?"

Eros watches me closely, and it's painful to witness his walls come back up. I hadn't even realized they'd inched down at some point during the day. Before I can change my mind, he's back to the coldly calculating man I've known him to be up to this point. "Take your time. I'll put together something to eat."

"Okay." I barely wait for him to pull on a pair of pants and leave the room before I grab my phone and rush into the bathroom. It seems silly to lock the door, but I'll take anything to make me feel more centered right now. I turn on the water and stare at myself in the mirror.

I look like a mess.

There's whisker burn on my neck and chest and, really, my entire body. Red marks from Eros's fingers pressing into my hips and thighs will likely turn into bruises later. The sensory memory threatens to overwhelm me, and I shiver. This is exactly why I shouldn't have slept with him. Instead of thinking about our next move and about how to counter whatever lies Aphrodite decides to spin, I'm thinking about how good it felt when he slid his hand between my legs and...

Gods.

I grip my phone tightly, but who am I supposed to call? Callisto? She's going to rip me a new one the first opportunity she gets. Persephone? She's already made her thoughts on this marriage clear; she's not going to have sympathy that I'm suddenly having second thoughts about the whole thing. Not to mention if she found out what the other option was...

No, I can't call her. I can't call anyone.

I take a deep breath and set the phone on the counter. This isn't the first time Olympus life has overwhelmed me. I already have the tools I need to steady the ground beneath my feet. I hope.

Despite my promise to be quick—not to mention the relatively late hour—I take a decently long shower and then put myself together, piece by piece. Hair dried and straightened. Subtle but flawless makeup. I duck into the spare bedroom and pull on a pair of leggings, knit socks, and my favorite oversize sweater. Relaxed, but photo ready. It's enough. It has to be.

I make myself take the time to stage a photograph in the fading sunlight filtering through Eros's giant windows. It's not up to my usual standards, and it takes me ten pictures to nail the soft and happy smile that I'm aiming for, but it'll do until I can get some more content created in the morning. I type out a happy, sappy caption as I head down the hallway.

I find Eros in the kitchen, sipping from a glass of wine and staring out the window. He glances over when I walk into the room, but his blank expression doesn't change. "Tomorrow, we're going out. The longer we stay closeted in the penthouse, the more opportunity we give my mother to create a narrative we don't want."

Relief and something akin to disappointment course through me. This is familiar territory; manipulating the paparazzi is what I'm good at. If we focus on that, I don't have to think about the fact that I really, really want to close the distance between us and kiss Eros for all I'm worth.

I tuck a strand of hair behind my ear. I can drive myself up the wall trying to anticipate what angle his mother will take, but at the end of the day, our best defense is to stick with our original plan. "Do you want the giddy newlywed experience or the poised and perfect one?"

"How are they different?"

"Giddy means that we visit the outdoor gardens in the university district and cuddle close while we walk the paths, followed by going to one of the smaller bars to get a little tipsy and pretend like we're the only ones in the room. Poised and perfect is dinner at the Dryad."

His brows rise. "Even I have a hard time getting into the Dryad on a moment's notice."

"I'm surprised you can get in at all. Pan hates Aphrodite, and I'm sure that extends to you as well."

Eros's slow smile affects me even more than it did the first few times I saw it. Now I know he looks exactly the same when he's planning out what delicious things he wants to do to my body. I fight back a shiver. He sees it—of course he does—and his smile widens. "Pan and I have an understanding."

That draws a surprised laugh from me. "Don't tell me you've seduced him, too."

"Psyche." Gods, every time he says my name, it's like an invitation to do something I'm sure to regret. "I'm hurt by your insistence that I'm moving through Olympus, leaving a trail of lovers behind me."

"Am I wrong?"

He chuckles and ducks his head a little. It's horrifyingly charming. "Depends on who you ask."

This is bad. I need to be focusing on the plan rather than how attractive Eros is when he's being self-effacing. "And if I ask Pan?"

"He'd argue that *he* seduced *me*."

Of course he would. Pan is even more notorious than Eros is for spreading his charms far and wide. I shake my head, amused despite myself. "Back to my original question; giddy or poised?"

"Giddy." He drops the smile, but something about it lingers in his eyes. "This is a love affair, and if we look too practiced, people will doubt that it's real and give my mother the opportunity to capitalize on their doubt. The fact that neither of us does the giddy, foolish thing normally will only help sell this story."

"I agree."

He crosses his arms over his chest. "Then why even give me an option? Why not simply lay out the plan?"

I can't quite hold his gaze. "You're in this, too. It's important that we're on the same page."

"Sure." He shrugs. "But we've already established that this is your domain more than it's mine."

"Still."

Eros drops his arms and moves toward me. It's everything I can do to plant my feet and not scramble away from him. Or at least that's what I tell myself as I watch him approach. I'm certainly not holding my breath, waiting to see what he'll do next. He leans down until our faces are even. "Silly me. I thought it might be because you're doubting your instincts, but you're not that ridiculous."

My skin heats in a way that has nothing to do with desire. "Excuse me?"

"You're doubting yourself. Stop it."

I straighten my spine and glare at him. "You don't know what you're talking about. I'm not doubting myself."

"Liar." He says it almost fondly. Eros turns away before I can form a response. "Food's ready."

I watch him pull a delicious-smelling casserole out of the oven, not sure if I want to let this go or not. "You don't know me."

"You keep saying that." He spoons plentiful portions onto two plates and passes me one. "I think we've established that I know enough."

I follow him around the corner to a small formal dining room. It's just as minimalist as the rest of the house—giant windows, a square steel and marble table, and a wall bare of anything but a large mirror with a geometric black and white frame. He sets his plate down and walks out of the room, reappearing a few moments later with his wineglass and a second one that he places in front of me. It feels very, very strange to sit in this room across from Eros. As if we're eating in a museum or something. "Are you sure you actually live here?"

He spares me a glance. "Not everyone leaves a trail of clutter behind them as evidence of their occupancy."

I tense, but there's no judgment in the sentence, just a simple statement. "I'm not a messy person."

"I said clutter, not mess. They're different." He stares at his plate. "Beyond that, I live here alone. There is no family to imprint their presence in every room the way it is at your mother's place."

"You keep bringing that up. Why?" I brace myself to defend my family. We might not always get along, but I'll be damned before I let anyone disparage us. Even Eros. Especially Eros.

But he surprises me. "It feels like a home. It's...novel."

"Novel," I repeat. "How can it be novel? You're only, what, twenty-eight?"

"You say that like you don't know."

I blush a little, because of course I know how old he is. We might not have *known* each other before now, but I have at least basic knowledge of everyone who is close to the various members of the Thirteen. "You haven't been living alone *so* long that you've forgotten your childhood home."

He fiddles with his fork. "You know who my mother is. Do you really think my childhood home was even remotely as warm as yours?"

"Well, it can't be that warm if it's designed like this place."

"What's wrong with this place?"

I flick my fingers at the mirror behind me. "What's with all the mirrors? I can theoretically understand it in the foyer as an art thing, and even in the bedroom as a kinky thing, but they're *everywhere*."

"Ah." He stares at his plate for a long moment. "I mostly let my interior decorator do their thing. It was easier, and it's not like I have strong opinions about it."

This interior decorator is someone hired by Aphrodite. I'd bet a significant amount of money on it. I hesitate, trying to parse my way through this without sounding like a complete asshole. "Eros, this is your home. You're allowed to put your stamp on it."

"Am I?" His mouth twists. "I suppose that depends on who you ask."

I open my mouth to keep arguing, but my brain catches up to my tongue before I can make a complete fool of myself. It's more than obvious who he's talking about. Still... "I know Aphrodite isn't a very good mother, but..."

He gives me a smile devoid of his normal charm. "There's no 'but' in that sentence, Psyche. I'm glad that you grew up in a place that feels like a home and that Demeter preserved that feeling even if things changed after you moved here. It's just not my experience." He goes back to eating as if the subject's closed.

I suppose it is.

I made fun of this penthouse the first night here. I *continued* to poke at his design choices, assuming that, at least in this, he is as clichéd as he pretends to be. The playboy millionaire with more money than taste, who mistakes minimalism for the peak of style. The more soulless, the better.

Except every time he talks about my mother's home, there's a thread of something in his tone that's almost like...longing.

I look around the dining room again, my mind whirling. "Would you be opposed to my making some changes?" I hold up a hand when he lifts his brows. "Nothing too intense. Just a few things to put a little bit of my stamp on the space, too." I honestly don't mind the sheer number of mirrors, but they need something to soften them.

The smile Eros gives me has my heart fluttering in my chest. "I'd like that."

"Good," I say softly. It's a small thing, but it feels very large. Too large for me to look at closely. Instead, I focus on my meal.

I eat slowly. The food is good, but it's the silence that comforts me. It's not strained. I have the strange feeling that Eros would be perfectly content occupying the same room for hours without talking if he had nothing to say. He might pretend to be the pretty playboy, but he doesn't run his mouth for the sole purpose of hearing himself talk.

I've always liked silence. I think it comes from living with three sisters and a mother who are all talkers. They talk when they're happy, sad, angry, or even bored. No one in my family would be content to eat a meal without filling the room with some kind of running commentary. There's a comfort in that, but when my stress level reaches a certain point, it becomes just one more thing that weighs on me. I like that Eros doesn't have the same urge. It makes this space feel almost safe.

A feeling I most certainly cannot afford.

I take a hasty sip of wine. Since Eros was in a sharing mood earlier, there's something I desperately want to know. Now seems as good a time as any to ask. "I'd like to ask you a question."

"I'll consider answering."

That's fair. I swallow hard. "Why do you do it? All the stuff your mom demands? This isn't the first time she's called for someone's head."

"Heart."

I blink. "What?"

"She didn't call for your head. She called for your heart." He takes another bite of food without looking at me.

Somehow, I know he's not speaking figuratively. The thought almost makes me laugh, but I manage to keep the hysterical sound inside. "Your mother is such a bitch."

"Glass houses, Psyche."

I start to argue, but the truth is that Demeter is just as scheming and ambitious as Aphrodite is. I have no doubts that Aphrodite would leave half of Olympus to starve if given the right motivation, and my mother *is* responsible for several individuals disappearing mysteriously. There might be no bodies and no murder investigations, but I'm certain she's behind them. Demeter just takes more care to ensure her sins can't be as easily traced back to her than Aphrodite does. I lift my wineglass. "Fair enough. But that's not an answer."

He shrugs. "It started out easily enough. She wanted me to ruin the last Apollo. I think I was seventeen at the time."

Shock nearly has me dropping my glass. "That was *you?*"

"Yeah." He says it without any boastfulness or pride. Just a statement of fact. "I didn't set it up, exactly, but I went to school with Daphne." His eyes go dark. "She was in a bad situation, and she knew no one would believe her word against Apollo unless there was proof."

I wasn't in Olympus then, but I know the story well enough. The old Apollo pissed off Aphrodite for some reason, and the next thing anyone knew, pictures of him and an underage girl—Daphne—were released anonymously to all the gossip sites. With this new knowledge, I can see how carefully those photos were chosen. Just explicit enough that no one could argue what was going on, but Daphne was wearing lingerie. "Did those photos exist before that point?" Or did two teenagers conspire to stage them?

"Yeah." He doesn't look at me. "She got them off Apollo's phone once we decided on a course of action. It wasn't ideal, but it got him away from her and it made my mother happy to see Apollo punished."

Olympus has few lines, especially for the Thirteen, but Daphne is Artemis's cousin, and *that* prompted a firestorm the likes of which Olympus had never seen. She demanded his head, and when the old Zeus wasn't willing to go that far, Artemis stirred up Athena, Hephaestus, Poseidon, and, no surprise, Aphrodite. Against those five, even Zeus had to do something. He didn't kill Apollo, but he came together with the rest of the Thirteen and stripped Apollo of his title.

Two weeks later, his body was found in the River Styx. Common opinion is that Artemis is responsible, but any proof washed away in the water and his killer was never found. Not that anyone looked too hard for answers.

I stare at Eros. "You're the one who came up with the idea to release those photos?" At *seventeen?*

Another of those shrugs that means everything and nothing. "Like I said, it was the only way."

The only way to serve Aphrodite's punishment.

The only way to help Daphne escape her situation.

"But..."

He sighs. "But what?"

"How did you go from *helping* people like Daphne to killing them?"

"The same way you boil a frog." I blink, and he clarifies. "A little bit at a time. The first person I killed was a man threatening my mother." He stares at his fork like it holds all the mysteries of the universe. "In hindsight, he really was a threat. I think he was a past lover, but he ended up stalking her and it was escalating to the point where she was legitimately afraid. She and Ares don't get along, so he wouldn't provide security. So I stepped in."

I don't point out that Aphrodite is more than capable of hiring her own security. Eros is smart. He knows that. "How old were you?"

"Nineteen."

My heart aches for him, both now and the boy he used to be. "I'm sorry."

"Don't be." He shrugs, but it's too stiff to be convincing. "By the time I realized the people *threatening* my mother weren't actually threats, my soul was stained too much to go back. The only path was forward." I don't know what my face is doing, but he shakes his head. "Don't pity me, Psyche. I haven't lost a single bit of sleep over the things I've done, to innocent people or not. I am as much a monster as she is."

I know that. Truly, I do. But I can't help hating her even more for grooming her son to be her personal fixer. He says it started at seventeen, but I know better. To get him to the point where he was willing to step in on her behalf, she would have started much younger. "You are her child. It's still wrong to use you like this."

"This is Olympus. There's more wrong than there's right. It's the way things are."

I understand he's correct, but it doesn't stop the surge of

resentment. Neither of us chose our roles. He's done unforgivable things at his mother's request. He might have been a child when she started, but he's no longer one. He could have stopped any time.

He stopped for me.

I stomp down on that thought before it can take me off the rails. It's too tempting, too seductive. Eros already admitted that he had his own reasons for giving me the option of a marriage instead of death. Yes, he desires me, but that's not enough to go against his mother. It can't be.

Best not to think about it too hard.

I push my food around on my plate. He keeps working so hard to set us apart, to remind me that he's a terrible human being and I'm... I'm not even sure. Good? The thought is laughable. I've made hard choices since arriving at Olympus, and I've done things that were petty and selfish and downright mean.

More... I don't want Eros to feel like he stands apart. I haven't killed anyone, but that doesn't mean I'm some angel. "You might not number me among the monsters, but I'm not entirely blameless."

He smiles like he's indulging me. "Oh yeah?"

I rush forward before I can change my mind. "Remember when that story was published on MuseWatch with the audio of Ares ranting about all of Zeus's children being failures?"

The surprise on Eros's face makes the confession more than worth it. He sits back in his chair and grins, admiration lighting his blue eyes. "That was you? I'd wondered. I thought it might be Helen—it has her sort of flare—but she claimed up and down and sideways that she had nothing to do with it. That audio was singlehandedly responsible for driving a wedge through the Zeus-Ares alliance that they never quite recovered from."

I know. I wish I could say that was one of my goals when I put my plan together, but the truth is much less ambitious. "He wouldn't leave Eurydice alone. He'd chase her around Zeus's parties and corner her every chance he got. No one would step in, not even my mother. All she could talk about was how useful an alliance with Ares would be for our family." The words taste foul on my tongue. I love my mother, but she can be unforgivably single-minded at times. "A marriage with Ares would have killed Eurydice. Probably not literally, but the thing that makes her *her* would have withered up and died. She's not like the rest of my sisters; she's soft. I wanted to give her space to preserve that for as long as possible."

His expression sobers. "I don't know if you've done her any favors on that note."

Sadness weighs at me. "We're all beginning to realize that now." We all have to grow up and face the reality of Olympus eventually, and I can't help but wondering if we should have torn the veil from my youngest sister's eyes earlier. Maybe she wouldn't have fallen in love with Orpheus and had her heart torn asunder. Maybe she would have seen him for what he is—a fickle artist forever in search of his muse. She might have served that purpose for a time, but it was never going to be permanent. "We all have to learn that lesson eventually."

"Some earlier than others." Eros tilts his wineglass, watching the red liquid shift within its confines. "You never made a misstep."

I almost laugh. "I made plenty. Even with my mother's warnings, I thought for sure Olympus couldn't be as cruel as she claimed. I was wrong." So much to encompass those three little words. *I was wrong.*

Everyone was so incredibly *nice* at first. Oh, not the other children of the Thirteen—they gave me and my sisters a wide berth—but those a little further out from the seat of power. So nice. So friendly. So sickly sweet. At least until I heard my so-called *friends* discussing how disgusted they were with me, my body, my looks, my country bumpkin ways. They thought I would be more like Helen or Perseus or the other popular children of the Thirteen. I was a waste of time and space.

I stopped trying to make friends after that. It was the first time I realized my mother might have a point with how she dealt with people outside the family. No one was to be trusted. Instead, they fell into one of two categories—potential enemy or potential ally.

Lessons in this city always hurt, and the intervening years haven't done much to soothe that ache. I really, really hope this situation with Eros isn't another hard lesson that I'm destined to learn through pain.

EROS

IT'S COLD AS A WITCH'S TIT. I'M A CREATURE OF SUMMER. I prefer the hot, lazy days where the sun holds court in the sky well into the night, everyone moving around the city in as few clothes as possible, and air that doesn't hurt my face. Given a choice, I would have picked nearly any other activity than walking the outdoor gardens in the university district.

Still.

I can't help appreciating how damn *good* Psyche looks in her fleece-lined leggings, slouchy oversize knit sweater, boots, and an honest-to-gods puffed jacket. Add in a knitted hat to match the sweater and she's downright fucking adorable. It makes me want to drag her back to my place—our place—and strip her out of that clothing, layer by layer.

She leans against my arm and smiles up at me as if I'm her favorite person in the world, and for a moment, I forget that this is pretend.

A click of a camera somewhere nearby reminds me.

I give her a warm smile of my own, and it's all too easy to convince myself that her rosy cheeks are in reaction to me, rather than the icy air. "Couldn't we have found somewhere warmer to show off how giddy in love we are?"

Her smile doesn't falter in the least. She leans into me and matches my low tone. "It's easier to pretend that we don't realize we're being followed outside." Psyche laughs a little. "Besides, I like the gardens in the winter."

I look around us. Some past Athena decided the university district really needed a giant, sprawling outdoor garden for students and professors to spend time in. There's a large greenhouse on the other side of the park, but Psyche seems intent on walking every path except the one that will lead us there. "I don't get it. There's nothing to see. Everything's dead."

"Eros." She smacks my arm lightly with her free hand. "That's very glass half-full of you. The garden isn't dead. It's sleeping."

I eye what appear to be bare sticks situated on the left side of the cobblestone path. "Looks dead to me."

"For someone who deals death on occasion, one would think you'd be better able to identify it." She says it so casually, as if she doesn't recognize the barbs attached to each word.

I'm a killer, and she needs to remember it. "Psyche."

"It's a reminder." She's not looking at me. She's studying the sticks as if they hold the secrets of the universe. "Nothing lasts forever. Not the hibernation over the winter, but not the beautiful blooms of summer, either. There are seasons to everything."

It doesn't require much to understand she's not talking about the garden at all. She's talking about herself. I slip my arm around her waist, tucking her in against my side. We might be pretending for the barely concealed paparazzi shadowing us, but the truth is that I like touching her. As much as I'd like to stay in the safety of our penthouse and keep working to seduce her out of her pants again, I'm not about to miss this opportunity to dig deeper into the enigma that is Psyche. "Your sisters all seem to have some kind of endgame when it comes to Olympus."

"Do they?"

We turn almost as one and continue wandering down the path, deeper into the *sleeping* garden. "Callisto would burn the city to the ground if no one stopped her. Hard lessons or no, Eurydice wants love. I thought Persephone would flee Olympus."

"Circumstances changed."

Circumstances. A strange way to say that Demeter essentially sold Persephone into a marriage with the old Zeus, sending her daughter fleeing over the River Styx and into Hades's arms. The tightness in Psyche's voice deters me from saying as much, though. That's fine. I don't really want to talk about her sisters. I want to talk about her. "You're the one I've never been able to figure out."

"Am I?"

I give her a little squeeze. "You damn well know you are. If I didn't know better, I'd say you were Demeter 2.0. You go about things in a very different way than your mother does, but the cunning and careful image manipulation is the same." She tenses, but I don't let her go. "That wasn't criticism. It's foolish to think honesty will get you anything but a knife in the back when you're dealing with the Thirteen and their inner circles."

"Maybe I'm exactly what I look like." A little bitterness seeps into her voice. "A socialite influencer on the prowl for a rich and powerful husband. Maybe you've played right into *my* hands."

I laugh. I can't help it. "If that's the truth, you're an even better actress than I expected."

"Thank you." She turns in my arms, still smiling at me as if I hold her heart in my hands. "Time for a photo op, Husband."

Husband.

Oh, I like that. I like that far too much.

I clasp her hips, bringing her as close to me as we can get with all the layers of clothing between us. Our exhales ghost the air between us, but for the first time since we got out of the car, I don't feel the cold. How can I when Psyche is so close?

There's no artifice in how eagerly I take her mouth. I'm not pretending to want her. She might be a damn good actress, but her little shiver and the way she melts against me aren't pretend, either. I know what she sounds like, feels like, looks like when she comes now. She's not faking her desire any more than I am.

She laces her arms around my neck and drifts her fingers over the sensitive spot at the nape of my neck even as she opens her mouth and lets me in. Psyche tastes like the fireball candy she had in the car, cinnamon and spice and too sexy by half. I lose myself in the stroke of her tongue against mine, in the way she fits against me so perfectly.

She's the one to break the kiss, leaning back just enough to let loose a surprisingly happy giggle. "Gods, Eros. You can't kiss me like that in public. You're going to get us in trouble."

True? Not true?

I can't be sure. Not when I'm half a second from dragging her into the greenhouse and finding a private corner to make her come a time or three. But no, I can't do that. We have observers, and the paparazzi in Olympus are relentless. No matter how giddy we're supposed to be right now, I'm not about to let photos of me with my hand down Psyche's leggings go public.

I press my forehead to hers, trying to get my body back under control. "*I'm* going to get us in trouble?"

"Yes." Her smile softens a little. "Obviously I'm an innocent bystander."

That's the thing. She's not entirely wrong. I don't normally waste time with guilt, but that must be the strange stabbing feeling in my side, like someone slipped a dagger between my ribs. Psyche had a plan of her own before my mother decided to punish her, pushed over the edge by a simple act of kindness Psyche showed *me*. I was never part of her plan. If I'm enjoying the perks of this hastily put-together marriage—and I am—it doesn't change the fact that it's not *her* plan.

"I'm sorry." I don't mean to say the words, but I *do* mean them. Possibly for the first time ever. "For all of it."

"You know, I almost believe you." She laces her arm through mine and turns us down the path. "It's a moot point now, regard-less. We're going to make the best of this situation."

We walk for a few minutes in silence. It's comfortable enough, and one glance at Psyche's face makes me think she's lost in thought and far from here. I don't mind. I doubt she realizes the significance, but I do.

She trusts me.

I let the knowledge roll over me, buoy me. I've done little to earn this woman's trust. Yes, I didn't kill her, but that's the literal bare minimum a person should do—and I can't even pretend I made that decision out of the goodness of my soul. It was just as selfish as everything else I've done. I wanted her, and this shitty situation provided me a way to take her.

All because she showed me the tiniest hint of kindness.

I might laugh if my chest wasn't so fucking tight. It's pathetic that I'm so starved for any kind of softer emotion that the second someone comes to me with gentle hands instead of sharp words, I'm willing to walk to the Underworld and back to keep them in my life.

If it was just that first night, maybe I could have resisted my darker impulses to bundle Psyche up and haul her back to my home like a dragon with his hoard, but then she showed up for that meeting intending to help me again. How could I let my mother snuff out such a compelling light?

I don't deserve Psyche's trust. With anyone else, it would just be a tool to leverage against them if the situation ever arose. With this woman?

I want to earn it.

Maybe a good way to start would to be to offer up some of my own in return.

The next time the path branches, I turn us back toward my car. "Let's go warm up and have a drink."

"I was thinking—"

It's more challenging than I would have guessed to cut in. "I'd like to take you somewhere."

She blinks. "Oh. Okay."

No reason for the flutter of nerves in my stomach. It's not like my regular spots are secrets, but I've never really wanted to share them with someone else before. In Olympus, I will always be recognized as Aphrodite's sharpest weapon. But in a few rare places, they see me as Eros. Just...Eros.

Even realizing that Psyche will always see the danger in me first, part of me wants her to see the rest. The man, fucked up though he is. She makes me feel...human...in a way I haven't in a very long time. Maybe ever.

I want her to see me as just Eros, too. Even if the idea terrifies me on a level I'm not prepared to deal with. How could she not turn away if she sees past the untouchable persona to the rough reality beneath? The broken bits I keep tucked away, lest they be used against me?

When we make it back to my car, I open the door for her and round to the driver's side. There are three photographers approaching, and they're no longer trying to pretend they're anything but paparazzi. They rush forward, and I'm a petty asshole, because I nearly take two of them out when I pull away from the curb.

Psyche snorts. "If we could avoid getting arrested, that would be ideal."

"If I was nice to them, they'd know something was up."

Her hazel eyes light up with mischief. "Gods forbid."

"Now you're getting the idea." I weave through the streets, heading south to the theater district. It's a few blocks that contain a trio of theaters that do a handful of productions each season. I can take or leave live performances, but actors in Olympus have a way of not giving a fuck that's difficult to find on this side of the river. The only thing they care about is *their* power hierarchy, and as long as Athena and Apollo keep them paid well, they don't bother with the rest of the Thirteen.

My mother, in particular, isn't overly fond of this area. She likes the theater well enough and dragged me to countless productions over the years in an effort to instill me with *culture*, but that began and ended with the shows themselves. She never lingers, and as such, this area has always been something of a refuge for me. I never have to worry about running into her when I'm here. I pull into the tiny parking lot behind the Bacchae and turn off the engine.

Psyche peers out the window. "Interesting choice."

"Have you ever been here before?"

She shakes her head. "I have season tickets to the theater, but we normally get drinks closer to home afterward." The Dimitriou women alternate their time out between their mother's neighborhood and the blocks around Dodona Tower, so it makes sense they would choose places more familiar to drink at.

I climb out of the car, but this time she doesn't wait for me to open her door before she joins me. There's still a little line between her dark brows. "I don't think the press spend much time here."

"They don't." I take her hand. "But the theater people are notorious gossips and so they'll do the work for us."

Her eyes light up. "I see. Clever."

"I live to please." We walk around the building and I purposefully slow down, watching Psyche as she takes in the outside of the Bacchae. Here in the theater district, they don't prize a pristine look the same way so much of the upper city do. They prefer *character* and the Bacchae has it in spades. The weathered exterior looks like it's stood here for time unknown, but the building is only twenty years old, and it had this faded paint job from the start.

I hold the door open for Psyche and follow her into the heat of the bar. She shrugs off her coat immediately, and after doing the same, I press my hand to the small of her back and guide her through the crowded tables to the small booth in the back corner. I'm glad it's open, because it's got the best seat in the house to appreciate everything the Bacchae has to offer.

She allows me to usher her into the booth and follow her in, her wide-eyed gaze on the wall. "Wow."

"The owner is something of a collector." I sit back and watch Psyche take in the objects crowding the walls. Glossy new posters of current productions sit side by side with ones faded from decades ago. A narrow ledge circles the room with glass cases filled with props and clothing, each painstakingly labeled with their production and year. The faint sounds of some musical soundtrack I'm not familiar with play in the background.

I should keep quiet and let her process, but I can't help speaking. "It's plenty busy now, but you should see it after the evening shows. The actors and actresses and stage crew come in, half of them still in some kind of stage makeup, and things get wild. The energy they bring is unlike anything I've ever seen. The shows are fine, I guess, but seeing the aftermath is a little like magic."

She finally drags her gaze away from a particularly intricate white gown and looks at me. "I'd like to come here sometime and see that."

"We will." It's a small promise, easily provided, but it doesn't change the fact that it *feels* profound.

"This place is important to you."

Of course she'd pick up on that immediately. She's too smart not to read between the lines, and I intentionally picked this place so I could share it with her. I tug her hat off and drop it on our pile of coats on the other side of the booth. Her hair is a little frizzy, but I like it. "Yes, it's important to me."

"Thank you for bringing me here." She smiles a little and smooths her hair down. "Thank you for sharing this with me."

My chest feels too tight, but I can't look away from her happy smile. "You shared the gardens with me. They mean something to you, right? A refuge of sorts."

"I don't know if I'd call it a refuge..." She sighs. "No, that's a lie. Sorry, habit." Psyche shakes her head, looking rueful. "Yes, the gardens are special to me. It's not a secret that I go there from time to time, but the reason I do is because it reminds me a little bit of life before moving to the city. It's nothing like the farm, of course, but growing things soothe me."

The sensation in my chest gets more intense, until I can barely breathe past it. "That's what this place is to me, too. No one here cares who I am or who my mother is. It lets me relax as much as anyone can relax in Olympus."

Psyche starts to say something, but she's interrupted when the bartender, a tall Latina whose dark hair is threaded with silver, heads in our direction with a smile. "What can I get you?"

I order my favorite red wine and Psyche asks for bourbon. She catches my raised eyebrows and blushes. "It's the perfect winter drink."

"I'm not arguing that." I know better than to make assumptions based on drink orders, but I can't help the surprise. From what I've seen, Psyche doesn't seem to party, but when she *does* drink, it's a very specific type of cocktail. "You don't normally drink bourbon."

"Correction: I don't normally drink bourbon in public." She gives a slightly bittersweet smile. "It's part of the image thing. Public Psyche likes fruity drinks and wine, depending on the time of day."

I shake my head. "The amount of thought you've put into your public image is staggering. I mean that as a compliment."

"Thank you." She shrugs. "It was necessary. You, of all people, understand just how effective armor a good public persona can be."

"Yeah." I stare out at the room. Instinct tells me to leave it at that, but I push past it. I didn't bring her here to shut her out now. "When they hate you, it's easier to pretend they hate the public version of you instead."

"Yes, exactly."

I glance at her. "You're willing to let that persona slip a bit with me?"

"It's a special occasion." She smiles slowly. "And I make a tidy sum on sponsorships from several wine companies. It can't hurt adding some whiskey sponsorships to the mix if and when we get photographed here."

She's intentionally navigating us back to safer territory. I appreciate it. The ground's feeling pretty fucking liquid beneath my feet right now. I search for something to say that won't toss us off the deep end again. "The wine sponsorships aren't the only ones you have."

Her smile widens. "No, they're not."

Likely another reason my mother zeroed in on Psyche. She's so damn successful at what she does, even more successful than Aphrodite. And Psyche doesn't have a team of people who're paid solely to make her look good.

The bartender arrives with our drinks and leaves an appetizer menu before departing again, making the rounds to the handful of occupied tables. There are two groups of people, and they're trying very hard to pretend like they're not watching us closely, but they keep putting their heads together and whispering while shooting furtive looks in our direction. No doubt pictures of us will be gracing their social media before too long.

I watch Psyche sip her bourbon and shiver, the color in her cheeks deepening. An answering heat pulses through me. "Bourbon looks good on you."

"Eros." She leans into me, her expression happy even as her words are dry. "You really don't have to say things like that. No one can hear you."

I dip my head until my lips nearly touch her ear. "I'm not saying them because I care about who's listening. I'm saying them because they're true."

"Eros, please."

I lean back enough to meet her eyes. The conversation from this morning plays through my head. We were both more than a little out of control, both more than a little skittish about how intense things have gotten so quickly. The smart play would be to slow down, to give each other space to shore up our defenses.

Fuck that. "Have you ever been seduced, Psyche? Truly seduced?"

She licks her lips. "Depends on your qualifications."

"That's a no."

She makes a face. "Fine. No."

I give her a slow smile, enjoying the way she shivers in response. "You're about to be."

PSYCHE

EROS IS DANGEROUS IN A THOUSAND DIFFERENT WAYS, BUT never more so than when he smiles at me like he is now. Like we're sharing secrets, like we're sharing *intimacy*. It's difficult to remind myself that it's all pretend. Yes, the desire between us is real, but that's just another tool to sell the story. It's a side effect, not the main goal.

Have I ever been seduced?

I want to laugh in his face. Olympus would happily strike me down if I let myself be seduced in anything but secret. The rest of the world might have moved on from archaic views of a woman's worth being linked to virginity, but Olympus hasn't. At least not in the upper city. After my first disastrous dating experience, all the rest were done in secret. A mutually assured destruction, at least with my femme partners. When you're spending so much time sneaking around to see each other, there's not much room for seduction.

The thought of allowing Eros to seduce me feels a little like what it must be like to jump out of a plane. It might end with a soft touching down...or a devastating embrace from gravity. I can't risk it.

I take too large a sip of my bourbon and have to twist away from Eros to cough as fire lances my throat and lungs. "Oh gods."

"They have nothing to do with it." His voice maintains that lower tone, the same one he uses when he's inside me. "Psyche, look at me."

Something uncomfortably like desperation lashes me. I grab on to the first subject that I can think of, one sure to distract me from the spell this man weaves around me with his very presence. "I'm surprised your mother hasn't made her first move yet."

His smile doesn't dim, but the heat disappears from his eyes. He winds a strand of my hair around his finger, keeping his head close to mine. "I'll see what I can find out tonight after we get home. There's no way she hasn't put something in motion; we just haven't seen evidence of it yet."

Home.

Now that's a terrifying thought. My mother's place has always been home to me. When I agreed to this marriage, it never occurred to me that I might start to consider Eros's penthouse home, too. Let alone that it would begin to happen so quickly.

Focus on anything but that. "You must have some theories about her plans. You've helped her with this kind of thing before." I need to remind myself why I must not, under any circumstances, fall for this man. No matter how much I enjoy what we do in bed. No matter how much I'm starting to appreciate his dry sense of humor and wit. No matter how drawn I am to the hints of vulnerability he shows me at the most unexpected of times. If anything, those traits just make him more of a threat, because I'm in danger of forgetting the path we took to get to this place.

He sighs. "I suspect she'll try to pry you out of my life first. There will be some kind of rumors to undermine the love story we're weaving, to suggest that you are in it for ulterior motives. Which, of course, makes me look like a fool, but I expect she's furious enough that she doesn't care." I don't know what expression my face makes, but he sighs again and elaborates. "She might be a temperamental monster, but she's smart. She knows I wouldn't have gone to these lengths unless I wanted to...unless I wanted *you*. She'll try to poison our relationship first so that I'll toss you out of my own volition. My mother doesn't have much of a heart, but in the tiny sliver that still exists, she does care about me."

Are you sure?

I don't voice the question. It's needlessly cruel, and he's already experienced enough of that without me adding to it. A parent who cares for their child doesn't use them as a fixer. Eros didn't magically come by his expertise; someone had to teach him. I would bet a significant amount of money that Aphrodite facilitated that. I don't know how early it started, but if he was ruining lives for her at seventeen, it began when he was young. While he was still impressionable and under her care. What kind of parent nurtures their ambition more than their child's mental and emotional well-being?

I have my answer, don't I?

The kind of parent Aphrodite is.

Probing into Eros's childhood to dismantle what little faith he has in his mother isn't on my agenda. It won't change anything about our current situation...and I can't shake the suspicion that it will hurt him. Instead, I focus on a different angle. "I have my own money. What other reason could I have for seducing sweet, innocent you into marrying me?"

"Revenge is the easiest to believe, even easier if word slips out that *your* mother commanded it."

"The powerful Demeter sending her daughter to climb into bed with the enemy's son in order to hurt Aphrodite." It's a reach, but if the story is compelling enough, Aphrodite might be onto something. In theory. I lift my brows. "Who is going to believe that *you*, playboy darling of Olympus, became so enamored with *me* that you threw caution to the wind and put a ring on my finger?" I know my strengths, but Olympus is all about the shiny surface. They'll see what they want to see, especially if it reinforces their beliefs of what power and beauty look like.

He catches my chin in a light grip, tilting my face up to meet his. "I don't know, Psyche. I'm feeling pretty fucking enamored right now."

Real?

Fake?

I can't tell, and that scares me. Almost as much as my desire for it to be real scares me. "You're doing a grand job of selling our romance," I finally manage.

He strokes his thumb over my cheekbone. "I gave you my word. No one will harm you while you're mine. Not even your reputation."

Silly to focus on that qualification. Didn't I just tell him this morning that I belong to no one but myself? "I'm not yours."

"That ring on your finger says otherwise."

I'd almost forgotten about the ring. No, that's a lie. I've felt its presence as if it weighs much more than it possibly could. Every time it shifts against my skin, every time the diamond catches the light, I'm reminded of what we've done.

The ring has nothing on Eros's gorgeous face. I can't look away from him. "By that logic, the ring on *your* finger makes you mine."

"Yes." He sounds far too satisfied with that. "I'm yours, Psyche. What will you do with me?"

The smart response would be to shut his question down. To remind him that we are not, in fact, jumping back into bed together at the first available opportunity. That this marriage is solely because my life is on the line and not for any other reason. It's difficult to remember that here, in the intimacy of this booth, in a little bar that Eros took me to because he likes this place. Because he feels safe here. "Do you bring all your lovers here?" I throw the words like a javelin, desperate to put some kind of space between us, even if it's emotional.

He doesn't move back. "I don't bring anyone here. Not like that. Sometimes Helen or Hermes will come drink with me, and Perseus used to tag along when we were younger, but like I said before, this is a..." Eros finally looks away, surveying the room with a strange expression on his face. "This is a safe space. As safe as one can get in Olympus."

I follow his gaze, guilt closing clammy hands around my throat. I catch sight of three separate phones pointed in our direction. "I'm sorry."

"Why?"

"I've never seen you photographed here and now you are, and it's because you're with me."

His lips curve a little. "I knew that would happen when I chose this place. There's nothing to apologize for."

Instead of abating, my guilt only gets stronger. "Surely you don't have so many safe places in this city that you can afford to lose one."

His small smile disappears. He searches my face. "Are you worried? About *me*?"

"Yes." I can't look away, can't break the growing intimacy of this moment. I thought I knew what was happening here, but now I'm not so sure. "I know how exhausting it can be to never let down your guard, and it's a really special place that allows it outside your home. You shouldn't have sacrificed that. Not for this. Not for me."

He cups my jaw and drags his thumb over my cheekbone. "You really *are* worried about me."

I don't understand why he's *not*. I can count on one hand how many public spaces are safe for me to be my true self at—and still have most of my fingers left over. Losing one would be devastating on a number of levels. "I'm sorry. If I'd realized—"

"Psyche." He shifts his hand to the spot where my neck meets my shoulder. It's a light touch but possessive all the same. "Being here doesn't burn this bridge for me. You have nothing to feel guilty over."

How can he not understand the implications? I wet my lips, trying to think of how to explain it. "The second those pictures go

live, you'll give the upper city something it loves above all else—
novelty. People will flock to this bar, most of them hoping to get a
chance to interact with you or your inner circle. It will become the
new hot spot, which means it will change the fundamental nature
of this place." I'd seen it happen before. I'd been the *cause* of it
happening before.

He shrugs. "It won't last forever, and it will give the Bacchae
a boost in income for the duration. In a few months, once they
realize I don't sit in this booth like a tiger in a cage, they'll move on
to the next big thing." He leans closer, still looking at me like I've
amused him. "That timeline will compress if we're seen frequent-
ing some other place."

"But…"

"The next time we're here after that, no one will pay us any
attention." He anticipates my argument. "I'm not the only one who
views this place as a safe space. The actors and crews won't like all
the people effectively playing tourist, and they won't share photos
again. If anything, doing this makes it safer in the long run."

I let the logic wash over me, let it reassure me. It actually makes
a lot of sense when he puts it that way. Slowly, oh so slowly, the
guilt fades. "I see."

"I like that you're worried about me."

I'm in trouble. If I didn't care about this man, I wouldn't care
that one of his safe spaces was compromised. He's supposed to
be the enemy, so it should be a *good* thing, not something to feel
guilt over. I start to retreat, but he tightens his grip on me ever so
slightly. I swallow hard, trying to tell myself that the fluttering of
my pulse is fear, but I know the truth. It's desire. Gods, everything

Eros does seems to ramp up my desire for him. Of course this would, too.

I lick my lips, achingly aware of how he follows the movement. I have to put distance between us, and I have to do it now. If he won't allow me to do it physically, then I have to use my words. "I'm not worried about you. I don't care about you at all."

"Liar." He leans down until his lips brush against mine. "Now give your new husband a proper kiss. Since you don't care about me at all, it shouldn't be a problem to keep control of yourself."

Oh, you bastard.

The challenge roars through me, drowning out the little voice whispering that this idea is even more ill-advised than marrying Eros in the first place. I grip his shirt and pull him the rest of the way to me, sealing our lips together. There's no easing into it, no light brushing of his mouth to mine. The kiss is a battleground. He seeks to conquer, and I refuse to bend. Give and take and take and take. The sounds of the room fade beneath the buzzing in my body. The room itself seems to disappear. There's only Eros and the taste of wine on his tongue and the feel of his body pressed against mine. Not enough. Not nearly enough.

A throat clearing has me jerking back. From the heat of my face, I must be crimson, but the flustered desire drains away when I realize who's standing over our table.

Aphrodite.

She looks just as flawless as she always does, her sleek blond hair falling in a perfect wave around her shoulders, her makeup understated but expert. She smiles at us, a curving of her crimson lips that doesn't reach her blue eyes. Funny how I never realized how similar Eros's cold eyes are to hers. The only difference is that Aphrodite's never warm.

What is she doing *here*?

And why come herself? She can hardly play the innocent party if she's going to show up and make a production of things.

Eros shifts back from me, and I get the strangest feeling that he's freeing up himself to move if he needs to. He does, however, take my hand, lacing his fingers through mine beneath the table. "Mother."

"Son." Her smile widens, a predator scenting prey. "You've been avoiding my calls."

"I got married yesterday. I think I can be forgiven. You, of all people, know how a wedding can take over a person's life."

"Hmmm." She leans forward and runs a critical eye over me. "I really don't understand why you chose *her*. Literally any of the other Dimitriou daughters would be better, even the feral one. She's..." She laughs, low and throaty. "Well, look at her."

The insult slides right off me. I've been dealing with variations of it since we first arrived in Olympus. I don't fit into their narrow definition of what acceptable beauty is, and there are plenty among the Thirteen's inner circles who aim for the low-hanging fruit of attacking my size whenever we interact. I can count the people whose opinions I actually care about on one hand, and Aphrodite sure as fuck doesn't number among them.

Eros, however, tenses and his tone goes positively frigid. "It's time for you to leave, Mother."

"Not until I've had my say." She picks up his wineglass and takes an idle sip.

A laugh slips free despite my best efforts. She really is

unimaginative, isn't she? When she frowns at me, I feel compelled to explain, if only to see the look on her face. "Why not lift your skirt and pee on his foot? It will accomplish the same thing."

"Crude thing, aren't you?"

"I prefer honest."

"I *honestly* don't care what you prefer." She sets down the glass with a clink, which is right about the moment I realize we have the undivided attention of everyone in the room. Wonderful.

I keep my smile in place, though it's a challenge. I don't want to smile at this woman. I want to throw my bourbon in her face and light a match. The sheer force of my violent thoughts nearly derails my concentration. I'm not one to let emotions get the best of me, but I've also never sat across the table from a person who wants my literal heart on a platter.

The blood would match her lipstick.

Aphrodite looks at Eros, who's still so tense, it's as if he's carved from stone. She sighs. "I suppose every child must have a rebellious stage. You've simply come to yours late."

"Don't."

She ignores him. "On occasion, it's a mother's role to save their children from themselves." Aphrodite smooths down her dress. "I've been cleaning up Eros's messes since he was a child. This is no different."

Eros's messes. As if he decided to wade into the muck of his own free will, rather than being shoved there by the one person in this godsdamned city who should have been protecting him. Now she'll do it again and pretend she's doing him a favor, rather than pursuing her own selfish agenda.

Fury unlike any I've ever known rages through me. "Aphrodite." I don't raise my voice, but I don't have to. She stops and looks back at me. I don't make her wait long. "It's a mistake to ignore your son's wishes. Attempting to ruin my reputation will splatter his as well."

"Don't make threats that you can't follow through on, little girl. You're swimming with the big fish now." Her smile widens. "You should be worrying about more than my son's *reputation*. A widower inspires all sorts of sympathy, especially if he was taken in by a little upstart slut."

A widower.

My mask slips. "But we're married."

"I don't see what that has to do with anything." She looks between us and bursts out laughing. "Oh, you sweet, simple children. Did you really think that farce of a ceremony would be enough to change your fate? It's barely a speed bump. Enjoy my son while you can, Psyche. This mistake will be rectified soon." She turns and strides out of the bar, every eye following her.

Fuck.

Eros exhales slowly. "Gods*damn* it." He tenses. "We need to get out of here. Right now."

I keep my smile in place because we're back to being the center of everyone's attention. "We can't leave yet."

"Psyche."

"We are a happy couple." I speak slowly, still smiling. "Your mother might not approve, but she's not the one we're trying to win over."

"*Win over?* Who gives a fuck about winning anyone over? She just said—" He takes a breath, and then another. After a small eternity, when I'm sure I've lost him, his shoulders relax and he slouches back against the booth next to me. I don't breathe a sigh of relief, but it's a close thing. Eros lifts our interlaced fingers to kiss my knuckles. "I'll keep you safe," he murmurs against my skin.

Gods help me, but I almost believe it. I thought I felt fear sitting across from Eros in that seedy little bar while he casually threatened me. It's nothing like I feel now. Aphrodite won't stop. Maybe I am the sweet, simple child she accused me of being because I am legitimately shocked. I was prepared to step to the line and battle for my reputation.

I didn't think she'd continue with her plan to *kill* me.

"The marriage was supposed to change things."

"I thought it would." The words are low and tight. "I thought it would be enough to deter her. It doesn't matter. We'll find a way forward. You have *me* now, and I'll be damned before I let anyone lay a finger on you."

I want to believe him. I want to so desperately, it makes me shake. Because of that desperation, I force myself to say, "You never told me what you get out of this." When he just looks at me, I make a vague motion with my free hand. "The wedding, the deception."

"I would think it's obvious." He brushes his lips to my knuckles again. "I get *you*."

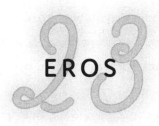

EROS

WE HAVE ANOTHER ROUND OF DRINKS BEFORE I PAY OUR tab and take Psyche home. She doesn't let her public persona slip once, but I can see the strain around the edges. All because of my mother. I knew she would try something eventually, but even I didn't expect *this*. She still intends to go through with the original plan. I don't know if me marrying Psyche was what pushed her too far, but there will be no talking her down from this ledge. She means to throw herself over it and drag us down in the process.

Psyche doesn't speak until we close the door of the penthouse behind us. "I thought the marriage would work."

"I did, too."

"Did you?" She hardly sounds like herself. "Or was this all part of the plan? Threaten me, humiliate my mother by marrying me, and then kill me?"

That stops me short. "You don't believe that."

"I don't know *what* to believe." Psyche drags her hands through her hair. "But I suppose you're right. If you intended to become a widower, Aphrodite would have no reason to ambush us." She glances at me, her expression softening. "Sorry. I'm so wrapped up in my head, I didn't ask how you're holding up."

My throat goes a little tight, but I breathe past it. "Don't worry about me. I'm not the one being threatened right now."

"Your mother just steamrolled right over you as if you were a child. That can't feel good."

It doesn't. It really fucking doesn't. But then, I have no illusions about the role I play in my mother's life. Always in support of her ambitions, her needs, her whims. She might tolerate my occasional pushing back, but I am a tool for her to pick up and use at her leisure.

I sigh. "My mother is a simple creature when it boils down to it. She lavishes praise and rewards on me when I do exactly what she wants, and she punishes me when I step out of line. I went against her will when I married you, so punishment it is." On the surface, I suppose that's how most people parent. I honestly have no idea. It just feels so fucking insidious with my mother.

"Eros, that's terrible."

I let her concern wash over me. It feels good, far better than I deserve. "Don't worry about me, Psyche. We'll find a way through this."

For a moment, I think she'll keep arguing, keep digging, but she finally nods. "We need to talk about next steps."

"Not yet." I take her hand. I enjoy touching her so much, and not even in a way that's confined to sex. It still feels a little baffling that I can do it whenever I want. This casual intimacy might be a small thing, but it's an experience I've never had before. More, touching her calms me in a way I'm not prepared to deal with. "I want to show you something."

"Eros." She gives an exasperated sigh. "I don't think showing me your dick right now will solve any of our problems."

"Ha-ha, very funny." I lead her to the locked door across from my safe room and pull her to stand before me. "Pay very close attention and memorize this." I type out the code slowly. "Repeat it back to me."

Psyche does, flawlessly. "What is this?"

Instead of answering with words, I push the door open and nudge her in ahead of me. I don't let her get far before I turn her back to the door. "This is reinforced. It can take machine-gun fire without punching through, at least long enough for Ares's people to show up. The walls are the same."

Her eyes go wide. "That's a lot of reinforcement."

"It's a safe room. If you're home alone for some reason and get spooked, come here. I keep several burner phones charged, so you can call out for help." I motion to the bright-red box near the door. "This will call Ares's forces."

If anything, her eyes get wider. "Not the police?"

"The police are for civilians." It stands to reason that she'd default to the police in a situation like this, though. The current Ares and Demeter don't get along, so of course she won't trust his private military with the safety of her family, even if that's their official role. Most of the Thirteen have some sort of private security they contract for themselves and their families, but we can't trust Aphrodite's people for obvious reason. No, it has to be Ares.

She gives herself a little shake. "I suppose that's fair." Psyche turns and looks at the trio of monitors set up around my chair, at the filing cabinets. "This isn't just a safe room."

"No, it's not just a safe room."

She glances at me. "You're putting an undeserved amount of faith in me by giving me access to all this."

I shrug with a nonchalance I don't feel. "I promised that I'd keep you safe. That promise extends to when you're not in my presence. This is one of the safest spots this side of the River Styx. Not even Hermes can get inside."

She looks at the room with new appreciation. "That *is* safe. I swear that woman is half ghost and can sift through the vents."

"Nothing so exciting. She's just an excellent thief and hacker." She was long before she became Hermes, but that part isn't known publicly. In fact, not much at all is known publicly about her. She prefers it that way.

"You talk like she's a friend."

"She...is. Or as near to it as one gets in this city."

Psyche's smile is bittersweet. "Olympus continues to be quite the qualifier."

"It's home."

"Yes, I suppose it is." She presses her lips together as if not sure what to say. "Thank you for showing me this. I promise to try not to abuse it."

That draws a laugh from me. "I appreciate your attempt at restraint." We go back into the hall and I have her input the code enough times that I'm sure she can do it under duress. We'll do this in a couple of days to be sure, but it's the bare minimum I can accomplish right now. It does little to combat how loose around the edges I feel at the thought of my mother's knife pointed in Psyche's direction. I promised that this marriage would change things, and in the end, it's changed nothing.

Aphrodite has made a liar out of me.

We end up taking the time to change into more comfortable clothing before retreating to the living room to talk strategy. As much as I don't want Psyche's idea of "organization" spilling all over the master bedroom, part of me intensely dislikes the way we have separate closets. I don't know what the fuck that's about. As she pointed out before, plenty of couples have separate *rooms*, and we have hardly anything resembling a traditional relationship.

Still.

Psyche sits on the other side of the couch, and I allow that space, but I reach down and grab her feet, lifting them to perch on my thigh. Her frown morphs into surprise as I take one foot and begin to massage it. "Oh gods, what are you doing?"

"Those heeled boots were sexy, but they look uncomfortable."

"They *are* uncomfortable, but that's the life of an influencer." She melts down against the couch until she's almost prone. "I can't think when you're doing that."

I dig my thumb into her arch, causing her to emit a damn-near-sexual moan. "Sure you can. We need to come up with a new plan."

She makes another little whimpering sound and rallies. "Pause."

I go still. "What? Pause? What are you talking about?"

"Just...pause." She pulls out her phone with a look of utter concentration on her face. "Can you tilt your head a little to the left so you catch the light? Yes, like that."

Bemused, I allow her to arrange me like a human-sized doll and snap a picture. She turns her phone to me without me asking her to show me. It's…really good. I look relaxed and happy, lounging on the couch with my wife's feet in my lap. "You're really good at this."

"I've been doing it long enough; I kind of have to be." She starts typing on her phone.

I won't have her full attention until she posts the picture, so I settle in to wait. It doesn't take her long. She sighs and sets her phone aside, giving me her full attention. "The plan—"

"I didn't mean about the social-influencer thing, though you are good at that. I meant the pictures. Do you ever use an actual camera?"

"Not really." Psyche shrugs. "I mean, there are photo shoots and stuff, but you can accomplish a lot with a camera phone these days. Besides, it's kind of a fun challenge to get the photos I want with just the phone."

"Consider me impressed." And I am. It seems like all I bring to this world is ugliness. Death and pain. It's never really bothered me before. Olympus might look gorgeous on the surface, but the pretty is only skin deep. Once you dig a little, all you find is rot.

Though that rule doesn't seem to apply to the woman with her feet in my lap. Psyche brings some beauty and positivity to the space she occupies. All her photo captions are uplifting, even the ones where she's admitting struggle. I thought it was a crock of shit when she first started making waves in Olympus, but the longer I'm with her, the more I realize how fucking genuine she is. Oh, she has her mask and she lies as well as I do, but that thread of kindness, that desire to bring light into the world instead of darkness? That's real.

"Eros." She says my name warmly, almost indulgently.

"Sorry, what were you saying?"

Psyche shakes her head. "Please focus. This is important."

She's right. I can't afford to get distracted, even by *her*. Really, focusing on anything but this conversation is an avoidance tactic. Now that my plan to keep Psyche safe—to keep her with me—has been proven a failure, there's really only one answer. "I can get you out of Olympus."

She goes still. "That's nearly impossible."

"It depends on who you know. Poseidon is a stickler for the rules, but not all his people are. With a hefty enough bribe, Triton will smuggle people out. If you leave Olympus, you'll be safe from my mother."

Psyche stares at me for a long moment. "But you won't be. If you think I should leave Olympus, then you should, too."

"My mother doesn't want to kill *me*." I should leave it at that, but I've trusted this woman with little bits and pieces of me already. What's one more? "Exile has been Aphrodite's punishment of choice more than once in the past, and I've been the person who enacted it. Those people would love a chance to get revenge. If I leave the city with you, it will just paint a different kind of target on your back, and I won't have the resources to even attempt to protect you like I can here." Not enough. No matter how hard I try, I'm never fucking enough. I can't keep Psyche safe without sending her away. I'm the reason she's in this messed-up situation to begin with.

"No."

I blink. "What?"

She looks as resolute as I've ever seen her. "No, I am not fleeing Olympus. My life is here. My *family* is here. I'm not letting that bitch—even if she is your mother—run me out of town. I'm not going anywhere."

"Damn it." I drag in a breath. "I will do everything in my power to protect you, but I might fail. I'm far better at killing than I am at playing bodyguard." I've never had to do the latter before, and never when the stakes were so high. "Money isn't an issue. We could get you set up. You wouldn't be able to see your family, but at least you'd be alive."

"Eros." She says my name so gently. "That might all be true, but if I run and leave Aphrodite in power, the next person she targets likely won't be as lucky to have the resources at my disposal. She'll continue to victimize people less powerful than her just because she can. She'll continue to use *you* to do it." Her hazel eyes go hard. "I won't allow that to happen. You deserve better than to be her weapon, and the people in this city deserve better than to walk on eggshells to avoid pissing Aphrodite off. We'll find a way to stop her. Together."

I'm ashamed of the sheer relief her words bring me. She's not leaving me. Not yet. Fuck, I'm such an asshole. "We have to adjust the plan."

"Yes. Starting with this Friday, when we attend Helen's party."

That gives me a little pause. "I thought you'd want to skip it considering what happened tonight."

"I do want to skip it, but it's not about what I want." She

shifts on the couch. It strikes me that this could be our lives if we were different people, in a different situation. Relaxing in my living room, her taking candid photos, talking about our days...

Longing hits me so hard, it steals my breath. I close my eyes and try to focus. "If you're staying in Olympus, it's the height of foolishness to leave the penthouse more than strictly necessary. My mother wants you dead; no reason to make it easier on her."

"Would you have gone if I weren't here?"

I frown. As tempting as it is to keep reminding Psyche how dangerous this course of action is, I answer honestly. "Yeah. I like Helen. She and Eris play the game differently than I do, but that goes with the territory of being born into the Kasios family. The events they put together are never boring, especially when one of them is trying to prove a point to Perseus or Zeus." Except Perseus *is* Zeus now. Damn it, one of these days that will click in my thoughts properly and I won't have to keep reminding myself.

"Exactly my point. We're fighting on two fronts now." She wiggles her foot until I pick it up and resume massaging. "We need time to figure out a way to deal with this renewed threat from your mother, and the only way to create that time is to have Olympus on our side. The original plan still has to stay in motion."

"That's reckless."

"We don't have a choice."

I concentrate on running my thumb up the sole of her foot until she lets loose that sexy little moan again. As tempting as it is to hole up in this penthouse for the foreseeable future, it will demolish our chances of playing out the epic love story we're supposed to be selling. More than that, I saw what happened last time one of Demeter's daughters was kept from her. She can't starve out the whole of the upper city in response to *this*, but she's got plenty of weapons in her arsenal.

And that's the *best*-case scenario.

Worst case, Demeter realizes why we entered into this marriage in the first place and goes after Aphrodite directly. There hasn't been a true war between members of the Thirteen in generations. Not even the last Zeus and last Hades, for all that their conflict ended with Hades's death. It was Ares and Hephaestus who warred all those decades ago, and they demolished several blocks of the upper city in the process. It was one of the few times in our history when Zeus, Poseidon, and Hades came together to quell the conflict. Zeus, of course, executed both Ares and Hephaestus in a particularly gruesome and public manner.

That Zeus had held his title for most of his life.

This one has been Zeus for a few months.

No matter what kind of heft the title carries, I don't know if Perseus can hold his own if a conflict spirals out of control between Demeter and Aphrodite.

No, Psyche is right. We don't have a choice. "Okay, we'll attend the party."

"I do have one question."

"Sure."

She twists her hair around her finger. "You're friends with the Kasios siblings, right? Why not just go to Zeus now and ask him to intervene? No matter how powerful Aphrodite is, she's not *Zeus* powerful."

I concentrate on rubbing her foot in a way that makes her

moan a little while I formulate an answer. "Perseus—Zeus—and I aren't as close as we were as kids, but even if we were, I don't think he could overlook the fact that the evidence against my mother also implicates me. He can't punish one and spare the other, because he'll have to justify any action he takes against another of the Thirteen."

"I suppose that makes sense." She tilts her head to the side. "We'll save going to Zeus as a last resort."

I hope it doesn't come to that. No matter how distant we've grown over the years, Perseus is dealing with enough without me dumping my problems into his lap and expecting him to fix them for me. We'll find another way, though.

In the meantime... "I have a question, too."

"Yes?"

"Why have you and your sisters put so much time and effort into holding yourselves apart from the rest of us? I understand avoiding *me* or some of the others, but Helen would have taken you under her wing in an instant."

"You think so?" Psyche makes a face but finally exhales. "I will admit that I have something of a chip on my shoulder when it comes to dealing with the children of the Thirteen. My experiences haven't been great."

We're a closed group. By the nature of the Thirteen, our number changes from time to time when the person holding the titles changes and brings their family with them, but there's a core group of us who have grown up together. Still... "Has Helen been cruel to you?" I can believe it of Eris, but Helen is a harder sell. She's not exactly warm, but she's better than most.

"No." Psyche says it so begrudgingly that I laugh. The sound is only partially in relief. I'd hate to have to rip my friend a new one because she was mean to my wife.

"I think you'd like Helen if you give her half a chance." I set her foot down and pick up the other.

She closes her eyes and seems to give herself over to the foot massage. "I'd like Helen, or the public version of Psyche would like Helen?"

"Both."

She exhales and opens her eyes. "This matters to you."

I'm surprised to find it does. I want to say that it's a simple game of numbers, and the more people on our side, the better off our position, but that's not strictly the truth. Nothing about this situation is simple, and the longer we're together, the more complicated it becomes. I expected to desire Psyche—I have from the start—but I didn't expect to like her or to feel so possessive that part of me wants to wrap her up and keep her away from the world while the other part wants to show her off at every opportunity. It's more than the fact that she's beautiful and has a sweet center that not even Olympus could mar. I *admire* her.

Which is why I tell her the truth. "Helen is as close to a sister as I have. More so than anyone else in Olympus, I trust her, and she trusts me. I..." I hesitate. "I would like it if you'd give her a chance."

"Not just because of the political gain?"

Of course she sees right through me. I give a rueful smile. "No, not just because of the political gain, though it never hurts to have a member of the Kasios family on your side."

She's silent for several minutes. "Okay. I'll give her a chance."

This feels more momentous than it likely should, but I can't help the fact that it feels right to have our lives start edging into each other. Or maybe that's just the selfish part of me that wants to tether this woman to me in as many ways as possible.

Psyche clears her throat. "We'll start with a two-pronged defense. The first thing we need is more alliances. I realize Zeus is out for the time being, but there are plenty of other powerful people in Olympus. The more we have on our side, the more risky it is for Aphrodite to strike."

"I can pretty much guarantee Helen's party will have a lot of powerful people, even if they're mostly the children of the Thirteen."

"That's a start." Psyche nods. "The second prong is getting the rest of Olympus on our side and cheering for us. The little social-media teasers have gotten that ball rolling, but doing an official interview will help speed things along."

I focus on her foot for a long moment. "That works for a short-term plan."

"Long-term will have to be adaptable." She closes her eyes, her expression becoming more and more relaxed. "I don't suppose your mother was bluffing about still wanting me dead?"

I wish I could let her believe that will happen, but I can't. "No. Aphrodite doesn't bluff."

"Then we'll just have to find a way to force her to call off this attack. Easy, right?" She laughs, the sound bitter. "At least my mother isn't rampaging this time."

"There is that. Have I mentioned lately that she's terrifying?"

"Pot, meet kettle."

I grin, but the expression fades quickly. "We'll find a way. My mother is hardly a rational individual, but she's only a danger because of how powerful she is. If we can find more allies and use the public's goodwill in our favor, it might be enough." It's still a long shot, but there's the tiniest chance that once she realizes she's outmatched, she'll cease any further attacks. Or at least keep it in the area of reputation, rather than literal life and death.

"Then we stick with this plan and adapt as necessary, depending on what she does." Psyche gives me a tired smile. "We'll figure it out, Eros. We're wonderfully matched when it comes to this. Between the two of us, we'll find a solution."

The casual faith she puts in me is staggering. My chest goes tight. "Yes. We will. I promise."

"Mmm."

It takes me several minutes to realize that Psyche has fallen asleep. Several more minutes pass before I force myself to set her foot down and rise. She looks different in sleep, something in her relaxing that I hadn't realized was tense. It's not that she seems younger, exactly, but that she's put down a burden she carries with her always.

I have the strangest urge to offer to carry it for her.

It's not late enough for me to sleep yet, which is just as well. I have a call to make. I leave Psyche on the couch for now and head to the safe room. Tomorrow, I'll drill her on the code again a few times to ensure it's properly memorized. I don't plan on leaving her unattended more often than strictly necessary, but I already know she's going to crave some independence before too long. I'm not sure how I'll handle security outside the penthouse; a problem for another day. I softly shut the door and do the last thing I want to right now.

I dial my mother.

I half expect her to ignore my call. Her favorite punishment is icing me out, depriving me of any contact or attention. When I was young and she'd do it, it always felt like she'd sliced me right down to the bone. Aphrodite is so much larger than life, and to a child—to *her* child—it's even truer. Having her turn away from me...

I give myself a shake. Her tactics don't work as well as they used to. Not since I grew up enough to realize she uses her love and her attention as both lure and punishment. But some things are impossible to shuck off, and I can't quite pull in a full breath until she answers.

She doesn't make me wait long. "So now you decide you're available for a conversation? I should block your number."

"You won't." It's an effort to keep my voice even. "How will you convey your disappointment in me then?"

She makes a sound suspiciously like a hiss. "Insolent child."

"I'm twenty-eight, Mother." I hurl the term like a weapon. "I'm more than capable of making my own choices, including who will be my bride."

"She wouldn't be your bride if you'd carved her heart out of her chest like I asked. I don't know why you're balking, Eros. It's not as if you didn't do that and worse to Polyphonte. Killed her right in front of her parents. Did you know her mother committed suicide this week? Tragic, that."

I'm not prepared for the guilt that swarms me. "That's different." The words feel like a lie on my tongue.

"It's really not. Did you convince yourself you're like that precious wife of yours?" She laughs. "Silly boy. You're nothing like her. You're like *me*. We are the only two people in this world who can understand each other, and you're putting that at risk for a little bitch with good hair. The moment that woman realizes what you're truly capable of, she'll turn from you. Don't you understand that I'm trying to *help* you?"

There are very few things I care about in this world. Most of the time, I hate that Aphrodite numbers among them. I'm old enough now, independent enough, to understand that she's constantly attempting to emotionally manipulate me. It's a good portion of the reason why I have systematically carved out the softer feelings from my personality, removing all possibility of traction. I thought those parts of me were gone forever, but Psyche's presence has them waking as if from a long slumber.

They won't serve me now. All they'll accomplish is giving my mother a foothold that I've worked too damn hard to eradicate.

"Mother," I say slowly. "If you cause any harm to come to my wife, you will regret it."

"Not as much as you're going to regret this marriage." Her tone goes just as cold as mine. "What were you thinking, Eros? I send you to remove the girl and you *marry* her? Have you lost your mind?"

"Plans changed."

"Not mine."

I know that. I don't know why I'm reaching out now, hoping

that I can work a miracle and change Aphrodite's mind. Still...I have to try. Reacting in fear will just give her a larger target to aim at. I have to be cold, colder than I ever have before. "I never ask you for anything. I'm asking you for this. Leave Psyche alone."

She's silent for so long, a foolish part of me starts to dare to hope that this is the moment things change. That, for once, my mother will put my needs above her selfish desires.

I really should know better after a lifetime of being her son. Finally, Aphrodite says, "I see that she's gotten to you. Pity."

"Mother."

"Do not say 'Mother' in that tone of voice. Not to me."

Something akin to panic tightens my chest. "Let me have her, and put this behind us and I'll never question you again. That's what you want, isn't it? A good little fixer who stops giving you attitude."

She takes a slow breath, and when she speaks again, she sounds almost calm. "Everything I do, Eros, I do for love." She hangs up before I can formulate a response.

I stare at my phone. "Fuck. *Fuck.*" I knew it wouldn't make a difference. I *knew* it, but I still tried. I close my eyes, but an image imprints itself on the back of my eyelids, of Psyche's body bent and broken, her hazel eyes gone blank with death, the thing that makes her *her* gone forever. I press my hand to my chest, hard, trying to breathe past the pain the image brings. I won't let it happen. I know all my mother's tricks. I just need to hold her off until we can come up with a plan to neutralize her for good.

I know how to neutralize her. She's the one who taught me.

I can't do it. I thought I had no lines left to cross, but not even

I can kill my own mother. No matter how evil she is. Not even to keep Psyche safe.

I leave the safe room with slow steps that increase in pace the closer I get to the living room. Psyche's only been out of my sight for ten minutes. She's fine. I know she's fine. But I don't breathe easy again until I walk into the room and find her exactly where I left her.

What the fuck is happening to me?

I gather her up into my arms, ignoring her sleepy protest that she's too heavy, and carry her into our bedroom. We end up in bed, me spooning her as she sinks back into sleep. I press my hand to her upper chest, counting her slow inhales and exhales until my nerves finally settle enough for sleep to take me.

PSYCHE

HELEN KASIOS LIVES IN THE SAME BUILDING AS THE REST of Zeus's family. I've never been there before. Usually when the past Zeus entertained, he did it in Dodona Tower. The new Zeus has entertained plenty since he took over, but it couldn't be clearer that he's just going through the motions. He doesn't crave the spotlight the way his late father did. Even when he was still called Perseus, he seemed more focused on the business aspect of things than his father ever was. The forty-day mourning period has come and gone, and people are already whispering about how resistant he seems to marrying someone and finally filling the Hera title. The last Zeus might have been monster incarnate, but he was charming and charismatic. He left large shoes to fill.

Of his four children, his youngest son, Hercules, managed to escape Olympus entirely. Perseus is now the new Zeus. And Helen and Eris are, as Eros said, insular. They've never crossed me that I'm aware of, but we haven't gotten close enough to each other to create friction.

That changes tonight.

Tonight, when Eros wants me to try.

Does he realize what he's asking of me? I glance at him in the elevator next to me, perfectly put together in a dove-gray suit and cream button-down shirt that offsets his golden skin. He catches my eye and gives our linked hands a squeeze. Yes, I suspect he knows exactly what he's asking of me.

I've survived—thrived, even—in Olympus because I kept my distance and trusted no one outside my family. I took the lessons I learned in the first year here and never looked back.

Now I'm swimming in deeper waters than I'm comfortable with. As the elevator doors slide open, revealing a classy hallway with lush gray carpet and soothing blue walls, I have to acknowledge that I'm not a shark at all. I'm a minnow playing dress-up.

I hope I can survive the night without getting eaten.

"Breathe," Eros murmurs.

Right. Breathe. Relax. Smile sweetly. Don't let them scent weakness.

I'm sure that's not what he intends to say, but I take it to heart all the same. Between one step and the next, I box up all my fears and insecurities and tuck them away. They'll still be waiting for me at the end of the night. I can ignore them until I'm back in the penthouse, those strong walls between me and the rest of the city.

The hallway contains four doors, and Eros leads me to the one at the end. He barely knocks before it's flung open by a glittering Helen. Literally glittering. The golden stuff coats her exposed skin—and there's a *lot* of exposed skin around her tiny dress of the same golden color—and even her long light-brown hair. It turns her beauty otherworldly, as if a literal goddess has wandered into our presence, but the squeal she gives when she sees us shatters the illusion. "You're here!"

She bounces up onto her toes to give Eros a kiss on the cheek, and I barely have time to process the hot flash of jealousy before she grabs my hand and pulls me forward to give me the same treatment. "I'm so happy to see you." She all but drags me into the apartment, leaving Eros to trail behind us.

I get flashes of the place. Elegant people in evening wear draped over equally elegant couches in the living room. A color scheme that makes me think of the stormy ocean—gray wooden floors, moody blue walls, lots of white and sandy-colored furniture. It's completely at odds with the shining woman attached to my hand.

She hauls me into a spotless kitchen with a full bar set up on the counter. "Pick your poison."

I almost say red wine, almost fall back to some sweet drink that will make my teeth ache. But I promised Eros I'd try, and so I take a tiny leap of faith. "Bourbon."

The smile Helen gives me is just as dazzling as her glitter-adorned body. "That's my girl. I knew I liked you."

"Correction, Helen; that's *my* girl."

I nearly breathe a sigh of relief when I realize Eros has joined us. He's got a strangely indulgent smile on his face, and I can't tell if he's faking it or not. Just like I can't tell how much of Helen's enthusiasm is really her. Persephone does a beaming sunshine thing when she's in public, and this kind of reminds me of that. But it's less soft warmth and more lightning in a bottle. I get the feeling she might explode at any moment in frenetic energy that is as likely to harm as it is to entertain.

Helen waves Eros's comment away as she pulls out a bottle of bourbon that's outstandingly expensive. "She might be wearing your ring—it's gorgeous, by the way—but you're practically a brother to me, so that makes her family." She beams at me. "I've always wanted a sister."

I blink. "You have a sister. She's standing right there." I point at Eris, who's wearing an ink spill of a dress and has her head close to a Black woman in a gorgeous—and tiny—red dress. I belatedly realize I recognize her as well. Hermes catches me looking and gives a cheery wave.

Helen snorts. "Eris isn't a sister. She's chaos personified."

That surprises a laugh out of me. "I have one of those, too."

"Callisto." She says the name like she's savoring it. "I wish she'd come around more. She seems interesting. You all do." She passes me the bourbon and pours a glass of red wine without asking Eros what he wants. Helen presses it into his hand and rounds the counter to stand a little too close. I'd take it personally, but I get the feeling that it's just how she is with everyone. She rakes her gaze over me. "You look outstanding. You *always* look outstanding."

I glance down at myself. I chose my dress carefully tonight. It's a deep-green wrap dress that makes my breasts look great and maximizes my curves. "Um, thanks."

"Oh, I'm obviously not telling you anything you don't already know, but it's still nice to hear, right?" She waves it away. Someone knocks on the door before she can continue. "I'll be back. Enjoy the party!" And then she's gone, trailing glitter behind her.

I feel like I've just been tossed around by a tornado and deposited somewhere completely different than where I started. It wasn't an entirely unpleasant experience, but it was disorienting in the extreme. I take too large a drink of my bourbon, but my nerves are in danger of getting the best of me. "Is she always like this?"

"No." Eros shrugs. "When she entertains, she ramps up."

Easy enough to read between those lines. She's got a public persona the same way we do. From what I've observed, she likes people to underestimate her, and they see a happy, pretty fool and don't look beneath the surface. I just hadn't realized her energy level was so...high. "I see."

Eros shifts close and pulls me into his arms. It feels horribly natural, as if we've been embracing much longer than a few days. I don't tense and I manage to smile up at him as if deeply in love. The warmth on his face never ceases to set me back on my heels, but I manage to mask my response. He leans down to speak in my ear. "An hour or two and then people will drift off to other parties or clubs."

Honestly, it's not a big ask to play this role with him for a few hours. This party might be filled with people I've spent years avoiding, but Hermes is the only member of the Thirteen in sight, and so it's still better than the events at Dodona Tower my mother insists on dragging me to.

I turn in Eros's arms. He doesn't let me go; he simply tucks me back against his chest and rests his chin on the top of my head. I don't understand why this feels as intimate as the embrace, but I'm not going to break his hold just because my heart is racing as if I just ran up a flight of stairs.

And then my attention lands on the man across the living room, and I forget all about Eros. "That motherfucker."

His arms tense around me, tugging me back a step when I would break free. "I didn't know he'd be here."

Orpheus.

The asshole whose selfishness not only broke Eurydice's heart but put her literal life in danger. They were dating seriously before that night, and she loved him with everything she had. The breakup has hit her hard, but Orpheus hasn't missed a beat in the intervening months. Every time I turn around, he's making headlines in MuseWatch with his partying and hooking up with one gorgeous person after another. Current speculation is that he's on the rebound and soothing the pain of a broken heart, but it's bullshit.

If he really loved Eurydice as much as he acted, he wouldn't have set her up. At the very least, he would have *apologized* for the harm he's caused.

Instead, he's here, wearing a designer suit and leaning against the wall next to a woman I recognize. Cassandra. From the smile on his handsome face, he's got his charm cranked up to a thousand. I might hate him, but even I have to admit it's a lot of charm. His mother is a Korean model who puts even Aphrodite to shame and his father is a Swedish businessman of some sort.

For her part, Cassandra seems bored by the whole experience. She's about my size, with a fall of brilliant red hair and a generous mouth that naturally turns down a little at the edges. She also has a reputation for taking no shit.

"Let me go," I say quietly.

"Psyche—"

I down the rest of my drink and turn to face Eros. I know this is a mistake, but I don't care—which seems to be a running trend with me these days. The alcohol is already buzzing my thoughts, feeding the anger I've been nursing for far too long. "Eurydice almost *died*. You weren't there that night. Persephone was. The man chasing her had a knife. The only reason she was in that position at all was because Orpheus sold her out to Zeus." Eros has his carefully blank expression in place. I hate it. I hate that he can keep his eyes on the endgame while I'm ready to pull a Callisto and find a knife to stab Orpheus with. "Let me go," I repeat.

For a second, I think he won't do it, but he finally releases me long enough to drape an arm over my shoulder. Between one blink and the next, his playboy smile is back in place. "Let's go have a chat."

I hesitate. "You know Orpheus?" Even as I voice the question, I realize how ridiculous it is. They don't exactly move in the same circles, but there's no way they haven't interacted before now. Apollo has been in his position for years now, so his younger brother Orpheus has been attending the same parties Eros and I have. It's how he and Eurydice met.

"Well enough."

I don't know what game he's playing at, and it's almost enough to distract me from my rage. Almost. I let Eros guide us toward Orpheus. He's so focused on Cassandra, he doesn't even look up until we're right next to him.

The way he blanches when he sees me almost makes me laugh. Or it would if I wasn't so busy trying not to scream. Eros gives my shoulder a little squeeze, his expression still perfectly relaxed.

"Orpheus, you know my wife, right?" He glances at me, all charming playboy. "Wasn't he dating your little sister?"

"*Wife?*" The man looks like he might be sick. "I didn't know you were dating."

"Not dating. Married." Eros's tone shifts, and the small hairs rise on the back of my neck. "I suppose that makes Eurydice my sister now, doesn't it?"

Orpheus sways a little. I can't tell if he's drunk or just that afraid of Eros. Maybe if I was a better person, I wouldn't get a petty thrill from the fact that he's nearly peeing his pants, but I want him to suffer. I turn to Eros and press my hand to his chest. "That's definitely what it means." I smile, letting an edge work its way into my expression. "I know how protective you are of your family, darling."

"I am. I really, truly am." He leans down a little, not quite getting in Orpheus's face but the threat is there all the same. "I'd be exceedingly put out if someone were to harm sweet little Eurydice. You understand, don't you?"

Cassandra stirs to life. Her dark eyes, enhanced with black eyeliner sharp enough to cut, narrow. "Are you threatening Apollo's little brother?"

"If I am?"

Her lips curve. "Don't let me stop you." She pushes off the wall and waves an idle hand in Orpheus's direction. "Good luck with that."

"Wait—"

I shake my head, anger still overriding my control. "Learn to read the room. You're not wanted here. Get out."

"Helen invited me." Even his sneer is attractive. If anything, the knowledge makes me angrier.

Eros looks over his shoulder. "Helen."

She appears at our side as if by magic. I half expect a cloud of glitter to cascade from her body and dress, but it all stays in place. She has a carefully neutral look on her face. "Is there a problem?"

"Orpheus has overstayed his welcome."

"Oh, that." She laughs, a merry tinkling sound. "Leave now, Orpheus."

He draws himself up, but if he thinks he can intimidate these two, he's more of a fool than I thought possible. "My brother will hear about this."

"Will he?" Helen cocks her head. "Is he also going to hear about the fact that you were chasing Cassandra around like a creep who doesn't understand the word 'no'? Because personally, I think Apollo would be *very* interested to hear about that."

Ah. So the rumors about Apollo and Cassandra are true, at least when it comes to his interest in her. From what I've seen, she's given him about as much attention as she gave Orpheus—as in only enough to escape his presence whenever he shows up. The fact that they work together only seems to complicate the issue.

Orpheus seems to realize he's outmatched and glares. "You can't treat me like this."

"Sweetheart." The softness in Helen's tone hides a vicious dagger. "Look around this room. Every one of us is related to the Thirteen in some way. You're not special here. Go play with your groupies and don't bother showing up for one of my parties again. It will be horribly embarrassing to require security to show you out."

He curses but turns and leaves, the eyes of every person in the room on him. It's only when the door shuts behind him that Helen flips her hair off her shoulder. "Gods, he's *such* an asshole. Why did I even invite him again?"

"Because you said he's an asshole whose face you'd like to ride," Eros says mildly.

"Ah. That." Helen snaps her fingers. "Right. I forgot." She gives me an apologetic look that seems genuine. "Obviously I wouldn't have touched him while he was with your sister, but I have horrible taste in men and better than questionable taste in women. It can't be helped."

"I...see." I don't hold it against her. Why would she care about Eurydice's emotional health? They don't know each other, and it's every person for themselves in this city—especially in this crowd. I paste a smile on my face. "No hard feelings."

"It's cute when you lie." Her smile goes sharp. "I meant what I said just now. He's dead to me. No more parties, no face-sitting. You're practically family at this point, and family sticks together, for better or worse."

I can't trust her. I can't trust anyone in this room, including Eros. But as I let Helen tow me to the dining room table to start a drinking game, I find myself wishing that I could.

EROS

MY WIFE IS DRUNK. EXCEEDINGLY DRUNK. SHE LEANS against me as I try to wrestle her coat on. Psyche is cute even while sloshed, and the irritation I might have felt if she were any other person is nowhere in evidence.

"I like her."

Psyche rests her face against my chest and smiles at Helen. "I like you, too."

Helen's relaxed for the first time since we arrived. Everyone is gone, even Eris, and she's let her frenetic alter ego dissipate. "You two can crash here if you want to."

It would be safer, but unfortunately, I have to weigh the small danger of traveling back to my penthouse against the sheer amount of damage staying could cause. I give her a look. "And when we're photographed leaving in the morning, they'll run a story about how we were engaged in some sordid threesome because the spark has already gone out of our marriage after only a week."

She shrugs. "If you were anyone else and she wasn't shit-housed, I'd consider it."

"Your compliments leave something to be desired." I chuckle a little as Psyche weaves away from me, and I have to loop an arm around her waist to keep her upright. "You shouldn't have played drinking games with my wife, though."

"She seemed like she was having fun."

"I was!" Psyche lurches, and I have to take two steps to counterbalance her.

Helen leans forward and grabs Psyche's hand. "Just so you know, we're sisters now. No takebacks."

Which is right around the time I realize that Helen isn't exactly sober, either. *Damn it.* "Lock the door behind me."

"Yes, Eros." She grins. "Marriage looks good on you. You seem happy. You should keep her."

I plan on it.

I can't say that aloud. Not here. Not now. Certainly not like this. "See you later." I shuffle Psyche out the door, pause long enough to listen to Helen throw the dead bolt, and then head for the elevator. Once we're closed inside it, I glance at Psyche. "Are you feeling sick?"

"No." She doesn't quite manage to open her eyes all the way. "Just goofy."

We'll see if that holds once we get into my car, but I can always crack a window and hopefully the cold night air will combat any motion sickness. I carefully adjust my grip on her as she sways. "Did you have fun?"

"Yes?" She shakes her head. "Gods, I'm drunk. I haven't

been this drunk since my twenty-first birthday. And that was only because Persephone and Callisto tricked me." She frowns. "I'm sorry. I was so nervous and then Helen was so bubbly, my drinks got away from me."

"They tend to do that at Helen's parties."

Psyche's spilling truth messily around, and there's a part of me that wants to press her for information. No, not information. I can't pretend it's anything but wanting to know what she really thinks of me. To find out if she's slipping closer and closer to falling for me the same way I've tossed myself past the point of no return while I wasn't paying attention. I manage to resist grilling her, but only barely.

She feels good in my arms, soft and sweet. She looks even better. I study our reflections in the mirrored elevator doors. We look...good together. Not just in the way that two attractive people do when they stand side by side. Psyche lays her head against my shoulder and closes her eyes. As if we're a real couple. The casual intimacy makes my chest ache with a longing so fierce, I can barely breathe past it.

If we can figure out a way around my mother's threat, if we can learn to live together... This could be us. All the time.

A real couple.

The ache in my chest gets stronger. I want this, want it so badly, I can't help pulling Psyche closer to me. Between the two of us, we'll find a way forward. We've already proven we're an outstanding team when we put our heads together.

My mother doesn't stand a chance.

Then the elevator doors open into the parking garage and my fledgling hope drains away.

Helen's building is very similar to mine when it comes to security. There are guards stationed both at the elevator entrances and the parking garage entrance itself. When we arrived, there was a woman in the booth next to the elevator.

It's empty now.

There might be a reasonable explanation for that, but I'm not willing to bet Psyche's life on it. I shift her to between me and the elevator, thinking fast. My car is three rows down. I can't see it from here. I certainly can't reach it, do a sweep to ensure it's safe, and get us out of here without letting Psyche out of my sight. If she were sober, maybe, but that ship has long since sailed.

Going back up to Helen's apartment might work, but it's a risk in a number of ways. Either I'm bringing trouble right to her or she's already nose-dived into her bed and she won't hear us even if I try to kick the damn door down. Neither is a good idea.

That leaves one option.

I muscle Psyche to the guard booth. The door hangs slightly open, yet another sign that something's gone terribly wrong. I push her inside and cup her face in my hands. "Psyche, I need you to sober up and I need you to do it now."

She blinks those big eyes at me and nods. "I'll try."

It's a lost cause, but if I can get her to focus for a few minutes, it will all work out. I take the phone and press it into her hands. "I need you to call the security desk and tell them there's been a breach. We don't know where the guard is. Can you do that?"

"Yes?"

Shit, I'm not certain, but it will have to do. I release her and move to the door. "Do not open this for anyone but me. Do you understand? Not a guard, not the head of security, not even Zeus himself."

"I wouldn't open it for Zeus. He seems like kind of an asshole."

I nod. "Definitely an asshole." Then there's nothing to do but leave her here and hope for the best. I step out of the booth and shut the door behind me. It automatically locks, a small relief. The glass is also bulletproof and the base is solid concrete, so even if someone rammed it with a car, it would do more damage to the vehicle than the booth itself. She's as safe as I can make her right now.

I knew I should have brought a gun. I rarely go anywhere without one, but hosts tend to frown on that sort of thing. With a few exceptions, Olympus parties like to keep the violence confined to words and power plays. The Thirteen and their inner circles like to pretend they're the pinnacle of class; they save the dirty work for the shadows in the darkest part of night.

I *do* have a gun in the car, though.

I move slowly down the middle of the parking aisle, doing my best to keep Psyche in sight. She's on the phone, her face a mask of drunken concentration, so I hope there will be reinforcements soon. I can't exactly trust the security in this building, not with her safety, but I can trust that Helen will skin them all alive if something happens to me. They know it and they won't risk any overt moves against me and mine.

But they might take their sweet time getting up here if my mother's gotten to them.

The parking garage is as well lit as a parking garage is capable of, which means it's got plenty of shadows. Every car I pass is exceedingly expensive and shines in the low light. The only sound is the scuff of my shoes against the concrete.

It's so tempting to assume I'm being paranoid. It's possible the security guard ran to the bathroom or something, but in all the years I've been visiting Helen, I've never seen that booth unmanned. I can't take the risk with Psyche's life.

I reach my car. It doesn't appear to be fucked with, but I glance around and then duck down to turn on my phone light and check the undercarriage. I don't honestly believe my mother is so angry she'll hurt *me*, but she's volatile enough that I can't take anything for granted. Five minutes later, I'm satisfied that no one has messed with my car.

Which is when I hear the first shot. It's barely a whisper of sound, a little whistle of a bullet passing through a silencer. A crack of glass. Psyche screams.

I'm up and moving in an instant. Sprinting down the main space is so fucking tempting, but it would paint a giant target on me. If I were the shooter, I'd wing me and use that to draw Psyche out of the booth. My mother might not want me dead, but I doubt she'd be furious over a flesh wound if it removed my wife from the picture.

I duck between the cars, moving as quickly as possible and keeping low to avoid being seen. Another shot. A third. Psyche's stopped screaming, but the glass hasn't shattered. She's still safe.

The shooter comes into view as I reach the end of the row. He's a short white guy wearing a nondescript pair of black jeans, black T-shirt, and black baseball hat. He glances around, obviously knowing I'm in the area, and I jerk back into the shadows between two cars. The man sweeps a slow circle as he reloads the gun before turning back to point it at the booth. He pulls the trigger, enlarging the spiderwebbed glass directly in front of Psyche's face.

Rage and fear short out my brain. I stop thinking, stop worrying about next steps. I charge him. He starts to turn, but I'm too fast. I take him down in a flying tackle that sends the gun skittering over the floor. It doesn't matter. I don't need it.

I don't give him a chance to flip me. I simply slam his face into the ground once, twice, a third time, and then once more for good measure. He goes limp. My hands are shaking. Why the fuck are my hands shaking? I kneel on his back, torn between ensuring he never gets up again and not wanting to show exactly how monstrous I am while I can feel Psyche watching me. Knowing what I'm capable of is one thing. Seeing it is entirely another.

"Eros!" Her voice is a little muffled by the glass, but there's no mistaking the fear there. I don't want to look, don't want to ever see that fear directed at *me* again. No matter how much I deserve it—and I do. I'm a fucking mess.

The sound of the booth door opening does what nothing else can; it gets me moving. I shove off the man and move to stand between him and Psyche.

But she's not looking at him. She stumbles into my arms and clings to me with a strength that takes my breath away. "You *idiot*. What were you thinking? He could have killed you."

Shock has my feet growing roots. "He was shooting at *you*."

She fists the front of my shirt and looks up at me with shining eyes. "Never do that again. If he shot you, I—"

The elevator doors open, cutting off whatever she'd been

about to say. Security personnel spill out into the area. Things happen quickly after that. Once they realize this is a Thirteen-on-Thirteen incident, they take the assassin into custody to await the arrival of Ares's people to sort things out. I leave my information and hustle Psyche into my car.

She slumps back against the seat, huddling in my coat. She's sobering up fast, and I hate how scared she looks, but I don't reach out for fear that she'll flinch away from me. I turn onto the street and head for my building. "I won't let anything happen to you."

She's got a white-knuckled grip on my coat. "Did you miss the part where I was worried about you?"

"I had things under control." When she still looks unconvinced, I try to elaborate. "Even if I didn't, my mother doesn't want *me* dead."

"All it takes is one bullet and it doesn't matter what Aphrodite wants." She closes her eyes but immediately opens them again and rolls down the window a bit. "I'm not sober enough to talk through this. I'm sorry."

"Don't be sorry." *I'm* sorry, but only that my mother managed to ruin what was a really good night. We were having fun before this, had carved out a tiny little escape in what was supposed to be a safe space. Psyche met some of my people, let her guard down a tiny bit, and all she got for her trouble was an attempt on her life. "This city is fucking poison."

"There will be consequences for tonight." Her eyes are sliding closed again, and this time she doesn't open them.

"There will," I say quietly.

Murder isn't legal in Olympus. Far from it. That doesn't

stop the Thirteen from having people like me who do their dirty work in the shadows, but it's an unspoken thing. By attacking Psyche in Helen's building, as she was leaving Helen's party, my mother has put our shit out in the open—or she will if the attack can even remotely be linked back to her. That's the big what-if right now. Zeus will get involved because his sister is tangentially involved. Ares will launch an investigation. No doubt Demeter and Persephone will be showing up on my doorstep the second they hear the news, which means Hades is involved as well.

Things were already messy, and they're only going to get messier.

I should be happy about this, but I can't shake the feeling that it's going to blow back on me somehow. My mother can be impulsive in the extreme, but she's not a fool. She'll have made sure none of this links directly to her—or at least doesn't directly link *only* to her.

No, someone else will pay the price for the night's events. I'm sure of it.

It doesn't matter how effectively Psyche argued for attending the party tonight. I knew the risk, knew my mother wouldn't stop. I just foolishly thought I could protect her. I didn't wager on Aphrodite being so bold as to attack us in Zeus's sister's parking garage, and Psyche could have been hurt as a result of my arrogance.

I've fucked up.

PSYCHE

I WAKE UP IN BED WITH A POUNDING HEADACHE. THE LAST thing I remember about last night was losing the battle to keep my eyes open in Eros's car. Which means he carried me to bed. Again. I groan and roll over to find a bottle of Gatorade and Tylenol pills sitting on the nightstand. No note, but why would there be? Eros is far too practical to try to make this gesture romantic.

And yet…it *feels* romantic.

He's taking care of me. Without flair, without showy moves. Just a simple act to meet my needs. It's strange and a little unnerving, and I like it far more than I should.

I manage to sit up and take the pills, and then I detour into the bathroom to brush the terrible taste from my mouth and take a quick shower. By the time I dress and go searching for Eros, I feel halfway human.

I find him in the safe room, pouring over some data on the computer monitors in front of him. He glances over as I walk in, and his small smile does nothing to detract from the circles beneath his blue eyes. I stop. "Have you slept at all?"

"No time." He turns back to the monitors. "We already have a summons from Perseus—Zeus—for later this morning. I know we wanted to hold him in reserve as a last resort, but that ship has sailed, and honestly, if he hadn't summoned me, I would have called him and arranged a meeting."

Because Aphrodite has escalated things. I think a part of me still believed she was bluffing until now. She's not, which means we need bigger guns than either Eros or I can bring to the fight. I take a slow breath. "What's the plan?"

"There's no hope of keeping this under wraps. Even if the assassin doesn't talk, we have to tell the truth or risk the entirety of the Thirteen coming down on us, which would put all our shit public. At least Zeus has motivation to find a solution behind closed doors."

The sinking in my chest is reflected in his face. "He's not going to side with us against Aphrodite. She's one of the Thirteen."

"There are specific laws within the Thirteen against going after the others and their families. That's what we'll play on." Eros sighs. "If it were the old Zeus, I'd agree with you that it's a long shot. But even if we're not really friends anymore, I've known Perseus since we were kids. He's not going to let my mother get away with this."

"Maybe. Or maybe he'll decide that the stability of Olympus is worth more than our lives."

"He won't let her kill you. No matter what else is true, Perseus isn't his father. Trust me, even if you don't trust him. We'll see what he has to say and go from there." Eros glances at his watch. "We need to leave in two hours."

I don't know how he can be so calm when something truly disastrous is welling up inside me. I have to get some distance between us, to move and expel some of this awful feeling inside me. The longer I stand here, the more the events of last night wash over me in waves. The fear when that man raised the gun and pointed it at my face, the horrible knowledge that the glass wouldn't hold forever... It was nothing compared to the terror I felt when Eros appeared and tackled the guy.

By nature, I face hard truths. I might lie to most people in this city, but I can't survive by lying to myself. I know what that fear means, even if I'm not ready to admit it to myself. "I have to go."

He jerks like I've struck him. "What? You can't leave."

"Not leave. Go." I'm not making sense. I know I'm not making sense, but I can't seem to help myself. Panic is clawing its way up my throat. I back through the door. "I just... I can't."

"Psyche, wait." Eros, my terrifying monster of a man, actually looks concerned about me, which only makes my panic worse. When did I start looking at him like a man and not an opponent? It's too much. It's certainly too soon.

I keep backing away, and he keeps following me, still looking confused and concerned. At least he keeps his distance, but it's not nearly enough for my state of mind. "Talk to me."

I shake my head. "I can't do this."

He shadows me down the hall, keeping a careful distance between us even as he reaches for me. "We'll find a way through. Her people won't touch you."

But they won't have to, will they? A hysterical laugh bubbles free. Aphrodite won't have to take my heart, because Eros is in danger of completing that mission already. He doesn't need my literal heart in his hands to crush me beyond repair. He's already too close, too overwhelming, too damn much. I back into the foyer, the room of mirrors, and jerk to a stop when faced with dozens of our reflections bounced across every available surface. "Eros, I—"

He moves faster than I expect and grabs my hands. A light touch, but I already know that if I yank against his hold, I won't be able to get free. "Please," I whisper.

"Talk to me," he repeats. "I can't fight what I can't see."

Oh gods, I really am falling in love with this man. I close my eyes and a single tear slips free. I can't control how I feel—I've already more than proven that—but at least I don't have to tell him. I don't know how he'd react, and I honestly can't stand the thought of coldness creeping into Eros's eyes in response.

Instead, I choose a different truth. "I'm scared."

He looks actually pained. "I'm sorry," he finally says. "I should have expected her to strike like that, and I didn't. It won't happen again. I realize that you have no reason to trust me because of what I am, but…"

"Because of what you are," I repeat. My fear welds itself into a fierce anger, the emotion so strong my entire body shakes. "What are you, Eros?"

He releases my wrist and takes a step back. The mirrors surrounding us show our images from all directions, and there's something apt about that, but I'm too focused on the man in front of me to chase the thought down. He looks away, but his attention snags on the reflection in the nearest mirror and he grimaces. "You know what I am."

"Indulge me."

His lips curve, but his eyes aren't happy. He flings a hand at the mirror to his right. "Failure." The mirror to his left. "Murderer." The one behind him. "Monster."

"Eros," I whisper. He's talked about being a monster more than a few times, and while I can admit that his past actions have been monstrous, I hate that he takes all the blame for it and ignores the conditions that brought him to that point. I can't change his mind. I'm not even sure if I should try.

But after what happened in that parking garage, I can't help but want to.

"You can't leave." He matches my low tone. "I'm sure you don't want to see my face right now, but this is the only place in Olympus I know you're safe from my mother. So... Please. Please don't leave."

"Eros," I repeat. "Would you like to know what I see when I look at you?"

He flinches. This cold, arrogant man *flinches* at my question. "I suppose it's the least I can do after everything I've put you through."

Oh, Eros.

I slip my hand into his. He's so tense, I can tell he's fighting not to pull away from me, to retreat to something resembling a safer distance. I turn us to face the mirror next to the front door. Eros is trying to shut down his expression, but he still looks pained as I take a deep breath. "I see someone loyal."

His hand spasms in mine. "Psyche—"

"I'm not finished." I turn us one mirror to the right. "I see someone ambitious."

"I don't know if that's really a virtue," he mutters.

But he allows me to move us to face the next mirror. "I see someone both clever and intelligent."

"Those are the same things."

"They're really not."

He gives me a tormented look. "Why are you doing this?"

Because I love you. I swallow hard. "Because you have only been told the negative about yourself for so long, that's all you believe. Every person contains a balance of both good and bad inside them. Even you. *Especially* you."

"Psyche..." He looks down at me like he's never seen me before. "I don't deserve you."

That fierce feeling inside me gets stronger. "I think we've established that I'm a flawed human being, the same as you."

"No. Not the same." He turns me to face the mirrors and steps behind me. We look good like this, even with him a little wild around the eyes and me shaking like a leaf. I never would have lined us up as a couple that fits, but our time together has more than proved me wrong.

Eros winds my hair around a fist, his eyes never leaving mine. "Do you know what I see when I look at you?"

I open my mouth to make a joke, but the words die before they leave my tongue. I lick my lips. "This isn't about me."

"Wrong, beautiful girl. It's always been about you." He drags in a breath, and I can feel the fine tremors in his body where he presses against my back. Eros speaks so softly, I almost miss the words. "I see a woman I don't deserve, but you make me want to be a better man so that one day I might deserve you. I see a *goddess*."

I turn in his arms. The words I promised myself I wouldn't say bubble up, and I do the only thing I can think of to keep them inside. I kiss him. The moment my lips touch Eros's, it's as if something explodes between us. He uses his hold in my hair to tilt my head back and take the kiss deeper. I will never, ever get enough of kissing Eros. He turns it into an art form, an intoxicating connection that goes straight to my head.

He breaks the kiss long enough to say, "I need you, Wife."

"Yes." I grab the hem of his shirt and push it up and over his head. "I need you, too."

"You have me." But he grabs my hands, stopping me from undoing the front of his pants. "Wait. Condom."

That's the smart, rational thing to consider, but I don't want to be smart or rational right now. "I know we said we wouldn't make this decision in the heat of the moment, but I don't want to use a condom." I hesitate. "Unless you want to."

There's that fine tremor again in his hands where they bracket my wrists. "Be sure."

I don't care if it's reckless; I'm already nodding. "I don't want anything between us. I just want you."

He takes me at my word. Eros reclaims my mouth as he gets busy stripping me out of my underwear and bra. His pants hit the floor a mere moment later and then his naked body is against mine, the delicious slide of his skin against mine going straight to my head. I dig my hands into his curls and tug, pulling him down to the floor on top of me.

I only get to enjoy the feeling of his weight pressing me against the cool marble floor for a moment before he pushes back to kneel between my spread legs. The expression on his face... I don't doubt for a moment that he sees me as the goddess he claims. My self-esteem is pretty healthy, but when Eros looks at me with such intensity, I feel like I could walk on water.

I want to give him the same feeling. I start to reach for him, but he gives a sharp shake of his head. "Not yet. If you touch me right now, I'm going to be inside you in the next breath."

"Sounds like a plan."

He shakes his head again. "Not yet," he repeats. Eros coasts his hands up my thighs, pressing them wide, continuing his path until he reaches my pussy. He presses two fingers into me and curses. "You're so fucking wet."

"You do that to me," I gasp, arching my back as he twists his wrist and strokes his fingertips against my G-spot. "More!"

"I'll give you more, Wife. I'll give you everything you need." He doesn't pick up his pace, though, and when I try to dig my heels into the ground to lift my hips, he plants a hand on my lower stomach to keep me exactly where he wants me. It feels so good, and it's only made hotter by how closely he watches me.

Eros turns his head. "Look."

I follow his gaze to find our reflections in the mirror. It's sexy to have him kneeling over me, strumming my pleasure higher and higher, but seeing it as if someone else were watching us? I almost combust on the spot. And then Eros starts circling my clit with his thumb and I *do* combust.

He barely lets me finish coming before he guides me onto my

stomach and then up onto my hands and knees. "I see you have a bit of an exhibitionist streak." He strokes a hand down my spine and I moan in response. "Or it is a voyeuristic streak?"

"Both." I lift my head to watch him shift behind me, his hands finding my hips and urging me into the position he wants me. I can't catch my breath, but I don't care. "But only with you. Only like this." A show performed and witnessed by only us.

"Good." The word is almost a growl. "I don't want to share you, beautiful girl."

"I don't want to share you, either." Not any part of this. Not with anyone else.

He closes his eyes for a beat. "Last chance, Psyche. Are you sure?"

No need to ask what he means. "No condom," I confirm.

Eros doesn't ask again. He shifts forward, guiding his cock to my entrance. I hold perfectly still, staring at the tormented expression on his face as he sinks into me, inch by inch. "You're so beautiful," I whisper.

He laughs a little, the sound choked. "It's only…" He drags in a breath. "I feel like it's the truth when you look at me like that."

"It *is* the truth."

He reclaims my hips and begins moving, sliding in and out of me in long, smooth strokes. It feels so good, I can barely keep my eyes open, wouldn't be able to if not for the show we're putting on for an audience of two. Eros puts every muscle on his impressive body to use, all with the intention of bringing me the most amount of pleasure. Before I can fully sink into the rhythm of his thrusts, he bends to brace one hand on the floor next to mine, and slides his other down my stomach to stroke my clit. "Dirty girl," he murmurs against my skin. "You complain about all the mirrors as if you don't get off on me fucking you in front of them."

I moan and arch my back, angling my hips to take him even deeper. "I suppose..." He picks up his pace, and I lose my breath. "I could be convinced...about the mirrors...to like them."

"You're a gift, Psyche Dimitriou. A fucking *gift*." He kisses my shoulder, my neck, the sensitive spot behind my ear. All while he keeps up those devastating little circles over my clit, the equally devastating strokes deep inside me.

I try to hold out. I truly do. I won't want this to end, don't want this perfect moment to fade back into reality and all the problems waiting for us.

My body has other ideas.

I cry out as I come hard, clamping around him. Eros curses as if I've surprised him and picks up his pace, driving into me until his strokes become uneven and he follows me over the edge.

He slumps down half on top of me. He's heavy, but I like it. It feels like he's continuing to anchor me to the here and now even as we relearn how to breathe.

Eros brushes my hair off my face. "Did I hurt you?"

My knees already ache in time with my racing heart. It's perfect. I leverage myself up enough to kiss him. "Thank you."

Something in him relaxes, and my pleasure-drugged brain realizes that he was actually worried this had somehow been too much. I reach up before I can find a reason not to. My fingers find his hair, and the little smile he gives me makes my heart lurch. I lick my lips. "I meant it about the mirrors. You've convinced me that they're an asset."

"I knew you'd come around." He turns his head and kisses my wrist. We lie like that for a long moment before he finally looks at his watch and grimaces. "Can you feel your legs yet? We need to get moving if we're not going to be late."

That pulls a laugh from me. "So arrogant."

"Is it arrogance if it's the truth?"

I'm still grinning as he climbs to his feet and pulls me up with him. "Yes. But don't stop. I like it."

EROS

WE MEET ZEUS IN DODONA TOWER.

It's a bit of a head trip. The last time I was here for a meeting, it was with the *last* Zeus. I've been around long enough to see several of the Thirteen switch people behind the titles, but part of me believed that old fucker would live forever. I know Perseus felt the same way; he was sure he'd have at least another decade before Zeus finally did us all a favor and kicked the bucket.

No one expected him to take a header out of his office window a few months ago.

Thankfully, the office where we meet Perseus—Zeus—isn't that same office. It's the one he's been working from for years now, ever since he took over most of the day-to-day tasks of running his father's company. *His* company now.

I glance at Psyche. No matter how unconventional, having sex in front of all those mirrors seems to have steadied the ground beneath her feet. She's lost the wild look in her eyes and has her public persona firmly in place. Calm, cool, and collected.

The only evidence of her nerves is her white-knuckled grip on my hand.

I'm not like her. I'm shit at comforting. I've never had to do it before, never had to search for the right words to say. Fuck, I've never wanted to. She gave me such a gift earlier that I can do nothing but try. "It will be okay."

"That remains to be seen."

"Perseus isn't Zeus."

She looks at me. "That's the thing, Eros. Perseus *is* Zeus. He might have been your friend up to this point, but now he's essentially the king of Olympus. That changes a person."

I know that. Of course I know that. But part of me rebels at it all the same. I was never as close to Perseus as I am to Helen or even Eris. I still *know* him.

"Let's go in." I open the door for her and hold it while she precedes me into the office. It looks nearly identical to every other office in this building. Steel, marble, glass, and little else. Perseus sits behind his massive desk, his fingers steepled in front of his mouth. He's always been a handsome fucker, and he won't thank me for saying it, but he really does have the look of his father. Athletic body, strong square jaw, golden-blond hair, the same cold blue eyes.

He motions to the chairs in front of the desk, and I wait for Psyche to sit before I take the empty one. Perseus looks between us before finally settling on me. "It's been two months since my father died. You couldn't have resisted started starting shit for longer?"

"You know me. I like to stir the pot." I relax back into the chair and give him an arrogant grin. "But in this case, if you want to start pointing fingers, you can take it up with Aphrodite."

"And yet I'm here, taking it up with you." He shoots a look at Psyche. "I don't suppose you were aware that your mother and I were negotiating for a marriage between you and me?"

Shock surges through me, quickly followed by a rage strong enough to burn this entire fucking skyscraper to the ground. Psyche had mentioned it during an early conversation, but I hadn't taken it seriously. With all the candidates throwing themselves at Perseus, he'd meant to go with the controversial choice of one of Demeter's daughters? "You've got to be joking me."

He ignores me, obviously waiting for an answer. Psyche draws herself up. "I suspected it was on the table, but my mother didn't see fit to inform me that things had gotten as far as negotiations."

"I figured as much, but knowing about a pending marriage didn't stop your sister from running into another man's arms."

Her voice goes frosty. "I am not my sister, and it wouldn't have made a difference if my mother was negotiating a marriage or not because I'd be dead. Or did you miss the attempt on my life last night?"

"Watch your tone, Psyche." He leans back. "I'm going to lay this out for you. I have no proof that Aphrodite is behind this attempt." He holds up a hand before I can cut in. "Before you tell me that she ordered you to kill Psyche, remember that if you admit as much to me, you'll share her punishment."

I tense, very carefully not looking at my wife. Perseus is pulling no punches. I didn't expect him to, but damn. All Psyche has to do is say I threatened her life, and she'll remove both me and Aphrodite with one fell swoop. And then she'll marry Perseus, marry *Zeus*, and become Hera.

It'd turn the tables in a way neither I nor my mother can do a damn thing about. I wouldn't blame Psyche for making that call. I desperately don't want her to, but I still wouldn't blame her.

"Did you call us here to tell us that you can do nothing?" Her voice hasn't thawed in the least. "Or do you actually plan to help?"

"I called you here to explain the situation. Demeter might be ready to scream for Aphrodite's head, but Aphrodite isn't the one who's insulted my family—and the position of Zeus—repeatedly. The only reason I haven't intervened to date is because the marriage negotiations were kept private."

I stare at him. Even with all the Olympus politics, I honestly thought he would side with us. "So we're on our own." It could be worse, but this is hardly the best-case scenario.

"Until you can bring me evidence that Aphrodite is breaking the laws against harming others among the Thirteen and their families, my hands are tied." He gives me a long look. "You'd be well advised to ensure *you* aren't implicated in that evidence."

Psyche snorts. "Your hands are only tied because you want them to be."

His expression doesn't change. "Every time one of the Thirteen titles is passed, there's a risk of unrest while the new person settles in. Not only has the title of Zeus passed to me, but Hades is now in play for the first time in over thirty years. Olympus needs stability right now, and replacing Aphrodite is not what stability looks like."

Not to mention there are several titles that might be flipped in the next couple of years already. Ares, in particular, has to be somewhere north of eighty. He's clinging to that title by his fingertips. In the next few years, he'll either kick the bucket or be forced to step down, and replacing Ares is such a fucking spectacle, something that can't be accomplished easily or quickly. Not when a tournament decides the winner.

Perseus is right. I hate that he's right. Unfortunately, he's also wagering on something that's got really shitty odds. "You might not have a choice about dealing with this. My mother won't stop."

"I'll speak to her."

I laugh, the sound bitter on my tongue. "Good luck."

Psyche has a strange look on her face. "If the marriage negotiations hadn't fallen through, what would you have done?"

He doesn't blink. "I'd have protected you and your family with all my power. That option is beyond us now. Even if you and Eros divorced tomorrow, the entire city believes you're a love match. If you married me now, it would paint me as the villain, and I have no interest in playing the part at this juncture."

He can't afford to. Perseus might be smart and savvy, but he doesn't have the sheer amount of charisma that allowed his father to lead all of Olympus around by its nose. Everything will be more difficult for him, including dealing with the veteran members of the Thirteen. There will be jockeying for power and influence and testing him to see how far they can push. He's not in an enviable position. That doesn't make me more inclined to forgive him for taking the easy route with this.

Then the full meaning of his words penetrate. He'd have protected both Psyche *and her family*. Which means that if he marries one of her sisters, he'll protect her. I shoot a look at her; from the tightening of her mouth, she understands what he's implying. She pushes slowly to her feet. "Stay away from my sisters."

"Tell that to your mother."

She clenches her hands, and I'm already moving, rising to my feet and stepping between her and Perseus. "Let it go. We have bigger things to worry about."

"There's nothing more important than my family, Eros." She leans around me to glare at him. "We'll be back, and we'll bring evidence that Aphrodite is behind this. *Without* implicating anyone else."

"I look forward to it."

I squeeze Psyche's hand. "Wait for me outside."

It's a testament to her anger that she doesn't bother to argue. She marches out of the office, shutting the door softly behind her. I turn to Perseus. "You'd break Eurydice, and making Callisto Dimitriou one of the Thirteen is a mistake no matter which way you look at it."

He doesn't move. "If I wanted your opinion, I'd ask for it."

"Perseus..."

"Eros." He sinks enough threat into my name to stop me short. "My name is Zeus. No matter what fondness I held for you before, I'm Zeus now. Every decision I make going forward has nothing to do with what Perseus wants and everything to do with what Zeus requires. Don't forget that."

A reminder I can't afford to ignore. I take a slow breath. "I'll keep that in mind."

"Do that." His eyes go hard. "If you bring danger to my sister's doorstep again, I'll kill you myself, law or no law."

"I'll keep that in mind, too." There's nothing else to say. "See you around, Zeus." I turn and leave the office.

Psyche falls into step next to me as we head for the elevator. Neither of us speaks until we're in my car and driving out of the parking garage. She exhales slowly. "That could have gone worse."

"Did you know about the marriage negotiations?" I don't mean to ask the question. I sure as fuck don't mean to let something resembling jealousy bleed into my tone.

"Not exactly. I knew my mother had her eye on a political marriage between us, but I was honestly bluffing before. I had no idea Zeus was even entertaining the idea." She leans back in the seat and twists to face me. "If I had realized my mother's ambitions were welcomed by Zeus, I would have married him instead of you and solved all my problems at once."

"And become Hera in the process."

"And saved my sisters from becoming Hera in the process," she corrects gently. "You know how the game is played, Eros. *You* play the game. You don't get to be angry about it after the fact."

She's right. I know she's right. It doesn't stop me from wanting to pull this car over, shove my hand up her skirt, and make her come until she forgets there was even a possibility of a marriage to Zeus. It's not rational, and it's damn near unforgivable with our current situation. I need to be focused on the future, on dealing with my mother's next attack, rather than what might have happened if Aphrodite's jealousy and rage hadn't gotten the best of her. I do *not* need to be picturing a wedding between my wife and Zeus. I sure as fuck don't need to be thinking about the wedding night, either. He'll be intent on securing his heir and a few spares. Zeus is one of three titles—Zeus, Poseidon, and Hades—who are passed from parent to eldest child.

The thought of Psyche's belly gone round with pregnancy...

No, I can't afford to think about any of that shit right now.

I make an effort to lighten my grip on the steering wheel. She's mine, at least for the time being. I have to keep my promise to ensure she's safe, which means focusing on the next few steps instead of what could have happened. "Where are we headed?"

"We have an interview." She glances at her phone. "And then we're going to speak with my mother."

Demeter.

Another powerful, dangerous woman who's only too happy to use her children as pawns in the Olympian power games. Yes, I have some things to say to Demeter. "Okay."

"Eros." Psyche reaches out almost hesitantly and touches my arm. "I need your head in the game. Are you with me?"

"Yes." It's even true. I've been compartmentalizing since I was a child. It's nothing new. My end goal hasn't changed, though now it's expanded to ensure that Zeus never touches Psyche. I can't tell her that, though. She'll say that I'm being irrational, that it's a moot point because our marriage has ensured he never will.

I don't care. I have no right to this jealousy, especially when Psyche is mine in every way that counts, but that doesn't stop me from wanting to brand my presence on her very skin. The more time I spend with her, the harder it is to control my baser urges. I feel like I have a monster inside me, rattling the cage of my control. Eventually it will break out, and then there will be a price to pay.

"Eros." She's quiet for several blocks before she takes what sounds like a fortifying breath. "It doesn't matter what I would have done if my mother reached her goals. It didn't happen. I married you, not Zeus. I am your wife, not his. I'm committed to seeing this through, so please stop thinking whatever is going through your head right now. We need Zeus's support, and these circumstances have already ensured that it's going to be nearly impossible to pull that off."

I'm committed to seeing this through.

I know she's talking about what is essentially our con. Marriage for as long as it takes to keep her and her family safe from my mother. She's not talking about forever.

But just for a moment, I really wish she were.

I'm not a dreamer by nature. I like facts and reality rather than the fantastic version of what could be. The *fact* is that Psyche only said yes at that altar because I forced her to. She didn't choose me; she *never* would have chosen me if given her freedom.

It doesn't matter. I won't let it matter. I've already decided to keep her, and now all that's left is paving that path forward between us. I want Psyche in my bed forever. I want the possibility of years spinning out between us, of new schemes and games and playing the public of Olympus to our whims.

I want...children.

The thought staggers me. It's not something I've put much consideration into. My father isn't around—Aphrodite doesn't allow for any competition, even in parenting—and my mother is hardly a perfect specimen of what good child-rearing looks like. Up until this point, I've always taken for granted that our line would end with me.

Not any longer.

I cover Psyche's hand with mine and give her a little squeeze. "My head is where it should be. We'll see this through."

And after?

After, I'll convince her that forever could be ours.

PSYCHE

THE INTERVIEW IS A NICE DISTRACTION. IT'S SO *NORMAL* IN the midst of a situation that's anything but. Eros manages to pull himself together enough to be charming, but I know him well enough now to recognize that he's a little off. It's a disconcerting realization, both that what happened with Zeus was enough to throw him off his game and that I can see the signs.

As agreed, Clio keeps to the subjects we outlined when I set this up. It's mostly softball questions about how we met and the wedding itself. A fair exchange for being the first to break with an interview. Most of the time, Olympus cares less about the real story than about whatever spin they want to put on things, but Clio isn't too bad for a reporter. I've known her since before she got her most recent promotion, and we've helped each other out countless times over the years.

She's a curvy Black woman with an impeccable style. Today she's wearing loose pleated gray trousers and a sleeveless cream blouse that does wonders for her silhouette. If I'm not mistaken,

I recognize Juliette's work. It seems she took my advice to try the designer out. Good.

Clio might be on the gossip circuit right now, but she's hungry for deeper stories than her column can provide. She's also smart enough to realize that she can't go chasing down those leads without the Thirteen turning on her. Not yet, anyway.

That doesn't stop her from collecting any and all information that comes her way, mining for a gold nugget in the midst of so much mud. I hope I have one for her today.

We wrap things up quickly, and I press a soft kiss to Eros's lips. "Do you mind waiting outside for a moment?"

He hesitates, but there's nothing to argue about. We're in my mother's building, and there are no windows in this boardroom. Clio is hardly an assassin; she wouldn't have many stories if she killed off her sources, and she's too ambitious to throw her future away for the chance Aphrodite might protect her. Eros seems to realize that and finally nods. "Don't be long, love."

"Wouldn't dream of it."

We watch him walk out, and Clio whistles the second the door closes. "Bold choice, Psyche."

"You have no idea." I manage not to blush, but it's a near thing. Clio isn't a friend and likely never will be, but we're aligned in a number of ways. "I have a tip for you."

She tilts her head to the side, her long black braids sliding over her shoulder. "Does this have to do with the real reason you went from avoiding Eros like the plague to having that giant diamond on your finger?"

"No." I won't break our cover, not even for Clio. Especially not for Clio. "This has to do with a feud between Aphrodite and Demeter."

"Old news." Clio waves that away. "They've been at each other's throats for years. There's nothing worth digging for there."

"You'd be surprised."

She raises her brows. "Okay, I'm intrigued. Surprise me."

"Aphrodite is so furious that her son married Demeter's daughter, she's taken out a hit."

Clio blinks. "That's quite the allegation. Do you have any proof?"

Not that I'm willing to share. Not enough. I give her a sardonic smile. "Since when do the gossip columns need proof?"

"Fair point." Her gaze goes distant, and I can already see how her impressive brain is considering the spin on this. "I'll need more in order to post anything. Aphrodite is a bitch and a half, and she won't hesitate to call for my job and slap me with a libel suit. Hearsay, even from you, isn't enough to take that risk."

I figured as much. I glance at the door. "There was a disturbance in Helen Kasios's building last night. Ares's people were called in to take custody of the assassin. They still have him."

Clio laughs softly. "Well, *that* I can work with. I can't promise to work fast, because I'll need to verify everything, but I'll ask some questions." She starts to gather up her purse. "Can I assume I'll get a call if there are any more *disturbances* that she might be connected to?"

"Yes, as long as you promise to give me a heads-up before you run the story."

"You have yourself a deal."

We shake on it. Eros is waiting in the hallway, and we head to the elevator while Clio strides out the front doors, an intense look on her face. Eros glances at me. "Do I want to know what you talked about?"

"Zeus wants things quieted down, but he won't take our word for it or step in unless we force his hand. Utilizing Clio is one way to go about it."

"It won't be enough. The gossip sites run scandalous stories all the time and no one blinks anymore. He'll write it off as fiction."

"He would...if that's the only thing we're going to do." I dredge up a smile, even though the last thing I feel like doing right now is smiling. "That's where phase two comes into play."

He shakes his head slowly. "You are truly terrifying, Wife."

Wife.

No reason to get a thrill from him calling me that. None at all. This marriage might be real, but it's not *real*. It doesn't matter if I've fallen for Eros; I have to remember that. I wait for the elevator doors to close to step away from him, needing a little distance. "I just hope I'm terrifying enough to pull this off. My mother puts me to shame." Though right now, I have enough anger that I'm not worried about the conversation we're about to have.

She tried to sell me to Zeus.

It's not even the potential marriage I have issue with. She didn't even *try* to talk to me about it, didn't trust me to recognize the value of making that play. She simply went over my head.

"I'll follow your lead." Eros watches me in the reflection of the elevator, but he makes no move to close the distance between us. Does he feel the pull even now? I do.

"Okay." I take a breath, straighten my spine, and march into my mother's penthouse the moment the elevator opens. I chose not to text her to let her know we were coming, but Mother always spends Saturday early evenings at home, usually getting ready for some event or other. I already checked her calendar, and she won't be leaving for another hour.

I lift my voice. "Mother!"

It takes exactly two minutes for her to appear. She's as perfectly put together as always, her dark hair pinned back, her makeup immaculate, her dark-green gown elegant and giving the earth mother vibe that she carefully curates for the public. She takes one look at Eros and shakes her head. "If you want to talk, he can wait downstairs."

"You don't have the high ground, Mother." I step forward. I catch sight of Callisto in the hallway leading to our bedrooms, but she makes no move to join the conversation. It's just as well that she hears this, too; it affects her, after all. "When were you going to tell me that you intended to marry me off to the new Zeus? When you ambushed me at the altar?"

Mother's too good to show surprise, but her pause speaks volume. "He told you."

"I've been to see him, yes."

Her gaze sharpens. "Why?"

"We'll get to why in a moment. Answer the question."

"I was going to speak with you about it this week, in fact. Negotiations had reached the final stages, and I intended to sit you down and walk you through the reasons why this is an excellent match." She holds my gaze. "Perseus isn't his father. I doubt you would have even needed to dispose of him. He's such a bore that you're more than capable of handling him." She flicks a disdainful look at Eros. "Or you would have been if you hadn't married this one."

Eros is wearing the same hard look he had when Zeus revealed the marriage plans. I can't read it at all. It's as if he's turned to a pillar of ice. I told him the truth in the car on the way over here; if my mother had come to me with these plans, I would have gone through with them. Her read on Perseus—on Zeus—is the same I have. He may be ruthless in the extreme, but he seems to genuinely care about his siblings, which is more than the old Zeus could say. He didn't care about anyone but himself. Perseus also has no violence in his past. I know; I looked.

But that doesn't mean I want one of my remaining single sisters marrying him. "Take the plans off the table."

"You know better." Mother shakes her head. "You've painted me into a corner with your actions."

Damn it, that's what I'm afraid of. I look over her shoulder, but Callisto has disappeared. It's just as well. The last thing we need is her getting it into her head to shove this Zeus out a window or something equally final. Succession would pass to Helen at that point, and while she seems great, she also seems so *young* in a number of ways. It would spell disaster for Olympus.

Love or hate the city, the fact remains that the Thirteen keep it running smoothly. Everyone has their roles, their own little slice of the pie. If they were normal people, those slices would be enough, but normal people don't aspire to be numbered among the Thirteen. No, every single one of them is ambitious and cutthroat and willing to step on others to propel themselves higher. Left to their own devices, they would be going to war with each other inside of a year. No matter what my personal feelings are when it comes to the title of Zeus, the truth is that it requires a formidable personality to keep the others in line.

In another ten years, Helen might be strong enough. She's not now.

There are days when I'd like to see this city burn to the ground, but ultimately, it's home. If I want to keep the people of Olympus as relatively safe as they are right now, that means Perseus needs to stay Zeus. No convenient accidents. No outright plans for murder. Not that I was really considering killing him…

As long as he stays the fuck away from Eurydice.

Callisto can take care of herself.

I can't worry about any of that now. I have to concentrate on surviving Aphrodite's wrath first. For that, I need my mother. "We'll discuss potential marriage plans later. Right now, there are more time-sensitive issues."

"I see." She sighs. "Come in. Having this conversation in the foyer is déclassé."

We follow her into the living room, Eros a glaring storm cloud at my back. His energy has changed in the few minutes we've been here. If I don't miss my guess, he's gone past frozen and straight into icy rage. And it's all pointed at my mother.

With that in mind, I grab his hand and tug him down onto the couch next to me. I don't *think* he'll harm her, but he's more than capable of it. There are times when I hate my mother, but she's still mine and I don't want her hurt.

I suspect that conflicted feeling is similar to what he feels for Aphrodite.

Mother sinks onto the chair across from us and arranges the skirt of her dress around her, the very picture of a queen in waiting. "Tell me what mess you've gotten yourself into."

"One could argue *you* got her into it." Eros's voice is hard.

I place my hand on his thigh and tell her. Everything. Oh, I leave out the sex because that's none of her business, but I walk her through the sequence of events over the last few days that brought us to this place. When I finish, my mother looks a little pale and absolutely furious.

She seems to make an effort to release her death grip on the arms of the chair. "I'll kill her."

"You won't," I cut in before Eros can. "We don't want her dead."

"And *you*." She turns hazel eyes, so similar to mine, on him. "Did you think my threats were without merit? You threatened my daughter. You—"

"Mother." I inject steel into my tone. "That's enough. Eros has not harmed me."

"I disagree. He harmed you with this marriage."

I let that go because this isn't an argument I'll win. "Regardless, it's done. If you try to remove Aphrodite, I'll bring my not-inconsiderable knowledge about you to the press. All the shady dealings and questionable moves. The stunt you pulled to try to get Persephone back to the upper city. The clean-up job on Zeus's death. Every bit."

She finally stops glaring at Eros and gives me her full attention.

"You're threatening *me* to keep the woman who wants you dead safe?"

"If you want to see it that way."

"Why?"

Because I love Eros and I don't want to see him harmed, even if it puts me at risk. Killing Aphrodite will harm my husband. He doesn't have to say as much for me to recognize that.

I don't say it. Even if they believed me, both of them would name me a fool for very different reasons. Mother never let something as mundane as emotions get in the way of her plans and ambitions. And Eros? The only thing Eros offered me was safety and sex. Nothing softer, nothing *more*.

"Because I am choosing the method of my revenge." That, at least, she should understand.

She finally nods. "I don't like it, but I will abide by your wishes in this." She points at Eros. "With the caveat that if something harms my daughter, I will burn your legacy to ash."

"Noted."

"I would like you to set up a meeting for me with Poseidon." I'd do it myself, but I can count on one hand how many times I've seen him at events in the last year, and even before then, he never did much mingling at Zeus's parties. If I show up to the shipyard without an invitation, I doubt I'll be able to get access to him.

Not to mention Poseidon notoriously loathes Eros, so there will be no help on that front.

Her brows snap together. "Poseidon? Your time would be better spent focusing on Hades or Zeus. Poseidon doesn't like power games."

I know. That's what I'm counting on. He mostly stays out of the intrigue native to the Thirteen, but he's a legacy title and carries the heft of power that brings. My mother has unique access to him because she handles feeding Olympus. While most of the food itself comes from the land surrounding the city, there are certain things that simply can't be homegrown. Poseidon is in charge of imports and exports, one of the few who can come and go from Olympus as he pleases. It's resulted in a decent working relationship between him and my mother.

We need both Poseidon and Hades in our corner before we circle back to Zeus. "Please, Mother."

She finally nods. "I'll see it done, though I can't promise it will be speedy. The man likes to dodge my calls when he can manage it."

"I'm sure you're more than capable of pinning him down."

"Of course I am." She rises. "Now, I have an event to finish getting ready for. You know where the door is." She pauses. "Thank you for telling me, Psyche."

"You can thank me by tossing out the negotiations with Zeus."

She gives me a tight smile and disappears down the hallway leading toward the master bedroom. I don't exactly breathe a sigh of relief when she's out of sight, but some of the fight goes out of me. I turn to Eros. "I—"

"We'll talk in the car." He jerks his chin at something over my shoulder, and I turn to find Callisto standing there.

I tense, half expecting her to threaten Eros like everyone else in my life seems to. But she turns a hard look at me. "Is it true? Mother's still got her eye on Hera for one of us?"

I swallow hard. "Yes, but—"

"Don't tell me that she'll back off. We both know she won't. If that situation with Persephone wasn't enough to dissuade her, nothing you do or say will." She flicks her fingers at Eros. "He's a monster, but he's no Hades."

"Thanks," he mutters.

"Callisto, we'll figure it out."

Her lips curve, but her eyes stay oh so cold. She crosses to me and grips my shoulders. "You and Persephone have been taking care of us long enough. I'll handle this."

True fear slashes through me. "You can't kill him."

"I know." She squeezes my shoulders and drops her hands.

"But—"

"Worry about yourself, Psyche. If Aphrodite lays one finger on you, I'll make what happened to the last Zeus look like a gentle death." She turns and walks away.

Shit. Shit. *Shit.*

"This is bad."

"Psyche." Eros waits for me to look at him. "You can't fight every battle at once. We have to prioritize, and right now we have more pressing things to worry about than your mother's potential marriage plans for your sisters. You can chase this down after we deal with Aphrodite."

He's right. I know he's right. But releasing years' worth of responsibility and worry is easier said than done. I've always worked with Persephone to manage Callisto's anger, to protect Eurydice from the worst Olympus has to offer. Letting that go is terrifying in a completely different way than dealing with Aphrodite.

But I allow Eros to steer me to the elevator and then through the lobby and out onto the street. I have to trust that my sister knows what she's doing and that she isn't about to land us in even deeper water.

I really, really hope Callisto proves that trust is founded. If she doesn't, we're in for a whole lot of trouble.

EROS

I TAKE PSYCHE HOME. THERE'S NOTHING ELSE TO BE DONE tonight, and she looks as rattled as I feel. I honestly expected Zeus to step in. Zeus is—*was*—a friend. I should have known better than to expect that to mean something in this godsdamned city.

We have laws for a reason, though, and everyone knows what happened the last time a member of the Thirteen turned against another. The last Hades—and his wife—were murdered, leading to thirty years of Olympus assuming that title had disappeared entirely. Those deaths were the reason we have the law against killing one another in the first place. It's supposed to safeguard both titles and their families.

It's *supposed* to mean that if anyone violates it, the full weight of the other members of the Thirteen will come down on them.

Admittedly, that would mean I'd see consequences for my part in my mother's schemes, but it's a small price to pay to ensure Psyche stays safe.

Strange how my priorities have shifted so much in such a short time.

I glance over to where my wife is staring out the window with a contemplative look on her face. Or maybe not so strange at all. I'm a selfish bastard. She matters to me, so of course I don't want her harmed. It's as simple and complicated as that.

When we make it up to my penthouse, Psyche slows in the entranceway and stares at the statue for a long moment. "My plan might not work. If Zeus and the others admit that Aphrodite did this, then they have to deal with it, and it's much easier to look the other way."

I walk up behind her and slip my arms around her waist, gently pulling her back to rest against my chest. "Hades will help you."

"I know. My sister will ensure that." She sighs. "But ultimately Hades is one man. Even with my mother involved, that's two of thirteen. Those aren't winning odds, no matter which way you look at it."

She's right. I close my eyes and inhale her cookie scent. We have to make this work. My mother is smart and savvy and ambitious, but when she has her sights set on someone, she becomes obsessed to the point where she sees nothing else. She *will* back down if we can get enough members of the Thirteen in our corner. I believe that. I *have* to believe that. But... "If our plan fails, I'll take care of it." No matter what means are necessary. I don't want to. Fuck, I don't want it to get to that point, but I won't let her hurt Psyche. That is my line in the sand, the one I will not cross, no matter who else pays the price. Even if it means *I* pay the price.

Psyche turns in my arms and clenches my shirt in her fists. "No, Eros. I won't let you do that. Not even if it means my life."

She's serious. Her sincerity is written there on her pretty face. Gods, this woman kills me. I pull her closer, as if the press of her body against mine is enough to banish my dark thoughts. It doesn't work. Of course it doesn't work. I let out a bitter laugh. "I lose regardless."

"What are you talking about?"

"Haven't you figured it out, Psyche? I care about you. Losing you will hurt me."

She shakes her head. "You're just saying that."

"No, I'm not." I take a slow breath and rest my forehead against hers. "When I'm with you, I feel human. I flat out fucking *feel*. Do you understand what that means for a person like me? I thought those parts were dead and buried so deep that they'd never see light again. I had to cut them down in order to continue to do the things required of me."

"Eros..."

But I'm not done. "Even with that, I don't know if I'm really capable of love, not in the way a normal person is. It doesn't matter. I care about you, and no amount of rationalizing that away is going to change the truth of it. So don't bother."

She lets out a little sound that might be a laugh—or possibly a sob. "We're such a mess."

"I think that goes without saying." I run my hand up her back. "I promised to keep you safe, and that's what I intend to do."

"What about you?"

I blink. "What do you mean, what about me?"

She leans back enough to look up at me. "Who's keeping you safe, Eros?"

"I don't understand the question."

She makes that strange little sound again. Now that I can see her face, I recognize it as a laugh. "No, you wouldn't, would you? You're so willing to cut your heart out to keep me safe, it never occurred to you that I'd feel the same way." She tugs on my shirt. "I won't let you bear the cost of hurting your own mother. We'll find another way."

"There might not be another way." It pains me to admit as much. This situation would be so much simpler if I truly had no heart to cut out, if I were as without feeling as my mother aspired to make me. "I don't want to argue. I'm stating facts."

Psyche's lips curve, but her eyes stay troubled. "So am I. I won't let you bear that burden. Not for me. Not for anyone. We'll find another way."

We could go round and round like this a thousand times, and it won't change the facts. I give Psyche a squeeze. "You should eat."

She makes a face. "That was a very artless change of subject."

"Nothing will be decided until tomorrow at the earliest, and you missed at least one meal today." Something I should have paid attention to, but there's been so much going on, I'm dropping balls. Even ones I can't afford to, like ensuring Psyche is taken care of. She's already proven herself to be driven and relentless when it comes to ensuring she lands on her feet. It's an asset, but it also means she's ignoring what she views as smaller needs while focused on the larger ones. "Come on."

I take her hand, enjoying the way she lets me. It's easier to focus on that point of contact, on measuring the steps it takes to bring us into the kitchen, than it is to circle back to what she said earlier.

She cares about me.

She cares if I'm harmed, even by my own actions.

I don't know what to do with that. Part of me wants to crow my victory to the heavens, and the rest just muddles over what the fuck she even means. I am not someone who needs to be protected. I am the knife in the dark, the threat ready to be leveled at any enemy that arises. What the fuck do I need a shield for?

Except that's what Psyche is offering, in her way. Perhaps not a shield; a better description of what she's offering me is a safe place to land. Both ideas are as foreign to me as sprouting wings from my back and taking flight.

"Sandwich?"

"Sure."

I get to work putting one together for each of us as she watches me. It strikes me all over again how *easy* it is to be with Psyche. Even when we're pushing at each other or fucking until I can't think straight, we've slid into each other's lives nearly seamlessly. It's a gift I never thought to expect. It makes me...want things. Things I was certain weren't for me.

Like children. "Did you mean it when you said you wanted kids, Psyche?"

She jolts. "What?"

I cut her sandwich in half and slide her plate across the counter to her. "It's a simple enough question."

"I..." She looks at her plate and then looks at me. "Yeah. I did. It wasn't just a ploy to make you empathize with me. I really do want a family."

A month ago, I would have laughed anyone out of the room if they suggested I might actually want the same. But ever since our conversation with Zeus, I haven't been able to get the image of that kind of future with Psyche out of my head. I want it all. It doesn't matter if she deserves better than me. No other partner is going to readily burn down the fucking world for her the way I will. I don't know if I'd be a good dad—it's not like I have anything resembling a role model for that—but I think we could muddle through parenting. Together.

I know better than to tell her where my head's at right now. We have a giant hurdle to get over before we can talk about anything resembling the future. Even then, if we successfully remove the threat my mother poses, that also removes any reason we have to be married to each other. I won't be able to make her stay; even I'm not ruthless enough to force her into forever if she wants her freedom.

Uncomfortable, desperate thoughts.

What the fuck am I going to do?

We finish eating in silence. What else is there to say? I simultaneously want to tether her to me forever and stay quiet to avoid saying something that neither of us can take back. Admitting to caring is one thing. Telling her the truth rumbling inside me is out of the question. I can barely admit it to myself.

I love her.

I try the words out as we brush our teeth, a slice of domesticity that must be so mundane for everyday couples but that I want to encase forever in my memory because this, too, is irreplaceable. All these little moments with her are new and novel, and if something happens to her or this blows up in my face, I'll have to sell this fucking penthouse and move away because Psyche's managed to imprint herself on every bit of space in the short time we've been together.

I'll never be able to sleep in my bed remembering all the pleasure we've dealt each other there. Never cook in my kitchen without replaying every word of every conversation we've had there. And the foyer? Forget about it.

She hasn't even had a chance to add items to the main space the way she plans. I won't be able to live here wondering what changes she would have made if given enough time. It will kill me.

"Eros."

I realize I've been staring at myself in the mirror far too long and shake my head. "It's nothing. I'm fine."

"Are you sure?"

No. Not even a little bit. I turn to her. It would be so simple to kiss her and do away with the need for any more words tonight. I know her body offers salvation that I can find nowhere else. But we've moved beyond just fucking, and I think we both know it. "Psyche."

She twists her hair around one finger, her brows pulling together into a frown. "Yes?"

"I..." Fuck, why is this so hard? I clear my throat and try again. "I need you tonight."

Her expression softens. "Okay."

That nearly makes me laugh; I would if there was enough air

in this room to fill my lungs. "You're not going to ask me what I need from you before agreeing?"

"No." She gives a small smile. "Why? Should I be terrified?"

If she knew what was going on in my head, the way I want to tie her to me in every way possible, she might be. I rub the back of my hand over my chest. "I...want to hold you tonight."

That seems to surprise her. "Hold me? I thought for sure you were about to propose some freaky sex stuff."

"Maybe later." I should. She's already admitted that she can't separate sex and emotional attachment, so seducing her is the surefire way to ensure she falls for me just as hard as I've fallen for her.

Tonight, though, it's not what I need. I need her body next to mine, the press of her against me, while I lie there and measure her steady breathing. I just need to fucking hold her. I look away, flushing despite my best efforts. "It's fine. Forget it."

"No." Her voice goes quiet. "No, I'm sorry. That was an asshole response." She steps close and slides her arms around me. It's criminal how perfectly Psyche fits against me. How am I supposed to move on with my life after knowing there's a person who's the other half of my puzzle? Damn it, I'm a mess right now.

She squeezes me. "With clothes or without?"

"Without."

Psyche laughs a little. "Okay. Come on." She releases me and walks out of the bathroom, leaving me to trail behind her. I do without hesitation, and as a result, I'm treated to the sight of my wife stripping as she walks toward our bed. She shoots me a look over her shoulder. "You were staring at my ass, weren't you?"

"Can you blame me? You have an excellent ass." Big and bitable.

"I know." She slides between the blankets and scoots over, making room for me.

I strip quickly and join her. The sheets are cool, and Psyche wastes no time plastering herself to me and pressing her nose to my neck. "You keep this place way too cold."

I settle onto my back with her draped half across my chest. This. This is what I need. I can feel her heartbeat through my ribs, her soft exhales against my skin. A reminder that she's here, she's safe, and she'll stay that way through the night.

She twines her legs around mine and snuggles closer. "Eros?"

"Yeah?" I sift my fingers through her hair, enjoying the weight of it against my palm.

"I meant what I said. I won't let it get to the point where you have to make that choice—the one between me and your mother. There's a solution here. I just need time to figure it out."

I close my eyes, letting the soft weight of her against me lull my racing thoughts to a standstill. "If anyone can find a way through, you can."

"Just...trust me, okay?"

"I do." It's even the truth. We don't have enough time, enough space, to come up with a better plan than we already have, but all of it hinges on Demeter getting us a meeting with Poseidon. "Sleep now."

"I will." She squeezes me tight. "We'll figure this out together. I promise."

As sleep rises up and takes me, I almost believe her.

PSYCHE

BY THE TIME MORNING ROLLS AROUND, I HAVE SOMETHING resembling a backup plan. It's not a good plan, and if I tell it to Eros, he might lock me into the panic room and throw away the key. Of all the things I never expected of this marriage, his protectiveness surprises me the most. It's not just in regard to the current situation with his mother. He's constantly…taking care of me.

It's not an act, either.

Eros has what he wants from me, everything he wants. We're married. We're having sex. Judging from the way Clio's story about us broke across multiple gossip sites this morning, we're successfully convincing Olympus that ours is a love story for the ages. He has absolutely no reason to lie to me, not in word and not in action.

Which means he meant what he said last night. He cares for me. I'm not foolish enough to think that caring translates to love, but it's more than I could have dreamed. It's almost enough to give me hope.

First, we have to survive the coming confrontation with Aphrodite.

My phone buzzes on the nightstand, and I angle myself enough to reach it without dislodging Eros where he's wrapped around me. He's held me like this all night, clinging as if he thinks I'll slip out of our bed under the cover of darkness and never return again.

Considering that's what my sister pulled with Hades when she rode off to save him from the last Zeus, Eros isn't too far off the mark there. I could tell him he has nothing to worry about on that front; trying to deal with Aphrodite in secret will just backfire a thousandfold. Keeping things below the radar is what got us into this trouble to begin with. It's time to bring everything out into the open.

I see my sister's name scrolling over the screen and swipe to answer the call. "Early for you, Persephone."

"Early, or late." She sounds a little breathless. "Why is Hades fielding calls from both Mother and Zeus this morning?"

They're working fast, which doesn't mean anything good. I had planned to call Persephone this morning and loop her in, but apparently I should have done it last night if I wanted a jump on things. I don't like that our mother is already up and maneuvering. The call with Poseidon must not have gone well. I sigh. "There's been a bit of trouble."

"More trouble than you up and marrying Eros without so much of a word of warning?"

"Persephone, I thought we were past that."

"It's been less than a week. We're not past it."

I roll my eyes, both frustrated and comforted by her overprotectiveness. Alone in this situation, it's something normal and expected. "If not Eros, it would have been Zeus."

She's silent for a long moment. "Tell me she didn't. Not again."

"Mother is single-minded. You know that. She has her heart set on establishing one of us as Hera."

She curses. "Okay, we'll deal with that later. Right now, I need to know what's happened with you, since that seems to be the more immediate issue."

"Aphrodite took a hit out on me." It feels good to say it aloud, almost cathartic.

"*What?*"

"Yes." I feel Eros tense a little, a silent acknowledgment that he's awake. "Zeus won't step in unless we have definitive proof, so we planned to get the support of Hades and Poseidon and force his hand. Even Aphrodite can't stand against those three."

She's silent for a beat. "It's not a bad plan as such things go, but it's not really a good one, either."

"I'm aware."

Another pause. "You have something in mind for backup."

My sister knows me so well. Normally, I'd appreciate her insight into what I'm considering, but I'm achingly aware of Eros against me, listening to everything. "We're set on trying this first," I finally say. It's even the truth. Just because I don't think it will work doesn't mean I'm correct. I desperately want to be wrong.

"Hades will stand in support of you."

That makes me smile. "You aren't going to talk to him first?"

"I don't need to. One, he's sitting right here, listening in like a nosy husband. And two, you're his sister-in-law and he likes you, so obviously he's going to do whatever it takes to ensure you stay safe. Right, Hades?"

I hear a deep murmured assent in the background. Well, that takes care of that. I didn't anticipate anything different, but I've been surprised enough in the last week that I can take nothing for granted. "Thank you."

"He'll let Zeus know, but you need to work on Poseidon. He stays out of this stuff, and it would take one rather large inciting incident to get him into the mix."

I'm all too aware of that. "Let Mother worry about that." We're both silent for a moment as we contemplate what our mother could possibly have to incite cooperation from that man. I shudder. "I have to get up and make some calls."

"Stay safe. We're here if you need us."

My throat goes tight, and I have to swallow hard to get the words out. "Love you."

"Love you too."

I toss the phone aside and turn in Eros's arms to face him. "You heard."

"I heard." He cuddles me close. For such an icy man, Eros certainly likes to touch me. Almost as much as I like being touched by him. He rests his chin on the top of my head. "One down, one to go."

I press a kiss to his chest, enjoying this closeness. It feels like we've turned a corner. I don't know what the future holds if we can get through this current mess, but a strange sort of hope takes up residence in my chest. I love him. He cares about me, which seems to indicate he could love me if given the opportunity. "Eros?"

"Yeah?"

It's tempting to keep my thoughts internal, but I've never been good at controlling my mouth around this man. Especially when his feelings hang in the balance. "Last night, you said you don't know how to love."

He tenses. "I don't."

"You're wrong."

Eros huffs out a strained laugh. "I think we can both agree I'm damaged goods."

"Stop that." I sit up. "Stop talking about yourself like that. I wouldn't let someone else talk about you so cruelly, and I'll be damned before I let you do it, either."

The shock on his face hurts my heart. "It's the truth."

"Eros, you love Helen."

He makes a face. "She's like a sister to me."

"I know." I press my hand to the center of his chest. "And you love her like a sister. That love counts. One could argue it counts even more than romantic love because there isn't sex in the mix, muddying things up."

He opens his mouth, hesitates, and finally covers my hand with his. "It's difficult to argue with that."

"Because I'm right." I take a deep breath. "Whether or not what we have gets to love, that's not something either of us can control." Even if it's too late for me on that note. "But never doubt that you're capable of it."

Eros studies my face for a long moment and then his face relaxes in a smile. "I really don't deserve you."

"You really don't." I laugh a little. "But not for the reasons you've stated previously. I'm just a gem of a human being."

"I know."

The moment spins out between us, and those three little unforgiveable words dance on the tip of my tongue. *I love you.* I can't say them. Not now, not after that conversation. It will look like I'm trying to manipulate him or, worse, that I expect him to say them back right now.

Desperate for a distraction, I clear my throat. "I'm starving."

That springs him into motion just like I suspected it would. "Let's get you fed, then."

An hour later, we've eaten and showered. We're plotting out the rest of our day when my phone rings. I hold my breath when I see my mother's name. "Hello?"

"Poseidon is out. I'm sorry, Psyche. I tried every bit of leverage I have, but he refuses to get involved."

Disappointment takes the bones right out of my legs. I barely manage to land on the chair instead of the floor. "I see."

"He's a young stubborn fool and he still thinks he can play the game his way instead of sinking down to the depths the rest of us occupy. If you give me some time—"

"Thank you, but that won't be necessary." Time is one thing we don't have. Even now, Aphrodite will no doubt be ordering the next assault. She's not one to take disappointment lightly, and from her point of view, I've bested her twice now. She won't let it happen a third time. "I'll take care of it."

"Psyche..." For the first time in as long as I can remember, my mother sounds unsure. "Let me help."

Horribly poisonous words threaten to surge forth. *I wouldn't be in this situation if Aphrodite didn't hate you so much. I wouldn't even be in Olympus if your ambition weren't so strong.* I don't say them. Ultimately, I bear nearly as much responsibility in this situation as the rest of the players. I could have been like Persephone and tried to find a way out of Olympus. That was never my goal. I've played the game, too, and now I need to play it better than I ever have before.

To fail is to die.

I inhale slowly. "I have things under control. I'll call you later." I hang up and glance over to find Eros watching me. "Poseidon won't offer his support."

"It was a long shot, but I hoped I was wrong." He's gone still the way he seems to when he's thinking hard, ice creeping into his features. "I'll take care of it."

"Eros, no." The strength rushes back into my body, born of pure panic. I cross to him and take his hands. "No. You can't hurt your mother."

"I don't want to." He sounds like he's in pain. "But we both know she won't stop." Eros slowly shakes his head. "There's no other way. We're running out of time."

I know that. I'm achingly aware of the seconds ticking by. "Eros, please." I skate my hands up his chest and cup his face. Gods, I think I'm going to cry. "I love you." A cruel move to say it now, underhanded and just as manipulative as I feared it would be. I don't care. I'll say worse to keep him from doing this. It's the truth, after all.

I thought he was still before; he's practically frozen in place now. "Say it again."

"Eros, I love you." The words spill so easily from my tongue. I dig my hands into his golden curls. "I love you."

He looks almost agonized. "I meant what I said earlier. I don't deserve it."

"Love doesn't much care whether you deserve it or not. It's not exactly a conditional thing—or at least it shouldn't be."

He coasts his hands over my hips. "I, in particular, don't deserve to be loved by you." Eros shudders out a breath. "But I don't give a fuck. You've said it. You can't take it back."

I find myself smiling even though it feels like my heart is breaking. "Please don't go. Please give me time to find another way." To put things in motion that will save him from this.

He covers my hands with his own and lifts them from his hair. Eros kisses one palm and then the other. "I promised to keep you safe. That's exactly what I'm going to do." He releases me and steps back. "Go to the panic room and stay there until I return. Don't open it for anyone but me."

I'm losing him. Maybe I lost him the moment Poseidon removed himself from the equation. I don't know, but I can feel Eros slipping through my fingers even though he's standing right in front of me. He might think himself a monster in truth, but if that were accurate, he wouldn't be able to care for me the way he does.

If he harms his mother, he'll lose what little there is left of his soul.

I can't let him do that, not for me. "Eros, please."

He kisses me gently. It feels like goodbye. "The safe room, Psyche. Promise me."

"I promise," I whisper. It's the first time I've lied to him since we were married.

He nods and releases me. "I won't be long."

I stand there, my heart sinking, and watch him pull on his coat and shoes. The sound of the door opening is obscenely loud in the quiet of the penthouse. I find myself counting softly. "One... Two... Three..." At twenty, I force myself to move.

The first step is the hardest. I'm taking a gamble of my own with this. Not only with my life but Eros might never forgive me for what I'm about to do.

It doesn't matter. I'll bear that price and gladly if it means I spare him from carrying the weight of harming one of the few people he cares about in this world.

I scramble for my phone, nearly dropping it in my haste. There's only one person I can call to pull this off, and it's a gamble of the highest order. I take a deep breath and dial.

When she answers, Helen sounds like she's been sleeping. "Hello?"

"Helen, I need Aphrodite's number."

"Hi, Psyche. So nice to talk to you. I'm doing great, thanks for asking."

I swallow down my need to scream. "Helen." I speak slowly. "Eros is in trouble, and I need Aphrodite's number. I don't have time to explain why."

She's silent for a beat. "I like you, Psyche, but Aphrodite will skin me alive if she finds out I gave her contact information to you. Ask Eros."

"Helen!" My voice spikes despite my best efforts to stay calm. "Eros is going to kill Aphrodite."

"*What?* He wouldn't. They have a toxic as fuck relationship, but she's his mother."

"I know. That's why I need her number and need it now."

Another pause, shorter this time. Finally, she says, "If this is all some ploy that will hurt him in the end, I'll grind you to dust. There will be nothing left of you when I'm done."

"If I fail with what I'm about to do, you're more than welcome to try. The number, Helen. Please."

She curses and rattles off the number. I hang up without saying goodbye. Time is of the essence, but I still allow myself a few seconds to take some breaths and get my head on straight. I only get one shot at this; I can't afford to screw it up.

My heartbeat isn't anywhere near normal as I dial Aphrodite's number. It's just as well. She won't believe me if I'm too calm. She's smart enough to sense that there's more to this than it seems, so it's my job to ensure she's too focused on the possibility of getting to me to worry about a trap. Or at least too arrogant to think that any trap of mine could hold her.

When she answers, she's as cold as ice. "Aphrodite speaking."

"I've changed my mind." I don't have to fake the quiver in my tone. "I didn't sign on for all this, and I want out. You can get me out of Olympus, can't you?"

She barely misses a beat. "Psyche? How lovely to hear from you. I'll admit I'm surprised you've reached out."

Damn it, I need this to move faster. I take a loud inhale. "I want out. You want me out. This serves both of us."

"And here I thought you were in a love match with my son." Her words drip acid.

"You know better."

Aphrodite laughs. "Yes, I do. You bit off more than you can

chew with Eros, but that's neither here nor there. What are you proposing?"

"Meet me at... I don't know, the gardens in the university district? If you can smuggle me out on the next shipment from the docks, you'll never see me again." The quiver in my voice gets stronger. "I didn't sign on for this. I don't want to die."

"Of course not, sweet girl. No one wants to die." She's silent as she seems to consider this. "I was under the impression that you had no plans to leave the city."

"It's not exactly easy to leave Olympus," I snap.

"Mm-hmm, that's true enough." Another pause. "I'll get you out. Meet me in the gardens tonight."

"No!" I realize I was too loud and silently curse myself. "Eros went out to run an errand. It has to be now. If I don't leave before he gets back, he'll keep me here."

Aphrodite sighs. "Yes, my son is rather tenacious when he's got his mind set on something. I suppose I can shift my plans for the day. I'll meet you in the gardens in an hour."

Barely long enough for me to get there with time to spare. I'm already moving to the door and yanking on my coat. "Okay. Thank you, Aphrodite."

I can hear the evil smile in her voice. "Not a problem, dear. Mother knows best, after all."

EROS

I'M NOT SURE WHAT SOMEONE IS SUPPOSED TO FEEL WHEN they're on their way to threaten and possibly kill their own mother. I feel nothing at all. Instead, I keep getting flashes of memories I thought long buried.

At eight, finding my mother crying on the couch. How she sobbed and told me the entire city was out to get her. I promised her that *I* would always protect her.

At thirteen, being able to perfectly detail all of my mother's enemies, the ones she told me wanted her dead. I parroted their personal details and supposed sins back to her, and she smiled at me as if I was her favorite person in the world.

At seventeen, when my mother asked me to do her a favor, just a tiny little thing. It was so godsdamn easy to ask the right questions that led to the truth about Apollo and Daphne. And then she showered her attention on me like the summer sun.

At eighteen, the first time I told her I wouldn't do what she asked. How quickly she withdrew her attention, her very presence, from me. How ruthlessly she punished me by withholding herself for days, weeks, until I finally buckled and did as she asked. My mother might be a monster, but she's the only family I have. I wasn't strong enough to withstand her icing me out. I had no one else.

At twenty-one, when I realized the lesson I should have years earlier: she doesn't really love me. I doubt she's actually capable of it. She sees me as a convenient tool to pick up and set down as the situation calls for it. All the soft moments, the tears, the hurt feelings, they were all weapons she wielded against me. Understanding that killed something in me, something I didn't think I'd ever reclaim, not until I met Psyche.

After that, Aphrodite resorted to stronger measures to bring me back in line whenever I pushed back against her.

Even with all the years of love and resentment that slid right into hate, the truth is that she's been the one constant in my life. Foil or guiding light, she's always been there. It never really occurred to me that one day she wouldn't be.

That one day mine would be the hand that brought her demise.

It takes me forty minutes to make it to her building. Though my mother spends most of her time in the area around Dodona Tower, she actually lives in the outskirts of the theater district. I've never been able to figure out if she actually likes the theater or if she just likes being a patron and muse to performers. Either way, it was her dragging me out to shows that eventually led to me finding the Bacchae.

She lives in a town house rather than one of the many skyscrapers that litter Olympus. It even has a small, fenced yard, and that's how I enter the property, letting myself in through the gate that borders the back alley. There should be security people watching over the space—at my insistence—but it seems she's dismissed them again. She hates having an entourage of armed people, and so she slips them off every chance she gets. It used to frustrate me to unspeakable levels.

Now, it works in my favor.

I pause in the yard. In the spring, it's an explosion of color and flowers, all perfectly curated and picture-ready. I never understood that. Aphrodite entertains endlessly, but she rarely does it in her home. She barely posts pictures of this space, either. It's almost as if all this beauty is just for her, but I can't think about that now.

I use my key to unlock the back door and slip inside without announcing myself. It's Sunday, so she should be home. Aphrodite ascribes to no church, and she likes lazy Sundays where she's not on display to the public.

Except the house feels strangely empty.

I wander from room to room, hating the cascade of memories each one brings. This was my childhood home, and if that childhood was often devoid of softness and safety, it wasn't all bad. I pause in the doorway to my old room. It's a relic from the past, exactly the way I left it when I moved out at eighteen, desperate to put some space between myself and my mother. A king-sized bed, ridiculously high-thread-count sheets, exactly one pillow occupying the great expanse of mattress.

Despite myself, I step into the room and look around. There are no posters on the walls, but I do have two framed paintings that my mother gifted me during a particularly angsty stage. Their artist's moniker is Death, which felt particularly apt at the time, and they show close-ups of battered hands drenched in color, giving the impression of violence just committed.

My desk holds a scattering of papers and pictures and random bullshit that teenagers accumulate. Notes from Helen. Old school assignments that I never got around to tossing. Notebooks filled with comments and insight gained during my first fledgling attempts at surveillance.

I open my closet and eye the gun safe tucked within. That's something I'd wager most teenagers *don't* accumulate. I crouch down and key in the combination more through force of habit than anything else. While I keep various weapons and poisons in my penthouse, using the stash Aphrodite keeps under her roof is better for this scenario. My mother won't feel a thing; she'll just get sleepy and then know nothing at all.

I can't think about the fact that it's the same poison I intended to use on Psyche.

There are a lot of things I can't think about right now.

I open the safe and frown. "What the fuck?"

One of the guns is missing. I hover my hand over the empty space. It was here two weeks ago when Aphrodite required my presence for dinner. Where the fuck is it now?

The small hairs on the back of my neck stand on end. Something's very wrong. I've let my emotions get the best of me, and they've clouded the one thing I *should* be thinking about. Or, rather, the question I should be asking.

Where the fuck is Aphrodite?

My phone buzzes in my pocket as I push to my feet. I fish it out, see Helen's name, and reject the call. I'll talk to her later.

Except my phone starts vibrating before I can put it back in my pocket. Helen again. I frown and answer. "I'm busy."

"Eros, I think Psyche is in trouble. Or maybe your mother is. I'm honestly not really sure, but something's going on and you need to know about it."

The feeling of dread weighing me down only gets worse. "Slow down and explain properly."

She takes a large breath as if she's been running. "Like an hour ago, Psyche called me and said she needed Aphrodite's number to keep you from doing something you couldn't take back. Which…I thought she was going to… Gods, I don't even know what I thought, but MuseWatch just reported seeing Psyche in the university gardens in one post and Aphrodite driving toward the university district, looking dressed to kill. I'm so sorry I took so long to put two and two together, but I think they're meeting, probably soon."

She wouldn't.

Except, as I picture the determined look on my wife's face, I realize she most definitely would. "You gave my mother's phone number to Psyche."

"I didn't know what else to do. Your mom is a bitch, but she's your mom. You can't… I can't sit by and let something happen to her. You'll regret it for the rest of your life." Because Helen's mother is dead, and there's no coming back from that. "I thought Psyche had a plan, but I didn't realize the plan would be confronting Aphrodite directly."

"There's no way you could have known."

"Is there anything I can do to help?"

I bite back the sharp retort that she's done enough. It's not

Helen's fault Psyche and I are in this mess. She just did what she thought was best, and I can't blame her for that. "Keep an eye on MuseWatch and let me know if there are any updates."

"I will." She hesitates. "Eros, I really am sorry."

"I know." I hang up, thinking hard.

If Psyche was seen at the university gardens and my mother is heading in that direction, that's where they'll meet. I'll have one chance to control this situation, and bringing in more people adds too many uncontrollable elements. I consider my options. If I drive, there are going to be added minutes trying to find a parking spot, and it will take time I can't afford.

I drag in a breath. No doubt my mother is driving. She never would have walked there from her house. That gives me time.

I start to run.

As my pounding strides eat up the blocks between me and the gardens, I can't help the frantic circling of my thoughts. Why would Psyche do this? Why would she *risk* this?

Except... I know why, don't I?

Love makes fools of us all. I never realized that would be so literal. We're both so intent on saving each other from pain and harm, we're throwing ourselves right into those very things. Psyche is cunning and so intelligent it drives me up the walls, but my mother is a different breed entirely. And she has a gun. I never would have thought she'd go so far as to dirty her own hands, but Psyche has outmaneuvered her at every turn. When cornered, Aphrodite won't hesitate to strike out.

To strike Psyche.

I can't lose her. I just fucking found her.

I'm panting and sweating by the time I reach the gardens. Where will Psyche have gone? I frantically think back to when we walked them. Was that just a few days ago? It feels like a lifetime. We walked deep enough down the paths that we couldn't be seen from the street, to what she said was her favorite part of the garden. I bet that's where she's at.

My body aches as I pick up my pace. My shoes weren't meant for running, but I barely feel the pain. Especially when I round a corner and find Psyche facing off with my mother. Aphrodite has *my* gun held in two hands, her stance shitty but it's not like she can miss at that range. My wife is all but cowering against those fucking twigs she told me are flowers.

I force myself to stop, to slow down to avoid surprising my mother into pulling the trigger, and lift my hands. "That's enough, Mother."

She doesn't look at me. "Turn around, Eros. I have this perfectly under control." Her voice is so perfectly controlled, she might have been commenting on the weather.

"I can't let you do this." I can't think, don't know how to play this to ensure she puts down the gun without pulling the trigger. All I have is panic, and panic will get Psyche killed. I inch closer. "Go home, Psyche. I'll deal with this."

"She has a gun!" Her voice shakes and she's half-crouched, her arms lifted as if that would be enough to stop a bullet. She's panicking, too, and there's not a damn thing I can do about it. "She's going to kill me!"

"She won't kill you. I won't let her." I desperately hope I'm not lying.

I take another slow step forward, but Aphrodite shakes her head. "No closer or I pull the trigger."

That stops me short, my heart lunging into the back of my throat. I have to find the right words to say, but my brain is pure static. I'm not close enough to lunge for the gun, though, so I have to try. "You'd risk Zeus's fury for this?"

"I'd do that and more." She doesn't take her gaze from Psyche. "But I'm not the one killing Demeter's daughter, Eros. *You* are."

Understanding dawns as I take her in. The old coat that I haven't seen on her in years. The leather gloves that will remove any trace of gun residue if she fires—and her fingerprints. Which means the only fingerprints on the gun registered to me are mine.

Fear, true fear, coats me in ice. She's really going to do it. She's not bluffing. "Why would I shoot my wife? I love her."

"Don't lie to me." Her pretty face twists into something horrible. "You don't love this little bitch. You're not capable of love. She was supposed to be dead, Eros. Her heart on a fucking platter. What the fuck is wrong with you that you would *marry* her?"

Psyche isn't crying, but she looks damn close. "Why would you want to kill me? I've never done anything to you!" She's shaking so hard, she has to clutch her hands in front of her chest.

Aphrodite turns her body a little to keep me in her line of sight as she glares down at my wife. "Your mother's done plenty. She needs to be taken down a few notches. She doesn't get to pick the next Hera. *I* do."

Psyche sniffles. "But that has nothing to do with me."

"It has everything to do with you." She leans down, sneering.

"Demeter really thinks that *you're* good enough to be married to Zeus. Look at you. You're nothing but a fat girl playing pretend."

"I didn't ask for this!"

"Wake up, little girl. No one asked for it in Olympus." She laughs, the sound wild and unhinged. "You don't get to swim with sharks and then cry about getting eaten. You tried to play the game and you lost." She shifts her stance, lifting the gun an inch. "Now you're going to pay the price."

"That's *enough*." I start forward, but she stops me with her finger on the trigger. If she were pointing it at me, I wouldn't hesitate. I'd take my chances. But I will not risk Psyche's life. "You don't get to talk to her like that. You don't get to attack her because she's better than you, prettier than you, both inside and out. Put the fucking gun down, Mother."

"We're done talking!"

Psyche sighs. "Yes, I suppose we are. I've got more than enough. So has the rest of Olympus." All the quiver is gone from her voice, her fear tucked away as if it never existed, leaving only cold calm and steely determination in its place. She reaches into the flower bed and extracts a phone from the space behind her. She holds it up to her face, and just for a moment, the calm flickers and she gives a trembling smile. "So, you see, everything is not okay. It's not okay at all. Aphrodite wants to kill me and frame my husband."

Aphrodite's jaw drops. "You're livestreaming us."

"One hundred thousand viewers and counting. Before the end of the day, all of Olympus will have heard you confess to trying to kill me." Psyche's trembling smile goes sharp. "Sharks aren't the only predators in the ocean, Aphrodite."

Holy fuck. Holy *fuck*. There will be no sweeping this under the rug, no pretending it never happened. She's just paved the way for a bloodless changing of power with the title Aphrodite; there's no way my mother will retain the role after this. Relief makes me giddy. "It's over. There's no coming back from this. It's finally over."

"It's not over until I say it's over!" Aphrodite turns fully to face Psyche, her expression going ugly and hateful. "If I go down, you're going down with me!"

"No!" I sprint forward, moving faster than I ever have. Even as I do, I know I won't be fast enough. There's too much distance between me and Aphrodite, too little distance between her finger and the trigger.

I don't count on Psyche.

She surges up, grabbing Aphrodite's wrists and shoving them up toward the sky as the gun goes off. She stomps on my mother's foot and yanks the gun from her hands, flinging it in the opposite direction. Aphrodite curses, but Psyche shoves her to the ground. The whole thing took two seconds.

I grab Psyche and pull her into my arms. I know she didn't get shot, but I can't help searching her body for wounds despite that. "Are you hurt?"

"I'm fine. I'm safe. We're both safe."

"Thank fuck." I point down at my mother, currently trying to sit up. "Do *not* move."

In the distance, sirens sound. Psyche presses her forehead to my chest for a long moment and then moves away. "Now, it's time for the final act."

PSYCHE

THINGS HAPPEN QUICKLY AFTER THAT. ARES'S PEOPLE arrive. Half of them cart Aphrodite off in a black van; the other half act as our escort to Dodona Tower to face Zeus. Good. I have some choice words to say to him.

Eros sits next to me in the back of the car. He hasn't said a word since Ares's people showed up. He's stayed close to me, but I can't read the expression on his face. He's iced me out. I open my mouth but decide against speaking before any words escape. We aren't alone, and this needs to play out before we can have anything resembling an honest conversation.

I don't know if he'll forgive me for lying to his face and going behind his back.

We reach Dodona Tower and are escorted up to Zeus's office. He's waiting for us in nearly the exact same position he was during our last meeting. He glances up as we walk through the doors, his gaze landing on the soldiers behind us. "Leave us."

They obey instantly. I've never had much desire to have power for the sake of power, but his ability to state commands and have people leap to obey is something that would be useful. Especially right now.

Zeus rubs his temples. For a moment, he almost looks tired, but it passes and then he's the implacable cold man he's always been in my presence. "When I said I needed evidence, I didn't mean I wanted you to stream that evidence to half of Olympus."

"The entirety of Olympus will have seen it by dinnertime." I clasp my hands in front of me, hoping he doesn't notice the way they shake. "Especially once MuseWatch picks it up, which we both know they will. A homicidal Aphrodite makes for juicy headlines."

"She'll be exiled." He sits back, blue eyes cold. "But then, that's what you wanted, isn't it?"

It's exactly what I wanted. Killing Aphrodite, whether sanctioned execution or no, will hurt Eros. He's shouldered enough hurt for a lifetime. I know I can't shield him from it forever, but I can do this. "Yes, that's what I wanted."

Zeus shifts his attention to Eros. "And you. There are plenty of crimes to lay at your feet. I should exile you as well. It's not only the Thirteen who will pay the price for breaking one of our most sacred laws; it's also anyone they loop into the plot."

"No!" I cry out before I can stop myself.

Zeus shakes his head slowly. "I would have done it. However, the situation has changed."

The shift is too unexpected. I stare at him blankly. What could have possibly changed that saves Eros from punishment? "Because it was livestreamed?"

"No." He gives me a long look. "Because you're family now,

and unfortunately, that allows you—and your husband—some leniency. As such, I will not be pursuing any sort of charges against either of you. However, this is your one and only warning. If you continue to plot and scheme and make my life difficult, I will make examples of both of you."

Family? I frown. "What are you talking about?"

He leans forward and presses a button on his phone. "Send her in."

Behind me, the door opens and familiar footsteps sound. Horror keeps my feet planted in place, but it doesn't save me from the truth as my oldest sister rounds me and Eros and moves to stand at Zeus's shoulder. Callisto is wearing a black dress, the sheer simplicity of the cut only serving to highlight her stark beauty. She doesn't touch Zeus, standing a careful foot away, but there's no denying what's happened.

It's written there on the giant diamond on her ring finger.

"No," I whisper.

For his part, Zeus doesn't seem overly smug. He just looks bored with this conversation. "The engagement will be announced in a few days. The wedding will be this spring. Under no circumstances are you to do anything to endanger that, or I *will* exile every member of your family." His gaze flicks to Eros. "As well as your husband."

"But—" I choke back my protest when Callisto shakes her head very slightly. When she said she'd take care of it, I was afraid she'd try to murder Zeus or something equally violent. I didn't think she'd agree to *marry* him. Her words from yesterday come back to me.

You and Persephone have been taking care of us long enough. I'll handle this.

I have to respect her choice; even if I don't understand it, I know Callisto too well to believe anyone forced her into this decision, not if she didn't want to do this.

I clear my throat. "Welcome to the family, Zeus."

"Better, but I expect smiles and happy words when we officially announce the engagement. You will be nothing less than effusive and supportive." He looks out the window for a long moment and then back at us. "That concludes things. You won't be allowed contact with Aphrodite until she's removed from the city. There will be a press conference in the morning that I do *not* want you to attend."

"You're going to spin the story."

"Of course I'm going to spin the story." He shakes his head. "Go home. Stay there. Keep making heart eyes at each other for at least a month. I don't care what you do after that, but you will keep to this timeline to avoid people asking uncomfortable questions. Do you understand me?"

"Yes," I whisper.

Zeus turns that cold gaze on Eros. "And you?"

"Loud and clear."

"Good. Now get out of my office."

I don't know if I'd have argued further. Eros doesn't give me a chance. He turns to me and, with a hand at the small of my back, guides me out of the room. It's a small touch but no less dominant for it. We don't speak as the elevator goes to the ground floor. Only then does he hesitate. "Are you up for the walk to our place?"

Our place.

He says it so freely, without hesitation or stumbling. As if the penthouse is really both of ours, rather than just his. As if this marriage was anything but a con. A month. A month is all we have left. After that, we'll have no reason to stay married. No reason except for the love that's threatening to rip a hole in my chest.

Eros told his mother he loved me. He told me he cared about me. But we've both spent so long pretending for other people, I don't know what's real and what's not anymore.

"I can walk."

"Okay." He loops his arm through mine and turns us in the direction of his building.

It takes half a block for my feelings to get the best of me. "Eros—"

"Not here."

Right. Not out on the street where anyone can overhear. I should be smiling up at him like the newlywed I am, but I can't manage it.

As long as I'm moving, I'm okay, but the second we get back into Eros's penthouse and he closes the door behind me, my knees give out.

He catches me before I hit the floor. Of course he does. Eros scoops me up and takes me into the bedroom that's become ours. Only then does he sit me on the bed and crouch before me. The ice is still present in his eyes, but the way he holds my hands is soft and sweet. "Breathe, Psyche."

"I am breathing." Except my voice is too high and thready. And I can't stop shaking. "What's wrong with me?"

"Adrenaline letdown." He rubs my hands gently. "It will pass."

Of course he would know. He's been in dangerous situations over and over again. I've only done it twice, and the feeling bubbling up inside me after the assassination attempt in the parking lot was nothing compared to this.

My throat is too tight, but I have to get the words out. "I'm sorry."

He frowns. "What are you talking about?"

"I'm sorry. You told me to stay here and I couldn't. I couldn't let you bear the burden of hurting her. She's your mother."

"She's a monster."

"That doesn't mean you don't love her."

He sighs and moves to join me on the bed. "No, that doesn't mean I don't love her, if you can call it that. I…" He curses. "I'm fucking furious with you. You put yourself in danger. You didn't fucking talk to me. I thought I was going to show up and find you dead. I can't… Psyche, I don't care what burdens I have to bear; they're more than worth it if you're safe."

I reach out tentatively and sink my fingers into his curls. "I had things under control."

"In hindsight, I'm aware of that, but there were so many variables." He shakes his head, the move tugging on my hold a little. "You were faking it, weren't you? Being that scared."

I shudder to think back to the moment I was crouching on the ground, staring down the barrel of a gun. "Only partly." I swallow hard. "She needed to think she'd won. She's too vain not to say all the ugly stuff out loud, and I needed that on the video."

Eros stares at me. "You're terrifying. Do you know that? Absolutely terrifying."

"I can't tell if that's a compliment or not."

"Neither can I." He leans down and presses his forehead to mine, a grounding touch that eases some of the tension in my chest. "So. A month left."

Just like that, it's back. "That's what Zeus said. I expect he doesn't want anything to detract from the narrative he's going to spin, and once he announces the engagement with Callisto—" I break off. "I can't believe she did this."

"Really? I can." He carefully extracts my hands from his hair and links his fingers through mine. "Your sister is going to be Hera."

"It seems that way." I can barely comprehend what that will look like. The last Zeus went through three Heras over his time with the title. Rumor is that he killed at least two of them, but no charges were ever leveled at him. As a result, the title of Hera has become something of an empty one. It technically still has duties and an area to rule like all the other Thirteen, but the last three people to hold it were overshadowed by Zeus. I don't know what my sister will do with the title, but I can guarantee she won't be the easy, biddable wife that *this* Zeus is no doubt hoping for.

But I don't want to talk about Callisto.

I take a slow breath and stare at our linked hands. "So much of this has been pretend. From the very start, we've been lying to the public."

"I'll give you a divorce."

That stops me short. I lift my head and blink at him. "What?"

"A divorce." The winter night outside the window is warmer

than Eros's voice. "You married me to keep safe from my mother. She's no longer a threat, and I know this isn't what you would have chosen for yourself. When the month is up, I'll get the divorce papers written up. You can have whatever you want. You've more than earned it."

I have to take my hands back from him to avoid doing something I'll regret. "Eros."

"Yeah?"

"Will you let me finish before you sprint to leap on your own sword to save me from big, bad you?"

Now it's his turn to blink. "I'm as much a monster as my mother. That's empirical fact."

"Did you mean what you said to your mother? Do you love me?"

"I don't see how that matters."

Gods, this man. I grab his face and bring it down to mine, nearly close enough to kiss. "Answer the question."

His huffed breath ghosts against my lips. "Yes, I meant it. I love you. But that's not a good enough reason to keep you chained to me. I'm a selfish bastard and I thought I could do it, but I can't bear the thought of you trapped. Not even by me."

I close my eyes. It's that or start crying all over him, which he'll misinterpret. "You might be a monster, Eros, but you're *my* monster. I love you, too. I don't want a godsdamned divorce. I just want you."

He's silent for so long, I open my eyes to find him staring at me. He reaches up and cups my jaw with a hand that trembles. "If you're serious—"

"I'm serious."

"Be sure, Psyche. If you really mean it, be sure. I can't... I don't have the strength to let you go twice."

I turn my head and kiss his palm. "You don't have to let me go at all."

"Thank fuck." He yanks me into his arms and holds me tightly. The same tremors that shook his hand work their way through his entire body.

I kiss his throat, his jaw, the corner of his mouth. "I'm here. I'll always be here." And then I'm kissing him properly. He hugs me tighter, as if he can't get close enough to me, and I feel the same way. Things could have gone so wrong today. They didn't, but that doesn't change the way I need this man. Right now. Tonight. Forever. I break the kiss long enough to say, "Eros."

He's already moving, pushing to his feet and yanking off his clothes. "I need you."

"Yes." I let him pull my dress over my head and toss it aside. Then he's there, bearing me back onto the mattress, his hands moving over my body as if to reassure himself that I'm whole, that I'm here. I push on his shoulders, and he lets me roll him onto his back and climb up to straddle his waist.

Gods, the way this man looks at me.

He grips my hips, devouring me with those fiery blue eyes. "You're enough to make me want to get into photography."

That surprises a laugh out me. "Eros, surely you're not suggesting taking dirty pictures of me."

"That's exactly what I'm suggesting." He cups my breasts and leans up to lavish kisses over them. "Just for us. Only ever just for us."

It strikes me all over again that we have *time*. We can act out every fantasy, explore every nuance of the thing that's flared to life between us. I roll my hips, rubbing myself along his length. "One condition."

"Name it."

I grin down at him, so happy I feel downright buoyant. "Take me in front of every mirror in this house, Husband. Let's put them to good use."

He pulls me down into a devastating kiss. "That will take years, Wife."

"Good."

He smiles against my lips. "That's my girl." Eros reaches between us, and I lift my hips so he can notch his cock at my entrance. I keep kissing him as I work myself down his length, guided along by his hands on my hips.

It's only when he's seated fully inside me that I sit up and brace my hands on his chest. "I love you."

His smile is wide and happy and free of any shadows. "Say it again."

I ride him slowly, reassuring both of us with touch and pleasure that this is real, that it's not going anywhere. "I love you."

Eros slides a hand down to press to my clit, so that every stroke winds my pleasure tighter, hotter. "Again, Wife."

"Again? Really?" I moan and pick up the pace.

"I'll never get tired of hearing you say it." He tightens his grip on my hip, urging me to move a little faster, chasing the orgasm I can already feel building deep inside me. "I love you, too. Psyche. So fucking much."

Between his words and his touch, I'm lost. My orgasm crashes through me, drawing a cry from my lips. "I love you!"

Eros topples me to the bed and then he's thrusting into me, harder and faster, his expression a mask of need and love. He wraps his arms around me, holding me to him as he grinds into me, chasing his pleasure. I dig my nails into his ass to pull him closer, needing this moment of connection as much as he does. When he comes, he buries his face in my neck.

He goes to slide off me, but I'm having none of it. I wrap my legs around his waist and hold him close. "Not yet. I'm not ready to let you go yet."

"You never have to let me go." He presses a kiss to my neck and leverages himself up so he can look down at me. Eros gives me a crooked smile. "Look at us. Beauty and her Beast. Happily ever after and everything. Maybe fairy tales do exist."

"You're much prettier than the Beast ever was."

He gives a rough laugh. "And yet much more of a beast than he could ever be."

"I don't care. Beast, monster, man, it doesn't matter to me. You're mine, Eros Ambrosia." I tilt my head up and brush a kiss over his lips. "And I'm yours."

EPILOGUE

EROS

"ARE YOU READY?"

"Almost." I finish buttoning up my shirt and check my appearance in the reflection. I look fine. Better than fine. This is a new suit, one of Juliette's designs, and the fit is so damn superior, I see why she charges what she does. The deep purple should be ridiculous, but it looks great. One wouldn't know by looking at me that my stomach is a mess of nerves.

Psyche leans against the doorway. She's as picture-ready as always, wearing a bright floral top with a deep-pink skirt that bells out to stop just below her knees. "Stop stalling or we're going to be late."

"We could always skip it." I stalk toward her. "I could strip you out of that cute skirt thing and lose track of time."

"Eros." She smiles, though her hazel eyes are serious. "You have nothing to be nervous about. It's just dinner at my mother's."

"It's *Sunday* dinner at your mother's, with your entire family." It's also the first one we've managed to make in the month since

Aphrodite was exiled. As Zeus feared, my mother created more than enough trouble on her way out. She named *Eris* as her heir, which sent the entire upper city into wave after wave of whispers. I hadn't even realized Eris was working beneath Aphrodite, though apparently she'd been doing it for years. Her appointment means two of the Thirteen are from the Kasios family, which has everyone speculating on how that will affect the power balance going forward.

Eris, of course, hasn't seen fit to reassure anyone. I suspect she's thriving off the chaos.

Demeter has been busy putting out political fires and circling the new Aphrodite warily, trying to figure out where they stand. And now Ares is sick, and it's not looking like he'll recover...

Yeah, shit has been fucked up in Olympus.

Ironic that it's been the happiest month of my life.

As I follow Psyche out of our room and into the kitchen to grab the wine I bought to bring to dinner, evidence of that happiness is everywhere I look. The key bowl Psyche bought at the winter market in the lower city with its jaunty color scheme of pink, yellow, and teal. The matching personalized glasses—a tumbler for her and a wineglass for me—on the drying rack, the stylized script etched into it reading *Hers* and *His*. She has entirely too much fun taking photographs of us drinking from those for her social media.

The dining room table always has fresh flowers on it, and they always seem to match whatever Psyche is wearing when she buys them. Even though I tease her about being vain, I love it. It feels like she leaves a little piece of her in the penthouse when she's out.

Every room has little things added. Extra pillows in our bedroom. A knit throw blanket in the living room, along with a stack of books that, judging from their broken spines, she's reread many times.

I stop in front of my favorite addition. Psyche rolls her eyes, but she's fully grinning now. "Every time!"

"We look good. It's a shame not to appreciate it." On the wall in the foyer, there's a larger-than-life print of the photo from our wedding. It's my personal favorite of the bunch, one of our first kiss as a married couple. Hermes did us a solid and ducked out of the way, though I didn't realize it at the time.

"You are such a sap." She nudges me with her shoulder. "Come on, Husband. We don't want to be late."

I loop my arm around her waist as we head down the elevator to the parking garage. It's so fucking *easy* being with Psyche, listening to her detail her plans to champion a new designer Juliette recommended who specializes in plus-sized clothing, that I forget to be nervous until we're parking outside her mother's building.

My chest gets tight as I stare at the front door. "What are the odds she decides to poison me?"

Psyche raises her brows. "We can pretend that you're actually worried about that if you like." She reaches across the center console and takes my hand. "Or we can talk about the real issue."

"Don't tell me Demeter isn't capable of poisoning someone."

"I wouldn't dream of it."

I give her a look. "Is that supposed to be reassuring? You're enjoying this."

"Only a little," she admits. "It's so rare to see you nervous."

"Psyche."

"Eros." She squeezes my hand. "I love you. My mother might have resisted the idea at first, but she's made her peace with it. She won't be more difficult than normal at this dinner, and homicide is stricken from the list of possibilities."

Psyche's family is important to her. The *most* important thing to her. She loves me, but her sisters are her bedrock. Even her mother, for all that they clash, holds a vital role in her life. If I can't make peace with them, true peace, it might become a wedge in the future. It might *hurt* her.

I swallow hard. "Let's go."

She releases me long enough to get out of the car and then reclaims my hand as we head into the building. I can pretend it's simply for the joy of touching me, but it's obvious she's offering her silent support. I appreciate it.

I've faced down innumerable dangerous situations. I've killed people. I've swum with the worst predators Olympus has to offer without blinking.

Of course it would be a family dinner that has me so nervous, I'm in danger of being sick.

Demeter's apartment is identical to what it looked like the last time we were here, one of the many trips to transport all of Psyche's wardrobe to our place. The spare bedroom already looks like a perfect replica of hers here, so I've commissioned a contractor to remodel the entire space as a closet. It's a surprise for her birthday next month. Once she approves the design, we'll start construction.

I expect Psyche to lead the way into the kitchen where I can hear Demeter and Persephone talking in low voices, but she veers away from that door and hauls me up the stairs. I curse when I catch my toe on a stair. "If you wanted a quickie, we could have done it in the car instead of your mother's house."

"Ha-ha, very funny. I want to show you something."

"Is it your—"

"*Eros*," she hisses, but she's obviously trying not to laugh. "Focus."

"I'd say I'm remarkably focused right now." The banter eases some of my tension. No matter what else today brings, *this* is the same. I let Psyche drag me along like her favorite toy until she stops in front of the picture wall. "Look."

This isn't the same as when I was here the first time. There are two new additions. The first is a black-framed photo of Hades and Persephone. She's wearing a white wedding gown that looks remarkably traditional. There's even a veil covering her blond hair. He, of course, is in a black-on-black suit, but he's not wearing his customary dour expression. Instead, he's staring down at his bride with an indulgent smile on his face. She's beaming at him, practically radiating light. It's so sweet it makes my teeth ache.

Psyche tugs my arm. "Yes, yes, my sister looks lovely. *This one*." She points to the second addition. There, next to the photo of Hades and Persephone, is one of me and Psyche. This one isn't from the ceremony but from the photos we posed for after the fact. I'm holding Psyche close and have one arm wrapped around her waist and the other hand tipping her chin up with the obvious intention of kissing her. She looks soft and happy and perfect.

And me?

My heart's in my eyes.

I don't miss the significance of this photo being here among these other happy photos of the Dimitriou women. Demeter might not have welcomed me to the family with open arms and sweet words, but by hanging this photo, she *is* welcoming me into the family.

I laugh, my throat a little tight. "Well, fuck."

"What?"

I can't really put this strange sensation into words. I've never had a family before, or at least a family where every interaction isn't transactional. A warm welcome, even this small, makes me feel strange and awkward, like I don't know what to do with my hands. "Your mother has a pointed way of welcoming someone into the family."

"She does, doesn't she?" Psyche leans against my arm. "Hey, you."

"Yeah?"

"I love you."

I press a quick kiss to her bright-pink lips. "I love you, too. Now let's go down and greet your mother properly."

We find the entire Dimitriou clan in the kitchen. And Hades, which surprises the fuck out of me. He lifts his brows when he sees me but otherwise seems content to occupy a corner away from the women moving around one another like a terrifyingly well-oiled machine. Psyche gives my hand one last squeeze and joins them seamlessly.

Eurydice stirs what appears to be marinara sauce while chatting with Persephone, who removes hot rolls from the oven.

Demeter tips steaming noodles into a strainer, gives it a good rinse, and weaves around Persephone to dump them into the sauce. Callisto is chopping vegetables for a salad with a speed that makes my stomach shrivel up. Psyche washes her hands and then starts transferring the chopped vegetables into the giant salad bowl filled with lettuce.

I inch back until I'm even with Hades, safely on the other side of the peninsula counter. "Are they always like this?" I murmur.

"Yes."

No one bumps into each other. No one even hesitates. And they manage it while all talking at once. It's overwhelming in the extreme. Not just the sheer competence; it's the fact that I can feel their love for each other in every word, every movement.

"So this is what family really looks like." I don't mean to say the words out loud. I sure as fuck don't mean for Hades to hear them.

He huffs out a dry laugh. "Yeah, it shocked the fuck out of me, too, the first few times. You get used to it." He hesitates. "It's even kind of nice sometimes, especially when they let you help."

It strikes me that Hades is another person in Olympus who wouldn't have much in the way of family experience. His parents died when he was a little kid. I glance at him. "Brave to step into that tornado."

"Just wait until you're in the middle of it."

Strangely enough, I can't wait.

Within ten minutes, the women have us hauling food to the table. Dinner is just as much a whirlwind as the preparing seemed to be. Psyche and her sisters talk over each other, with Demeter interjecting dry comments at regular intervals. It's chaotic and more than a little overwhelming.

But Hades is right. It's...nice.

I can *feel* the love they hold for each other, even when Persephone and Callisto start bickering over a misremembered instance of sibling injustice. I'm content to pick at my food and soak up the energy. This is what family feels like. What *home* feels like.

I like it.

Once everyone's eaten their fill, Hades clears his throat. "We'll do dishes."

"Smart boys." Demeter's smile is knife-sharp. "We'll be in the living room."

Hades heads into the kitchen and the women whisk out of the room. All except Psyche. She glances after her family and takes my hand. "Are you doing okay? I know we can be a lot at first. If we need to leave—"

"I'm good." The love I feel for this woman about bursts out of my chest. Of course she'd pause to check in on me, to offer to leave early even though she's obviously enjoying herself. I squeeze her hand. "Better than good. Go enjoy your mother and sisters. We'll be in once we've finished the dishes."

"If you're sure..."

"I am."

She finally nods, her lips curving in a slow grin. "Oh, by the way, I almost forgot. I have a surprise for you when we get home." She leans close and lowers her voice. "I bought some new lingerie. Play nice and I'll let you tear it off me with your teeth."

"You little asshole," I breathe. I have to adjust my pants a little, which makes her smirk. Even her damn smirk is sexy. "Just for that, I *am* going to tear it off with my teeth, strip by lacy strip."

"Oh no, not that," she says, deadpan.

I laugh. It's big and freeing and banishes the last of the nerves that clung through dinner. A beautiful wife who is everything I never dreamed of deserving. A loving family that seems all too ready to draw me into their circle. I really am the luckiest son of a bitch in Olympus.

ACKNOWLEDGMENTS

A massive thanks to all my readers. I wouldn't be able to do this without your support, and I am constantly humbled and so incredibly grateful for your response to the sexy little stories I enjoy writing so much.

Huge thanks to my editorial team at Sourcebooks for helping me craft *Electric Idol* into the best version of itself. Mary Altman and Christa Désir, your insight was exactly what I needed! Thanks to Jessica Smith, Rachel Gilmer, Jocelyn Travis, and Susie Benton.

Thank you to Dawn Adams for the design! This book feels so special because of it. Big, BIG thanks to Stefani Sloma and Katie Stutz for your support with marketing and PR. You've gone above and beyond! Thanks to Liz Otte for talking up this series so much!

Thank you, as always, to my agent, Laura Bradford, for always being in my corner!

Thanks to my team in the very unofficial sense. Piper J. Drake, you suggested having a literal "take the heart" moment and it really made all the difference in this book. Thanks to Asa Maria

Bradley and Jenny Nordbak for always being only a text away when I get stuck or just have a bonkers idea. Big appreciation to Andie J. Christopher and Nisha Sharma for keeping me fed on TikToks. Many, many thanks to the WordMakers group for writing with me, day in and day out, and always believing me when I say "It'll be FINE" even when I'm barely reining in my scattered chaos.

Last but never least, thank you to my family for keeping me tethered to reality, or at least some approximation of it. Thanks to the kids for weathering truly unprecedented times (really, would love to get back to something resembling *precedented*) with all of us stuck under one roof for thirteen months and counting. All my love to Tim for being the best partner a person could ever dream of. Your support and belief in me has kept me going through ups and downs and loop-de-loops. You really are romance hero material!

ABOUT THE AUTHOR

Katee Robert is a *New York Times* and *USA Today* bestselling author of contemporary romance and romantic suspense. *Entertainment Weekly* calls her writing "unspeakably hot." Her books have sold over a million copies. She lives in the Pacific Northwest with her husband, children, a cat who thinks he's a dog, and two Great Danes who think they're lap dogs. You can visit her at kateerobert.com or on Twitter @katee_robert.

WICKED BEAUTY

BY KATEE ROBERT

Olympus has never felt so wicked...

In Olympus, you either have the power to rule...or you are ruled. Achilles Kallis may have been born with nothing, but as a child he vowed he would claw his way into the poisonous city's inner circle. Now that a coveted role has opened to anyone with the strength to claim it, he and his partner, Patroclus Fotos, plan to compete and double their odds of winning. Neither expect infamous beauty Helen Kasios to be part of the prize...or for the complicated fire that burns the moment she looks their way.

Zeus may have decided Helen is his to give to away, but she has her own plans. She enters into the competition as a middle finger to the meddling Thirteen rulers, effectively vying for her own hand in marriage. Unfortunately, there are those who would rather see her dead than lead the city. The only people she can trust are the ones she can't keep her hands off—Achilles and Patroclus. But can she really believe they have her best interests at heart when every stolen kiss is a battlefield?

"Deliciously inventive."

—*Publishers Weekly* Starred Review for *Neon Gods*

For more info about Sourcebooks's
books and authors, visit:
sourcebooks.com

A PROMISE OF FIRE

BY AMANDA BOUCHET

A fierce woman cursed with powerful magic,
abducted by a dangerous warlord determined
to save his country, igniting a forbidden
attraction that will make them burn.

Cat Fisa isn't who she pretends to be. She's perfectly content living disguised as a soothsayer in a traveling circus, avoiding the destiny the Gods—and her dangerous family—have saddled her with. As far as she's concerned, the magic humming within her blood can live and die with her. She won't be a pawn in anyone's game.

But then she locks eyes with an ambitious warlord from the magic-deprived south and her illusion of safety is shattered forever.

Griffin knows Cat is the Kingmaker—the woman who divines truth through lies—and he wants her to be a powerful weapon for his newly conquered realm. Kidnapping her off the street is simple enough, but keeping her by his side is infuriatingly tough. Cat fights him at every turn, showing a ferocity of spirit that burns hot...and leaves him desperate for more. But can he ever hope to prove to his once-captive that he wants her there by his side as his equal, his companion—and maybe someday, his Queen?

KINGDOMS WILL RISE AND FALL FOR HER.

For more info about Sourcebooks's
books and authors, visit:
sourcebooks.com

ALSO BY
KATEE ROBERT

Dark Olympus
Neon Gods